DRIFTERS

ALSO BY KEVIN EMERSON

Chronicle of the Dark Star:

Last Day on Mars

The Oceans between Stars

The Shores Beyond Time

The Fellowship for Alien Detection

The Oliver Nocturne series

Carlos Is Gonna Get It

FOR YA READERS

The Atlanteans trilogy

Any Second

The Exile trilogy

Breakout

DRIFTERS

KEVIN EMERSON

WALDEN POND PRESS
An Imprint of HarperCollins*Publishers*

Walden Pond Press is an imprint of HarperCollins Publishers.

Drifters

For information address HarperCollins Children's Books, a division of HarperCollins Publishers, 195 Broadway, New York, NY 10007.
www.harpercollinschildrens.com

Library of Congress Control Number: 2021950858
ISBN 978-0-06-297696-3

Typography by Carla Weise
22 23 24 25 26 PC/LSCH 10 9 8 7 6 5 4 3 2 1
❖
First Edition

For all those hoping to be seen

WELCOME TO
FAR HAVEN
WASHINGTON
Potter's Beach
Jetty Park
Bunkers
Bluff Trail
Shipwreck
Bathhouse Ruins
Fort Riley State Park
Satellite Beach
Beach Trail

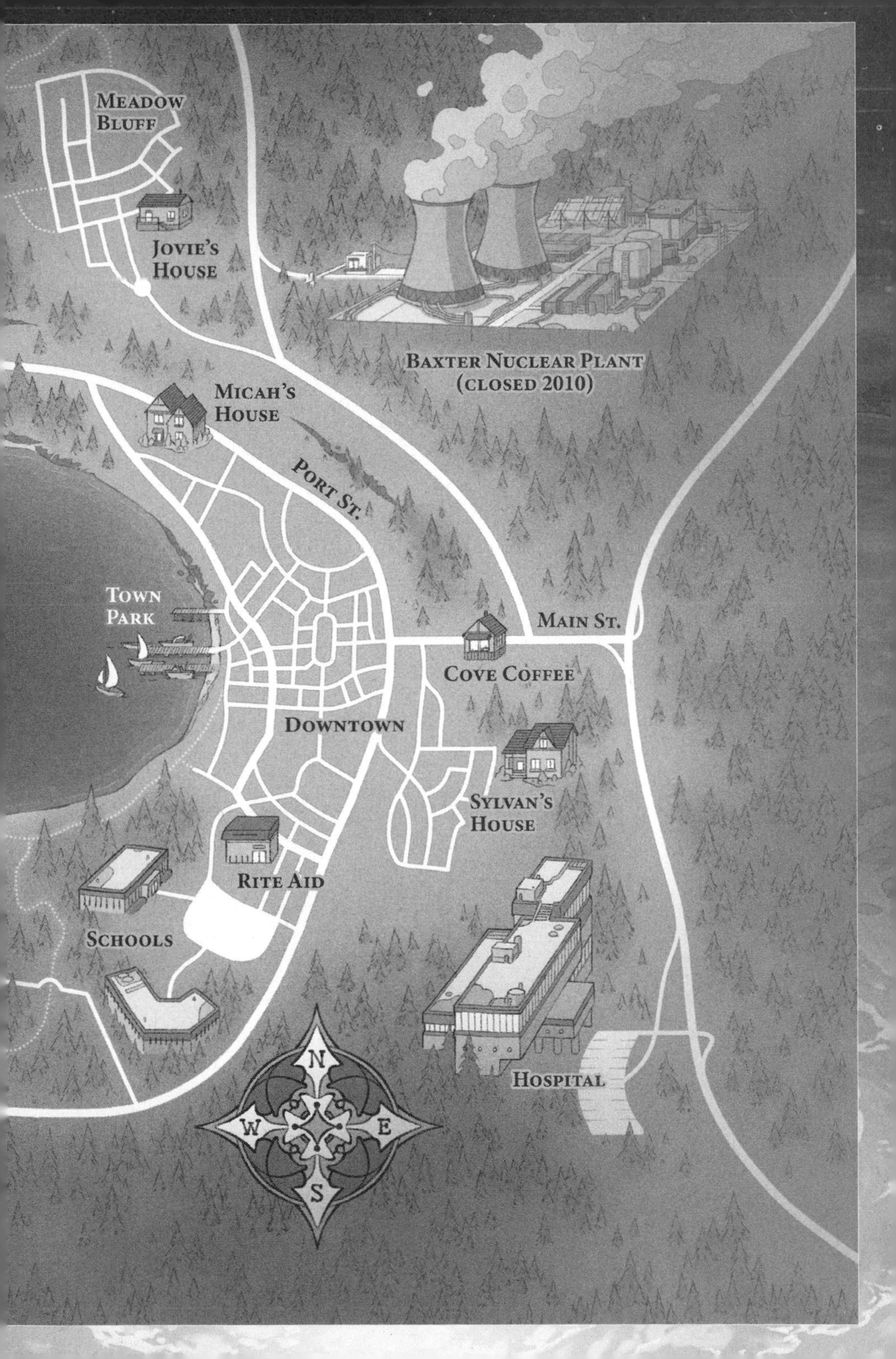

Meadow Bluff
Jovie's House
Baxter Nuclear Plant
(closed 2010)
Micah's House
Port St.
Town Park
Main St.
Cove Coffee
Downtown
Sylvan's House
Rite Aid
Schools
Hospital
N
W
E
S

CONTENTS

DRIFTERS

PROLOGUE

FIRST TRIAL, JANUARY 1898

PROJECT BARRICADE

REFERENCE CODE: 7

ARTIFACT #06450-1

SOURCE: U.S. NAVAL ARCHIVES

CLASSIFIED: TOP SECRET

Concerning the Tragic and Unexplainable Circumstances of the Sinking of the Trading Vessel ENDURANCE, an account by reporter Stephen Peters

28 January 1898

Dearest Willa,

I cannot imagine what wild rumors have reached you regarding my fate, and I hope this letter can bring you some comfort. How I long to deliver these words in person, to feel your loving embrace once more, but alas, I fear that my condition is unlikely to improve, and there is little hope of finding passage home in the short time I have left.

Before I continue, darling, I must make a solemn request: given what has transpired, I suspect this correspondence will be the only account of the Endurance's end. Therefore, I beg you, once you have read this, please deliver it to the naval authorities, and please stress to them that, though the events described herein may suggest fantasy or madness, I swear upon my father's name that all of what follows is true.

Now, for my grim tale: as you will recall from my previous letter, I joined the crew in San Diego on the tenth of December for the journey north to Skagway, in order to file a firsthand accounting of this Klondike gold rush that has of late gripped the imagination. The voyage began most amicably; I have always felt a certain ease among the swarthy clientele of such vessels, perhaps even more so than in the stuffy parlors of our fair city, and so I found the weeks at sea aboard the Endurance quite pleasant, until the fateful night of the twenty-third of January, when tragedy struck.

The hour was nigh seven. I had, as usual, declined the invitations to join the nightly round of card games, and was tucked into my hammock, attempting to organize my notes from the journey so far, when I heard the warning bell ringing on deck: three sharp tones.

Of course the bell did not always indicate danger. Sometimes, it was for a pod of humpback, which our navigator would want to chart for the whalers. Other times, for some sight of interest; there was no shortage of wild and breathtaking coastline along this journey, and the remains of spectacular shipwrecks to match.

And yet as I rose, I felt a portentous chill, and saw a similar disquiet on the other men's faces as we made our way up the narrow stairway to the main deck. For what, at this dark hour, could justify raising all hands, other than danger?

"What is it, Barson?" the captain called to the first mate, who was perched in the crow's nest.

"It's there, sir," Barson replied, pointing two o'clock off starboard. "But what it may be, I cannot say."

We crowded to the railing. The sea was relatively calm, the moonless sky clear and twinkling with uncountable stars. I could just make out the features of the coastline: a wide beach and a high bluff.

which ended sharply at what might have been the mouth of an inlet.

"There!" a crewman shouted, pointing at the water between us and the beach.

And here you must take my word, though you are sure to doubt: there was a ghostly light shimmering beneath the surface. It fluttered and danced and seemed to spiral in a vortex . . . and it was spreading quickly, causing a riot of waves above it.

"Could be a bioluminescence," said Mr. Partridge, our science officer. "Or some phosphorescence from thermal vents, though I'm not sure—"

"It is none of those things," said the captain gravely. He stared at the growing light with a calm, almost innocent visage, which at the time I found perplexing. As a disciple of our new scientific age, I spent those precious final moments engaged in fruitless theorizing: Was this a new manner of diving bell, or some technology known only to the mind of Edison himself? But somehow, the captain knew better. "Bring us hard to port, Mr. Wells," he ordered. "All hands to the rigging!"

Some of the crew took heel to their stations, but others remained at the railing with me, our eyes fixated on the light as if in a trance. And it grew ever more fascinating: blooming and pulsing, a brilliant golden-white. The water boiled, the waves becoming giant and chaotic, and the light shone bright enough to burn spots in my eyes and cause an unnatural heat on my face. At the same time, a storm was brewing overhead, dark clouds gathering in a spiral, as if this light were drawing foul weather to it.

"Now, curse you!" the captain shouted. "Move!"

Boots shotgunned on the boards, ropes groaned, pulleys whined. But we had barely begun our maneuvers when the first riotous wave reached us. The bow heaved, then fell steeply, sending us staggering for balance.

The Endurance was thrown off its line, and so we came broadside to the next wave, which loomed high above the deck rails.

"Hang on!" Barson shouted from above.

For the briefest moment, I saw in that great wave a view that challenged the imagination: a disk of pure darkness had begun to grow within the center of the brilliant vortex, like the pupil of some otherworldly eye. And yet this pupil seemed more like a window: through it, I saw stars, same as the night sky above, but also green swirls of ethereal fire, and closer, a great, hulking darkness, like the blot of a cloud against a moonless night, as if some presence lurked on the other side—for I swear to you, Willa, that was what it seemed I was witnessing, a portal into another realm. I know not how else to describe it.

Then that great wave curled overhead and broke upon us. I lost hold of the rail and was swept across the deck by the frigid, raging sea. It was sheer luck that I slammed into the mast with enough force to slow my pace; otherwise, I would have been carried overboard like so many of the crew. Instead, I was left prone against the far railing, choking and gasping for breath.

I wiped the salt from my eyes and raised my head to see that the brilliant light had only grown. It was all around us now, not just beneath the water but everywhere, such that I could no longer see the fore or aft of the ship, nor the sails—they may have already been ripped away by that point—nor even the sky above. There was only that blinding brightness.

"Ahh!" A nearby crewman shrieked, and when I gazed at him, I witnessed a horrifying sight. His eyes had clouded over with a milky-white film, becoming pearlescent, unseeing, like something from one of Poe's ghastly tales. He began to speak in wordless tones, his fingers clawing at his face, before he collapsed to the deck.

The light had grown so bright it seemed to spear through the very fiber of every board, of the air itself, but that dark pupil had grown in kind, and from within it, a figure now appeared, walking forward as if out of nowhere. A human form in a heavy blue suit, similar to what a deep-sea diver might wear, and yet lined with flashing lights, as if it were somehow electrified. The figure stopped right in the middle of the deck, looking this way and that.

I realized that I could no longer hear the waves, the wind, even the creaking of the ship. There was only a rhythmic whooshing, like breathing through a pipe, and a steady hum as if made by an enormous windmill. Then a series of urgent sounds: at first, I heard only strange clicks and chirps, but somehow, these unearthly noises began to form themselves into words in my mind, a voice, edged with fear, and sounding as if it were coming through some manner of megaphone.

"Report! What do you see, Admiral?"

"I'm not sure," a woman's voice replied from inside the suit. "I'm still taking readings—"

"Be gone, Moon Man!"

I turned to see our captain braced against the ladder to the aft deck, one arm held to shield his eyes, the other aiming his pistol at the otherworldly figure.

"No, don't—!" I shouted, not quite knowing why, yet feeling certain that no good could come from adding a bullet to this equation.

How right I found myself to be, when the captain fired anyway.

"Ah!" the woman in the suit cried, stumbling backward.

A furious tone began to blare, like a siren.

"Abort the trial!" the frightened man's voice shouted. "Bring her back, now!"

The woman staggered, a jet of steam shooting from her suit. "Close it!" she shouted. "Close it!"

That humming sound intensified, concussing my ears. The siren wailed. The last thing I perceived was the blue-suited figure staggering into that pupil of darkness, the light shrinking around her.

And then all at once, the light collapsed in on itself and vanished, and the humming ceased, leaving a hollow space in our ears, in the night itself—and also where half our ship had once been. Just beyond my feet, the entire center of the deck and the decks below had completely vaporized. There was the briefest moment of pause . . .

Then, with a titanic roar, the sea consumed what was left of the Endurance. I heard the screams of crewmen, the splintering of wood, before I myself was plunged beneath the surface. I struggled to swim, not knowing which way was up, my limbs slamming into broken timbers. A fathomless cold and dark squeezed me in its grip. . . .

Truth be told, I know not how I survived. Some pure instinct must have kept me swimming, held the air in my lungs just long enough for a forgiving wave to carry me to shore. There I awoke at dawn, flat on my back in the surf, unable to move due to a broken leg and a punctured abdomen. I shivered incessantly from the ocean cold, and yet I discovered that my arms, legs, and face were covered with red burns, as if I had been exposed to some intense heat. And while I could still see, a milky fog had accosted my vision.

I feared I might not live out the day, lying there, soon to be food for the crabs and gulls, but a whaling party of Coast Salish people happened upon me, and brought me back to their camp. They have made room for me by their fire and at their table, but despite their best efforts, my wounds are too severe, and foretell my end.

There are, to my knowledge, no other survivors.

My dear, it has taken all my meager strength to write this. I know my tale skirts the boundary of imagination itself, and I would forgive you, of course, for suspecting that I have conjured it while in the grip of some mad fever. Yet I implore you to see this note to the authorities so that other ships may avoid this same fate. For I cannot shake a feeling that this will happen again. There is something about this place, this coastline: you can feel it in the mist. As if some essential border, some comforting gravity that we take for granted as part of our very existence, is missing here. It feels as though, were you to slip just a bit, you could drift away, to where, I do not know. . . .

My rescuers seem to sense it as well. While the gulf between our languages is vast, I have learned that their village is to the north, and that while they visit this place to hunt, they would prefer not to linger. I might suggest that those seeking to settle this region follow their lead, and avoid this spot as well.

Now, dearest Willa, I fear my hour grows late, and the time has come for me to say goodbye. And while I know this will land tragically in your heart, please know that I am ready, and that wherever I end up, I shall wait for you there.

Be strong, my darling. And live well. . . .

All My Love,

Stephen

PART I

A HOLE IN THE WORLD

1

THE INTERVIEW: PART I

JANUARY 18, 2022

Picture a spark of light, like a firework shooting skyward in the moment before it explodes. This spark is traveling through the pure darkness of starless space. The only other lights are a few other distant sparks, headed in roughly the same direction.

As we move closer, we see that this single spark is actually a cluster of lights. And each of these lights is, in fact, an entire galaxy, a hundred billion fire diamonds of dazzling colors, from red to blue to white, spinning around a bright center.

Now picture a single blue dot orbiting a single white star. The dot is moving at sixty-seven thousand miles per hour in its orbit, and the star is moving at nearly five hundred thousand miles per hour around its galactic center. This galaxy is racing at one point three million miles per hour toward a mysterious presence—we call it the great attractor—that draws us, for reasons we cannot know, across the dark sea of space.

And yet.

Despite all that, it is possible, on this little blue dot, inside its blanket of atmosphere, in a tiny town huddled at the edge of a great ocean, in a small, crowded living room—

To feel like you are not moving at all. As if the universe itself has ground to a halt.

This was how fourteen-year-old Sylvan Reynolds felt on a winter night in 2022, in the town of Far Haven, on the coast of Washington State, as Dr. Wells began to speak.

"Thank you for agreeing to meet with us again."

Sylvan sat on one of the couches. Dr. Wells sat directly across from him, in a chair from the dining table, her tablet balanced on her knees. Her assistant stood behind her, tapping his phone.

"Sure." Sylvan glanced at his parents over on the other couch. His mother, Beverly, smiled supportively, but her eyes darted with worry. His father, Greg, sat with his arms crossed, glowering at the visitors.

"I'd like to revisit the events surrounding the disappearance of Jovie Williams," Dr. Wells said. "Now, as I'm sure you know, what we're discussing here is very sensitive. We do need to have your word that—"

"We signed your papers," Dad snapped. "Isn't that enough?"

"Easy, Greg," said Sheriff Marks, who leaned against the entryway to the living room. "We're all here for the same reason."

Dad narrowed his eyes at her. "You sure about that?"

"I understand your concerns, Mr. Reynolds," said Dr. Wells. "But our goal is the same as it's always been: the safety of the people of Far Haven."

Not all *the people*, Sylvan thought. He glanced at the logo on Dr. Wells's tablet: a slanted capital *B* inside a parallelogram with rounded corners. It was the logo of Barsuda Solutions. Their vehicles and their workers in black jumpsuits and hard hats were as common a sight around Far Haven as trash trucks and Amazon vans, and had been for as long as Sylvan could remember. Technically, they'd arrived when he was two, in order to clean up the accident at the Baxter nuclear plant, and to monitor the health of the town's water supply ever since.

At least, that was the tale everyone had been told.

Sylvan, however, knew the real story: one of wild lights in the water, thrashing helicopter blades over the beach, and, of course, that night, nearly four years ago now, when the ground had shaken, and his friend had vanished.

A friend who, if Dr. Wells had her way, he would never see again.

"If you really cared about us," Dad was going on, "you would've moved everyone out of this town a decade ago."

"There was a relocation incentive program," said Dr. Wells.

"Which only helped if you could already afford it," said Dad.

Sylvan felt a wave of embarrassment hearing Dad talk like that, even if he understood. You rarely met anyone who said they *wanted* to live in Far Haven. Most everyone seemed to agree that life was better in the sparkling vacation towns elsewhere along the coast, or the gleaming cities of Seattle or Portland, each a few hours away, but no one from here could really afford to live in those places. Far Haven was somewhere you ended up, rather than somewhere you chose to be. A place you couldn't escape from, even if you wanted to.

Only Sylvan knew how close to the truth that really was.

"I understand this has been difficult," said Dr. Wells. She flashed what was maybe supposed to be a kind smile at Sylvan's parents. Really, Sylvan thought she just looked bored. "Now . . ." She adjusted her glasses. "According to the case file, you weren't with Jovie the night she went missing, which was . . ." She scrolled with her finger. "January 22, 2018. Is that correct?"

"No," Sylvan said immediately. "I mean, yes, correct. I wasn't with her."

Relax! he thought. *You sound nervous.* But he could feel the sweat creeping down his arms, the adrenaline blooming in his gut. Back in elementary school, he'd never been one of those kids who got in trouble, disobeyed his parents, lied to people. How things had changed over the past four years. Now he knew all too well what it felt like to be that kid sitting in class, or at home, hoping you wouldn't get busted. "Sorry," he added, "it was a long time ago."

"That's all right." Dr. Wells gave him a smile that seemed more genuine.

Sylvan smiled back, feeling a sliver of ease. And yet he heard Jovie's voice in his head, like a ghost across time: *We can't trust anyone except each other.*

"And do you remember the last time you saw Jovie?" Dr. Wells asked.

"Yeah." Sylvan scrunched his face like it was taking him a second to remember, as if he hadn't thought about these very details every single day—*4 times 365 minus 4 equals . . . 1,456 days, except plus 1 for the 2020 leap year, so 1,457*—and the lies he had carefully prepared. "It was outside school that morning. She rode by on her bike."

"And did you two interact at all?"

"Well, we weren't *supposed* to talk," Sylvan said, flashing a glance at his mom, who looked away. "But she did say hi, and I said hi back, and she rubbed my hat I think." Like an older sister, like someone who got him in a way that neither his actual older sister, nor his parents, ever seemed to. Sylvan looked away for a moment, willing back the lump in his throat.

"And that was it," said Dr. Wells.

"I think I said, 'Have a good day'"—*"Don't go." That's what I really said, and I should have said it a hundred more times*—"And she said, 'You too,' and that was it."

"Same as he told you four years ago," Dad growled.

"I'm aware of that," said Dr. Wells. Her smile faded for a moment, and she reaffixed the band holding her dark red hair. "But we're looking for the slightest detail we might have missed. Memories tend to re-sort themselves over time; things that seemed unimportant in the moment find their way to the surface. Especially when we're talking about events that took place more than a quarter of your lifetime ago."

"Twenty-eight point six percent," Sylvan said under his breath.

"What's that?"

"Nothing."

Dr. Wells continued: "The police found Jovie's bike at the state park the next morning, in what was left of the old bunkers. Did you ever go up there with her?"

"No." This was true.

"Did she ever talk about that place?"

"No." A bit less true.

"Also the same answers he gave you before," Dad muttered.

Dr. Wells nodded tersely. "The police came to the conclusion that she died in the landslide, though no body was ever recovered. Do you think that's what happened to her?"

"I don't know." This was a total lie. And the next words that came out were ones that surprised Sylvan himself: "Do you?"

For just a moment, Dr. Wells gave him a knowing look. "Did Jovie tell you why she might have been going up to the bunkers that night?"

Sylvan wondered what would happen if he told Dr. Wells the whole story: about how the events leading up to January 2018 had begun decades, if not centuries, beforehand. What if he mentioned the drifters? Sylvan felt certain Dr. Wells would know exactly what he was talking about. And that was the game they were playing here tonight: Who knew what, and when, and what would it mean for *this* year? Because one thing was for certain: what had happened in Far Haven four years ago was about to happen again, and both of them knew it.

But instead, he simply said, "She didn't say, but I bet she was looking for Micah." He could almost see Jovie nodding with approval. *Nice. Let's see how she reacts to that.*

And sure enough, Dr. Wells's expression turned blank for just a moment. Then she flinched, almost like she'd just returned from a daydream. "I'm sorry, who?"

"Micah Rogers," said Sylvan. Inside he felt a small swell of relief. *Okay, good. I might still be a step ahead of her.* "A girl in Jovie's eighth grade class?" he continued. "She'd disappeared the September before."

Dr. Wells's face scrunched. She tapped her tablet screen, her fingernails clicking. Sylvan saw his parents exchange a perplexed glance.

"Ah right, here she is: Micah Rogers, age thirteen, reported missing September twenty-first, 2017. I must have forgotten." She looked at Sylvan. "Funny how that happens, isn't it?"

Very funny, Sylvan thought.

Dr. Wells typed rapidly as she talked: "Jovie and Micah were good friends."

"*Best* friends," said Sylvan, "except they'd had a fight before Micah disappeared. Jovie kept looking for her, though, even after everyone else had given up. She wouldn't let it go."

"Did you know Micah?"

"I knew who she was. I mean, I was only ten back then, and she and Jovie were thirteen. They weren't really hanging out with fifth graders."

Dr. Wells stopped typing and seemed to be reviewing her notes. "Okay, so Jovie was looking for Micah. Why don't you start there."

"What do you want to know?"

Dr. Wells looked at him. Her gaze sharpened and her

smile widened, her teeth perfect. Sylvan suddenly had a frigid feeling like this wasn't a game at all—instead, he was a mouse that had just been dropped into a tank with a snake.

"Tell me everything."

2

THE EMPTY SEAT

JANUARY 2, 2018
492 HOURS TO BREACH

Four years earlier, on the first day back after the school holiday break, Jovie Williams set off on her bike through the winter dark. A briny mist smudged the streetlights and coated her face. She'd worn her long underwear beneath her jeans, hoodie, and puffer jacket, but she still shivered in the predawn chill. Her eyes were heavy with sleep; school didn't start for two hours, yet here she was, out the door before Mom had even gotten home from work, determined to keep doing something that, with each passing week, seemed more and more hopeless.

Her bike chain creaked with each turn of her pedals. The old thing needed a tune-up, but there wasn't a bike shop in Far Haven anymore. Or a dad. And though Jovie had watched a couple of videos on how she could do it herself, Mom hadn't had time to take her to the Fred Meyer for the right supplies, and it turned out that kitchen vegetable oil didn't really work on a bike chain. Fortunately, her early start meant there was no one around to notice; most of the houses in her neighborhood of Meadow Bluff were still dark.

Jovie reached the state road and veered onto the bike trail beside it. High on the hillside, red lights blinked atop the concrete cooling towers of the old Baxter nuclear plant, which had loomed silently over town since the accident in 2010. Jovie barely remembered it, as she'd only been five, but her mom had said it was a pretty scary time. Radioactive cooling water had leaked into the soil and contaminated wells, streams, and beaches. Three people had died, and a handful of others had gotten sick. Everyone in Far Haven had to take anti-radiation medication for a few months, and many of their neighbors' wells had to be moved. Some houses were even condemned.

The one thing Jovie did recall was peering out her window as the cleanup workers from Barsuda Solutions skulked around her yard wearing black protective suits with astronaut-style helmets, reading meters and sticking long silver wands into the ground. But that was so long ago, it seemed more like a spooky dream than a real memory.

A few months later, the county and state had declared

that the crisis was over and everyone was safe, but even now, eight years later, Jovie and her mom kept two shelves of bottled water in the basement, and their well had a monitor on it that a Barsuda worker stopped by periodically to check. And there always seemed to be at least one spot around town, either a part of the beach or the forest, or some home or building, that Barsuda had taped off and blocked with their vans in order to do further testing or cleanup.

As for the plant, it was supposed to have been torn down years ago, but as Jovie's mom often said, this was *only* Far Haven, and so there it still stood, the concrete towers slowly crumbling, their sides covered in blackberry and ivy like they were ancient ruins.

Jovie glided down the hill to Main Street, catching a glimpse now and then of the cove, and the lighthouse blinking weakly at the end of its jetty. When she reached the bottom of the hill, she turned toward downtown. The only cars out this early were headed in the opposite direction, toward jobs elsewhere. She passed a series of dark buildings—the former hardware store, the former ice cream factory, and the former bowling alley—before reaching the KFC/Taco Bell, its lights so bright, it was like arriving at a spaceport.

Definitely the place where you'd make your stand against the zombies, Micah had joked one time. They used to talk about making a horror movie, Jovie running the camera, Micah building off her starring role in the middle school spring production, which she'd gotten even though they'd only been in sixth grade. Whether it would be zombies, mutants, merpeople, or some combination had never been quite decided. Just something caused by the old radiation. *We wouldn't even need to build sets*, Micah had said, looking around at Far Haven's patchwork of closed and dilapidated buildings with her wry smile. *It's perfect.*

Jovie coasted over to the crosswalk and parked her bike. Here she reached into her backpack and removed a flyer and a roll of packing tape. She stepped to the utility pole and positioned the paper at eye level. One rain-wrinkled corner remained of the last one she'd hung in this same spot, two weeks ago.

The tape barely stuck to the damp, staple-studded wood—a staple gun would have worked better, but they cost almost twenty bucks, and would also set off the metal detectors at school—and so she had to wrap the tape around the entire pole so it would stick to itself, a move that made it look like she was giving the pole a hug. Of course, a car passed as she was doing this.

Jovie stepped back to check the placement of the flyer and felt a familiar lurch in her abdomen, like an elevator suddenly in free fall. There was Micah's grinning face, cropped from a selfie they'd taken back in March during their last sleepover, her eyes sparkling with that ridiculous eye shadow they'd gotten at the dollar store. The text above the photo read:

HAVE YOU SEEN THIS GIRL?

And then below:

MICAH ROGERS, AGE 13, MISSING SINCE SEPTEMBER 21.

Beneath that was the police department's hotline number and the link for the web page that Micah's parents had set up.

Jovie heard footsteps coming from behind her. A man was approaching the crosswalk: black raincoat, shoulder bag, earbuds, on his way to the commuter bus stop across the street. Jovie watched him pass right by the pole without even a glance.

Her insides sank, but the man's lack of attention wasn't uncommon. After all, who had time to think about a girl who had gone missing so long ago now that it had officially happened last year?

And yet Jovie could still picture the moment when she'd walked into first period that September morning and noticed that Micah's seat was empty. That in and of itself hadn't been all that troubling, but by the time Jovie had gotten to the next class they'd shared, period five, and found Micah's seat empty there, too, the rumors had already been blazing through the halls: Police had been spotted in the main office and at Micah's house. Isla and Corey, Micah's friends—her *new* friends, the ones who had replaced Jovie last spring—had been seen sitting on the bench outside Principal Martinez's office. Did they know something? Were they involved somehow? *Suspects?*

But it had turned out they'd had no contact with Micah that morning, nor since that pool party at Braiden Sandberg's back in July, the one Micah had reportedly left in tears.

In fact, no one at school seemed to have been in contact with Micah at all leading up to her disappearance. That included Jovie. She'd wanted to talk to her during those first couple weeks of school; Micah had seemed down, and looked lonely. Jovie had almost texted her, but she hadn't been sure what to say, and besides, the last time she'd reached out, sometime late in the spring, Micah hadn't responded.

There had been a school-wide email that September afternoon. Then every phone buzzing with an emergency alert.

State police and investigators.

News vans and reporters.

A rising panic, like the entire town was short of breath. . . .

On her way home from school, Jovie had paused on the hill up to her neighborhood, leaning against her handlebars to watch the teams of officers and dogs and volunteers combing the shores of the cove. She'd seen on the news that they'd searched the beaches, the woods in the state park, even the fenced-off forest around Baxter.

The next day: Micah on the front page of the *Far Haven Herald.*

The next week: articles about Micah on the *Seattle Times* and *Portland Tribune* websites, and her class picture on a poster board outside the school library, surrounded by notes and flowers.

For almost a month, Micah's face had been everywhere, her name on the tip of everyone's tongue. . . .

And then it had begun.

The regional headlines had turned to wildfires, to elections, to holiday gift guides. Micah was *only* a girl from Far Haven, after all. But the articles in the *Herald* had dwindled in length, too. Because what else was there to say? There had been no new leads, no new evidence. Soon, the principal had stopped including updates in his weekly email. The poster board by the library had been taken down on the night of the school's fall concert and never put back up. Even Micah's parents had stopped posting updates to the web page, and stopped running ads.

By December, it was as if Micah was no longer missing; she was simply *gone.* The only sign of her that remained was the empty seat in her classes, which still hadn't been filled.

Jovie couldn't believe it: That was *it*? Shouldn't the police have been trying harder? Posing new theories, looking for new clues? Surely the search should have been getting more intense the longer Micah was missing, not less.

But there was nothing.

One afternoon, frustrated by the lack of any new articles, Jovie had repurposed an unused journal-sized notebook she'd won in a school library raffle and started a list of her own:

Causes of Micah's Disappearance

- ACCIDENT: Drowning? Hit-and-run? Fall? Lost in the woods?
- ABDUCTION: Stranger? Family? Friend?
- RAN AWAY: Relationship? Problems at home? Bad friends?

And yet just by making this list, Jovie had quickly understood the predicament the police were in, as she was almost immediately able to cross out nearly every possibility.

~~ACCIDENT~~

While an accident was possible, Micah almost certainly hadn't drowned; she was a strong swimmer, the cove had been searched thoroughly, and she definitely knew better than to swim out in the open ocean, with its frigid water and treacherous currents, not to mention the enormous driftwood logs that could be lurking within the waves at any time.

On top of that, Micah had last been seen by her parents at dinner on the night of her disappearance. She'd gone up to her room at about eight, and as far as they knew, she'd been in there all night. It was only the next morning that they'd realized she was gone. It seemed weird to Jovie that neither of them had stopped by to say good night, or crossed paths with her somewhere in the house, but still, the point was, even if Micah had been crazy enough to go swimming, she wouldn't have taken it to the double-crazy extreme of going in the dark.

But assuming that she had sneaked out in the night, the other possibilities for an accident didn't make sense, either. Micah almost always biked around town, but her bike had been safely in the garage, which meant she would have been on foot. She could have been hit by a car, but every roadside in town had been searched. Maybe a fall from some height? But the only real danger spot would've been the high bluff at Fort Riley State Park. Micah did love the view from atop the old World War II bunkers up there, but every inch of the bluff and the beach below had been searched. She liked the tunnels in those bunkers, too—she and Jovie had gotten lost for almost two hours up there back in fifth grade, a frightening ordeal, but one that had somehow made Micah only love that spot more; *it's the perfect location for the final scene of our movie*, she had said of the dank tunnels—but the bunkers had also been searched. As had the woods. Abandoned buildings. Basically everywhere.

ABDUCTION

An abduction couldn't be completely ruled out, but there was simply no evidence for it. Every member of Micah's family had been interviewed, as well as anyone who'd been in the same places as her leading up to her disappearance. And of course, there had been no ransom note or any such thing.

You did hear stories about teens meeting people online, secret boyfriends or girlfriends who turned out to be creepy adults or psychos or both, but Micah's phone records and social media accounts had been searched as well. There was still a chance that a total stranger had taken her, though no suspicious types had been seen in town that night or any of the previous days.

All of which left only one possibility:

RAN AWAY

Micah hadn't seemed like the type to run away, but Jovie couldn't be sure—a lot could have changed in the five months since Micah had stopped hanging out with her. Maybe something had happened to Micah that Jovie didn't know about. It certainly had seemed like she was starting to change before that.

But still: Why would she leave? They already knew it hadn't been for a romance; there would have been *some* digital fingerprint of that. And if something bad had been going on at home—Micah's parents hadn't seemed all that happy when Jovie had known them, but Jovie felt nearly certain there hadn't been anything dangerous or abusive going on, unless, again, it had started in those last few months—wouldn't that have come to light during the official investigation?

So all Jovie could come back to was that very last thing on her list:

Bad friends?

Isla and Corey. Those five months. Could something have happened with them that made Micah want to run away? Could it have been whatever happened at Braiden's party?

Jovie actually had a theory about that: on the night of the party, which she hadn't even known was happening, Jovie had stumbled across a photo, posted by Isla, that showed Micah beside the pool, dripping wet, as if she'd just climbed out, except instead of a bathing suit, she'd been wearing a nice crop top and what Jovie knew were her most stylish white jeans. In the photo, she was turned toward the camera, a look of shock on her face. The text of the post had read *first date FAIL!* beneath which was a string of comments featuring laughing emojis and face-palm emojis and OMGs.

Jovie had also found a post on Micah's account from a few hours earlier, a selfie she'd taken before leaving for the party, in which she looked absolutely perfect the way that Micah always seemed to pull off so easily. The caption had read: *Putting myself out there.*

Both posts had vanished by later that night.

Jovie suspected that Micah had been going to the party specifically to see Braiden. She had mentioned to Jovie once that she sort of had a crush on him. Jovie had agreed that he was pretty cute, if not also pretty cocky. His photos always looked so posed.

So, had falling in the pool been an accident—or had someone, perhaps even her new besties, Isla or Corey, pushed her in? Jovie wouldn't put it past them. Either way, it broke Jovie's heart to think how embarrassing that must have been, even for Micah, who was way more comfortable around others than Jovie was. And yet Jovie couldn't help also thinking, *That's what you get when you choose friends like that over me.* This was not a thought she'd been proud of, but she'd had it.

All that said, Braiden's party had been nearly two months before Micah had actually disappeared. If that event had really been awful enough to make Micah want to run away, why had she waited?

Also, based on what Jovie had read online, most runaways ended up coming back, or landing with a relative or a friend somewhere else. The fact that Micah hadn't suggested a twist that threatened to turn Jovie's entire list upside down: What if Micah had run away *and then* something bad had happened to her? Those possibilities seemed endless and dark, and without a lead to go on, there was almost no way to narrow them down.

Jovie had thought about asking Isla and Corey or maybe even Braiden about the party, just to see if there were any other important details from that night, but the thought of approaching them and their sneering faces made her nerves buzz like exposed wires. Besides, they'd already been interviewed by the principal and the police.

And so, just like that, the case was at a dead end.

Actually, there was one more thing, a possibility hidden in plain sight on Jovie's list, one that made her throat tight and her eyes well with tears:

What if *Bad friends* didn't mean Isla and Corey?

What if the bad friend was Jovie? If they'd stayed friends after their fight last April, if Jovie had just been there for Micah when she needed someone . . .

But she pushed ME out, Jovie reminded herself. Micah was the one who'd chosen Isla and Corey, who'd started to dress different and act different. Jovie hadn't done that; she hadn't done anything! She'd just been left behind by her best friend. Who could blame her for not trying harder?

And yet that knot of guilt remained. She and Micah had been best friends since kindergarten. They'd been at each other's birthday parties, played on the same soccer team and been in the same dance class, gone to summer camp together, gotten sick on too many sour candies from the Walgreens, gotten scolded for staying up too late at sleepovers, and shared a hundred ice-cream cones and sandwiches and mochas.

Micah had even been there, a year and a half ago now, listening through the wall with Jovie as her dad walked out, finally and for good, after the last bitter, tear-filled fight with Mom.

Sure, they'd had their rough spots along the way, as any friends did. They'd gone weeks without speaking, one time for most of a summer, but they'd always ended up back together. And so who could blame Jovie for believing, right up until that September morning, that eventually, that same gravity would bring them back into one another's orbit again?

But it hadn't happened, which left Jovie wondering: What if all those comforting phrases like *things will come full circle* or *she'll come back around* weren't true at all? Maybe nothing in life actually moved in a circle. Technically, even Earth itself didn't. Sure, it was orbiting around the sun, which was, yes, spinning around the Milky Way, but the entire galaxy was actually hurtling at millions of miles per hour through space, toward some distant spot Jovie couldn't remember the name of. Those circles were really spirals. Yesterday wasn't just in the past—it was millions of miles behind you.

Maybe things didn't come back around. Maybe things just *went*.

A best friend. A father.

Or, Jovie thought, *it's me. They just leave me.*

She sniffed and wiped her eyes. Ugh, it didn't do any good to think like this! Hanging flyers, that was still something she could do. And the sky had lightened to a dim gray, which meant she needed to get moving.

She biked on into Far Haven's historic downtown: a few charming blocks of cobblestone sidewalks and quaint buildings that could almost make you feel like you were in one of the coast's fancier vacation towns . . . until you noticed that nearly every other storefront was boarded up.

She hung a flyer on the bulletin board in one of the few thriving spots: the Salt & Sand Mercantile, a combination café and grocery store inside a creaky old Victorian house where she and Micah had gone countless times after school. She hung another on the post office window, then on the board outside the Red Apple grocery store, as well as a few on streetlight poles, before heading back out to Port Street, where she coasted into the parking lot of the Gas 'N Go.

At the far corner of the lot was Cove Coffee, the tiny stand—it was really just a converted garden shed—where Jovie worked a few mornings a week. Technically, she wasn't old enough to have a job yet, but Elena, her boss, paid her under the table, and while it wasn't very much, the money helped.

She circled around the line of cars at the ordering window and parked by the door on the other side. Inside,

Elena was making multiple drinks, the espresso machine humming and steaming, the coffeepot burbling, the shed full of the spicy scent of coffee mixed with car exhaust.

"Hey," Jovie said.

"Oh!" Elena jumped. "You startled me. Didn't I give you the week off? Not that I couldn't use you, if you have a sec!" She glanced at the mirror that allowed them to see the line at the ordering window. Cove Coffee owed most of its success to the fact that it was on *this* side of Main Street, so it caught all the people racing away from Far Haven each morning.

"I have to get to school. Just stopping by to put up a flyer." She waved the paper.

"Ooh, new band?" Elena asked.

"No." Jovie had briefly been the singer in an after-school rock band in sixth grade, which had been fun except for the actual performing part, which had terrified her. "It's for my friend—"

"What's that?" Elena said out the window. "Almond milk? Sure, no problem." She turned to Jovie and held out a cup. "Want a mocha?" She lowered her voice: "The customer's always right, even when they change their mind at the last minute."

"Sure, thanks."

Elena bent to the little refrigerator beneath the counter. "I want to hear more about this band sometime. You're so talented."

"It's not . . ." Jovie trailed off. "Okay, bye." She closed the door and felt a surge of frustration. Of course, Elena had been distracted. But that band had been almost two years ago. It was like people didn't even *want* to remember Micah.

She hung the flyer on the bulletin board beside the ordering window. As she squeezed by the cars, none of the waiting drivers seemed to notice her, all just looking at their phones. She drank her mocha as quickly as she could, grateful for the burst of warmth and sugar, and continued on up the long hill toward school, her bike chain grinding away.

Far Haven's elementary, middle, and high schools were located on the same campus, separated by wide, mud-slicked playfields. Jovie locked her bike and hurried into the middle school with the last stragglers, but stopped at the bulletin board by the office, where one of her last remaining flyers would go.

The board had been cleared off over break, and there were no pushpins to be found, so she used a short piece of her packing tape. Its tearing sound attracted a quizzical look from Ms. Daly, the receptionist in the office. You had to have permission to hang flyers, but Jovie had gotten a pass in the fall. If Ms. Daly said anything, she still had it somewhere in her binder.

The second bell rang. Jovie quickly rubbed the tape down and hurried off.

Everyone was already seated when she slipped into her language arts class. As Jovie crossed the room, her eye was drawn to the empty seat at the front table, a hole in the world that caused a hollow feeling inside her. It still seemed as if it had happened yesterday.

"Good morning, Jovie," said Ms. Neary, standing by the front board. "No tardies on the first day back, but try to be seated by the second bell, okay?"

"Yup," Jovie said, her cheeks flushed. She could feel Isla's and Corey's eyes on her from across the room, never missing a chance to revel in someone else's awkwardness.

The morning passed in a dull blur. Jovie moved from one class to the next in a daze, feeling like she was barely there, invisible to everyone else, except for a shoulder bump or two in the halls.

On her way to lunch, she passed the office and saw that the bulletin board had been freshly covered with two large posters, one announcing a Valentine's Day dance, the other for auditions for the spring drama production.

She could just imagine turning to Micah, seeing her inspecting that poster hungrily, putting the audition dates into her phone . . .

Jovie's flyer had been removed.

For a moment, she just stood there. What was the point? Spending so much of her time, using up her precious money from the coffee stand on printing and tape, if no one noticed, if no one even cared?

But then she found herself in fifth period, earth science, and there at the front corner table was Micah's empty seat. No matter if anyone else noticed it or not, *she* did.

Just keep trying, she told herself. Even if the search felt hopeless, the idea of giving up felt even worse.

THE PRINCIPAL'S OFFICE

JANUARY 5, 2018
420 HOURS TO BREACH

Friday morning, Jovie woke up to heavy rain, which meant she'd have to leave early so that she could catch the school bus, which picked her up first before making a wide circuit around the northern end of town. She rushed around her room gathering her things and had just crossed the short hall to the kitchen when she heard Mom's car pulling into the driveway, home from her overnight shift at the casino.

Jovie had been planning to just get a muffin at school—they only cost a dollar—but Mom would be hungry, so she opened the refrigerator. Dad used to be in charge of breakfasts, and of course, as Mom frequently noted, she hadn't *had* to work nights until he'd left. So, the job had fallen to Jovie.

"Hey," she said as Mom stepped in.

Mom dropped her keys and purse on the counter, her gaze somewhere between the floor and deep space. She had her wireless earbuds in, which she wore basically all the time.

Jovie quickly placed the eggs, milk, English muffins, and butter on the counter. "Mom," she said, a bit louder.

Mom seemed to startle and squinted at Jovie. She felt a squeeze of adrenaline, a weird momentary fear that her mom didn't even recognize her. "Oh, hey." Mom plucked out her earbuds and yawned. "So exhausted I didn't even notice you."

"How was work?"

"Long and slow." Mom got a juice glass and squeezed by Jovie to the fridge. In the pale light of the open door, she unscrewed the cap on a wine bottle and filled the glass. "Vampire dinner," she said, her usual joke.

"Want some human breakfast, too?" Jovie asked.

"That would be great." Mom slumped into a chair at their little dining table, which was pressed against the kitchen wall, and started scrolling through her phone.

Jovie opened the old propane camping stove, its lid squealing on rusted hinges. It sat atop the electric stove, which had stopped working a couple of months ago. Mom kept saying she was going to call someone. But if you ignored the giant sticker on the side of the stove that warned *DO NOT USE INDOORS*, the camping one worked fine.

She turned on the vent, lit the stove, flicked butter into a frying pan, and cracked three eggs on top. As they began to pop and splatter, she mixed them with one of the disposable sporks Mom brought home by the pocketful from the casino. Each one came wrapped in plastic with a napkin and salt-and-pepper packets. *The fewer dishes, the better*, Mom always said. Dad had been in charge of the dishes, too.

"Do you have to go to the studio today?" Jovie asked as she slid the English muffin halves into the toaster.

Mom sighed. "I don't have any students, but Colin says there's a problem with the heat, so I'm meeting a contractor at three."

Mom still ran the Far Haven Music and Dance Academy, a business she and Dad had started before Jovie was born. Jovie had spent countless hours there when she was younger—taking piano and voice lessons, but more often just hanging out in the lobby after school, a crowd of students and parents bustling around her. Mom and Colin were the only instructors left now, with just a handful of students each. Jovie had heard more than one person ask if Mom ever considered closing the place, including Dad. *There are still kids who need it*, Mom always replied, and to Dad, she'd added, *even if you don't*.

"Think you'll sleep?" Jovie asked.

"I should get a few hours in—" Mom coughed, damp and sharp, into her elbow. "Once I shower all this smoke off me."

Jovie scooped half the eggs onto a plate and added half an English muffin, which she quickly smeared butter on. She put the plate by her mom and tore open a fresh spork packet. "Here you go."

"Thanks," Mom said absently, still scrolling through a blur of gifs and angry headlines. "Are you working this morning?"

"Elena gave me the week off." Jovie had told Mom this at least twice already. She opened a cabinet to get her lunch. "We're out of granola bars."

"I'll put it on the list. Where were you yesterday? You weren't home when I left."

Jovie grabbed a few little bags of oyster crackers, more spoils from the casino, and tossed them in her backpack. Not exactly a healthy lunch, but it would have to do. "I stopped at the library to print more flyers."

Mom's face remained glued to her phone. "For what?"

Jovie paused in the middle of the kitchen. "About Micah," she said crossly.

Mom looked up at her. "Who?"

Jovie frowned, while at the same time feeling that empty rush, the elevator falling in her belly. "*Micah.* My best friend?"

For a moment, Mom just looked at her. Then her

phone buzzed with an alert and her eyes slid back to it. "Oh, right," she said, shaking her head. "Sorry. What are the flyers for?"

"What do you mean—"

Jovie was cut off by the sharp crack of Mom's phone slapping against the table. Her glass toppled over onto her plate, the bloodred wine seeping into her eggs. She made a low moaning sound and rubbed at her temples.

"What is it?" Jovie asked. "Another headache?"

Mom didn't reply for a moment. She'd been having what she'd described as "pulsing" headaches for a while now. She said they made her eyes hurt, and sometimes caused these bright flashes in her vision. Finally, she breathed deep. "They've been bad lately."

"I have some ibuprofen in my bag," Jovie offered.

"I'm fine." Mom waved her hand. "Lots of people say they're acting up because of the time of year."

Mom was referring to the people online who suspected that the cause of any health problem in town, from headaches to cancer, might actually be the leftover radiation from the Baxter accident. Jovie knew from her science classes that radiation could linger in the water and soil for years, and that the wet winter weather was one of the things that could dredge it up. But those same teachers had always emphasized that the water and the town were safe now, and that the data Barsuda Solutions collected from the wells and soil and beaches, all of which was available to the public, proved as much. In fact, no one in Far Haven had actually gotten sick because of Baxter in many years.

And yet whenever Jovie had tried to convey this to Mom, she just dismissed it with statements like *Nobody knows for sure*, which was true—and also how science worked—but shouldn't the actual evidence have counted for more than the wild online theories?

It seemed to Jovie as if Barsuda was one of the voices in town you could actually trust, unlike so many businesses that had closed abruptly over the years, from stores to movie theaters to an entire logging company. Unlike their last mayor, who'd been accused of stealing money.

In addition to their monitoring, Barsuda also did things to be part of town. One of their young interns had visited Jovie's sixth grade class—Micah had gone on about how cute he was, even drawing a heroic, anime-style version of him in her journal—and he talked about Barsuda's program to protect the local wildlife from any radiation effects. The whole class had gotten school binders with a big *B* logo on them. Barsuda had also sponsored the town's little July 4th parade, had funded the waterfront park by the cove, and had built new bleachers at the baseball fields. Their little office in town even had the best candy on Halloween.

Mom was still rubbing her head when her phone buzzed. "Hey, it's trash day. Could you put it out before you go? Recycling, too."

"Okay." Jovie eyed her breakfast plate, the clock on the microwave . . . and opted to put the food in a plastic container. School muffin it would be after all. She rinsed the pan and gathered the trash and recycling to put by the door.

As she slid on her jacket, she realized that her earbuds were still charging. She hurried back to her room, and as she passed through the kitchen again, Mom looked up. "Are you working this morning?"

"You already asked me that!" Jovie snapped. Mom flinched, and Jovie felt a surge of guilt. "Sorry."

"No, I'm sorry, it's my head." Mom yawned again. "Have a good day."

"Thanks." Jovie paused in the doorway and looked back at Mom, sitting there, her body crooked over her phone, face ghostly in its light. She felt a wave of sadness mixed with anger, like she wished Mom was doing better, but was also annoyed that she wasn't. Sure, there were the headaches, and the long nights at work, but also Dad had been gone awhile now, and Mom had wanted it that way. *So get over it*, Jovie thought, but also *I'm sorry*. Two voices speaking at once. The feelings overlapped and rose up in her like a wave, and all she could do was mumble "Bye" and slip out the door.

Outside, she took a deep breath, then rolled out the bins. As she started up the street, she noticed their next-door neighbor Ruth, who was in her eighties and lived alone, standing on her front path. She was holding the slim plastic bag with her newspaper and looking out into the misty dark. She did this sometimes, just sort of frozen in place, ever since she'd had a stroke a couple of years ago. Jovie liked Ruth, who was nothing but sweet to her, and yet the sight of her like this always caused a little spike of fear: Was this how Mom would end up? How *she* would end up, someday?

"Hi, Ruth," Jovie called.

Ruth flinched and looked over, the streetlight reflecting on her large glasses. "Oh, hi, dear," she said. She looked down at her paper as if remembering why she'd come out. Then she smiled. "Will I see you today?"

"No, tomorrow." Jovie helped Ruth with small jobs around the house, getting paid hopefully in cash, though sometimes just in baked goods.

"The sixth," Ruth said, nodding to herself as if puzzle pieces were fitting together. "Today is the fifth."

"That's right. See you then!" Jovie rushed on, but looked over her shoulder just to be sure that Ruth was making her way back inside.

Jovie barely made the bus, and sat slumped against the window for the bumpy, nearly forty-five minute ride to school. As she walked inside, she stopped to hang a fresh flyer on the bulletin board, just as she'd done each day this week. Whoever had put up those posters did not seem to care for her putting her new flyers directly on top of them and had removed each one, but the way Jovie saw it, *her* flyer had been there first.

Ten minutes into first period, Ms. Neary was interrupted by the classroom phone.

"Sorry, everyone." She answered and listened for a moment. Jovie returned to copying the class notes—

"Jovie." Ms. Neary was looking right at her. "Mr. Martinez wants to see you."

Eyes speared her from all sides. Jovie's cheeks burned as she gathered her things. "Sorry," she mumbled to Ms. Neary, and hurried out.

Her stomach churned as she walked through the empty halls. This had to be about the flyers. She remembered the way Ms. Daly had been eyeing her, and sure enough, her flyer from moments ago was already gone. She shifted her backpack around as she walked, hauled out her binder, and started leafing through it for the pass.

"You can head down to his office," Ms. Daly said, not looking up as Jovie entered.

Pass clutched tight, Jovie walked down the narrow hallway. The bench outside the principal's office was empty. His door was open.

"Hi, Jovie." Mr. Martinez stood by his desk. He motioned to the two chairs in front of it. "Have a seat."

Jovie slid into one, her heart hammering. Mr. Martinez eased himself into his chair and exhaled hard through his nose. He straightened his tie, slipped on his glasses, and picked up her latest flyer from his desk. "Did you make this?"

"Yeah—" Her voice came out like a croak. She cleared her throat. "Yes."

"And . . ." Mr. Martinez picked up the three other flyers. "These, too, I'm guessing." Mr. Martinez stacked the flyers, laid them on his desk, and laced his fingers together.

"I have a pass," said Jovie. She slid the paper across his desk. "Ms. Daly gave it to me in October."

Mr. Martinez eyed the pass but didn't take it. "Jovie . . ." He scrutinized the flyer and seemed to be searching for words. "I'm trying to understand. Is this part of a project? I can't imagine it's some kind of prank. That would seem unlike you."

"What?" Jovie said, stunned.

"'Have you seen this girl?'" Mr. Martinez read. "Micah Rogers. I thought maybe it was related to a book you're reading in class or something. A creative assignment. But Ms. Neary doesn't know a thing about it."

"A book?" said Jovie, her chest constricting. "That's Micah. She goes—I mean, she went to school here."

Mr. Martinez looked from her to the flyer. His brow furrowed, then he shook his head and gave her a kind smile. "You've been having some trouble at home." He glanced at his computer screen. "Your dad left. I can only imagine how hard that's been."

Jovie shrank in her seat. "I guess, but . . ."

"Have you talked to Mr. Sommers about this?"

The school counselor? "No. What does that have to do with Micah?"

Mr. Martinez adjusted his glasses. "I'm sorry, Jovie, I just—I know you're a good kid, so I'm looking for a way to understand this. Putting up flyers about a fake missing person could be triggering to members of our community—"

"It's—it's not fake," Jovie stammered. "Micah's real. She went missing on September twenty-first."

"Jovie—"

"Her seat is still empty in my classes!" Jovie knew she shouldn't be raising her voice at the principal, but she couldn't help it. Why was he saying these things?

Mr. Martinez peered at her like she was a puzzle he couldn't solve. "Look, I'm willing to skip calling home about this, but I really do think you should talk to Mr. Sommers."

"But . . ." Jovie blinked back tears. "The police were here," she said. "You talked to them."

Mr. Martinez laughed incredulously. "The police? Jovie . . . Mr. Sommers has lots of experience with what you're going through. I'm going to make you an appointment—"

"I'm telling the truth!" The tears ran down Jovie's

cheeks. She felt like she was floating in her own head, like there was no solid ground, no gravity. This made no sense! Something had to be going on here.

She thought of how Mom had reacted this morning when she'd mentioned Micah, how Elena had misheard her yesterday, the way people walked by her flyers without looking at them, and how there hadn't been any new stories about the case. . . . But then Mom *had* seemed to remember. How could she jog Mr. Martinez's memory now? Where might there be something to remind him that Micah existed?

"Our grades!" Jovie pointed at his monitor. "You can see them from here, right?"

Mr. Martinez blinked at her. "Well, yes."

"Look up Micah Rogers." Jovie reached across the desk and tapped the stack of flyers. "Search for that name, just one time, and then I promise I'll go to Mr. Sommers, or detention, or whatever you want. *Please.*"

Mr. Martinez bit his lip. Another deep exhale through his nostrils. "If you weren't one of our best students . . ." He slid his keyboard closer, checked the flyer, and typed in Micah's name slowly, letter by letter. Jovie watched the search results blink in his glasses.

He stared. His eyes narrowed.

"Is she there?" Jovie asked.

"I, um . . ." Mr. Martinez winced and kind of flinched, almost like something had poked him in the eye. "Okay, well, I guess I should apologize. I—wow." He glanced at Jovie for a moment, then back to the screen, shaking his head. "I'm so sorry, Jovie, you're right. There she is: Micah Rogers. I—I don't know how I could've forgotten her." He took off his glasses and wiped them with the cuff of his shirt. "I guess with the holidays, or something. My god," he said to himself in almost a whisper. "Micah . . ."

Jovie felt a cool flood of relief surging through her, except: "Did you really forget her?" she asked.

"No, of course not, I, um—I should call the police." Mr. Martinez shuffled everything on his desk, as if his hands needed something to do. "Get an update. The last time I spoke to the sheriff about this, she, um . . ." His brow furrowed again. Jovie saw beads of sweat there. He picked up the flyer, gazing once more at Micah's photo. "Thank you very much for bringing this to my attention. You should get back to class."

"Wait," said Jovie, her heart beating even faster now. "What's going on?"

Mr. Martinez answered as if his thoughts were miles away. "Everything's fine." He kept staring at the flyer, his lips moving soundlessly. It looked like he was saying *Micah*, over and over. Then he waved a hand at her. "I'll look into this and come find you later. It's all right. It'll be all right. Don't worry."

Jovie stood and Mr. Martinez barely seemed to notice,

so she left him there. She was out of the office and half-way back to class before she stopped in the middle of the hall, stunned. *What just happened?* No matter what Mr. Martinez said, he *had* forgotten Micah. As if she'd never even existed. How was that possible?

Back in class, she nudged Thomas, who sat beside her. "Hey, do you remember Micah Rogers?"

"Who?" he said, looking up from his phone, which he had beneath the table.

"Micah. She sat *right there*."

Thomas followed her gesture. He peered at the empty seat for a moment, then looked back at his phone. "What are you talking about?"

"What *am* I talking about?" Jovie said to herself.

"Huh?"

"Nothing."

But this wasn't nothing.

Somehow, she seemed to be the only person who remembered Micah had ever existed.

Jovie spent the morning in a daze. She eyed her class-mates, her teachers. Did any of them remember Micah at all? She hoped Mr. Martinez would have some answers, now that she'd jogged his memory. But by midday, he still hadn't come to find her.

On her way to lunch, Jovie stopped by the office again.

"Oh, he left," Ms. Daly said. "Stepped out this

morning, then called to take the rest of the day off. He wasn't feeling well."

"Oh." *If I forgot a student at my own school, I'd be sick, too,* she thought darkly.

She headed for the library, where she preferred to eat lunch. There was a blue couch by the courtyard window that had an outlet beside it for charging her phone. She plugged it in, and as she ate her oyster crackers, her body simmered with anxious energy.

What if it wasn't just Mr. Martinez, Thomas, Elena, her mom? What if it really was everyone in town, even the police? If this was really happening, if everyone had actually forgotten Micah . . .

Then I'm the only one who can help her.

But how?

THE WARNING

JANUARY 10, 2018
299 HOURS TO BREACH

Five days later, the urgent fire that Jovie had felt after her strange encounter with Mr. Martinez had all but died out to a black cinder.

She'd spent a number of hours over the weekend researching what might cause one person, or many people, to lose their memory, but once again, she'd barely finished making a list in her notebook when she'd been able to cross off every item.

Possible Reasons for Memory Loss

- ~~DEMENTIA~~—only in older people
- ~~ALZHEIMER'S~~—also very rare under 65
- ~~STRESS~~—causes some forgetfulness, but not serious enough

- ~~THINGS IN THE ENVIRONMENT: LEAD, PCBS, RADIATION?~~ Lots of bad stuff, but memory loss isn't really common

Nothing hinted at the kind of thing she'd witnessed in the principal's office. And while she hadn't quite had the nerve to start asking the strangers who pulled up to the coffee stand if they remembered Micah, or to do something rash like go to the police station and ask there, she *had* tried Mom again, this time showing her one of her flyers. After a moment, Mom had seemed to remember Micah, but just like with Mr. Martinez, Jovie couldn't shake the suspicion that if she hadn't brought it up, Mom might never have thought of Micah again. Mr. Martinez's memory didn't seem to stick, either. When Jovie got to school on Monday, he'd said hi to her in the hall as if everything was normal, as if their conversation the week before had never happened.

All of it began to make Jovie feel like *she* was the weird one. Maybe it really was just the amount of time Micah had been missing: the spiral of days and weeks and months leaving her further and further back in everyone's memory.

Maybe there was no fighting it.

School got out an hour early on Wednesdays, which made it the one afternoon of the dark winter weeks when Jovie could spend some time outside in reasonable daylight. But instead of planning to print and hang more flyers—because, Jovie thought dejectedly, what was the point?—that morning, she decided on a different afternoon plan, one that might actually make her feel better.

Before she left for school, she stuck her head into Mom's room. Mom had called in sick to the casino the night before, complaining that her headache had gotten worse. Jovie wondered how well she'd slept. A storm had passed through in the night, with howling winds that rattled the house, waking Jovie up. She'd even seen flashes of lightning out her window, a rare occurrence on the Washington coast. And once she was awake, she'd tossed and turned, thinking about Micah for what seemed like hours.

Mom rolled over as Jovie leaned into the dark room. "What is it?" she asked, her voice thick with sleep.

"Sorry," Jovie said, yawning from exhaustion. "Just wanted to see if you were feeling better."

"I'm fine, honey."

"Is the headache gone?"

"Mostly. My eyes still hurt. I just need more rest. I have students later." She rolled toward the wall. "Have a good day."

"Okay, bye." Jovie took the cue and gently closed the door. She was back in the kitchen before she remembered she'd wanted to tell Mom about her afternoon plan. Rather than disturb her again, she left a sticky note on the counter:

Going to Potter's Beach after school
Home by 5

After school, Jovie biked through downtown. As she coasted over the cobblestone streets, her phone began to buzz. She slid it from her jeans pocket and saw that it was a call from an unknown number, which she quickly muted. Her battery was under 10 percent, as usual by this time of day, and she already had it in low-power mode.

As she glided past Salt & Sand, she paused, briefly considering a mood-enhancing mocha. People were bustling in and out, and Jovie could smell the aromas of espresso and cinnamon. Their prices were really high; she and Micah used to split their order. But the little metal tables by the front steps, their favorite seats, were open. . . .

"This situation needs ice cream," she remembered Micah saying the day Jovie's dad had left. Jovie had wanted to shrink down to a singularity, but Micah had insisted they come down here and get cones of birthday cake ice cream.

"Feel better?" Micah had asked as they sat at those tables.

"Yeah."

"No you don't. It completely sucks."

Jovie had nodded and started to tear up again.

"Ice cream has healing powers," Micah had said. "We can have it every day this week. My treat." Then she'd started a game where they rated each passerby's outfit pass/fail, Jovie shooting quick videos of each contender and adding cool filters, while Micah added a fashion reporter's narration, like the street was a red-carpet runway. By the end, they'd both been in stitches.

Jovie pushed off on her bike, leaving the empty tables behind her. It just wouldn't be the same today.

She continued on out of town, along the north shore of the cove. After a mile, the road crested the hill and Jovie was buffeted by a stiff, salty breeze. A wide meadow spread out before her, rolling down to the bluff, which was much shorter here than it was down at the state park. Beyond was the wide sea, feathered in whitecaps. The mist had retreated enough today to reveal a stripe of golden horizon. The little lighthouse flashed weakly at the end of its jetty. Far off, a tanker ship blinked.

Jovie reached a small parking lot, where an old RV and a rusted camper van had been parked for months. There was no bike rack, so she hoisted her bike onto her shoulder and carried it down a rickety wooden staircase to the beach, past a sign that read *Danger: Shellfish can be contaminated. Check county website before harvesting.* There was a Barsuda logo in the corner.

Jovie reached the sand and leaned her bike against one of the enormous driftwood logs piled along the base of the bluff. Many of them were wide enough to walk along, their sides bleached and smooth, like the bones of great leviathans.

In between them, smaller logs had been arranged into makeshift shelters and forts. The one she and Micah had built back in sixth grade, and visited many times thereafter, was still standing, a little ways up the beach, though one side had partially collapsed. It had been Jovie's favorite spot, and probably Micah's second favorite, after the bunkers.

Jovie started toward it, but paused. The last time they'd been there had been almost exactly a year ago. They'd been flying Jovie's little drone, nicknamed Beryl, and had spotted migrating whales.

"We should name them," Micah had said, pointing her finger dramatically at each of the three great creatures and making her deep-in-thought face, one of her many theatrical expressions. After her star turn in sixth grade, everyone thought of her as the best actor in school, and she'd even gone to a special Shakespeare camp that summer, though oddly, she hadn't participated in the big production last spring.

Jovie had been trying to think of interesting aquatic names when Micah had said, "How about . . . Julius, Alejandra . . . and Steve."

"Steve?" They'd cracked up, sitting there in the fort, cozy against that day's furious wind, holding cups of hot chocolate from Micah's thermos, their gloves dotted with crumbs from the macaroons they'd bought at Salt & Sand. When Jovie had let Micah fly Beryl, she'd gotten so close to the whales that the spray from one of their blowholes had speckled the lens.

The fort wouldn't be the same today, either.

Jovie trudged across the sand, shivering in the whipping wind, and kneeled just above the edge of the surf, beside a lone log that was pointed at the water. A trio of wildly colorful butterflies had been drawn on it in chalk, their lower edges smudged by the highest-reaching waves.

She opened her pack, swapped her bike helmet for a knit hat, and removed Beryl from its nest of bubble wrapping. The drone had been a birthday present from Dad, the first birthday after he and Mom had split. Actually, it had arrived a day late, and in an Amazon box with a few other things, but it did matter that Dad had remembered, sort of—not in time to have it arrive *on* her birthday, or to have it gift wrapped or, you know, to actually bring it himself, but at least it was a gift she'd wanted, and something he'd been part of; he'd taken her to the science center in Olympia for the day once, and she'd loved the drone-flying exhibit there.

"Ready, buddy?" she said, unfolding Beryl's wings and locking them into place.

She turned on the remote control. The drone's propellers hummed and it lifted from the beach in its wobbling way. Jovie used the twin joysticks to guide it out over the water.

From overhead, the waves looked smooth, like contour lines on a map, their curves mirroring the coastline. A little ways out, Jovie smiled at the sight of a sea lion, its snout sticking just out of the water, its long oval body lazing beneath the surface. She watched it for a minute before sending Beryl farther out, on the hunt for bigger prey.

Just then, her phone buzzed with another call. Jovie got it out and saw that same unknown number. She probably ought to see if they'd left a message . . . and yet before she could get to her voicemail, the icon for her phone battery flashed red, and the phone died.

"Come on." She stabbed at the screen, pushed the buttons: nothing. The cold air always made her sketchy battery even worse. She should have kept it in a warmer pocket.

She had just tucked away the useless device when the remote began to beep, informing her that she was nearing the edge of Beryl's range. Jovie flew a little ways north, then south, but there was no sign of whales.

She glanced back at their old fort. Silly to think she'd have the same luck today. Things like that had always worked out better with Micah. And yet before she could avoid it, the memory of that whale-watching afternoon bled forward three months to April, when Micah had been on the band trip to Disneyland and Jovie had watched in social media fireworks as she lost her best friend to Isla and Corey.

I don't know, maybe because they're FUN.

A text from after the trip that Jovie could still picture.

They want to, you know, actually DO stuff.

Hadn't this been doing stuff? Sitting here at the beach that day? And who was this person texting her? She'd sounded nothing like the friend Jovie had shared ice creams and whale spotting with.

Jovie had replied defensively:

Sorry that I don't want to DO stuff like shoplifting.

She'd seen Isla's vague posts about the hotel gift shop.

You wouldn't understand. You weren't there.

And Jovie had felt that same old insecurity, like she wouldn't have understood even if she *had* been there. When Micah got around others, she seemed to grow to the size of the moment. Funnier, prettier, up for anything. It was like there was more of her, enough for everyone, energy that you just wanted to be around, while in the same situations, Jovie felt the opposite: shrinking, unsure of her words, her hair, her face. Instead of growing brighter, she felt like the light was leaving her, like one of those illustrations of stars on the edges of black holes, their shining plasma being sucked into darkness. . . . Sometimes, it felt like if she stayed exposed to a group for too long, she might vanish completely. Why couldn't Jovie bloom like Micah did? Why did she have to wither?

It had been getting worse, too, throughout middle

school. Jovie hadn't done any music since that after-school band, had stopped playing soccer, too. She'd even stopped riding horses on Sundays, though that had been a money-saving decision, or as Mom put it, *your father's fault*. She knew all these choices had something to do with her parents splitting up, even though that had made her want to be home less, but also, she couldn't shake the feeling that she was *wrong* somehow. Lacking something everyone else had. Why would Micah even want to hang out with someone like her?

And yet Micah had never seemed to mind. She could go supernova with ease in a group, but when she and Jovie were alone, it was like they were the only two people on the planet. At Salt & Sand, in their driftwood fort, it had been just them, and it had seemed perfect.

Then Disneyland. Suddenly, that balance had changed. And it had hurt so much. Before last April, Jovie couldn't remember feeling alone when she was alone. Ever since, it was like that black hole was around all the time, her light dimming, a constant chill. It hurt to be left behind. To not be chosen. But more than that, it hurt to know that what you thought was everything wasn't enough for someone else.

She probably should have been mad at Micah for dropping her, but all she could feel was how much she missed her.

Jovie wiped her eyes and brought Beryl in. She sighed,

and another thought whispered in her mind, the same one that always arrived right after those painful ones:

There has to be something I missed.

There just had to be.

Beryl had nearly reached shore when Jovie noticed a sound like a voice. She turned and spotted a tall older man just down the beach, walking slowly in her direction. She'd seen him before on previous visits. He was wearing a long brown duster coat that, because of his height, looked too short on him. He also had on high rubber boots, one of those plaid hats with earflaps, and big headphones that were connected by a spiral cord to the metal detector he was swinging back and forth. Over the breeze, Jovie could hear that he was humming to himself.

She brought Beryl down to her lap and started putting her away, noticing now how quickly the afternoon had dimmed to dusk. The mist had thickened, and the waves had taken on an inky darkness.

"Hey there."

Jovie looked up to see that the tall man had stopped behind her.

"See anything good?" he asked, smiling broadly. He was far enough from her that he had to speak up over the wind and surf, and yet the steep angle of the beach made it feel as if he was looming over her.

"Just a sea lion," Jovie said, zipping up her pack and standing up.

The man peered past her, raising a hand to shade his eyes. "Uh-huh. Saw some whales yesterday." His mouth moved like he was chewing on something. There was a glint of light by his temple. Was that aluminum foil under his hat? Then he flinched, like he was snapping out of a trance, and held up his detector. It had what appeared to be a triangular shard of glass, roughly a foot long, affixed near the handle with many layers of duct tape. "I'm coming up empty today, too," he said. "Normally, it's good hunting after a storm, but last night's storm was a bit *abnormal*, wasn't it?"

"I guess," Jovie said, thinking of the lightning outside her window.

"I'm Harrison. I own the Treasure Trove."

"Right." Jovie knew the place. It was a ramshackle little house downtown, stuffed with dusty junk. She and Micah had been in there, and though they'd never actually bought anything, it was kinda neat, in a pirate-y, shipwreck-y sort of way. "Nice to meet you."

"Uh-huh." Harrison didn't move. He kept looking at her, grinning. Jovie noticed now that his teeth seemed to be stained blue.

She felt a tingle in her legs, like she should get going. Harrison didn't seem threatening, but he was still a strange man, acting oddly, on this otherwise empty beach. And it was getting dark. "Well, I gotta go." She started down the beach to circle around him—

"You're the one who puts up the flyers about the missing girl, aren't you?"

Jovie froze. "You've seen them?"

"Oh sure," said Harrison. "But you're not going to find her that way, you know."

Jovie peered at him. "Why not?"

"You can't find someone who nobody is looking for."

A nervous chill surged through Jovie. "No one remembers her," she said hesitantly.

Harrison's expression lit up. "Uh-huh."

"Do you . . . do you remember Micah?"

"No, but I can tell that you do." He gazed out at the ocean with an odd, detached look. "Uh-huh," he said again, absently. "That's the question."

"What is?" Jovie asked. "You mean why everybody forgot about her?"

"No." Harrison tapped his head. The foil in his hat made a crinkling sound. "Why do we *remember*?"

A tremor of fear quaked in Jovie's belly. "What do you mean?"

"Most people just forget," he said. "They have it easy. But some of us are cursed with memory. . . ." He blinked rapidly, like he was snapping out of a trance. "I can help you."

Jovie's heart had started to pound. "Do you know what happened to her?"

Harrison shook his head, and Jovie thought she saw

tears rimming his eyes. "No. Nobody does. Not really. The only question you can answer is why they left," he said, sniffling. "They're already going before they're gone. That's where you have to look."

Jovie could barely follow. But she thought of what he'd said a moment ago: *we*. "Did you lose someone too?" she asked.

Harrison answered with a nod.

"Someone who everyone else forgot?"

A more emphatic nod.

"What happened to them?"

Harrison just stood there for a moment, looking out at the water. Finally, he spoke in nearly a whisper: "It's coming. Just like it did before. You have to be careful. Don't get too close. All it does is take. Don't let it take you, too."

"I don't understand—"

"Jovie!" The voice reached her ears over the wind. Jovie spotted a woman standing at the top of the staircase, waving her arms.

Her heart skipped a beat. She didn't think she recognized the woman, and yet Jovie immediately thought of those calls she'd been getting before her phone died. . . .

"Time to go," Harrison said dreamily, then turned and continued up the beach.

Jovie looked from him to the woman. She was still waving. Meanwhile, Harrison had started humming and swinging his detector back and forth.

"Wait—" Jovie called halfheartedly, but then she returned to her bike and climbed the stairs to find out what was so urgent.

"Hey," the woman said as Jovie reached her. "Thank goodness I found you." She was smartly dressed in boots and black jeans and a nice hiking-style raincoat. "I'm Beverly Reynolds. My son takes clarinet lessons with your mom." Beverly started down the path toward a car parked in the middle of the lot. "I tried calling you."

"Sorry." Jovie followed her, catching her breath. "My phone died. What is it?"

"Something's happened to your mom," Beverly said over her shoulder. "I'm here to take you to the hospital."

5

THE EMERGENCY ROOM

JANUARY 10, 2018
290 HOURS TO BREACH

"We showed up for a lesson and she wasn't there," Beverly said as they reached the car. She opened the driver's-side door and leaned in. "Sylvan, let Jovie sit in front."

Jovie spied a boy through the windshield. He was younger, likely in elementary school, and had his eyes fixed on a handheld game console. He brushed his hair away from his glasses as he looked up, and when he saw Jovie, he startled, as if he hadn't quite realized she was there. He hurriedly gathered up his things.

"Colin tried to call her, but she didn't answer," Beverly continued, speaking over the wind. "He had a student coming in, so I said I'd go by your house. I wasn't trying to pry, but I looked in the kitchen window and that's when I saw your mother. She was lying on the floor. I called an ambulance, and the paramedics found that note you left, and Colin gave me your number. When you didn't answer, I came here."

Jovie listened, stunned. "Is she okay?"

"I think she will be." Beverly opened the car's back hatch. "Will your bike fit in here?"

"Yeah." Jovie lifted her bike in.

Beverly peered beneath the hatch. "No, honey, use the door," she said, but Sylvan was already clambering over the front seat into the back.

Beverly shut the hatch and they got in the car, Jovie taking the passenger seat.

"Was it her headaches?" Jovie asked.

"I'm not sure." Beverly backed out and accelerated up the road. "What kind of headaches has she been having?"

"She said she saw flashes in her vision. She stayed home sick from work last night . . ." A wave of guilt rushed through Jovie. Had she been so tired from the storm that she'd missed something this morning? Some sign that Mom was worse than usual?

"That will be good information to pass along to the doctors. She regained consciousness as they were getting her onto the stretcher, but—" Beverly seemed to catch herself.

"What?" Jovie asked.

"Tell her about the eyes, Mom," Sylvan said. Jovie

craned her neck and found him gazing at her, yet at the same time his thumbs were still flying over his console.

Beverly flashed a flustered glance at him in the rear-view mirror. "It was only for a second, and I can't be totally sure what I saw."

"What do you mean?"

"Your mom had eyes like a night wraith," Sylvan said.

"Sylvan!" Beverly snapped. "Sylvan and I were there beside your mother as they were wheeling her to the ambulance. She opened her eyes for a moment, and . . . it looked like they had turned white. I know that sounds strange, um . . . Had she been treated for cataracts, or had any other issues with her vision?"

"Her eyes are fine," Jovie said. "I mean, I thought they were. She said they hurt this morning, but . . ."

"We'll know more when we get there. I work for the hospital—I'm at a different clinic, but I know one of the doctors working in the ER today. Your mom's in good hands."

"Thanks," Jovie said quietly. She breathed deep, but her insides were churning. All of this felt unreal.

Beverly glanced back at Sylvan again and said, under her breath, "You need to remember that the real world is not one of your *Shadow Realm* games."

"Sorry," he muttered.

They drove on quietly, just the hum of the road and the plinking electronic sounds from Sylvan's console.

The hospital was on a hilltop off the state highway. By the time they pulled into the parking lot, it was nearly dark. The mist had blown in and gathered around the streetlights, turning them into softly glowing moons. As they crossed the wet pavement toward the blindingly bright ER entrance, Jovie started to tremble. She didn't want to go in. She just wanted to go home, and for none of this to be happening.

The doors whooshed open, and they were greeted by a gust of warm air with a chemical smell. Brilliant white floors reflected stark white ceiling lights. It wasn't the chaos you always saw on TV shows, but instead, an almost eerie stillness. There was a long desk ahead of them with multiple staff sitting at screens. To one side was a set of double doors; to the other was a brown-carpeted waiting area with almost every chair filled.

"Okay, you guys wait here," Beverly said. "I'll find someone to talk to." She headed toward the desk.

Sylvan made his way to the only pair of empty seats in the waiting area, but Jovie felt frozen, looking at the slouched bodies and forlorn faces. She could feel the sickness and dread in the air . . . but then Sylvan waved emphatically, which caused a couple of people to look up, and Jovie felt a burst of embarrassment and hurried over.

They sat squeezed between a young family beside Sylvan, the daughter asleep across her parents' laps, and, beside Jovie, a crooked old man with tubes snaking from his nose down to an oxygen tank. Jovie tried not to react to his powdery smell or the gentle wheeze of his breaths. A loud, virulent cough a few chairs over, the din of two newspeople shouting angrily on the TV in the corner . . . each thing made her heart pound harder.

Jovie got out her phone, then remembered it was dead. She dug into her backpack for her cable, only to realize that the nearest outlet was on the other side of the old man.

"Want a charger?" Sylvan held out a small silver stick, still playing his game with the other hand.

"Thanks." Jovie plugged her phone into it. She spied Beverly heading back through the double doors. As they swung shut, the emergency room became still once more. And yet Jovie felt a tingling sensation on the back of her neck, almost like she was being watched.

Just then, the outer doors whooshed open, startling her, and a man came in, pushing a woman in a wheelchair.

Jovie shook her head. She had to *relax*.

"What are you playing?" she asked Sylvan. He was controlling a character who was doing battle with a horde of shimmering creatures in a cave.

"*Shadow Realm: Reanimated*," he said. "Do you know it?"

"Not really."

"So far I think it's the third-best game in the series.

There have been seven total. Wanna try?"

"That's okay." Jovie eyed the double doors: no movement yet. "I've seen you around the music school."

"I've been taking lessons with your mom for a couple years," Sylvan said without looking up.

"What grade are you in?"

"Fifth. But I'll be eleven in . . . ten days, thirteen hours. Then only six more months until middle school. One hundred and sixty-two days, not counting summer."

"Wow. Cool."

Sylvan added quietly, "With summer, it's two thirty-eight." He bent close to the console, his thumbs clacking feverishly. The device buzzed with impact effects, and Jovie saw that Sylvan's character was using a massive battle-ax gleaming with magic to finish off some sort of enormous demon. The demon split in two and then evaporated in a shimmering silver cloud, and the game switched to a cutscene.

Sylvan looked up. "You were my reading buddy in second grade."

For a moment, Jovie didn't know what he was talking about, but then the memory came to her. Back when she was in fifth grade, her class visited the younger kids once a month and read with them, sitting on pillows on the floor. Suddenly, there he was in her mind: a smaller, round-faced version of the boy beside her now. "Oh yeah."

"That was cool," Sylvan said. "You were a really good reader."

"Thanks." Jovie didn't think of herself that way—she got lost when reading, more often than not, except for graphic novels—but also the thing she remembered most about those reading-buddy times was how she and Micah, who had been sitting with her own second grader nearby, would do weird character voices to make one another laugh. Micah had been more emphatic about it, while Jovie had been more tentative, but she'd played along. "We read that book about the trolls, right?" Jovie said, remembering the deep voice Micah had made.

"Yeah! That was fun," Sylvan said. He looked like he wanted to say more, but then bent back over his console and started the next battle.

Jovie's gaze returned to the double doors. What was going on back there? Was it taking so long because her mom's condition was worsening? What if she was dying?

They're already going before they're gone. Harrison's strange words from the beach drifted back into her head.

Jovie reached into her backpack and fished her investigation notebook from the very bottom, where it had been all week. The cover had a glossy photo of a palm tree on a crystal-white beach, the palm tree embossed, the sand coated with a gritty-textured glitter. Micah had helped her pick it from the raffle prize box, as the two of them often spent time looking at social media accounts with travel photos, the more tropical, the better. She slid the pen out of the spiral rings, opened to a new page, and wrote:

Harrison _____—owner of the Treasure Trove

- Knew I was looking for Micah
- About Micah: "They're already going before they're gone"
- He lost someone who people forgot about, too?
- Said "It's coming, just like it did before"—what does this mean?

"What's that?"

Sylvan was eyeing her list. Jovie quickly put her hand over it. "Nothing, just doing a project."

"Oh, okay," he said, as if this was a relief to hear.

Jovie turned to him. "Hey, do you remember a girl named Micah Rogers? She was in my grade, and she was there on those reading-buddy days."

Sylvan's face scrunched. "I don't think so. The only older kids I know are in my coding class. And a few who I see online, playing *Shadow Realm*. But I'm not really sure if any of them are from around here. Everybody in *Shadow Realm* uses aliases like—"

"She went missing," Jovie said over him.

"Oh. Who?"

"Micah. My friend. Back in September."

"I don't think I heard about that."

"Right." Jovie tapped her pen against her notebook.

"What happened to her?" Sylvan asked.

Jovie shook her head. "I don't know. And it's like everyone's forgotten her."

"Well, I don't think Harrison Westervelt—that's his last name, by the way." Sylvan tapped the blank space Jovie had left at the top of her page. "I don't think you need to worry about him. He's not like a kidnapper or anything, if that was what you were thinking. At least, I don't think so."

"I wasn't thinking anything yet," Jovie said. She looked at her page. "It wasn't actually an interview; he just started talking to me on the beach." Something in the way Sylvan had spoken made Jovie curious. "What do you know about him?"

Sylvan looked at her with mild surprise. "I mean, all kinds of weird stuff has happened to him. First of all, his dad spent most of his life in jail, and his mom died in an explosion."

"An explosion? Wait, are you talking about the Baxter accident?"

"No, that wasn't an explosion . . ." Sylvan sat up and turned off his console. "You've heard of the Vanescere Bathhouse, right? It blew up in 1962?"

"I have no idea what that is."

Sylvan whistled dramatically. "Okay . . . well, that's when Harrison's mom died, but there's even more than that. His wife and son drowned in the Ascension Camp incident. You *must* have heard of that."

"Uh, no?"

"Nineteen ninety-four?" Sylvan said, incredulous. "A freak storm washed away a bunch of people camped on the beach? Harrison was the main organizer of the event. He got sued because of it and ended up nearly broke."

"How do *you* know about all this?"

"Oh, so last year I started reading those I Survived books." Sylvan pushed up his glasses. "You know, the ones about different tragedies? Like the *Titanic* and stuff?"

"Sort of." Jovie remembered seeing them on kids' desks in school.

"I burned through, like, all of them," Sylvan went on, his voice picking up speed, "and so then for a final project in social studies—we were studying Washington state history—my teacher let me write my own, about the Baxter accident. But when I started reading about that, I learned about all this crazy stuff that's happened in town. Far Haven has a pretty weird history, it turns out. I was thinking that I would make a bunch of YouTube videos about it all, but I haven't gotten around to it yet. Actually, it's more like I keep forgetting to start. I don't know. The point is"—Sylvan tapped Jovie's list—"Harrison hasn't just lost someone, he's lost a *lot* of people."

"Okay, but what's that have to do with Micah? She wasn't even alive when those things happened."

Sylvan shrugged. "Yeah, well, maybe Harrison thinks there's some sort of connection. He's been through a lot and he's kinda odd. But who knows? Maybe he's right, and there's a pattern of missing persons in town or something."

"Nobody's said anything about that kind of thing," said Jovie.

"Sure," said Sylvan, "but sometimes it takes a while to put the pieces together. A lot of times, they don't catch serial killers until like, decades later."

"There's not a serial killer!" Jovie snapped.

"Sorry, I just meant as an example . . . like of how sometimes things are connected but you don't know it yet."

"Well, you're the big history expert," Jovie said. "Have *you* heard of a pattern of missing people in town?"

"No. Unless nobody remembers them. You said everybody's forgotten about your friend, um . . ."

"Micah."

"Right."

A chill ran through Jovie. "That's crazy," she muttered.

"I just mean it as a theory," said Sylvan, turning on his game again. "That's what detectives do, right? Consider every possible theory?"

"We're not detectives," Jovie said.

Sylvan just shrugged, his thumbs flying. The console chirped with the sounds of death and mystical combat.

Jovie shook her head, her thoughts in a jumble. None of this made sense. At the same time, she clicked her pen and added another note to her page about Harrison:

Could there be more forgotten people?

But even if that were the case, how would she ever find out about it?

She put her notebook away and sighed, looking from the double doors to the front desk. Why was this taking so long?

"I lost someone, too." Sylvan was still playing, his hair falling in front of his face.

"Oh." Jovie wasn't sure what to say, but then, Sylvan wouldn't have said anything if he didn't want to talk about it. "Who?"

He paused the level. "My older sister, Charlotte. I mean, she's not actually missing or anything. She's just down in LA." Sylvan's voice lowered to barely above a murmur. "She's not really around ever. I mean, why would she be? She's nineteen and she's such a good singer and actor, I get it, plus, she and Mom are always going at it, but . . . it *feels* like I lost her."

"I'm sorry," said Jovie.

Sylvan's eyes flashed up and then back down. "Here's Mom now."

Beverly had appeared from behind the double doors, along with another woman, who wore a white lab coat and carried a tablet. As they approached, Beverly pointed Jovie out.

"Can you keep an eye on my stuff?" Jovie asked Sylvan, getting to her feet.

"Sure," he said, returning to his game.

Jovie moved to the edge of the waiting area, and her heart tripped over itself as she saw the grave expressions on the two women's faces.

THE GIFT

JANUARY 10, 2018
289 HOURS TO BREACH

"Jovie, this is Dr. Aaron," Beverly said as the two women arrived in front of her.

"Hi," Jovie said, her voice barely above a whisper. "Is my mom okay?"

"She's stable," said Dr. Aaron. She had a kind expression, but one that gave Jovie no hint whether the news was good or bad. "You can come back and see her now."

"I'll catch up," said Beverly, going over to Sylvan.

Jovie followed Dr. Aaron through the double doors. The hall on the other side was a stark contrast to the quiet of the waiting area: cluttered with medical equipment and people hurrying this way and that. With every step, Jovie felt like she was in the way.

"Your mother's conscious now, but in and out of sleep," Dr. Aaron said. "Based on the bump on her head, we think she passed out. Could have been a light-headed spell, or dehydration. . . ."

"So she's going to be all right?"

Dr. Aaron stopped beside a doorway and looked at Jovie seriously. "Your mom has some other symptoms that, to be honest, we don't quite understand."

"Can I see her?"

"Yes, I just want you to be ready." Dr. Aaron put a hand on Jovie's shoulder. "Beverly said she'd described the condition of your mom's eyes. . . . It's still going to come as a bit of a shock."

Jovie nodded, her stomach in a knot.

Dr. Aaron stepped into the dimly lit room. Mom was in a half-reclined bed, her head to the side, eyes closed. She wore a hospital gown, a thin gray blanket over her. Her face was pale, her eye sockets deep in shadows, as if she'd somehow aged twenty years since Jovie saw her that morning.

Dr. Aaron moved to the side of the bed, but for a moment Jovie just stood there in the doorway. The blinking lights and strange mechanical sounds made it seem as if she was stepping into a spaceship, one that was here to take her mom away.

They're already going before they're gone. Jovie had a sudden terrified feeling, like this had already been happening for a while and she hadn't quite noticed, and now it was too late.

Mom snapped up and her eyes flashed open. She blinked rapidly. "Who's there?"

Jovie flinched in shock: her mom's eyes were completely covered in a milky-white film.

"Hey there, Alex," Dr. Aaron said gently. "I have Jovie with me."

"Jovie . . ." Mom's head turned, her ghostly eyes darting back and forth. "Where are you?" Her voice was paper-thin.

Jovie willed herself to step closer and took Mom's hand. "Right here, Mom." At least her skin felt warm, normal, alive.

Mom shook her head, her white eyes glinting like pearls. "I can't see you. Doctor, do you know anything yet?"

"We're waiting on the results of the tests."

"My legs still hurt," she said.

"I know. Hopefully the pain relievers will help."

Tears slipped from her milky eyes. "I want to go home."

"Not just yet." Dr. Aaron checked the readings on the monitors and tapped them into her tablet. "All your vitals look good. Just hang in there."

"It's gonna be okay, Mom," Jovie said, and yet she could barely breathe.

Mom shut her eyes and made a hissing sound.

"What is it?" said Jovie.

"More flashes?" Dr. Aaron asked.

Mom nodded. "It's too bright."

"We'll keep the lights down." She moved to the wall and dimmed them further. "Just try to rest, okay?"

Mom nodded again, her face still pained. Dr. Aaron motioned for Jovie to follow her out.

"See you soon, Mom," Jovie said, rubbing Mom's hand a last time and yet also hating how she felt thankful that her eyes remained closed. She reached the door and looked back, a lump in her throat. She had a sudden feeling like this was her fault, like she should have been taking better care of Mom. Irrational thoughts spiraled in her head: *Please don't take her. Please don't go. . . .*

Beverly was waiting in the hall. She patted Jovie's shoulder.

"Will her eyes get better?" Jovie asked.

"She'll need to have surgery to remove the cataracts," said Dr. Aaron. "Given their aggressive nature, we've scheduled an emergency procedure for tonight."

"Aggressive?" Jovie asked, her belly lurching with worry.

Dr. Aaron slid her finger over her tablet and shook her head. "Cataracts usually take at least a few months to form, and even that is uncommon. More often, they take years. But these developed in a matter of hours."

"Have you ever seen that before?" Beverly asked.

Dr. Aaron looked down the hall before lowering her voice. "It shouldn't even be possible."

"Then what's happening?" Jovie asked.

"That's what we're going to find out," said Dr. Aaron. "We heard she's been experiencing bad headaches? Migraines?"

Jovie swallowed. "I think so. She's had them for a while."

"Well, her other symptoms—the weakness and fainting, the white flashes in her vision—all of those could be related to migraines. But not the cataracts."

"Is it a tumor?" Jovie asked. Wasn't that usually what weird symptoms meant?

Dr. Aaron pursed her lips. "We certainly don't want to jump to any conclusions. If there is anything abnormal like that, we'll know shortly. In the meantime, I need to look into what other tests we can run."

"What about the radiation?" Jovie asked, thinking of the things Mom had said. "We live close to the plant—"

But Dr. Aaron was already shaking her head. "If your mom had any exposure, we would've known from the monitoring. And even so, existing radiation levels would be far too low to cause anything like this."

"But something had to cause it," Beverly said, her brows knitted in thought.

Dr. Aaron nodded. "I wish we had more answers right now."

"Can I stay?" Jovie asked.

"Of course," said Dr. Aaron. "Is there another family member we can contact?"

"My dad," Jovie said. "He works late, though. I'm not sure when he'd be able to get here." And she worried that when he did show up, he'd be annoyed about it. He'd say he wasn't, of course, but Jovie could always feel it.

"I could call him," said Beverly, as if reading Jovie's apprehension. "I'm sure I can convey the seriousness of the situation to him."

Jovie nodded. "Thank you."

Dr. Aaron checked her watch. "Surgery is scheduled for eight. Hang in there until we know more, okay?" She walked briskly up the hall.

Beverly led her back to the waiting area. Jovie gave Beverly her dad's number and then dropped back into her seat.

"How'd it go?" Sylvan asked, still playing his game.

"I don't know." Jovie felt a simmering urge to scream, not at anyone in particular, but at everyone and everything. Or maybe just to cry. She held her breath. She pictured her mom in that spaceship room, her eyes. . . .

"My mom said that your mom's cataracts are super strange," said Sylvan.

"Yeah," said Jovie, her heart still pounding.

"Did your house get struck by lightning?"

"What? No. Why'd you ask that?"

"I heard that the lightning last night caused weird electrical surges around town. Not just power outages, either—some of my friends online, their whole computers got wiped."

"Abnormal," Jovie said faintly. That was the word Harrison had used for the storm. "But lightning doesn't cause cataracts, does it?"

Sylvan shrugged. "It's still weird, though, right?"

He got back to his game. Jovie sat there for a lost moment and felt the sting of tears again. She leaned forward to get a tissue from her backpack—

And froze.

The top of her bag was partially open. Hadn't she zipped it up when she'd gone to see Mom? She was almost certain she had, though she had been distracted.

She eyed Sylvan. "Did you open my bag?"

"Huh?" he said absently.

"Nothing." Jovie glanced at the old man beside her, but he was asleep, his head lolled over. Not exactly the bag-snooping type. *Maybe I just forgot to close it*, Jovie thought. She reached down and unzipped it farther to check on her stuff—

And froze again. There was something inside her bag. Something that hadn't been there a few minutes ago.

"What's up?" Sylvan had paused his game.

"I'm not sure." Jovie reached in gingerly and removed the object. It was a polished wooden box, about six inches long and three inches wide, with golden hinges and a golden latch. The wood was a deep maroon color, and while it appeared to be in good condition, Jovie thought it also seemed very old; there were thin cracks here and there in the lacquer, and a slight warping to the wood. Some tarnish, too, on the hardware.

"Ooh, what is that?" Sylvan asked.

"I don't know." *More importantly*, Jovie thought, *what is it doing in my bag?*

"Open it," he urged.

Jovie peered around the ER, her mind tingling with that same odd sensation she'd had shortly after they arrived. . . . Who had put this here? Her eyes moved from face to face in the waiting area, but everyone was either asleep or gazing into their phones, and the front-desk staff was busy on their computers. Everything looked normal, but it didn't feel that way. Jovie's heart pounded, and she felt a burning flush inside that made her head swim.

"Come on." Sylvan reached over.

Jovie moved the box away. "I'll do it."

"Sorry."

"No, it's okay, just . . ." She unfastened the latch and flipped up the lid. The inside of the box was lined with stiff black felt, molded to cradle a small cylindrical object, about five inches long and made of a smooth, dark-silver metal. Jovie plucked the cylinder from its snug fitting. It seemed heavy for its size. At one end, it had a small glass circle that seemed to be an eyepiece. The other end had a convex lens as wide as the cylinder.

"It looks like a little spyglass," said Sylvan.

Jovie frowned. "This isn't the 1800s." Except that was exactly what it looked like.

"Maybe it's a kaleidoscope?"

Jovie held it to her eye and looked through the small hole. "Definitely not a kaleidoscope." There was no color design. Instead, she simply saw what appeared to be the waiting room, but it wasn't magnified, either, as a spyglass would have done; at least, she didn't *think* it was. She couldn't be sure because the view through the device was completely blurry, like looking through frosted glass, and there were faint swirls of oily rainbow colors around the edges.

She lowered the cylinder and looked for a way to twist it into focus, but there was none.

"You try." She handed it to Sylvan and then peered around the empty ER again, her nerves tingling.

Sylvan held the device to his eye. "Maybe it's supposed to work like a spyglass, but the lenses need to be calibrated."

"How do you do that?" Jovie asked.

"I don't know. I just feel like I've heard that about things with lenses. Microscopes and stuff. My science teacher might know."

"Is that Ms. Harter? Is she still at the elementary school?"

"Yeah." Sylvan lowered the spyglass and ran his finger along it lengthwise. "Hey, there's something here." He peered at it. "There are words. Look."

Jovie took the sypglass. There was writing etched into the side. The letters were very small, simple print with rough endings and jagged curves, as if they'd been done by hand:

PROPERTY OF F.D.L.

"Who's F.D.L.?" asked Sylvan.

"No idea." Jovie handed Sylvan the glass and did a quick search on her phone. "I'm not getting any people, or like, organizations or anything. It could stand for 'fall down laughing' or a bunch of other random things, but . . ."

Sylvan looked around the ER. "I'm pretty sure there wasn't anyone messing with your bag. I was in the middle of a level, but . . . Could someone have put it in there before we got here?" He whirled around to face her. "What if it was Harrison? I mean, he owns an antiques place."

"He never got close to my bag," Jovie said, thinking back to the beach. She took the spyglass back and looked through it again: still just a useless blur. Then she put it in her lap and turned her attention to the box. She inspected the sides, then the bottom. Other than scuffs and hairline cracks in the old wood, there were no other markings.

As she held it upside down, something slipped from the seam between the felt lining and the wood. A tiny paper square, flitting like a moth as it fell between Jovie and Sylvan.

He doubled over, plucked it off the floor, and held it out to her. It was an inch-wide strip of lined paper, like from a notebook, folded three times. Jovie unfurled it, revealing a single sentence in black ink. The print letters looked like they'd been written by someone her age. She held it out so Sylvan could see, too:

LOOK AT WHAT IS LOST

"Okay," said Sylvan. "What's that supposed to mean?"

A nervous vibration grew more urgent in Jovie's stomach. "Micah."

"But it doesn't say *for*, it says *at*."

"Huh?"

"It doesn't say to look *for* something lost," said Sylvan, "it says to look *at* something lost."

"How would you do that?" Jovie wondered. "If something's lost, you don't know where it is."

"Yeah, that is weird. Still . . ." Sylvan's face was dead serious. "Someone must have given this to you on purpose."

Jovie felt a cold sweat blooming. "Because I remember," she said quietly.

"They gave it to us so we can help," said Sylvan. "Maybe we're the only ones who can find, um—"

"Micah," Jovie said.

"Right." Sylvan smacked his forehead with his palm. "Sorry."

"No, it's not your fault. Here . . ." Jovie got out her notebook, turned to the next blank page, and wrote:

Jovie's missing friend = Micah Rogers

She tore out the page, folded it in half, and handed it to him.

Sylvan opened the paper carefully, then closed it again and looked at her hopefully. "Does this mean I'm on the case?"

"There's no case," Jovie said.

"Come on," said Sylvan, the slightest childish note in his voice. "You're looking for someone who's missing—that makes you a detective. And a detective needs a partner." He counted on his fingers. "Holmes had Watson, Batman had Robin, Nancy Drew had George. I know all kinds of history stuff, and I'm good at researching things. I can help you. Please?"

Sylvan's hopeful expression made him look younger than ever. Jovie smiled at him briefly, but then glanced around the room again, that same prickly feeling lingering on the back of her neck. Whatever was going on here felt eerie, maybe even dangerous. She probably shouldn't be involving a ten-year-old. And yet it was nice having someone to talk to, someone who actually wanted to help. There was no harm in talking stuff out, right? "Sure," she said. "Do you have a phone? We could trade numbers."

"No," said Sylvan, "but I can message from my computer."

"Okay, here." Jovie took the paper back from Sylvan and wrote her number on it, too.

"Awesome," Sylvan said to himself. "We should come up with a name for our detective agency, you know, like—"

"Let's do that later," said Jovie, slumping back into her chair. Her whole body felt heavy.

"Oh, right. Sure."

Jovie looked from the spyglass to the double doors, and thought of her mom with those frightening eyes. . . . It all felt like too much. Tears slid down her cheeks.

"It's going to be okay," Sylvan said. "We'll figure it out."

She reached over and patted his shoulder. "Thanks."

He smiled and looked away, his face reddening.

A moment later, Beverly emerged from the double doors. Jovie packed the spyglass away.

"Your dad is on his way," Beverly said, handing them each a bag of M&M's. "He said he would text you, and bring takeout. Sylvan and I are going to go, but Dr. Aaron will be out to check on you. You can just stay right here, okay?"

"Thanks."

"Your mom is in good hands. Come on, Sylvan."

"See ya," Sylvan said as he stood. When they got to the door, he looked back and waved at Jovie, the notebook page she'd given him clutched tightly between his fingers.

Jovie tried to pass the time looking at her phone, but her eyes kept darting to the double doors and around the waiting room. She wondered about Mom and about who had given her the strange device.

And why.

7

THE NEW STUDENT

JANUARY 11, 2018
276 HOURS TO BREACH

Jovie woke the next morning to odd sounds from the kitchen. She shuffled out of her room and found Dad amid the sizzle of sausages, the gurgle of the electric kettle, and the hum of the toaster.

"Hey," he said over his shoulder, standing there in his sweatpants and that same old hoodie with the ripped sleeve, as if Jovie had stepped through a portal to two years ago. She rubbed her eyes and felt a squeezing inside; it smelled so good in here, felt so warm, and yet she stood there for a moment, unable to move.

"I couldn't find the mocha mix," Dad said, scraping a spatula in the frying pan. "Have you graduated to coffee?"

"We ran out," Jovie said. "I can just get something at the stand."

"Ah, okay. Food will be ready in a minute; I had trouble getting this thing lit. Has your mom tried to get the stove fixed?"

"She called somebody, I think."

Dad nodded to himself and turned to her, his hair its old morning mess, a tired grin on his face. "Sit. I'll bring it over."

Jovie moved to the table. She and Dad had been at the hospital until nearly eleven o'clock, and Mom's surgery had been successful. She was coming home tonight.

Dad darted from the toaster to the kettle to the stove to the fridge, making the tiny space feel like a diner kitchen. He brought her a plate of sausage and eggs and an English muffin, each side expertly half-mooned with butter and strawberry jam. He'd added raspberries in the corner; they hadn't had berries in the house in months, but he'd arrived with the groceries that, in his words, "I didn't think you'd have."

"Thanks," Jovie said, trying to smile. This was nice, and yet her insides squeezed tighter. Not only did this feel good, Dad seemed to be enjoying himself, too. But that probably had to do with Mom not being around. She remembered sensing this, back then.

"So, you have everything you need for the day?" Dad had started cleaning up while taking bites from his own plate on the counter.

"Uh-huh." Jovie ran her fingers over her backpack. The top pocket was stretched around the box with the spyglass. Even though she'd searched online last night for what it might be and had no luck, she still wanted it with her. It had to mean something.

"And this Mrs. Reynolds person will take you to the hospital to get Mom?"

"Yeah. You'll be gone when we get home?" Jovie had already noticed his bag by the door.

Dad shrugged. "I gotta get back to the office."

"Can I still come over Saturday?"

"Ah, can we do next weekend? I had to reschedule all my morning meetings, and band practice last night." There was that tone, something else Jovie remembered, as if this—as if she—was an inconvenience, even though he'd say that wasn't what he meant.

"Fine," Jovie said.

Dad dried his hands and gave Jovie a plastic container. "Tuna sandwich. Gotta have a good lunch."

I might have good lunches if you were still around, she thought, but all she said was, "Okay."

He rubbed her back. "By tonight, everything will be back to normal."

Jovie nearly burst into tears. She ate quickly and dressed to go.

Dad gave her a hug by the door. "See you next weekend?"

"Yeah," Jovie said, leaning against his shoulder. His sweater smelled the same. Ugh.

She got out the door as fast as she could and pedaled hard through the chilly wind. When she arrived at the coffee stand, Elena was already there, opening the back of her minivan.

"Good morning!" she said, pulling out the boxes of the pastries she got from the Manager's Special rack at the Fred Meyer. "It's nice of you to come in. I would've been happy to let you have the morning off, with your mom and all."

"It's fine," Jovie said. She'd messaged Elena from the hospital, in case she'd ended up there all night. She still felt bleary with exhaustion now, but it was a relief to be out of the house.

"How's she doing?"

"Okay," Jovie said, crouching to loosen the nut on her bike's front wheel. Removing it was the only way to fit the bike in the stand; there was nowhere to lock it outside, and theft had been a growing issue in town lately. "She's coming home tonight."

"Well, that's good news," said Elena.

Headlights blazed from behind them, making Elena shield her eyes. A car had stopped just beyond the coffee stand, as if waiting for them to open. "Ooh. Someone's an early bird. Always in a hurry to get out of Far Haven, aren't they?"

"Yeah." Jovie thought of her dad, already miles away.

Elena unlocked the stand and put the baked goods

on the narrow counter inside. Then she looked around the little space, pointing with her finger and speaking quietly: "Scab pot . . . S-C-A-B . . ." She noticed Jovie eyeing her. "Oh, ha, it's a little mnemonic I came up with for making sure we have everything. My doctor says they help with memory." She counted on her fingers: "Soy milk, cow milk, almond milk, beans . . . pastries, oat milk, tea. Scab pot."

"Are you having memory problems?" Jovie asked.

"Not really," said Elena, "but I have been kinda forgetful lately. Could just be that I'm so distracted by the kids, or tired after the holidays. Anyway, I've been making these silly abbreviations for everything. I don't know, I think they help."

"Is that common?" Jovie wondered aloud. "I mean, do you know other people having memory problems, like, lately?"

Elena shrugged. "Rob and I both feel like the twins have ruined our minds, but no, I don't think so. Why?"

Jovie decided to just ask directly: "Do you remember Micah Rogers? She was my age. She disappeared last September?"

"Oh, jeez. That doesn't ring a bell. Was she from Far Haven?"

"Yeah." Jovie felt a fresh wave of both satisfaction—Elena's answer fit with what she'd suspected—but also disappointment, as this was all still very weird.

"Wow, well, you would have thought that'd be bigger news," Elena was saying.

It was, Jovie didn't say. "So you don't think memory loss is, like, a common thing in town."

Elena had gone back to her inventory, saying her mnemonic quietly and pointing around the stand. "Not that I've ever heard of—Oh!" She checked her phone. "Hey, speaking of almost forgetting: Would you mind opening solo?" She stepped quickly toward the door. "The twins are starting their new day care, and Rob has a meeting this morning. I should've already left."

"Um, sure." Jovie didn't love being at the stand by herself, but she was used to Elena leaving her while she ran one errand or another, and it was pretty cramped when they were both here, anyway.

"Great. Thanks a ton." She patted Jovie's shoulder. "There are sixteen pastries," she said. "Feel free to have one!"

Jovie tucked her bike and wheel in back. "Thanks, I'm good today." At least Dad had saved her a dollar fifty. Coffees were free, but Elena only gave her half off on pastries.

Elena returned to her van. "So I'll be back to relieve you at . . ." She checked her watch. "What time do you need to leave for school again?"

"Eight," Jovie said, not adding *same as every other day*.

"Whoo, okay. I'll do my best."

"Thanks." Except why was she saying thank you for just being able to get to school on time?

As Elena's minivan drove off, the waiting car pulled closer, as if urging her to open. Jovie turned on the space heater, started a pot of coffee, and unlocked the small safe. She removed the card-swiping system, only to realize that Elena hadn't left the tablet they used for payments, which meant Jovie would have to use her phone, and thus her own data, even though she really couldn't afford to go over her limit again.

She sighed in frustration and felt a sudden, electric urge to just grab her bike and go. To get away from this dumb stand, from everything. To ride until she reached a place where people didn't forget a missing girl, or even what time Jovie started school, who didn't rush to leave her. Somewhere she could feel more . . . *something*. Noticed? Like she mattered, to anyone?

They're already going before they're gone. Harrison's words made her shudder now. Was this how it had started for Micah? All the strangeness aside, Jovie wondered if it was that simple: maybe Micah had run away because she felt like she *had* to, like she couldn't take it anymore, like there was almost no reason not to.

At times like this, Jovie could understand that.

Except . . . it *hadn't* been that simple with Micah. Elena's reaction just now proved it. Which was why Jovie needed to grit her teeth and sling coffee drinks for an hour and a half, and then she could get to school, where she'd decided it was time to do something she'd been afraid to do ever since Micah disappeared. The one thing she could think of that might offer some clue to whatever mysterious thing had happened. *The only question you can answer is why they left.* Jovie needed to know what she'd missed in those last six months.

It was time to talk to Isla and Corey.

Elena barely returned in time, and Jovie biked to school as fast as she could. She made it to first period, but not early enough to talk to Isla and Corey beforehand, so her pulse raced nervously all morning, until just before science, the next class she shared with them.

Jovie spotted them standing at Isla's locker, which was just across the hall from the classroom. Her legs tingled as she approached, urging her to turn and run. *No,* she told herself, *you can do this.* She should have done this long before now.

"Hey," Jovie said as she reached them.

Isla and Corey turned, and their eyes narrowed in unison.

"What?" said Isla. Her big dark curls framed her face, and her eyes flashed with glittery makeup. She wore a turtleneck sweater and nice ripped jeans and looked like she'd taken at least an hour to get ready for school. It was about as far as you could get from Jovie's look: hair tied back, her same hoodie, and faded black jeans with rips she'd had to make herself.

Jovie held steady. "I wanted to ask you guys something about Micah."

They both looked at her blankly. Corey stood chewing on a turquoise pen cap. She had lighter, straight hair that was dyed with magenta streaks. Her cream-white puffer jacket looked expensive, and only seemed to highlight how threadbare Jovie's was.

When neither of them reacted after another moment, Jovie pulled out the flyer she had ready in her notebook and unfolded it. "This is Micah. Do you remember her?"

They both peered at the photo.

Jovie started to worry: What if they didn't remember at all? "You knew her," she said. "Last year."

Finally, their eyes began to soften, and Jovie saw recognition slowly spreading on their faces. They glanced at one another.

"Micah . . . ," Corey said, almost to herself.

But Isla's scowl quickly returned. "The police already asked us about her. We didn't do anything to her, and we don't know where she went."

Jovie suddenly felt silly standing there with her little notebook, but she fought off the feeling. "Right . . . It's just that *nobody* knows what really happened to her, so I'm trying to figure it out."

Corey was still staring at the flyer. "We weren't even

friends with her anymore, really, once school started," she said.

"Okay," Jovie pushed on, "but why not?"

Isla's brow scrunched. "I don't know. We just weren't."

"Did something happen, or—"

The first bell rang, cutting them off.

Isla nudged Corey with her elbow and took a step toward the door.

"No, wait." Jovie shook the flyer in front of them again. "Micah—what happened to make you stop being friends with her?"

"There wasn't, like, a *thing*," Corey said. "We just stopped."

"Was it about what happened at Braiden's party?"

Isla grinned and rolled her eyes while flashing a look at Corey, but Corey just blushed and looked away. "We didn't even hang out with her that day," said Isla. "Nobody did."

"But—"

"Look, Jovie," said Isla. "We were having fun, and then, I don't know, we weren't. We don't know anything else."

"Didn't she run away or something?" Corey asked.

"Maybe," Jovie said.

She took the flyer from Jovie and gazed at it. "She got really quiet a lot. Like she was sad but she wouldn't say why."

"Girls." Jovie looked over her shoulder to see Ms. Kim waving them in. "Second bell means you're tardy."

Jovie turned back to Isla and Corey. "But I don't get it. You guys looked like you were having the best time ever on the band trip. What changed?"

"Maybe you should have asked her yourself," Isla snapped, "instead of being, like, the worst friend ever." She nudged Corey and they walked toward the door.

The words hit Jovie like a lightning bolt. "What?"

Corey turned midstride and said, "You guys had that big fight or something. . . ."

They strode into class, leaving Jovie standing there with her notebook as blank as her thoughts. *What fight?*

The second bell rang and Jovie hurried to her seat, but once class began, she just sat there, stunned. Isla and Corey were alternately whispering to one another and scowling at Jovie, but soon, they settled in to work. Jovie wondered if they'd already forgotten Micah again.

She thought back to last April. Everything had been fine, and then came the band trip, and all those posts with Micah and Isla and Corey. Was she forgetting something that happened right before the trip? Did the memory loss affect her after all? But that didn't make sense; she was the only one who *did* remember, every detail, she was sure. The only drama she could recall from that month was her own parents getting into a fight about her birthday, but that had had nothing to do with Micah.

Maybe Isla and Corey were just making it up to hurt her. But what if Micah really had told them Jovie was a bad friend? Why would she have done that?

Jovie felt a sinking inside. She looked out the window and watched a strengthening rain pelt cars and sidewalks. The sky was heavy. The raindrops were heavy. What good was her silly investigation? Even if Micah was out there, and did need someone to find her . . . what if she didn't even want that person to be Jovie?

But then why am I the one who remembers? And why had someone given her a spyglass to look for something lost?

It doesn't say to look for *something lost*, she remembered Sylvan saying, *it says to look* at *something lost*.

Jovie's gaze drifted across the classroom, to Micah's empty seat at the front corner table.

She glanced around the room, making sure everyone was still busily taking notes. *This is silly*, she thought, but she reached into her backpack anyway, opened the box, and slipped the spyglass free. When Ms. Kim turned toward the board, Jovie raised it to her eye and aimed it at the space where Micah had once been.

All she saw was that blurry view, same as before—

Wait.

The blur started to ripple. It swirled in waves edged with oily rainbow colors. Lines sharpened, clarified. A shape was coming into focus, and Jovie had just a moment to form a wild thought—*Is it her? Is it Micah??*—before the view through the glass stilled. Everything in the room remained blurry and out of focus except for one thing.

Jovie nearly jumped. Adrenaline flooded through her. She lowered the spyglass. Blinked. Looked at the empty seat.

Raised the spyglass to her eye again.

The seat wasn't empty.

A boy was sitting there. A boy who was perfectly in focus through the spyglass, and yet—she lowered it one more time to be sure—utterly invisible without it.

8

THE TRAIL

JANUARY 11, 2018
273 HOURS TO BREACH

Someone sighed nearby and Jovie instantly lowered the spyglass. It was just Kaya in the seat beside her, reacting to something on her phone.

Jovie's heart pounded. She looked at the empty seat. There was no way she'd really just seen that. But after a deep breath, she raised the spyglass to her eye again.

And there he was.

A boy who looked about her age, with thick black hair, wearing a black hoodie with a rip in the sleeve, dirty sneakers, and worn jeans. He had a ratty canvas backpack resting against his chair, and a notebook and pencil out on the desk, and he was sitting there taking notes as if he were just another student in the class, except he wasn't. He—

A student cleared their throat. Jovie lowered the spyglass again. From two tables over, Corey was eyeing her, brow arched. Jovie dropped her eyes and picked up her pencil, but as soon as Corey had returned to taking notes, she immediately looked again.

The boy was still there, still the only thing in focus, perfectly so, against a blurry background. She noticed, too, that there was a faint rainbow shimmer around him, almost as if glowing mist was rising from his skin and fading away into the blur.

This was impossible! What was he doing here, in Micah's seat? And who was he? Someone invisible to everyone else, who could only be seen through a spyglass. . . .

Look at what is lost. This boy. He was lost to . . . sight. Was it possible he was lost to memory as well? Could this be what had happened to Micah? Was she also here, somewhere, still in Far Haven, but unseen, unremembered by anyone? Jovie's heart began to pound. Did this boy know where she was? He was sitting in her seat, after all.

But people can't be invisible! Jovie nearly shouted at herself. Except, clearly, they could. Jovie was seeing it, and she'd experienced everyone forgetting Micah, too. This. Was. Happening. And she was the only one who knew.

She, and whoever had given her the spyglass.

"Jovie?"

Jovie's hand snapped down to her lap. Ms. Kim was

eyeing her. Every head in class turned in her direction.

"Is that a novel new way of taking notes?" Ms. Kim asked.

Jovie's face burned. "Sorry." She slid the spyglass into her pocket and stared straight ahead. Had the boy seen what she'd been doing? Between that and Ms. Kim's eye falling on her now and then, she didn't dare take the glass out for the rest of class.

The thirty remaining minutes dragged on forever. Jovie sat there breathing hard, breaking out in a nervous sweat. How could you take notes on the different categories of igneous rock when there was an invisible boy sitting in your missing friend's seat? Jovie's eyes kept darting to the empty seat, looking for any indication that there was, in fact, someone sitting there, but without the spyglass, the chair appeared empty. No notebook or pen or backpack, either. What if he got up and left at some point during class? What if she could never find him again?

When the bell sounded, Jovie threw her backpack up onto her desk, ducked behind it, and risked looking through the spyglass again. Reality rippled and focused and, to her great relief, the boy appeared once more. He was stuffing away his notebook and getting to his feet, like he was in no particular hurry.

Jovie lowered the spyglass, grabbed her pack, and pushed for the door. Outside the classroom, she hurried across the hall and ducked into a recessed doorway. She raised the spyglass and watched the stream of students exiting. There he was, walking out among her classmates just like any other student, and when Jovie lowered the spyglass, she saw that there was a person-sized gap in the crowd as it moved up the hall, as if the other students sensed his presence somehow and were giving him space. Through the glass again: the boy walking along, untouched.

Jovie pocketed the spyglass and started up the crowded hall. She rose to her tiptoes every few steps, keeping her eye on that gap as it bobbed up the hall like an invisible balloon. When she reached the next intersection, she slid beside a trophy case. The hallway had gotten even more crowded, but Jovie spotted the gap up ahead, and through the spyglass saw the boy heading for the cafeteria. He slid right past the students lined up outside the lunch line door.

Jovie hurried to the doorway, her body surging with energy, and peered in through the spyglass, fretting that she'd look ridiculous to everyone in line, but they were all just looking at their phones anyway. She watched the boy pluck two premade sandwiches and drop them into his backpack, followed by two apples, energy bars, and milks, then walk right out without paying.

She hurried into the main cafeteria and positioned herself by one of the pillars. She scanned the room with the spyglass and spotted the boy at the dessert stand. He added two packages of brownies to his bag and headed toward the exit.

There were snickers from the tables around her, and Jovie noticed someone pointing at her. Whatever. She followed the boy.

As she approached the teacher who sat by the cafeteria doors, she tried to look normal, casual. *Just on my way to eat in the library, like any other day.* There weren't enough students coming in for her to see where the boy was by his negative space. But as long as she kept pace—

Just then, a shoulder slammed into hers as a younger boy rushed by.

"Hold on a sec," the teacher said, rising from her seat, and Jovie's way was blocked by the two of them. "Only eighth graders can leave without a pass."

"Can I go to the restroom?" the boy asked, panting and clutching his stomach. "I don't feel so good."

"Oh, all right. Do you think it's something you ate? Do you need to see the nurse?"

"I don't know," the student said. "I just need to go to the restroom now!" He staggered a bit.

Jovie bounced on her feet. She didn't want to push around them, but she was going to lose the invisible boy.

"Okay, go," the teacher finally said, patting his shoulder.

The boy careened out, and Jovie gave the teacher a quick wave as she passed.

After the slapping of the restroom door, the hallway outside the cafeteria was eerily silent. Jovie raised the spyglass. The invisible boy was nowhere to be seen.

No! He'd been gathering food. . . . Maybe he was leaving? She hurried to the main entrance. There was no one around, but then she heard a light click: one of the main doors latching shut.

There he was, outside, heading down the steps. Jovie almost darted after him . . . but she couldn't just stroll past the main office and leave school without being noticed. She glanced at the clock on the wall. Nineteen minutes left before sixth period. There was an exit by the gym that was usually deserted. . . .

She hurried up the hall, and a moment later emerged into the stiff wind of a chilly gray afternoon. The boy was heading out to the main road. Jovie realized she'd still have to walk right past the front of the school to keep up her pursuit, so she got out her phone and held it to her ear as if she was making a call; she could always claim she was checking on her mom in the hospital.

Then she was past the school. No one was calling to her, running after her. Her feeling of relief cooled quickly, however, and a shiver passed through her. That had been too easy, as if she, too, was invisible. The feeling almost made her turn back, but she kept going.

The boy was heading down the hill toward town. Jovie checked her phone. Still sixteen minutes. She set a timer for ten minutes, so she'd have time to hurry back. Then she picked up the pace, checking the boy's position every few seconds. He walked in no hurry, passing right by the occasional oblivious pedestrian. A block down the hill, he went into the Rite Aid. Once he was inside, Jovie jogged to catch up.

She found him again in the food aisle, loading more items into his backpack. Then he walked to the pharmacy counter and hopped right over it. His sneakers slapped on the tile, but the pharmacist, who was standing right there, continued to ring up a customer, neither of them reacting. The boy examined the contents of the small cubbies on the wall and selected two orange pill bottles before hopping back over the counter. On his way out of the store, something he'd taken set off the shoplifting detectors, but the workers just looked around, perplexed.

Jovie hurried outside and followed him down the hill. She checked her phone. Four more minutes. . . . Should she try to get his attention? Talk to him? Maybe that would freak him out. Also, she wasn't sure if he was dangerous, though she didn't think so. But how had this happened to him? And was invisibility, like, contagious?

Just a block later, the boy turned onto a short lane that ended at a thickly wooded area with a trailhead. As Jovie rounded the corner, she saw him disappear into the gloomy shadows beneath the pines. The state park was in that direction. She stared at the dark trail, her body buzzing with energy. She needed to keep going, see where he went. The park trails led to the bluff and the bunkers, one of Micah's favorite spots.

Jovie thought of the last time they were up there. It was the summer before seventh grade, when they'd been old enough to bike out there on their own. The bunkers consisted of concrete rooms dug into the hillside, with giant cannons and lookout towers on top. Inside was a labyrinth of chambers, all empty and dark now, as well as tunnels that led out to platforms sticking out of the face of the bluff. They'd sat atop one of the towers with a pile of snacks and watched the sun go down, talking about places they'd love to travel.

If Micah really was like this boy, still here but unseen, could that be where she'd been hiding out? Did she know him? Was that why he was gathering so many supplies? Jovie gazed at the spyglass in her palm. If she followed him right now, she could find out—

Just then, the alarm on her phone started to beep, nearly making Jovie jump. If she didn't show up in sixth period . . . what if the school started looking for her? Called her dad, or the police. *Or what if they don't notice I'm gone at all?*

That shiver returned, more urgent this time. Jovie gazed at the dark mouth of the trail, her legs tingling to go farther. . . .

She turned and headed back toward school.

THE OUTBREAK

JANUARY 11, 2018
268 HOURS TO BREACH

Jovie barely made it to class on time, and her thoughts were swirling for the rest of the afternoon. Who was that boy? How had he gotten that way? Did he know anything about Micah?

Now and then she glanced around at her classmates, going about their days with no idea of what had been right among them. It made her feel like some sort of astronaut, one who had traveled leagues and had life-changing adventures only to return home and find everything just as it was, with no one around who could truly understand. It was exhilarating, but also desperately lonely.

And though she kept the spyglass hidden in her pocket, Jovie's hand kept returning to the warm metal, and she wondered, could it show her Micah, if she just knew where to look?

Her phone buzzed at one point during seventh period, and checking it in the hall afterward, she found a new message:

Hi Jovie this is Sylvan. I asked Ms. Harter if she knew about calibrating lenses and she said she could take a look at it after school today. Could you come by?

He added:

P.S. In case you're wondering, I'm writing from one of the library computers during choice time.

Jovie started to reply immediately, but paused. It had been nice talking to Sylvan last night, and she couldn't wait to tell him what had just happened, but all of this was far stranger now, maybe too strange for her to be involving a fifth grader who still had "choice time" every day. And yet maybe Ms. Harter could shed some light on how this spyglass worked, and what it meant that she could see that boy. . . .

Okay sounds good.

She added:

Also, very secret agent of you. ;)

Sylvan replied with three starry-eyed emojis, then wrote:

If you're here right when the bell rings, we

can show her before my mom gets here. Do you remember where Ms. Harter's room is?

Yeah. I'll try to get there fast. I have info to share with you too.

The middle school day ended just before the elementary school let out. When the last bell sounded, Jovie hurried out of school and down the walk. A line of buses was idling in front of the elementary school, and there were kids everywhere on the lawn and by the bike racks, their parents milling around.

Jovie was so lost in her thoughts that it took a young boy careening into her for her to notice what was happening around her.

"Hey!" Jovie stumbled and turned—and watched the boy drop to his knees and vomit onto the grass.

The wet retching sound made Jovie's stomach turn. But then she saw another boy leaning against his bike and vomiting over the handlebars. A girl staggered off a bus and barfed on the sidewalk. Two more kids in the grass by the playground, a girl hanging on to the front doorway and barfing on the steps, another kid slipping in it and falling. Jovie saw one of the teachers trying to comfort a student, only to drop to her knees and vomit herself.

Jovie held her breath against the sour stench all around her. Some of the students seemed to be fine, like her, but more than half of them were getting sick. Looking back over her shoulder at the middle school, she spotted older students in a similar state, hunched over on the front steps, on their knees in the grass. Now a car pulled over on the drive and two high schoolers bolted for the curb.

A siren wailed in the distance.

"Jovie!" She spun to see Beverly jogging across the parking lot toward the school. "Are you all right?"

"Fine," said Jovie, trying not to gag. "What's happening?"

Beverly's eyes darted around the scene. "I have no idea. Food poisoning, some sort of bacterial outbreak . . . Have you seen Sylvan?"

"Not yet."

"Okay, wait out here. It might be a norovirus, so best not to touch anyone." She rushed toward the front steps.

Jovie crossed the parking lot swiftly to unlock her bike. The strained sounds of vomiting were coming from all sides, and there were kids sprawled everywhere, their parents rushing this way and that. The siren grew to a shriek, and a fire truck pulled into the drive. First responders hurried toward the front doors of the elementary school, pulling on rubber gloves and masks. A second truck arrived a moment later, siren blaring.

Beverly finally appeared in the doorway. Sylvan was slumped against her, his face gray. Jovie met them at the car. "Well, we were going to the hospital anyway." With her free hand, she thumbed a message into her phone.

"How are you doing?" Jovie asked Sylvan.

His eyes tracked up to her weakly. There was a yellowish stain on his plaid shirt. "Not great."

As Jovie put her bike in the back of the car, Beverly got Sylvan a grocery bag. He barfed into it just as they were pulling out of the school drive, the sour odor overpowering.

"It's okay, honey," Beverly said, glancing worriedly in the rearview mirror. She accelerated out onto the main street, hands gripping the wheel, and gunned it through two yellow lights. An ambulance raced past them, then another. The moment they parked in the ER lot, Sylvan moaned, popped open the door, and vomited again, half into the bag and half on the pavement.

Dr. Aaron met them just inside. "We've got you all set up," she said, putting a hand on Sylvan's back and guiding them toward the double doors. "How many do you think there are?"

"Dozens, at least," said Beverly.

"Word is, they're setting up a treatment tent on-site, then bringing the more serious cases here. Jovie, your mom is ready to go. But if you could just . . . we'll—"

"It's okay," said Jovie. "I'll wait."

They disappeared through the doors. Jovie retreated to the waiting area, which was mostly empty today, and took the same seat she had sat in before. She looked online and found a few posts on social media about the outbreak, but aside from a few sick-faced selfies and stories, no one seemed to know the cause yet.

The ER might have been empty, but nurses and doctors were moving at a frantic pace in and out of the double doors, checking with the front desk.

Sitting there, Jovie felt that eerie feeling returning. She fished the spyglass from her pocket and looked around the room. All was a blur, but she couldn't shake the disquieting sensation now that there was more she couldn't see.

She got out her notebook and started a new page:

The Lost Boy

- Invisible except through the spyglass
- Not a ghost—has presence, can open doors and pick things up
- Didn't look familiar—isn't from school? So from where?
- Are there others?
- Hypothesis: IF spyglass sees him, and spyglass was given to me, THEN Micah might be invisible, too?

Jovie tapped her pen on that last line. *Please be true*, she thought.

Sirens grew in the distance, and a moment later, an ambulance arrived. Masked paramedics guided a group of four kids inside, each holding a white sick bag.

They had just passed into the back area when two more vehicles pulled up to the entrance, only Jovie was surprised to see that these weren't ambulances, they were black Barsuda Solutions vans. A group of eight workers got out and walked briskly through the front doors. Most of them were in the usual black jumpsuits with the white *B* logo, small on their chest pocket and large on their backs, but they were led by two people in professional suits: a woman with thick-framed glasses, her dark red hair pulled back in a clip, and a lanky guy whose jacket and tie seemed to hang off him. Every member of the team had a black shoulder bag with the Barsuda logo on the side.

Jovie wondered what they were doing here. Did it mean that the outbreak had something to do with the radiation? The red-haired woman nodded to the front desk, and the group strode through the double doors.

Ten minutes passed, and more and more patients arrived: mostly students with their parents, but also some adults, too. Jovie recognized a few teachers among them. By the time Dr. Aaron appeared and waved to get her attention, the waiting area was packed with worried parents.

"I sent upstairs for your mom," Dr. Aaron said as she led Jovie into the back, walking so quickly that Jovie nearly had to jog to keep up. They passed rooms that had been divided into curtained-off areas, each with a kid in a bed. Jovie noticed Barsuda workers here and there, holding tablets and studying the monitors by the patients. She spied Sylvan, Beverly beside him. He looked like he was asleep.

They reached an intersection, and out of the corner of her eye, Jovie saw the woman and man in suits standing by a computer workstation studying a screen, its pale blue light on their faces. The woman looked up, as if sensing Jovie's gaze, and it almost seemed as if she narrowed her eyes at her—

"Jovie!"

She saw her mom at the other end of the hall, sitting in a wheelchair. Mom was in her sweatshirt and pants, her hair tied back, and she wore a pair of large black sunglasses to help her eyes recover.

"I'll let Beverly know where to find you guys," said Dr. Aaron, and she strode off.

Jovie hurried over to Mom and hugged her. "How are you?"

Mom sighed. "Apparently, I've been worse." Her speech was a little slow. She lowered the sunglasses for a moment. "How do they look?"

"Good," said Jovie. Mom's eyes looked tired but were otherwise back to normal; it was hard to imagine they'd ever been that frightening white.

Mom slid the glasses back up. "These bright lights are still hard." She looked around Jovie. "I heard there might have been food poisoning at school. Are you feeling okay?"

"I'm fine," said Jovie.

"Was it the lunches?" Mom asked. "Did you have one?"

"No, I . . . didn't have time to eat. But Dad made me a sandwich anyway." Jovie looked away, wishing she hadn't mentioned that.

"Oh, did he," Mom said in that tone Jovie knew too well. "Did he bring you a pony, too?"

"He left this morning," Jovie said under her breath, thinking of breakfast, but also of his bag, already packed.

Mom sighed. "Well, I hope Beverly shows up soon. I need to rest up for work tomorrow."

"She's with Sylvan. He's pretty sick," Jovie said, feeling a flash of annoyance. "You're going back to work so soon? Is that a good idea?"

Mom scoffed as if this was obvious. "I've already burned two sick days because of this."

Mom's tone left little room for argument. Jovie heard the retching sound of someone throwing up in a nearby room. Looking up the hall, she noticed that those well-dressed Barsuda people were gone.

Beverly appeared a moment later. "Hey, there you are," she said, pulling off a pair of gloves. "Ready?"

"Definitely," said Mom.

"Is Sylvan all right?" Jovie asked.

"He is. It's salmonella, apparently. They think it was in the school water supply, but . . ." Beverly trailed off, looking down at one of the two charts she'd brought with her.

"What?" Jovie asked.

"Dr. Aaron says this salmonella strain is super virulent. Like, it caused symptoms in just a couple hours, which is really strange."

"Mom's sickness came on really fast, too," said Jovie. "Do you think they're related?"

Beverly shook her head. "I don't see how they could be." She led the way down the hall as Jovie pushed Mom's wheelchair. "My husband, Greg, is coming to take you guys home. He should be here in a few minutes."

"Could I say hi to Sylvan?" Jovie asked.

"Sure. He was actually asking about you." Beverly motioned to a doorway. "But just for a minute, okay? He should rest. I'll bring your mom out front."

The room had been divided into three sections. A sour smell greeted Jovie as she stepped into the narrow space where Sylvan reclined. A Barsuda worker was there, reading Sylvan's monitor and tapping her tablet. When she saw Jovie, she smiled and moved on to another patient.

"Hey, Sylvan," Jovie said quietly. "How's it going?"

His eyes fluttered open. He was wearing a hospital gown and had an IV attached to his arm. His face was slack and pale. He looked so young. "Hey," he croaked. "I don't think there's anything left in my body. Sorry it was so gross."

"Don't be. Your mom says you'll be better soon."

He nodded. "We didn't get to study the spyglass. . . ."

Jovie leaned closer and lowered her voice. "We don't need to. It works."

"Works?" He reached for his glasses on the table beside him and slid them on. "You fixed the lenses? How—"

"No." Jovie checked over her shoulder before she continued. "Remember how it said to look *at* something lost? I looked at Micah's empty seat and saw someone. A boy who only appears through the spyglass."

Sylvan narrowed his eyes. "A boy . . . who's lost?"

"He was invisible, but he was really there. He left during lunch and went up the trails to the state park."

"Whoa," Sylvan said. "Are you sure that's what you saw?"

"Positive."

"And you think it's related to . . . um . . ."

"Micah," Jovie reminded him. "I think so. Message me when you're home, okay?"

"Okay." Sylvan swallowed weakly, his head falling back. "I'm glad you didn't get sick."

"I'm sorry you did. Rest up."

Jovie found Mom and Beverly at the front desk. The nurse in front of them was typing.

"Was he awake?" Beverly asked Jovie.

"Yeah, he seemed okay."

She continued looking over a chart on the counter. "Everything looks good here, Alex," she said to Jovie's mom.

"Uh-huh," said Mom. She was scrolling through her phone.

"No lingering effects, or—" Beverly paused and peered at the page for a moment. She ran her finger over something. "Carlo, can I just peek at Sylvan's chart again?"

"Sure," the nurse said, handing it back.

Beverly put the charts side by side and flipped to the second page of both. She produced her phone, tapped quickly, and frowned at the results. "Carlo, what's a code seven? It doesn't come up in the database."

"Never heard of it," said Carlo.

"Me neither, but it's on both of these charts."

Carlo typed. "It's not coming up for me, either. Could be a temporary code."

"But for what?" Beverly flipped the pages of both charts. "These two cases have nothing in common."

"Here it is." Carlo turned his screen, and Beverly leaned over the counter. "There's no explanation for what it means," said Carlo. "There's just a local phone number in the description field. Looks like it's a county prefix. Probably at the health department."

"Is that weird?" Jovie asked.

"I'm not sure," Beverly said, except her brow was furrowed like she thought it was.

"Want me to give the number a ring?" Carlo asked.

"Nah, you're busy enough. I'll give it a try later." Beverly typed the number into her phone, and glanced at the two charts one last time before sliding them over. She turned to Jovie. "Ready to go?"

"Is something wrong?" Jovie asked. "With that code?"

"Probably not. It's just new to me." She smiled, but Jovie thought it looked forced.

They pushed Mom outside, through another arriving group of sick kids and parents, and found Greg waiting in the parking lot.

By the time they got home, it was dark, the clouds low, the air heavy with mist. Mom reclined on the couch, in and out of sleep, while Jovie heated up fish sticks and quesadillas. They'd just started an episode of their favorite baking show when Mom fell fast asleep, snoring lightly.

Jovie picked at her dinner and tried to do her homework, but she couldn't focus. She became aware of the stillness around her, of how utterly alone she felt on this couch in this room on this ground on this planet. She could have been invisible right then, and no one would have known. The thought caused a tremor of fear.

But then she wondered about that boy: he hadn't seemed to be afraid, or even trying to get anyone's attention, almost like he was used to being that way. Or okay with it. Why would he feel like that?

And if this really was what had happened to Micah, what could have caused it? How did you become forgotten by everyone around you? Had it been quick, like

Micah woke up one morning and suddenly, no one saw her? Or had it happened gradually: a missed *hello* here, a friendship ending there . . . so slowly she might not have even known it, until it was just how she was? *They're already going before they're gone.* Had this been happening to Micah when she and Jovie were still friends? Was it something Jovie could have noticed?

Maybe not—*because you're the worst friend ever.*

Isla's stinging words burst back into her thoughts. If this really had happened to Micah, had Jovie been part of the reason? Had it been her *fault*?

No, Jovie told herself. *She* still remembered Micah, when Isla and Corey and the principal and her mom didn't. That had to matter.

She fished the spyglass from her pocket and turned it over in her fingers. She thought of the bunkers, dark and damp now, and wondered if Micah was really out there somewhere. . . .

Just then, her phone buzzed. It was Sylvan:

Mom brought me my tablet. Any more invisible people???

No, how are you feeling? Any news?

No updates yet. I feel like an empty water bottle. What are you doing?

Jovie smiled. She told him about the baking show she was watching, and he told her about the level he was playing in *Shadow Realm*, and it was nice to be sitting here, texting with someone in the light of the TV, even if it was just Sylvan. Jovie had almost forgotten what that felt like. They talked for almost an hour, and afterward, Jovie finally got some math done, and fell asleep.

10

THE ROOFTOP

JANUARY 12, 2018
252 HOURS TO BREACH

The next morning, Jovie stepped out into the dark on her way to school, only to nearly topple down the stairs. A thin layer of ice coated the steps and the driveway and glistened on the tree branches. She noticed now that the rain was making a prickling sound, the frozen droplets bouncing off her jacket. Fortunately, her bike was mostly ice-free, tucked beneath the eave, and when she got out to the street, she found that the pavement hadn't frozen over—a good thing, considering it was too late to get the bus.

She was just about to push off when she heard a clattering sound and a moan, and spotted her elderly neighbor, Ruth, lying on her side against her front steps. Jovie hurried over.

"Ruth! Are you okay?" She dropped her bike and knelt beside her. A bag of rock salt and a metal scooper were lying on the ground.

Ruth made a weak, sighing sound. "I wanted to make sure the path was safe for the paper girl."

"Did you hurt yourself?" Jovie asked, not pointing out that Ruth's newspaper had been delivered by a guy who tossed it out his car window for as long as Jovie could remember.

"I don't think so," she said. She started to push herself up but winced sharply and grabbed her wrist.

"Here, let me help you inside."

"But I need to finish the salt before she gets here."

"I'll do it," said Jovie.

"Thank you, sweetie," said Ruth as Jovie helped her to her feet. "John always took care of the salt." Her uninjured hand traveled to the collar of her coat, to the little gold locket around her neck. She'd shown it to Jovie many times; inside was an old color photo of her and her husband, John, on some tropical beach.

They moved slowly up the steps, and Jovie held the door as Ruth tottered inside. "He always read the *Farmers' Almanac*, knew what was coming before Mr. Wright did." Mark Wright was one of the current forecasters on Seattle's local news. Given that John had died something like twenty years ago, Jovie doubted whether these facts quite lined up, but it was often that way with

Ruth; her memories were mostly there, but they were like puzzle pieces loose in a box.

Jovie guided Ruth to her little kitchen table, which was eternally cluttered with stacks of mail and whatever seasonal craft project she was working on. Today it was little stuffed felt hearts for Valentine's Day. Ruth sat in her usual spot with a view out the front window. A teacup was still steaming there.

"Do you want some ice for your wrist?" Jovie asked.

"No, I think it will be fine," she said, twisting it. "When I was a little girl, the doctor said to have a glass of milk each morning. I haven't missed one since, and no broken bones." She sighed and gazed out the window into the ice-bejeweled dark. "Mr. Wright did say we would have a big winter."

"Oh yeah?" Jovie checked the time. She didn't want to be late, but she also wanted to be sure Ruth would be okay when she left.

"They say there is climate change, but then this winter is colder. I just don't know."

"Mm-hmm." Ruth brought up climate change a lot, but whenever Jovie tried to convey what she'd learned about it, Ruth didn't seem to follow, partly because it stressed the limits of her English. Ruth was originally from Korea, and she'd met John during the war there. In the summer, she'd sit out on her back porch chatting away with her overseas relatives; it was a sound Jovie associated with warm nights and late light.

"It would take a lot to beat the winter of sixty-six, though," Ruth went on. "We were stuck at home for over a week. We really missed the bathhouse that winter."

Jovie had taken a quick look at her social media. "Uh-huh," she said.

Ruth shook her head and made a clucking sound. "Such a shame. It was a grand place. Though if it hadn't been for John, we might have been there the night of the explosion."

Jovie looked up, remembering what Sylvan had said in the waiting room the other night. "You remember the explosion at the bathhouse?"

Ruth nodded. "John didn't get along well with the owner. He always had a good nose for a scam, so we were no longer members at that point, but . . ." Ruth went silent for a moment. "We knew so many people back then. Now I don't remember any of their names." Her hand moved to her locket again. "Sometimes I feel like I'm all alone in the world."

"I'm sorry," Jovie said, a lump in her throat. She remembered Sylvan saying that Harrison's mother had died in the explosion, and she wondered if she was one of the people Ruth was referring to.

But then Ruth was shaking her head and looking out the window. "That Mr. Wright should read the *Farmers' Almanac*."

This was often how it went with Ruth: her thoughts trailing off as if the box of puzzle pieces had been shaken.

"I should go," Jovie said. "I'll finish the salt, okay?"

"Thank you, dear. And will I see you Saturday?"

"It's Sunday this weekend, but yes."

Jovie let herself out and spread a few more scoops of salt onto the walkway. She biked through the spiky frozen rain, arriving at school soaked, and sat through class shivering and noting how dry everyone else was, how their hair wasn't wet and helmet-matted.

Near the end of first period, when everyone was taking notes and Ms. Neary was turned toward the board, Jovie aimed the spyglass at Micah's seat, but it was empty today. Same in science.

A whisper of doubt crept through her thoughts: Had what happened yesterday even been real? Of course it had been, and yet as the morning went on, she felt more and more as if she'd dreamed it.

She was eating her lunch on the blue couch in the library, drinking the bottled water everyone had been given on the way in—there was a large team from Barsuda spread around the school grounds confirming that the school water was no longer tainted—and waiting for her phone to charge back to life, when she sensed someone walking up to her.

"Hey."

Jovie looked up to see Corey standing there, checking

over her shoulder. Isla was nowhere in sight.

"I, um, remembered something, about Micah. I thought you should know."

"Oh, okay." Jovie pulled her notebook from her bag.

Corey sat down on the couch beside her. She glanced at a paper in her hand, and Jovie saw that it was her flyer, folded up small so that it just showed Micah's face. "It's weird. I have to keep looking at this to remember her," Corey said, and her lips moved as if she was saying *Micah* to herself.

"It's not just you . . . ," Jovie said, but then decided against trying to explain it further. "What did you want to tell me?"

Corey bit her lip. "Isla said we didn't hang out with Micah at Braiden's party, but that's not really true. I did, but . . . it was weird."

"Weird, how?"

"Well, the party was at the pool at Braiden's condo complex. Isla and I had already been there for a little while when Micah arrived. We hadn't really hung out with her since before school ended."

"Oh." Jovie remembered Corey mentioning that they hadn't been hanging out anymore by the start of the school year, but in her mind, Jovie had still pictured the three of them frolicking around having some great summer. "Why not? Did something happen?"

"It wasn't one thing," said Corey. "More just like,

she started acting weird, not showing up for stuff, or she would drop out of text threads with no responses. I don't know. I think we were both kind of annoyed by it? Like we felt like she was ignoring us." She glanced at the photo. "But it's also like we thought about her less." Corey shook her head, as if she were loosening cobwebs. "But anyway, then she showed up at Braiden's and we were like, *whoa*, first of all because she was even there, but then also because she was all done up."

"I saw that photo Isla posted," said Jovie. "Did somebody push Micah in?"

"That was an accident, actually," said Corey. "Braiden and Todd were just running past her, goofing around, and Micah got bumped. I made Isla take that photo down. I mean, it did seem funny at first, or just, like, shocking, but then Micah was really upset. I think Braiden offered her a towel, but she just left. At least, I think that's when she left." Corey looked away and was quiet for a moment.

Jovie tapped her pen against her notebook. "Is that it? That's what you wanted to tell me?"

"No," Corey said, and she lowered her voice. "It's what happened *before* that that was strange." She looked warily around the library again.

"Corey," said Jovie, "you can tell me."

Corey nodded. "Well, um, after we saw Micah arrive at the party, I lost track of her. To be honest, I think I kinda forgot she was even there. I think maybe we all did." She shook her head dismissively. "I know that doesn't make any sense."

"It's okay. Keep going."

"Well, the party went on for a while, and then Isla was off hanging out with Sara—we'd been fighting about dumb stuff—so I was on my own, and that's when I noticed Micah again . . . up on the roof."

"The roof?"

"The pool has a little clubhouse next to it," Corey said, "and you can get up there from the fence in back and even jump to the pool from there, but nobody was going up that day because Braiden's parents and a couple other adults were around. But then there was Micah, just standing right at the edge of the roof, up on her tip-toes, almost like she was about to try to jump, but that didn't make sense since she was all dressed up and every-thing."

"Were you the only one who saw her up there?"

"Yeah. And that was the first weird thing. She was practically right above a big group of people, and it was like, nobody noticed. Just me."

Jovie's pulse had started to race. "But you could *see* her."

Corey looked at her, confused. "Yeah, what do you mean?"

"Nothing. Then what happened?"

"Well, like I said, I was having drama, so I climbed up

there and was like, 'Micah, are you okay?' And she was like, yeah. Except she said it in this kind of out-of-it way. So I asked her why she was standing near the edge and she was like, 'To get the best view of them.' I didn't know what she meant, but then I saw that from where she was, you could just see between the condos, and there was a view of the top of the bluff."

"The bluff," Jovie echoed. "You mean like the high part at Fort Riley? Where the bunkers are?"

"Yeah."

The bunkers again, Jovie thought. "What did she mean by 'them'?" Jovie asked. "Like, the actual bunkers? Or could you see people sitting up there or something?"

Corey shook her head. "From Braiden's you're too far away to see any of that. But Micah kept getting up on her toes, like she was trying to see better, and she was so close to falling that I grabbed her arm and pulled her back. She seemed shocked when I did that, and I noticed that her eyes were kind of red and glazed."

"Like she was drunk or something?" Jovie asked. Micah had never tried alcohol when they were friends, nor had Jovie, but she knew that Isla and Corey and others in that group had.

"That's exactly what I asked her," said Corey. "There were rumors that Parker and Allen were going to try to sneak stuff in, but I hadn't seen anyone actually drinking—well, except for the parents. You know how they get." She rolled her eyes. "But Micah said no, and got this really weird look, like very serious, and she was like, 'Do YOU see them?' And she pointed out toward the bluff and said, 'I keep trying to follow them.' But like I said, I couldn't see anyone out there."

Or maybe they couldn't be seen. Jovie thought again of that invisible boy, of the trail he'd taken in that direction. "Did she say who she was trying to follow?"

Corey bit her lip again and looked around the room as if to be sure there was still no one listening. "I'm not sure it was a *who*," she said.

"What do you mean?"

"Well . . . we were standing there, and all of a sudden, she looked up at the sky and was like '*Ooh!*' And she pointed and said something like, 'There's one!' And she made an arc with her finger like something was flying over us, except there was nothing there."

"Flying," Jovie repeated.

"Yeah, and she was grinning, and had this sorta dreamy look, and she was like, 'They're so beautiful.' And I was like, 'What are you talking about,' and she said, 'The lights.'"

"You mean like planes?" said Jovie.

"No, I think she meant something closer. The way she was acting, it was like they were right overhead, and flying out toward the bluff. When I told her I couldn't see them, she was like, 'Try,' but I still didn't see anything.

And she said this other thing, like, 'Maybe there's a storm coming. That's what attracts them.' Or something, I'm not sure. I was still trying to figure out what she was even seeing."

"It wasn't lightning, was it?" Jovie was thinking of Tuesday night's storm, the one Harrison had called "abnormal."

But Corey shook her head. "No, it was like, a totally clear night."

Jovie glanced at her blank page. She didn't even know what to write down. "Did she say any more about what the lights were? What they looked like?"

Corey scratched her fingernail on her jeans for a moment.

"Corey?"

Her face scrunched like she was confused. "I don't remember."

"Was there anything else that she said?"

"No, I mean, like, I really don't remember." She held up the flyer again and looked at it, whispering *Micah*. "I was up there with her, and I was looking at the sky, and the sunset, and she was there, talking about the lights, and then . . . it was just me. That's the next thing I remember. Like she'd left or something, and I hadn't noticed." Corey frowned. "So I climbed back down, and I didn't see her again until she was in the pool."

Jovie thought of the invisible boy, of that negative space

in the hallway, surrounded by students. "When you say you didn't see her, like, do you mean you didn't see her around the pool at all?"

"Yeah. That's actually what Braiden and Todd said, too, after they bumped her. 'I'm sorry! I literally didn't know you were there!' Which was just them making excuses, I know."

"Maybe not," said Jovie.

Corey peered at her for a moment, but then she just sighed. "When I explain it now, it sounds dumb, but, I don't know. It felt really strange . . . I just thought I should tell you. I'm sure there's no way it has anything to do with why she disappeared. I mean, she probably ran off because of her dad."

Jovie cocked her head. "What happened with her dad?"

"I think he drank too much, right?"

"Oh, um, I think so?" Jovie didn't remember Micah saying anything about that.

"He didn't hurt Micah or anything," Corey went on, "but I think he'd lost his job and gotten sick a few times. And then obviously there was that night after band."

"What night?"

"After our last dress rehearsal before Disney. He left her at the school parking lot for like, two hours. He was at the casino or something and kept saying he was coming, and when he finally showed up, he was in *bad* shape."

Jovie felt like her mind had gone blank. None of this sounded familiar at all. She did remember now that Micah's dad almost always had a drink in his hand and seemed particularly red-faced and loud when she'd be over for dinner in a way that sometimes annoyed Micah's mom, but those moments had only made Micah roll her eyes. Maybe it had gotten worse after they'd stopped hanging out. Or had Jovie missed it? Was this how she'd been the *worst friend ever*?

"I thought maybe she ran away because of him," Corey continued, "but then it's like, I didn't think about her at all. That makes me sound like a terrible friend."

"You're not," said Jovie. She closed her notebook and ran her finger over the embossed palm tree, the gritty sand. There had to be something to what Corey was saying, and yet at the same time, she felt further from Micah than ever. "Thanks for telling me about this."

"Sure." Corey stood up. "Thanks for . . . um, reminding me about her. Do you think any of that will help?"

"It's all helpful." *If only I knew how.*

After Corey left, the wheels kept turning in Jovie's mind. Whatever had been going on with Micah, she had seen something at Braiden's, something no one else could see, and she'd wanted to follow it to the bluff, to the bunkers. Where that boy had been heading, with food and medicine. She could just picture Micah up there now, sitting where they'd sat that summer night. . . .

Jovie sent a message to her mom:

Hey, I have a lot of homework so I'm going to go to the library after school. Is that okay?

Mom would say yes. The public library had better internet than their house, and they let you sign out laptops in the building, all of which made getting her homework done easier than doing it at home on their shared tablet. It also made it the perfect cover for what Jovie was really planning.

11

THE BLUFF

JANUARY 12, 2018
244 HOURS TO BREACH

Jovie stood beside her bike at the end of the road, peering into the gloomy shadows beneath the tall pines. Other than the dripping of the trees, the woods ahead of her were as silent as a held breath. She looked over her shoulder; no one was around. She held the spyglass to her eye and looked up the trail: only a dim blur. Checked her phone: three thirty. She had just over an hour until it would be dark.

Am I really doing this?

She felt like she was wound so tight, she might snap, and yet she couldn't stop picturing Micah up at the bunkers. Everything—from the spyglass to the lost boy to Corey's story—pointed in this direction.

Jovie started in.

The silence closed around her, the only sounds her footfalls and her tires on the dirt path as she walked her bike. The drip-drip from the branches, the whisper of the wind in the tops of the trees. And the pounding of her heart.

The trail bored through the shadows, and soon Jovie reached a T-shaped intersection. To the right, the trail led back down to town. To the left, it followed the ridge-line above the cove, climbing to the high point of the bluff, where the bunkers were. She continued in that direction.

The trail rose steadily. Seabirds made lonely calls. Down at the cove, a fishing boat's engine gurgled. Jovie spotted a collection of tents on the narrow beach with tarps strung between them and a curl of smoke rising. She scanned the camp with the spyglass, but all was a blur.

She reached a little metal bridge over a narrow ravine, where a small waterfall tumbled toward the cove. Though the bridge was relatively new, Jovie noticed that it had been tagged with graffiti. The shapes were surprising: there was a large, golden spiral shape resembling a galaxy on the step leading to the bridge, and a stream of rain-bow colored butterflies along one of the railings—where had Jovie seen butterflies recently? But what caught her eye and gave her a chill was a series of silver-gray figures on the floor with no details, faceless and featureless. The thought flashed through her mind: *invisible people*. The angle of their bodies suggested they were walking in this same direction.

The trail grew steeper and the whistling of the wind increased. The trees were shorter up here, their limbs bent from lives standing up to the ocean wind. Soon, it became too narrow and rocky to push her bike, so Jovie hoisted it onto her shoulder. By the time she emerged from the trees on the high bluff top, she was out of breath, her face red and her shoulder aching.

A gust of wind blew her back a step and coated her face with far-flung sea spray. She was standing at the edge of a mowed field beside a parking lot. There was only one person here today, a guy flying a kite.

Across from her, built into the bluff, were the concrete bunkers: long, low, rectangular chambers, stacked two high. There were ladders here and there connecting the levels, and thick metal doors on sliders that closed off some of the chambers. Squat lookout towers were positioned at regular intervals above the bunkers, along the grassy top of the bluff. There were also wide, round platforms, one of which still supported a giant cannon, painted green.

Half the bunkers had been restored, and were freshly painted and open to the public, though there was no one exploring them today. The other half were cordoned off by chain-link fencing, their walls crumbling and streaked with rust and graffiti. The lookout tower where Jovie and Micah had hung out for picnics was above the unrestored section.

Jovie could picture the last time they'd been up there, the summer before seventh grade. They'd been perched atop the tower waiting for sunset, the sea stretching in all directions. Jovie remembered that at first, Micah had been disappointed; she'd wanted to explore the bunkers again, but Jovie hadn't wanted to venture too far inside. The memory of getting lost in them still haunted her, and on that summer night, only two months after her dad left, her anxiety had been like an engine stuck constantly revving.

Micah had never seemed fazed by those dark hours underground. Jovie remembered her being scared in the moment, but soon after, she'd begun recalling it as an adventure and she seemed to have no fear of going in again. As if for Micah, something dangerous and unknown was an invitation to look closer. But Jovie couldn't shake the feeling that they'd been lucky that day, that given another chance, those bunkers would swallow them up. She hadn't wanted to say this—it had felt so *lame*—but Micah had sensed it as they stood at the entrance.

So they'd gone straight to the lookout tower, and sat eating the snacks they'd gotten from Salt & Sand, while looking at the itineraries of cruise ships, reading about three-week jaunts to the South Pacific, and three-month excursions that sailed on to India and the Mediterranean.

"Singing and dancing by night," Micah had said, imagining herself as a performer on the ship, "and a celebrity by day when you walk around. Not a bad way to see the world. After next week, I'll have the résumé." Micah was leaving for her Shakespeare camp up in Seattle the following week. The kind of thing that only the best actors got into. "What about you?"

"Oh." Jovie had just been imagining them as passengers, sharing a stateroom with bunks, sitting on their balcony with matching sunglasses, eating pizza by the pool. "Um . . ."

"You don't want to be serving food or cleaning rooms," Micah said. "Those jobs are brutal. How about social coordinator?"

"Sure." Jovie had never been on a cruise and had no idea what that job entailed, but the title made her skin crawl. She imagined scowling faces disappointed with her suggestions. "Could I work in a gift shop?" People purchasing souvenirs were usually in a better mood.

"Ooh, sure," Micah said. "Then you'd get discounts on lots of sundries. I like your thinking." Jovie wasn't sure what "sundries" were, either.

"Maybe when we get off in Bali or Delhi, we'll just stay there," Micah said. "We'll be expats. I bet there's a theater company I could join in one of those former British colonies. You could bust out those old singing skills. By the time we make it back to the States, we could be world-renowned."

"Yeah," Jovie said. Again, she'd just been imagining a vacation, but there was that difference in the reach of their imaginations: Jovie, a two-week cruise; Micah, a life around the world.

Their talk of running away like that had never been serious, of course, but now it made Jovie wonder: Had that conversation, or even picking out her notebook with the tropical cover, been a sign that Micah was destined to leave?

But she hadn't left, Jovie reminded herself, not in the way they'd talked about that night. What had happened to Micah was no globe-trotting adventure, Jovie was sure of it.

She got out the spyglass and slowly scanned the field and the parking lot. All a blur. She moved it slowly over the bunker entrances and back across the top of the bluff. More of the same—

Wait. As she passed over the last lookout tower, the very one where she and Micah had been, the view began to ripple, a shape crystallizing. . . .

A girl was sitting up there. She was facing the sea, leaning back on her palms, her legs dangling over the edge. She wore a long gray coat, loose-fitting jeans with the cuffs rolled up above hiking boots, and a black knit hat. Strands of long hair were flying back in the wind.

Jovie's heart tripped over itself. She lowered the spyglass and the top of the tower appeared empty, but when she raised it to her eye again, there she was: a girl who was invisible, just like that boy. She was the right height, it seemed. Could it be—

"Hey."

The voice came from right behind her. Jovie spun and took a frantic step away, but her foot tangled in her bike and she tumbled backward, landing in the soaked, muddy grass.

The path was empty behind her. Jovie suddenly realized her hands were empty. She patted frantically at her jacket and legs. Where was the spyglass?

Just then, she felt a warm, tingling sensation on her arm. Her vision swam for a moment, and when it cleared, there was the invisible boy.

He was standing over her and grasping her forearm. Jovie felt frozen, almost afraid to breathe. He broke into a faint smile. "Let me help you up." He pulled, and Jovie got to her feet and immediately stepped away from him.

"Thanks," she said, catching her breath.

He was wearing the same black hoodie and jeans, the hoodie unzipped, a faded T-shirt for that old band Nirvana beneath it. His backpack hung off one shoulder, and Jovie saw now that she was just a bit taller than him.

He brushed his mop of dark hair out of his eyes. "Are you okay?"

"Yeah, I think so." Jovie's tailbone hurt, and she could feel the damp cold seeping through her jeans. She scanned the grass around her. "I dropped something."

"You mean this." The boy held the spyglass in his palm.

Jovie nearly lunged, but forced herself to hold out her hand casually. "Can I have it?"

The boy turned it over in his fingers for a moment, but then handed it over. "Will you tell me what it is?"

Jovie clutched the warm metal in her fist, relief washing over her. "I don't really know," she said. "It lets me . . . um . . ."

"Lets you see me? Is that why you're up here?"

"Yeah, and . . ." She glanced at the bunkers. "I saw a girl up there, too."

The boy brushed back his mop of dark hair and held his hand up to shade his eyes. "That's Jeanine."

"Jeanine," Jovie repeated, hope cooling to ice crystals inside her. "And she's like you?"

"She's a bit older, but yeah." The boy motioned to the spyglass. "Where did you get that?"

"Someone gave it to me the other night," said Jovie. "I didn't see who. . . ." The boy was nodding, as if to him, those circumstances were entirely possible, and Jovie wondered: "It wasn't you, was it?"

"Nope. And it wouldn't have been any of the others, either."

"Others?"

He nodded. "We're . . . well, I guess we call ourselves drifters."

Jovie followed his gaze toward the bunkers. "So there are even more like you?"

"Yeah. I'm Mason." He held out his hand and they shook. "You're not getting like, an electric shock or anything, are you?"

"No—"

"Just the look on your face."

"Sorry. This is all just . . ." Jovie crossed her arms. "Drifters," she repeated. "And you're all invisible?"

"More like forgotten," Mason said. "It's like we've lost our connection to the world. And the world has lost its memory of us."

"But how can that happen?"

Mason shrugged. "That is the big question. I'm guessing you saw me at school yesterday?"

"You were sitting in my friend's old seat," said Jovie. "She's been missing for months, and it's like no one remembers her. I thought maybe the same thing that happened to you happened to her, or something."

The boy narrowed his eyes at her. "But you remember her."

"Yeah. Is that weird?"

"If your friend is a drifter, that would be pretty weird, but not impossible, I guess. What's her name?"

"Micah."

"Doesn't sound familiar, but . . ."

Mason pushed up his sweatshirt sleeve. He wore a wide silver bracelet with what Jovie first thought was a watch face on it, but then she saw that it was just a polished black stone. Above that, there was a long list of words written on his skin in black ink. The ones by the crook of his arm were in medium-sized letters, but they got increasingly smaller closer to his wrist, like he'd been trying to squeeze more in. There were dozens, and Jovie thought they looked like names. Many of the ones near his elbow had lines through them, as if they'd been crossed out.

"I don't have a Micah here."

"I have a picture." Jovie got out her phone and scrolled to the photo she'd used for her flyers. Mason peered at it for a long moment, and Jovie felt a slight burst of hope. "Do you recognize her?"

But he shook his head. "I thought I did for a second, but no, she's not here. But that doesn't mean she *wasn't* here. When did she disappear?"

"September twenty-first."

"Yeah, okay, see, I didn't get here till after that. We can ask Carina, though. She's kind of our leader, and she keeps the official list. I just like to keep my own, in case something happens to her. But if your friend was here, she'll know. Come on." He started across the field.

Jovie didn't move right away. "But . . . where would she be now, if she's not here?"

"That's a longer answer. I can tell you on the way."

"How many of you are there?"

"About twenty at the moment. It's not dangerous—"

Mason paused and cocked his head like he was listening. Jovie thought she heard something on the wind, the faintest impression of a voice. She raised the spyglass and saw that Jeanine was standing and had her hands to her mouth like she was shouting in their direction.

"Look, I need to get back," Mason said seriously. "You coming or not?"

"I . . ." Jovie felt both frozen solid and burning with energy. She checked her phone: a half hour before it would start getting dark. *But I'm close.* The thought vibrated through her, louder than all her fears. "Yeah. Just one sec."

She opened her messages and quickly typed a note to Sylvan:

> Hey, I'm at Fort Riley State Park. I'm going to check out the bunkers with the spyglass. I got lost in them once, so I just wanted to let someone know where I was. If you don't hear from me in about an hour, maybe just check in, okay? Haha.

Hopefully that wouldn't worry him too much. She sent the message and caught up to Mason, pushing her bike across the damp, windswept field. As she walked, she glanced at the man over by the parking lot flying his kite. To him, she must have looked like she was walking alone. And if she talked to Mason, it would look like she was talking to herself. . . .

"So," she said anyway, "had you been to school before?"

"A few other times," Mason said. "I never thought I'd say this, but I missed it. I mean, not the homework and tests, but I don't have to worry about those."

"Did you know you picked Micah's seat?"

"No. It was the only empty chair in the room. But it did also feel sort of unnoticed. How'd you know I'd be up here?"

"I followed you to the pharmacy, and then to the trail."

"Ah," he said. "Just so you know, the medicine you saw me steal is for my dad. And the other stuff, well, it's not like you can pay for anything when you're like this. I try to only take things from places that can afford it. You know, not from small shops or people or anything."

"The school probably doesn't notice a few missing sandwiches," Jovie reasoned.

"That's what I figured. And the people here really need it."

"And this same thing has happened to all of you? Becoming invisible?"

"Yeah. How it happens is a little different for everyone," said Mason. "For me and my dad, it started last spring. He lost his job; he said it was layoffs, but it turns out it was really that he was addicted to painkillers. By summer, we ended up homeless, moving from spot to spot, camping with other people. And it's like, one day you look up and realize you've faded out of everybody's mind, even though you're right there. They don't see you, don't remember you at all. It's like you're a ghost."

"That sounds terrifying," Jovie said.

"At the very beginning, it actually seemed kinda cool. You can go wherever you want, take what you want . . . but that gets old pretty fast, and mostly what you feel is lonely, like you don't belong anywhere. And it's weird: you don't feel like you can do anything about it—trying to get people's attention doesn't work; the best you can do is freak them out, like they're being haunted—but it also isn't really on your mind to try. It's more like . . . you're in this current, and it feels natural to just let it take you."

A chill ran through Jovie. "Like you're going before you're gone."

"That's a pretty good description. Did you just come up with that?"

"No, it was this guy Harrison. He's like, a beachcomber."

"Oh," said Mason, "you mean the tinfoil hat guy with

the metal detector? I think I've seen him around. He seems pretty out of it."

"Yeah, but I think he might know something about all this. He's the only person who knew I was looking for Micah, and it sounded like maybe he lost someone, too, but . . . I don't know. I didn't get to talk to him for long, and he didn't make a lot of sense. We were thinking that maybe he was the one who gave me the spyglass, but I don't see how he could have."

Mason nodded thoughtfully. "Got it. Who's 'we'?"

"Me and my friend Sylvan. He's been helping me look for Micah."

"Ah." Mason looked down at the grass.

"He's just a kid," Jovie added quickly, feeling her face flush. "In like, fifth grade. He happened to be with me when I got the spyglass, so I've been talking to him about it." As the words came out, Jovie felt a twinge of guilt for being so dismissive of Sylvan. She didn't even know why she'd said it that way.

"It's nice having someone to talk to," Mason said, and a shadow seemed to pass over his face.

They reached the chain link fence that blocked off the unrestored section of the bunkers. Mason pulled up a corner, ducked under, then held it higher so Jovie could push her bike through.

"So you said there are over twenty of you. Are you all from Far Haven?"

"No," Mason said. "Me and my dad are from Seattle. I think the farthest person is from Spokane."

"Why did you all come here?"

"It's more like we ended up here. My dad and I never even talked about it, we just . . . at some point, started heading this way, walking, taking buses, sitting on the backs of trains, just following the current, like there was some force pulling us here."

Jovie looked into the dark concrete rooms before them. "Coming from the bunkers?"

"No." Mason motioned toward the sea. "From out there somewhere."

Jovie didn't know what to say to that, and before she could think of anything, Mason turned toward the grassy slope beside the bunkers. "Hey, what's up?" he said, seemingly to no one.

Jovie heard faint footfalls. She raised the spyglass and saw Jeanine making her way down to them. She had a freckled face and curly hair tied back beneath a knit hat. She looked a couple years older than them, and gave off a confident yet weary energy.

"It's Carina," Jeanine said worriedly as she reached them. Then she eyed Jovie. "Who's this?"

"Jovie, this is Jeanine," said Mason, making an introductory motion with his hand. "Jeanine, this is—"

"Not one of us," Jeanine said.

"Sorry," Jovie said immediately, not even knowing what

she was apologizing for. She lowered the spyglass and realized she could see Jeanine without it now. "Someone gave me this, to find you," she said, feeling the urge to justify her presence. "I mean, to find my friend." She pointed to Mason. "And that's how I found him—"

Jeanine's glare whipped back to Mason. "Did you go to the school again?"

Mason looked away sheepishly.

"Dude, Carina told you not to do that! It's not safe."

"I didn't expect there to be someone there who could see me," he said.

Jeanine looked across the field. "How do you know she wasn't followed?"

"Because *I* followed *her*. She's looking for someone who might have gotten caught in the drift. If somebody was looking for *you*, wouldn't you want them to find you?"

A pained shadow crossed Jeanine's face. She bit her lip and looked away. "Carina and Rian are still on the beach. I think they've got a tough one down there, and it will be dark soon."

"You want me to go?" said Mason.

Jeanine rolled her eyes. "I'd already be down there, but I'm on watch. Hurry, okay?"

Mason turned to Jovie. "I guess we can meet up another time, if you—"

"Can I come with you?" said Jovie. "I mean, if that's all right." She glanced at Jeanine, who scowled.

"Yeah, sure," said Mason, his mouth angling up in a grin. The smile had a surprising effect, bunching up his eyes; almost goofy, but not. It passed quickly across Jovie's mind that it made him look cute, and her face began to burn. *Stop it!* she shouted at herself. That was the last thing she needed to be thinking about.

Jeanine eyed the two of them and huffed. "Whatever." She turned and climbed the slope.

"It's this way." Mason started along a path that led around the hillside.

Jovie leaned her bike against the bunker wall and started after him. She glanced at the lone kite-flyer out on the field, and almost wished he would look this way, a check-in with the known world . . . but he didn't, and she followed Mason up the sandy path toward the edge of the bluff.

12

THE WOMAN IN THE WAVES

JANUARY 12, 2018
243 HOURS TO BREACH

They reached the edge of the bluff and stopped. A steep rocky slope dropped down, down, to a narrow beach far below. In the misty distance to the south was the wide, flat expanse of Satellite Beach. The lighthouse gleamed weakly to the north. The wind whipped off the ocean, strong enough to steal Jovie's breath, and salt stung her eyes.

Mason pointed down at the beach. "There they are. Try your spyglass."

"I can see them without it," Jovie said, squinting into the wind. There were two figures, one standing on the beach, the other out in the waves. They seemed faint in her vision. Another gust of wind made her shiver, and she had an odd sensation like the wind was moving through her, like she was more hollow then before. She felt a burst of fear. Was this how the drift began?

"It's okay," Mason said, as if he could hear her thoughts. "I think you can see them because you're aware of us right now, not because you're *like* us."

"Okay," Jovie said, but as Mason started down the steep, zigzagging trail to the beach, Jovie felt that chill lingering. *You should go back, right now.* The thought was urgent in her mind, and yet so was the certainty that she was closer than ever to finding Micah, after all this time. *And I can trust him*, she thought, and hoped this intuition was right.

They descended the sandy switchbacks. Jovie's thoughts continued to race, and almost immediately, a new worry occurred to her. "So," she said, "those names on your arm . . . A lot of them are crossed out."

"Yeah," said Mason. "Drifters end up here, but they don't stay here. Not forever, anyway. You keep feeling that pull, and then, eventually, you move on."

They reached the base of the trail and clambered over the driftwood pile, then started across the sand toward the two figures.

"Move on to where?" Jovie said.

"Out of this world, or beyond it. Nobody's exactly sure how to describe it, because no one's ever come back."

Jovie halted in the sand. "Are you serious?"

Mason motioned to the figures just ahead. "See for yourself."

They reached the young man standing at the edge of the waves. He wore a rough wool sweater and a brightly striped knit hat with an oversized pom-pom, and was holding on to a thick rope. One end was tied to a giant log up the beach, and it stretched out through the waves to the other figure.

"Rian," Mason called. "What's happening?"

Rian turned around and Jovie flinched; his face was covered by a large, clear mask held in place by leather straps. The mask had a convex shape that distorted his facial features like a giant magnifying glass.

"It's not great," Rian said.

"This is Jovie," Mason said. "She's looking for a friend who might have been a drifter. She was maybe here in the fall."

Rian looked uncertainly at Jovie. "She still remembers her?"

"I do," Jovie said.

Rian eyed her for another moment, then turned his attention back to the rope and the waves.

"Does Carina need help?" Mason asked.

"Yeah. She's got a real faint one, and the riptide is strong." He pulled off the mask and handed it to Mason, who slipped it over his head.

"Ooh, yeah."

"There's someone else out there?" Jovie asked. She could only see the woman she guessed was Carina, standing waist-deep in the surf. She wore a maroon raincoat and had a salt-and-pepper braid snaking out from her hood. But when Jovie looked through the spyglass, she could just make out another figure, a woman. She was faint, nearly transparent, and misty rainbow energy shimmered around her. Carina was holding her by the arm, as if trying to pull her back toward shore.

Mason handed the mask back. "Okay, I'll go."

"Nah, you take the line," said Rian. "I'm already soaked anyway."

Jovie noticed Rian eyeing her spyglass. But then he handed over the rope to Mason and started to trudge out into the waves. Mason planted his feet in the sand and gripped the rope with both hands.

"I don't get it," said Jovie. She looked at the faint woman again through the spyglass. She was facing away from the beach, almost like she wanted to walk farther into the water. "What's she doing?"

"Trying to keep going, to stay in the drift," said Mason. "To let it take her across."

"Across what?"

"Carina calls it the gradient. It's like a doorway, or a border, between this world and another."

"And this is an actual thing?" Jovie asked.

Mason nodded. "It is."

"So if you weren't here to get that woman, you're saying she would cross this gradient? And that means, like, vanishing completely?"

"Yeah, but today, she'd just drown. The gradient only opens now and then. It makes a storm when it does, and that's the only time that drifters can actually cross it. But that doesn't change the fact that she feels its pull, like it's calling her."

"There was a storm last week," Jovie said.

"Yeah, we lost four people that night."

Rian had reached Carina. Through the spyglass, Jovie saw that they had the faint woman between them and were trying to guide her to shore, but she was still tugging toward the open sea.

Now a large wave crashed over them, and Mason staggered with the pull of the rope.

"Here, let me help." Jovie stepped behind him, grabbed the cold, sandy rope, and dug in her heels.

Carina and Rian fought through the surf, each with a hand on the rope as Jovie and Mason pulled. As they got closer, Jovie could just make out the faint woman between them with her naked eye. Finally, they staggered out of the water, soaked and coated in sand.

"Thanks for coming down," Carina said to Mason. Then she turned to the woman. "It's all right now."

Rian retrieved a heavy blanket from where the rope was tied off. He put it over the woman's shoulders. She was drenched, wearing a sweatshirt and joggers. Her eyes were sunken, her dark eye shadow smudged on her face. Jovie thought she looked about Mom's age. She was so frail, and even though she was easier to see now, she still seemed like some sort of ghost.

"You're safe here," Carina said. "What's your name?"

The woman blinked like she was coming out of a trance. "I don't know."

Carina rubbed her shoulder. "It will come to you."

The woman twisted to look back at the water. "Did you see the lights?" she asked through chattering teeth, her gaze haunted.

Jovie's heart skipped a beat. *The lights*. What Micah had said to Corey.

"No, honey, we didn't, but it's okay, we know about them."

The woman sniffled and wiped her eyes. "I wanted to follow them, I was supposed to go, I—"

"Shh." Carina hugged her, rubbing her damp head.

Rian had coiled the rope, and now handed Carina a worn shoulder bag. He looked warily up and down the beach. "Sunset in twenty," he said. "We need to go."

Jovie noticed that the gray hues of the sky had begun to dim, and the water had taken on a dark metallic tone.

"Right. Let's get back." Carina guided the woman up the beach, Rian falling into step beside them.

Jovie and Mason followed. She glanced uneasily out at

the sea. "Why would she want to go?"

"For some people . . . it feels like you should," said Mason, and his voice quieted. "Like you belong over there more than here. Like it would be better if you went."

Jovie noticed the way he was looking out at the water, as if this idea didn't sound as terrifying to him as it did to her. "Have you felt that?"

"Sometimes. Mostly just when I first got here." Mason motioned to the faint woman. "She'll snap out of it. Carina will help her reconnect."

Jovie shivered, imagining Micah walking into the waves. What if she'd been feeling this pull? Like she didn't belong in this world anymore and . . . what if she'd followed it into the sea and drowned?

"I don't think this is what happened to your friend," Mason said, again as if reading her thoughts.

"But that woman said she saw lights that she wanted to follow. Did she mean like, flying lights?"

"Yeah, some drifters have described that, why?"

"I think Micah was seeing those." The thought made Jovie's breath hitch. "So if she's not here, then does that mean she . . ."

"It could just mean she's not here *yet*," said Mason. "This all happens at a different speed for everyone. Some people drift in a matter of days. Others hang on for months. But part of it is always being forgotten. And you still remember her."

"Okay," said Jovie, but the thought gave her little relief. "But no one else does."

"That might mean she doesn't have much time left," said Mason. "But it also means it's not too late."

They walked quickly, passing the trail where Mason and Jovie had come down. Both Carina and Rian kept looking over their shoulders. Jovie wondered who they were looking out for, especially when the drifters couldn't be seen.

They reached a different switchbacking trail and climbed up it to one of the concrete platforms that stuck out of the side of the bluff. A tunnel led from it into darkness. They paused on the platform, everyone breathing hard.

"Looks like we're clear," Rian said, looking up and down the beach.

Carina nodded in relief. "Take her inside and start a recounting, okay?"

"Got it." Rian ushered the woman into the tunnel.

"We try to get them to picture their old life," Mason explained to Jovie. "It helps you to reconnect. Carina did that for me."

"Just like someone did for me when I arrived," Carina added.

"Will it work?" Jovie asked.

"Most of the time it helps," said Carina, "but not always. Sometimes, a person is just too lost." Carina slipped on the glass mask and looked up and down the beach. "Hopefully that's it for the night." She removed the mask and turned to Jovie. "So, Rian tells me you're looking for a friend who might be one of us."

Mason explained how he and Jovie had met. "Jeanine already told me I shouldn't have been at the school," he added.

Carina flashed a patient smile. "I was going to say. . . ." She turned to the tunnel. "Let's talk more inside. And check my list for your friend."

Jovie followed Carina, with Mason behind her. The light in the tunnel dimmed quickly to total darkness, and the space was tinged with a dank, moldy smell. The sound of wind and waves faded away until there was only their breaths and their footfalls slapping on the concrete. They turned at an intersection and then again, and Jovie found that old fear returning from when they'd gotten lost. She wouldn't be able to find her way back out. This dark would swallow her up—

"Here." Mason touched her arm gently and she nearly jumped. "Sorry."

"It's okay," Jovie said, gulping air.

He guided her hand to the wall and her fingers brushed over something carved. Jovie held up her phone light and saw a small arrow etched in the concrete. "These mark the way," Mason said.

"Thanks." Jovie looked back at him and smiled, and

he smiled back, and Jovie averted her eyes, mortified that despite this situation, the thought had just flashed across her mind a second time: yup, definitely cute. *Oh my god, stop it!* she shouted at herself. She could just imagine what Micah would have said, all of it totally embarrassing.

Now she spotted a warm glow flickering up ahead, along with shadows of movement. She heard sounds of shuffling fabric, of plates and utensils, the snap and pop of something cooking.

The passageway opened into a large, circular room with a giant metal structure in the center, a cylindrical shaft surrounded by enormous gears, and a metal staircase spiraling around it. The ceiling was made of heavy metal panels. Jovie guessed they were beneath one of the old cannon mounts.

Light glowed from camping lanterns and battery-powered strings. Elongated shadows danced on the walls, and Jovie saw a collection of sullen faces, from teens to elderly people, all of them pausing what they were doing to look up and eye her suspiciously. They had straggly hair beneath dirty hats, unshaven faces, frayed coats, dirty jeans, and worn boots. Jovie stuck close to Carina and Mason and kept her gaze firmly on the floor.

"I don't think they're happy to see me," she said under her breath.

"They're just worried," said Mason. "Nobody like you has been here before."

Tarps had been strung up to create makeshift rooms around the perimeter. Sleeping bags and mats were laid out in each one, and there were piles of clothes and cooking supplies. A few people huddled around camp stoves in the center of the room. A large, dented pot bubbled, and Jovie smelled something salty like soup.

How was this possible? How could all these people have just been . . . lost? The thought terrified Jovie and opened a deep well of sadness inside her. Once again she had that strange, unbalanced feeling, like this room, too, could be some sort of spaceship, like she had left Earth completely, only the darkness of space outside these metal walls.

"I just need to do a head count," said Carina.

"I'm going to check on my dad," Mason said. "We'll meet you at your bunk."

Jovie followed Mason to one of the tarp-walled rooms. He breathed deep and knelt beside two sleeping bags. Inside one, a thin man was curled on his side.

"Dad," Mason said tenderly. "Paul, how are you feeling?" The man made a faint sound. Mason held a hand to his forehead, then rummaged through their supplies.

Jovie knelt beside him. "What's wrong with him?"

Mason produced the pill bottles from the pharmacy. "It's withdrawal from the painkillers he was hooked on. A few weeks ago, I started replacing them with B vitamins that looked the same. That was a trick Carina told me about. He's been a wreck ever since—that's what these pills are for." Mason held up the bottles. "This is an anti-nausea medication, and this is a muscle relaxant. Promethazine and baclofen. They sound like alien wizards." Mason shook a pill from each. "Hopefully he'll start to pull out of it soon."

"That must have been hard," said Jovie.

Mason shrugged. "Not as hard as seeing him that way. I think he was having a hard time for a lot of years before he told anyone." He grabbed a cup from the pile of supplies in the corner, placed the pills inside and crushed them with a spoon. Then he produced a bottle of sports drink from his bag and added some.

"Hey, drink this."

Paul mumbled and rolled over. His eyes creaked half open. "Mason . . . ," he said wearily. "I missed you, buddy."

"Me too. Here you go." He held the cup to his dad's lips while trying to lift the back of his head with his other hand. "Time to drink up, come on."

Paul made a mumbling sound and cowered deeper into his sleeping bag. Mason handed Jovie the cup and pulled him up by his shoulders. He groaned but didn't resist, and Jovie heard a rattling in his chest as he breathed in. Mason scooted around and got his dad's head in his lap, then pressed the cup to his lips. The first bit dribbled down his chin, but then he began to swallow. When he was finished, he rolled back onto his side.

“Okay, that should help,” said Mason, sliding out from beneath his sleeping father and casting a worried look at him.

“This is really tough, what you’re doing,” Jovie said, wondering if she would have been able to do this, to hold her mom’s head, if she’d needed her to.

“It sucks to see him like this,” Mason said, getting to his feet. Then, quieter, “I never wanted things to turn out this way. I know it’s not my fault, but I still feel like if I’d just done things differently . . .”

“I know what you mean,” said Jovie. “My parents always say it wasn’t my fault that they split up, but . . . I still felt like it was. At least partly.” Jovie thought of the fights she’d overheard, and the certainty she’d felt, now and then, that she should have been able to stop it, that if she’d been a better daughter somehow, she could have kept them together. “But,” she added, “it wasn’t up to us, was it?”

Mason shrugged. “No, but it can feel like it is, especially when you realize that adults don’t have all the answers.”

Jovie looked around and felt a surge of frustration. “This isn’t right. You shouldn’t be here. Your dad needs to be in a hospital. Nobody should be living like this, forgotten and worried they’re going to be taken from this world. There has to be a way to stop this.”

“I know,” said Mason. “But no one here has the power to fight it. We don’t even really know what this force is that we're fighting. And so we just . . . exist out here, trying to get from day to day, trying not to let something worse happen." Mason bit his lip. "I want to help all of them."

"Me too," said Jovie.

"Well, maybe we can figure it out together." Mason pulled the sleeping bag up over his dad's shoulder. "Come on. Let's go see if Carina knows anything about your friend."

They crossed the room to Carina's tarp-walled space. The floor was piled with similar camping supplies, but also stacks of books, which had been sealed in plastic bags. Carina was kneeling on the floor. "Everyone's still here," she said. "Twenty-two with our newest addition." She reached into a long, jagged crack where the curved wall met the floor and pulled out a large resealable plastic bag. She carefully removed a small spiral notebook and flipped through pages of names and dates. Most of them were crossed out. "When did your friend go missing?"

"September twenty-first," Jovie said. "Micah Rogers."

Carina nodded as she ran her finger down the pages. "When I got here in July, there were only two others." She motioned around the bunker. "Now, as you can see, it's a full house, and that's even without the ones we've lost in the storms."

Jovie watched Carina flip to the next page. Her

heart had begun to gallop. But then another page, and another . . . until she reached blank lines.

"I'm sorry," Carina said. "I don't see her here. It's possible she's one of the 'unknowns,' people who were never able to remember their names, but I don't think any of them were teens. And they've all passed along now."

"Here's a picture." Jovie said, holding out her phone.

Carina studied it but shook her head. "She doesn't look familiar."

Jovie felt a lump in her throat. "But she could still be around somewhere, right?"

Carina closed the notebook. "It's possible. Are you sure this is what happened to her?"

"Not exactly." Jovie's gaze fell. She felt like her insides were seeping out of her. "This was the only lead I had to go on." And yet, she thought bitterly, had it really even been a lead? A spyglass from a stranger, a secondhand story about Micah gazing out in the direction of these bunkers . . . Maybe Jovie's search had never actually left the dead end where she'd started.

"I'm sorry we couldn't help more." Carina sealed the notebook and the large glass mask in the bag and slid it back into the crack in the wall.

"If she is a drifter," Jovie said, "but she's not here yet, where could she be?"

"It's hard to say. If she still feels some connection to her old life, she might be near places where she felt like she belonged. Have you tried her favorite spots, or even her house?"

"You mean she might still be there?" *Like a ghost*, Jovie thought. She pictured Micah sitting invisible at Salt & Sand, or in her bedroom.

"I lingered around my house for a while," said Carina, "but being unable to connect to my partner, or to the space, watching everyone lose their memory of me . . . Eventually I gave in to the drift. Was your friend lonely? Was she losing touch? That's usually how it starts."

"I don't really know," said Jovie. "We hadn't talked in a while."

"Well, even if she isn't there any longer, there may still be some clue as to where she is now."

"I thought maybe she ran away," Jovie said.

"She might have tried," said Mason, "but it wouldn't do any good."

"We haven't even been able to move our camp to a safer distance from the beach," said Carina. "The drift always brings us right back here to the edge, whether we like it or not."

"We're like the sticks that get stuck at the top of the waterfall," said Mason.

"That's a pretty scary place to be," Jovie said.

"It is," Carina said. "I don't blame the drifters who look forward to crossing the gradient. Spend enough time here with this lack of warmth, this constant wind through you, and you can't help but hope there's something more welcoming over there, something that wants us."

"Is that what you think?" Jovie asked.

Carina didn't answer for a moment. When she did, her voice was quieter. "I want to believe there's another world. But I can't shake the fear that we are simply unraveling."

Jovie imagined Micah evaporating into dust, like something out of a movie. "That's not possible. Is it?"

"None of this should be," Carina said. She got to her feet. "And I'm determined to keep us hanging on, here, until I can find a way to save us."

"What can I do to help?" said Jovie.

"First, you can show me that device you have."

Jovie handed her the spyglass, and Carina held it to her eye for a moment. "This seems to work similarly to our mask. Both items function as a kind of spectrometer, I believe, filtering out certain wavelengths of light, so you can see parts of the spectrum that you usually can't. Who gave this to you?"

"I don't know. It has someone's initials on it."

Carina ran her finger over the inscription. "I can't think of anyone in camp whose name matches F.D.L."

"Who do you think might have made it?"

Carina pursed her lips. "Someone who knows a great deal more about what's going on here than we do." She handed the spyglass back to Jovie.

"But this isn't just something to do with wavelengths," said Jovie.

"No," said Carina. "But it *is* like we're out of phase with the rest of the world."

Jovie turned the spyglass over in her fingers. "We could use this to show someone you're here. Like the police, or—"

"No," Carina said firmly. "We can't afford to be discovered now, not with so many here."

"But," Jovie said, "don't you want to be found?"

"Yes," said Carina, "but not while those agents are looking for us."

"Who do you mean?" Jovie asked.

"The ones who sweep the beaches at night," said Mason. "They look and act like military, except I've seen them around town. You know, with that 'B' logo? They have tech that lets them see drifters—"

"Wait," said Jovie, "you mean Barsuda? The cleanup company?"

Carina smiled grimly. "Cleaning up their own mess, maybe. As far as we can tell, they're the ones who are causing this."

"But they're here because of the nuclear plant."

"That may be what they say," said Carina, "but each night before one of the storms has occurred, they've closed the beach and set up their equipment. It's a major operation. We can't get too close to the gradient, so we've only watched from a safe distance, but it's only once they're set up that this swirling light appears in the water and the storm begins. And whatever they're trying to do seems to be working—each storm has been stronger than the last . . . which means we lose more of our people."

"And they know this is happening?" Jovie said, motioning around to the other drifters.

Carina nodded. "Whenever they find one of us on the beaches, they scan us with these . . . probes. I'm not sure what else to call them." A note of fear had entered her voice. "Makes you feel like you're being x-rayed while you're standing there, like you're hollowed out. They study us like we're *things*. And they certainly don't seem to feel any remorse for what the gradient has done to us, or have any interest in helping."

Jovie could barely wrap her thoughts around this. The same Barsuda that had always been around, coming to her school, her backyard . . . "Why would they be doing such a thing?"

"We don't know," said Carina. "But I would be careful now that you know about us, and have that." She motioned to the spyglass.

Jovie felt a fresh burst of fear. She checked her phone. "I should probably get going."

"Yes, and I have to get dinner organized," said Carina.

"I'll walk you out," said Mason.

Jovie looked around the dark room, still catching wary

looks. "Is there anything I could do? Get you supplies or something?"

"Mason and some of the others have that covered," said Carina. "You just concentrate on finding your friend, ideally before the next storm. She may not be able to resist its pull."

"When will that be?"

"All we know is that it will be soon," said Carina. "A week, maybe less. As the storms get stronger, they also happen more often. There may come a time when they're too strong and too frequent for any of us to resist."

"We still have time," Mason said.

"I hope so. Good luck," Carina said to Jovie.

"Thanks," said Jovie. "You too."

Mason led Jovie up a series of dark tunnels. There were guide arrows etched in the walls here, too. Soon, a square of light appeared, and they emerged into one of the outer chambers of the bunkers that was open to the field.

The sky had turned a deep twilight, and the street-lights were on. Jovie's phone buzzed with a message from Sylvan as it reconnected to service:

It's been an hour are you alive please say yes!

Jovie turned to Mason and looked past him down the tunnel. "Will you be all right?"

"For now," he said, though he didn't sound convinced.

"I think I should go to Micah's house this weekend with this." Jovie held out the spyglass. "I'm not getting my hopes up that she'll be there or anything, but like Carina said, maybe there will be some clues. Would you want to come with me? You might see something I'd miss."

"Sure," said Mason. "When?"

"I have to work tomorrow afternoon, so I was thinking Sunday. Or . . . am I just going to forget about you by then?"

"Here, maybe this will help." Mason dug into his pocket and pulled out a black marker.

"Are you adding me to your list?"

"No. For you." He motioned to Jovie's arm. "Would that be okay?"

"Oh. Sure." Jovie pushed up her sleeve, thinking she would take the marker, but then Mason held her elbow and wrote his name in small print on the inside of her forearm. When the gentle press of the marker lifted from her skin, she realized she'd been holding her breath. "You have neat writing," she said, before immediately cursing at herself for saying the stupidest thing ever.

"Thanks. There, all done." Then he added in a raspy, serious voice, "You now bear the mark of the drifters."

Jovie half laughed. "Okay . . ."

Mason's face fell. "Sorry, that was dumb."

"No, it wasn't," she said, thinking, *Awkward!* "Hey, I do know one way I could help: I work at Cove Coffee, by the Gas 'N Go. I can't make two dozen drinks, but . . .

do you like mochas? Because my mochas *have* been described as legendary."

Mason grinned. "Well, now I have to try one. I'll be there."

"If you're not busy."

"I literally have no other plans. I don't even have a calendar."

She started toward her bike. "Okay. Good. Tomorrow: Mocha. Sunday: Micah."

"It's a date—sorry, I just meant that's what we'll do, for sure."

"Okay," Jovie said, feeling her cheeks flush.

Mason gave her a little wave and started into the shadows. Jovie watched him fade into the darkness. Then she hauled her bike out into the windswept twilight. She messaged Sylvan:

Hi. I'm alive. Just leaving now.

She coasted across the grass to the parking lot. As she gained speed through the dark, the damp wind prickled her face, and with each deep breath, she had that feeling again as if she was returning to reality from some faraway world. At the same time, that chill remained inside her. It was possible that she was closer to finding Micah than ever before . . . but she was also closer to something dangerous, something that could take a person from this world. And to continue her search, Jovie wondered how much closer she would have to get.

13

THE CYCLE

JANUARY 13, 2018
218 HOURS TO BREACH

Saturday morning, Jovie sat at the kitchen table eating cereal, her investigation notebook open to a new page. For a moment, she just stared at it . . . and then a tingle in her mind made her push up her sweatshirt sleeve. *Mason*, she said to herself in relief, reading the name there in black ink. Had she forgotten it? Not completely, but . . . almost. She could no longer remember the names of the other people she'd met, but she could still picture their faces, and those of the drifters she'd seen in the bunkers. And remembering Mason was enough to give her thoughts focus. She began to write:

Drifters

- Lost connection with the world

- The Gradient: Opens during storms = drifters vanish.
- Could Barsuda be responsible? What are they doing? Why?
- IF Micah is a drifter, THEN where is she now?

When she'd gotten home last night, she'd even looked around her house with the spyglass, but of course, why would Micah have been here? Still, she had to be somewhere, and Jovie had until the next storm to figure out where.

Outside was a rare crisp blue sky. Jovie stopped at Salt & Sand on her way to the coffee stand. The outside tables were full, so she found a safe spot inside by one of the grocery shelves and scanned the store. Micah wasn't there, either, though the place was busy with the nice weather, so there wasn't much room for a person to hang out, no matter how invisible.

At the coffee stand, Jovie served one upbeat customer after the next. Everyone had a little more light in their smile, more jokes in their banter, more tips to toss into the jar, and yet Jovie found herself irritated by them. How could all these people be so happy, their lives just *fine*, when up in those bunkers, there were people living, quite literally, on the edge of the world? It wasn't fair.

By midday, the rush of cheery customers had died down, and Jovie had time to make her own mocha. She was sipping her drink, scrolling through social media and listening to music, when suddenly, something brushed lightly against her arm, making her jump. Her first thought was that it was a bug or a spider, but she didn't see anything on the counter. She paused her music and heard a sound like a whisper from outside the window. "Mason?"

And then there was a shimmering impression of him, and then he was there, almost as if she'd blinked him into existence. "Hey," he said with an uncertain smile. "Sorry, I didn't mean to scare you."

"That's okay," Jovie said, catching her breath. "How are you?" As she said it, she reached to remove her earbuds, but then glanced out at the road, realizing that to any cars passing by, she would look like she was talking to herself. At least with her earbuds in, it might seem like she was on her phone.

"Good, just finished getting some supplies." Mason tugged the straps of his full backpack. He was sitting on a red mountain bike.

"Where'd you get that bike?"

"It's not stolen," Mason said quickly, "just indefinitely borrowed from the rack outside the Goodwill store."

"I'm pretty sure that's stealing."

"Yeah, but not from a person."

"Okay. But from a future person. Whoever was going to buy it."

Mason shrugged. "So I'm a fourth-dimensional thief."

Jovie smirked at him and checked to make sure no cars were coming. "Mocha?" she asked.

"Definitely. How are you doing? You know, after yesterday."

Jovie started the espresso. "I am dealing pretty well. Kind of annoyed at all these chipper people, though. They have no clue what's really going on."

"They literally don't," said Mason. "You can't really blame them."

"I guess not," said Jovie. "I still feel like they could be trying harder to notice . . . or something."

A car arrived at the stand.

"I'll give you this over at the door," Jovie said, and Mason moved around the front of the stand. It was two cars later before she could finally bring the mocha to him. "Sorry, got a little busy."

"That's okay," Mason said, and sipped the drink. "Hmmm . . ."

"Oh, did it get cold?"

"No, it's good. . . ." Mason made a deep-in-thought face and stroked his chin. "But is it *legendary*?"

"Come on!" said Jovie, rolling her eyes.

He grinned. "I'm just kidding. It's awesome. I—"

Another car approached.

"Sorry," said Jovie.

"It's fine," Mason said. "Some of this stuff needs to

get back to the coolers, anyway. Do you still want to meet up tomorrow?"

"Yeah." The car had reached the window. "Here." She grabbed her notebook and pen, quickly jotted down her address on a blank page at the back, and tore it out. "Meet at noon in front of my house?"

Mason folded the paper carefully. "Done."

"Okay, gotta run," said Jovie, waving quickly and darting over to the window. She didn't see Mason leave.

Her shift finished at three. She had just reassembled her front bike wheel and was locking the door to the stand when she caught a glimpse of a familiar figure over by the gas pumps.

Harrison was standing by a beat-up old Jeep, filling the tank and looking in her direction. Was he grinning at her?

Jovie remembered his odd comment about the last storm being *abnormal*, a comment that carried a lot more meaning with all that she'd learned since that afternoon. . . .

She got on her bike and glided over to him. When he saw her approaching, Harrison's grin suddenly faded. He looked this way and that, hands fidgeting like he didn't know what to do with them. As she stopped in front of him, he crossed his arms and smiled again, but it looked forced.

"Hey," she said, getting off her bike. She produced the spyglass from her pocket and held it out. "Did you give me this?"

Harrison peered at the device. Jovie noted that the Mariners cap he was wearing today was also lined with tinfoil. He fished in his pocket, popped something into his mouth, then held his palm out to Jovie. In it was a blue capsule. "Want one?"

"No," Jovie said. "What is that?"

"Prussian blue." He ate that capsule, too. "Have to be ready." He pointed at the spyglass. "Can you see them with that?"

Jovie looked from the spyglass to Harrison. "Yes. So you knew my friend was one of them?"

"One of who?"

"The drifters."

"Drifters? Who are they?" Harrison looked perplexed.

Jovie lowered her voice. "The invisible people. You know, the ones who are 'going before they're gone,' like you said?"

Harrison looked this way and that with a worried expression. "There are invisible people? Where?"

Jovie felt perplexed now, too. She waved the spyglass at him. "Did you give me this or not?"

Harrison shook his head. "I didn't give you that. I've never seen anything like that. Well, not since Arthur."

"Who's Arthur?"

Harrison's gaze fell to the pavement. "He thought he knew," he said absently. "We all think we know, until it's too late."

Great, Jovie thought. What was he talking about now? "You said you could help me find Micah."

Harrison's eyes snapped up to her. "Did you?"

"No."

"Oh, I'm sorry." He sighed. "That's a shame. Not much time now before the cycle ends."

Jovie narrowed her eyes at him. "What cycle?"

Harrison shrugged as if the answer were obvious. "Uh-huh, the storms," he said. "They grow stronger and stronger until the eye opens, until he can see into our souls, and then . . ." He made a shape in the air with his hands, like an explosion. "Boom. Until next time."

"Who can see into our souls? Do you mean Barsuda? Because I heard—"

Harrison cut her off with an incredulous laugh and made a face like he'd eaten something sour. "Obfuscators! Opportunists!" he said, shaking his head. "No, the eye of the Blue Bathymetrist." These words made his expression darken, and he wiped at his eyes. "People who don't remember, they're the lucky ones. But for you and me, every day is a struggle."

Jovie had a discouraging feeling that each question she asked was going to lead to an even more confusing answer. "Does this have something to do with the gradient?"

Harrison just scowled and waved his hand at her. Tears rimmed his eyes now.

"You lost your wife and son," Jovie tried, remembering what Sylvan had told her. "Is what happened to them related to this? To what happened to Micah? Is that why you talked to me?"

Harrison took a deep breath. "I told you, what matters is that I lost them before that. Should have seen it. Shouldn't have brought them so close." He grasped at the air. "Lost them," he said, looking away and mouthing the same words, again and again. *Lost them, lost them.*

He seemed so sad, and yet at the same time, Jovie wanted to shout at him to please, just once, make some sense! But it didn't seem like Harrison *wouldn't*—more like he *couldn't*. Maybe he was still hurting too much. "I don't understand," Jovie said as gently as she could. "You're saying these storms are part of a cycle, and then, what, they'll stop for a while?"

"For years, like clockwork," Harrison said absently.

"So, storms like this have happened before?"

But Harrison was looking dreamily past her. "Half my life since I lost them. Can't screw it up this time," he said. "Uh-huh. Not after what I saw. Can't screw it up, or—" Harrison's eyes suddenly darted out toward the street. He gasped and Jovie saw his face blanch.

She followed his gaze to the cars lined up at the red light, and saw a black Barsuda van. It was hard to be sure with the glare on the window, but it seemed as if the driver was looking in their direction.

Jovie felt a surge of worry, that feeling like she'd been caught doing something wrong. There was a commotion, and by the time she turned back to Harrison, he had yanked the gas nozzle out of his car.

"What's wrong?"

"Don't talk to me anymore!" he hissed, opening the car door, the gas cap still open.

"Why, because of Barsuda?" Jovie asked. He'd sounded so dismissive of them just a moment ago. "Do you know what they're up to?"

"They'll know about you, with a device like that," Harrison said frantically. "Should never have talked to you. You'll ruin everything!"

"Wait, please. I don't understand—"

"Leave me alone!" He slid into the front seat and started the car.

Jovie glanced at the Barsuda van again, then hurried over and knocked on Harrison's window. "I need to know what you're talking about!"

Harrison looked at her through the window, chewing urgently, blue dribbling from the corner of his mouth, his eyes wide with fear. Then he shifted the car into drive and lurched away. Jovie threw herself back against the gas pump, narrowly rescuing her feet from the rear tire. Harrison's Jeep swerved out onto the road and roared off.

When she looked over at the light, it had turned green. The Barsuda van was moving along normally with traffic, and the driver seemed to be looking straight ahead.

Jovie brushed herself off and got on her bike. As she rode home, she tried to make sense of what Harrison had said. Cycles were things that repeated. Was he saying the gradient had opened before? *Lost them.* Sylvan had told her what year Harrison lost his family in an accident, but she couldn't remember it; she'd have to ask him.

Jovie pedaled up the hill to her neighborhood, her thoughts in a fog—

To find a Barsuda van parked on her street.

She coasted slowly by it and saw that there was no one inside. *Relax*, she told herself. Seeing a van on her street was nothing new—lots of these houses had well monitors that needed to be checked—but her heart still raced as she pulled into her driveway.

She wheeled her bike through the fence gate, and had just started locking it to the post beneath the eave when she heard footsteps.

She whirled to see a man rounding the corner from her backyard. He was dressed in a Barsuda jumpsuit and carrying a toolbox. He had salt-and-pepper hair and a neatly trimmed beard, and of course, it wasn't unusual for Barsuda to be in her yard, as they had to check the well. But what *was* different was the enormous pair of goggles he was wearing, like something you might use for VR gaming, only these had individual lenses for each eye, large and convex, so he resembled a giant insect. As he lumbered toward her, he looked at her with those bug eyes and Jovie felt like cornered prey.

"Hello there," the man said as he strode past.

"H-Hi," Jovie stammered, and the man strolled out to his van without looking back. She bolted inside.

Mom looked up from the kitchen table, still in her bathrobe. "What is it?"

"Nothing," Jovie said, catching her breath and trying to sound normal. "It's just chilly out." She peered out the kitchen window at the truck. Those goggles . . . Their lenses were too similar to her spyglass and the drifters' mask. Did that mean Barsuda really did know about them, maybe even knew that *Jovie* knew? "Everything okay here?"

"Yeah. Why?"

"Just, uh, that Barsuda guy."

"Oh, him." Mom scrolled on her phone as she talked. "He came to the door a little while ago and said he was here to update the monitor. Said it would be quick. He seemed nice enough, asked if I was feeling better, so . . ."

"He asked about your health?" said Jovie. "Like, about how you were sick?"

"Yeah," said Mom. "I saw them around at the hospital."

But they weren't there the night you were admitted, Jovie thought. How would Barsuda have known about Mom's illness?

"Anyway, he was probably just making nice to cover up the fact that he's out there faking the data so they can avoid a lawsuit after the other night."

Mom often tossed out comments like this, and Jovie would normally let them go, but . . . "What do you mean by that?"

"Hmm?" Mom said, looking up from her phone.

"That Barsuda would be, like, faking the data?"

"It was in the *Herald* this morning. Barsuda said the salmonella outbreak at the school happened because radiation from Baxter leaked into some old pipes and mutated the bacteria. They also said that same bacteria was responsible for my"—Mom made air quotes with her fingers—"'*temporary blindness*.' Ridiculous."

"Why is that ridiculous?" Jovie asked, even though she remembered Dr. Aaron saying the Baxter radiation couldn't be responsible for Mom's sickness. And Beverly had dismissed the idea that the salmonella and Mom's case were related . . . but there was one way that the two cases *were* connected: code 7, Jovie remembered, on the medical charts. Actually, there were two ways: both illnesses had happened after the storm. What if the two cases were related, but not for the reason Barsuda was saying? What if they were related to the gradient opening? If Barsuda really was behind that, like the drifters said . . . could the illnesses actually be Barsuda's fault?

"Well"—Mom tapped her phone as if it contained the

evidence—"there's a lot of suspicion that the whole Baxter accident was a cover for something else in the first place."

Jovie could hear that excited agitation in Mom's voice, the way she got about the wild conspiracy theories she read online—there had been a time when they weren't buying any foods with corn syrup in them because Mom had heard it caused some kind of brain tumor—and on any other day, this was when Jovie would have found a reason to change the subject or leave the room. . . . "Like what?" she asked instead.

"First of all," said Mom, "why do they monitor wells like ours, when the radiation was all on the beaches?"

"The beaches," Jovie repeated, thinking now of how different parts of the coastline had been closed for cleanup over the years.

Mom sat up, seeming the most energized she'd been since her surgery. "The most popular theory is that what we were *told* was a radiation leak was actually a nuclear submarine accident. So, you know, it's a cover-up. I mean, there have been crazier theories, like that Barsuda is actually *adding* radiation to the water supply so they can track us all with isotopes or something, but that stuff's a little too out there, I think."

Too out there, Jovie thought. Just imagine what Mom would have thought of Jovie's last couple of days.

"What time is your father picking you up?" Mom asked.

Jovie had to tear her gaze away from the window. "Oh. He's not."

Mom sighed. "He canceled again?"

"No." A familiar nauseous feeling rose inside her at having to defend one of them to the other. "He had stuff to catch up on because he was here while you were in the hospital."

"God forbid he do any more than is required of him."

The comment felt like a heavy stone tossed into a lake, scattering Jovie's thoughts about the drifters and Barsuda. "I'll be in my room," she muttered, and stalked down the hall. She nearly slammed her door, but caught herself. That would just rile Mom up.

Jovie cast a wary glance out her window—she could see the metal top of the well sticking up in the back corner of the yard—then sat on her bed and pressed herself into the corner so she'd be as far out of view through the window as possible. There, she did a search online for "Barsuda Solutions." She found their website, but not surprisingly, it offered no clues about gradients or drifters. In fact, it didn't say much at all. The home page had their name and logo, along with a photo of two smiling workers in jumpsuits standing beside a van. Below that was a place to enter the site, but you had to log in, and there didn't appear to be any way to sign up for an account or anything. There was an address and a phone number for their little office in town at the very bottom of the page. Jovie had never really thought about it, but based on their vans and all, she'd always just assumed that Barsuda had a bigger headquarters somewhere, and like, a 1-800 phone number or something. That little Far Haven location couldn't be it, could it?

She looked farther down the search results. The few that came up led to documents that, again, you needed a password to access. They seemed to all be on government websites about energy or defense. Which made sense, Jovie supposed, given that Barsuda claimed to specialize in nuclear accidents. She did find mention of them working at one other place, an experimental energy site in a town called Juliette, in Arizona. But otherwise, there was nothing to indicate that they were anything more than what they said they were. And yet, after her encounter outside, and her talk with Mom, Jovie felt certain that there was quite a bit more to them, indeed.

She put the search aside for the moment and called Sylvan. She'd filled him in on the events at the bunker over text last night, and they'd planned to chat more today.

His face appeared in a dark room with holiday lights strung behind him. He was wearing a gaming headset. "Hi!" he said, and immediately narrowed his eyes. "What happened? You look freaked out."

"Oh, you know, just a regular old morning in Far Haven." Jovie explained about the Barsuda worker.

"Do you think they're watching you?"

"It sure seems like it. Have you seen them around your place?"

"No, why?" Sylvan sounded worried. "Wait, do you think they're listening in on your phone? Do they know I'm your partner?"

"Probably not. Just keep your eyes peeled," Jovie said, not wanting to freak him out. "How are you feeling?"

"Pretty much back to normal." Sylvan picked up a glass, finished its contents, and made a dramatic *ah* sound. "I've had one hundred and ninety-two ounces of water since I got home yesterday afternoon."

"Ha ha," said Jovie.

Sylvan's smile shrank. "It's true. You're supposed to have sixty-four a day normally, and I missed an entire one, so I've been catching up."

"Nice, well, that's impressive."

"I may have to run out to the bathroom."

"Got it."

"So, listen." Sylvan looked over his shoulder and then lowered his voice. "I heard Mom and Dad talking this morning. Mom said she thinks the town's story isn't true."

"You mean the one in the *Herald*?" said Jovie. "My mom told me about it."

"Yeah. Mom said there were actually three other cataracts cases the night before your mom's, only Dr. Aaron was never told about them. Almost like they'd been hidden."

"No way. Were they all code sevens?"

"Yeah, but my mom still can't find out what that means. Nobody at the hospital seems to know, either, or if they do, they're not saying."

Jovie thought for a moment. "I think maybe code seven cases are caused by the gradient opening. Did your mom say if there are any other kinds of cases that are labeled that way? Like besides cataracts and salmonella?"

"No, why?"

"I don't know, I was just thinking that if we can piece together these symptoms, it might help us understand what the gradient is, and how it makes people like Micah drift."

"Who?" Sylvan said. But then he looked down, and jolted back up. "Micah Rogers!" He held up the square of paper Jovie had given him. "I remind myself every hour or so. But yes! That's good. And if you could link code seven to Barsuda, you'd have a story you could take to like, the *Herald*, or maybe something bigger like CNN. Or, ooh! We could do a series of videos uncovering the truth and post them! Things like that get tons of views—"

"I'm not sure posting videos is the best idea," said Jovie. "If Barsuda really is behind this, they are trying to keep it secret, and videos are very public."

"You think they'd come after us?"

"I don't know what they'd do. But if we could find a connection, we could take it to a news station, or the police or something."

"Wait a minute," said Sylvan, his eyes widening. "If there *is* a connection between the illnesses and the gradient . . . does that mean I'm going to become a drifter?"

"No," Jovie said immediately, except the thought caused a flash of fear. She glanced at her door, thinking of Mom. But then she remembered: "The drifters didn't say anything about that. They said drifting was gradual and you don't even know it's happening at first. These illnesses are pretty serious, and they were sudden. I think drifting is something different."

Sylvan exhaled. "Okay. Well, next time my mom leaves on an errand, I can get on her computer and look up the code seven cases. She always leaves it logged in so she can finish her charts."

"Do you think you can do that soon?"

"Yeah, sometime this weekend for sure. Why?"

"Just that Micah may not have long. Maybe only until the next storm."

"When's that?"

"I'm not sure, but I think it's soon." Jovie thought again of the faces of the drifters in the bunker, their forlorn gazes. She thought of that woman trying to walk into the ocean, trying to follow those lights . . . What if Micah reached that point even sooner than the next storm? Mason had made it sound like Jovie's memory of Micah made that unlikely, but how could they be sure? Nervous energy brewed in her belly. There had to be a way that these strange puzzle pieces fit together that would lead her to Micah. If only she could see it!

"Did you try looking around town for Micah this morning?" Sylvan asked.

"Yeah, no luck, though. But I did run into Harrison again."

"Oh, really? Did you ask him about the spyglass?"

"He said he'd never seen it before. And he said he didn't know about drifters, either. Except then he freaked out because he thought Barsuda was watching him, too. He did say one thing, though: that these gradient storms are part of a cycle, and he made it sound like that's what killed his family."

"A gradient storm?" said Sylvan. "You mean in 1994? The Ascension Camp tragedy *was* a freak storm!" he added breathlessly.

Something occurred to Jovie now. "If it was the gradient," she said, "maybe there were code seven cases then, too. That might give us more to go on."

"Ooh! I can look. When can we talk again?"

"We're going to Micah's to look for clues tomorrow. How about after that?"

Sylvan's face fell a little. "You mean you and, um . . . ?"

"Mason, yes, the drifter I told you about."

"Right," said Sylvan. "*Him.*"

"He knows more about what to look for than I do," Jovie said patiently.

"Well, maybe."

Jovie resisted rolling her eyes. "I'll call you right after, okay? And Sylvan, thank you. I couldn't do this without you."

This made a smile crack the corner of Sylvan's mouth. "Okay. Let me know how it's going tomorrow!"

"Will do."

14

THE ORDER

JANUARY 14, 2018
204 HOURS TO BREACH

The Barsuda van left Saturday evening, but as Jovie walked her bike over to Ruth's house on Sunday morning, it was back by the curb. A different person was sitting in the van this time: a younger woman. She didn't look up as Jovie passed by. Again, not out of the ordinary, and she wasn't wearing strange goggles, but . . .

The clouds had returned, bringing light rain and a chilly breeze. Jovie was just leaning her bike beside Ruth's front steps, her newspaper in hand, when something brushed her arm.

She whirled to find Mason standing there, bike beside him.

"Sorry. I'm trying to figure out how to do that without scaring you."

"That's okay," she said, catching her breath. "You're early."

"Yeah," said Mason, "I couldn't sleep, and then I was done getting supplies pretty quick, so I just came over this way."

Jovie glanced nervously at the Barsuda van. She lowered her voice and tried not to look like she was talking to someone. "They've been there since yesterday. The guy had a pair of goggles. . . . I think they work like my spyglass."

Mason frowned. "Have they said anything to you?"

"Nope. They're just *there*. How's everyone doing back at camp?"

"The same. We found another drifter when I got back yesterday. Didn't lose anyone."

"And your dad?"

"He's holding steady. I think his symptoms were a little better this morning, but he's still pretty disoriented. How's your mom?"

"Doing better. Back to being grumpy and annoying."

Mason looked away. "She's probably trying her best."

"Oh." Jovie felt a wave of embarrassment. "I mean, I guess so."

"Should we go to Micah's?"

"I actually have to help my neighbor Ruth first," Jovie said, motioning to the door. "It won't take long, but I told her I would, and . . ." She stopped herself before adding that also, she kinda needed the money that Ruth would hopefully give her.

"That's nice of you," Mason said. "I can just wait out here."

"Or come in," said Jovie. "Ruth has lived in town forever, so I was going to try to see if she knew anything about the drifters or the gradient. I ran into Harrison again yesterday, and he made it sound like these storms are part of a cycle, like it's happened here before."

"Oh." Mason peered at her. "He told you that?"

"Well, not exactly. Everything he says is super confusing. But Sylvan and I were thinking it might have been a gradient storm that killed his family."

Mason's expression had clouded over. "Jeez," he said. "That's . . . intense."

"I know. Harrison also made it sound like the cycle is going to end soon. Which might be a good thing, for you guys?"

Mason shrugged. "If we can make it through the storms."

"Right, well, anyway, maybe Ruth will know something." She started up the steps, but Mason hesitated. "Come on, she won't even know you're there." Jovie glanced at the Barsuda van. "Also, it will keep you out of sight."

"Yeah, I guess you're right," Mason said.

Jovie rang the bell, and after a long moment, Ruth

appeared and let her in, Mason slipping in right behind her. Ruth had three jobs waiting: decorate the mantel with a string of little light-up cupids that had rosy cheeks and eerie smiles; take the last boxes of Christmas lights to the basement; and fish Ruth's snow boots out from the garage.

"Here they are," said Jovie, returning with the boots. "Where do you want these, Ruth?"

Ruth was sitting at the little kitchen table going through her bills. She had on her big octagonal glasses and a shawl. She had paused and was gazing through the living room, out the front bay window. "No mail on Sundays," she said. "Such a shame."

"Yeah," said Jovie.

Ruth turned to her with a slight look of surprise. "Oh, my boots. Put them by the front door. Were they hard to find?"

"Nah," said Jovie. In truth, she'd had to face down a legion of spiders, and her throat was constricted from the powdery mold on all the cardboard boxes. As she brought the boots over, she looked at Mason, who was sitting on the couch. "Bored yet?" she whispered.

Mason smiled. "I'm good."

"It won't be much longer. Time to get some intel." She headed back to the kitchen and summoned her nerve. "Hey, Ruth, have you ever heard about people going missing here in town?"

Ruth flipped from one bill to the next, her bracelets jangling loosely on her veiny wrists. "Missing . . . like they run away? Lois Denning's husband ran off with that floozy from the bank. Rhonda, I think her name was."

"No, I mean more like getting lost and disappearing."

"Oh." Ruth tore open an envelope and unfolded its contents. She stared at the paper for a long moment. "Like crossing the gradient to Planet Elysia."

"What?" Jovie glanced at Mason, who leaned forward.

Ruth looked up. She blinked behind her large glasses, which magnified her eyes. "Hmm?"

"You said something about a gradient?"

"Yes, and Planet Elysia," said Ruth, pronouncing it *ee-LEE-see-uh*. The word made her look out the window.

"What is that?" Jovie asked.

"I . . . I don't know." Her gaze stayed distant, and then she shook her head. "Sorry, I get confused. Something from a movie, I think. You know, I have forgotten more movies than you have ever seen." She picked up the next bill. "The ones they made back in the sixties were so much better than the ones today."

"Right," said Jovie, "it's just that I've heard that term 'gradient' before."

Ruth paused again. After a still moment, she sniffled, then picked up the pink handkerchief on the table and dabbed her eyes.

"Ruth?"

"Oh my . . ." She put down the cloth and fiddled with her gold locket. The tears fell harder.

"Hey." Jovie went over and patted her shoulder.

Ruth looked up at Jovie with a confused expression. "Where's the book?" she asked, her voice suddenly urgent. She pushed to her feet with surprising speed, only to teeter like she might fall.

"Whoa." Jovie grabbed her arm. "What book?"

"The blue book. With my memories. Arthur's book."

She started urgently toward the living room, Jovie keeping her steady as she padded across the thick ivory carpet in her stocking feet.

"Who's Arthur?" Jovie asked, remembering that Harrison had said the same name yesterday.

Ruth proceeded to her bookcase as if she hadn't heard and ran her bony finger along the sagging rows of faded spines. "Where is it?"

"Do you remember what the book is called?" Jovie asked.

"I don't . . ." She kept running her finger, stooping to the next shelf down. "John would know. John always knew." She bent farther, her breathing becoming more agitated. "Where did it go?"

"Is it something to do with the gradient?"

"Well, of course. That's where I keep the picture of all of us. From that winter, before the explosion."

"You mean . . . at the bathhouse?" Jovie said.

Ruth huffed and dropped to her knees, a surprisingly spritely move. "I swear, if Helena put it in the donation box . . . I told her to check with me. . . ."

"Who's the picture of?"

"All of us. The Order," said Ruth curtly, like the questions were annoying.

"The Order?"

"Order of the Evanescent . . . that's what Arthur called it. He owned the bathhouse. He was *very* into creative names, you'd know that if you *read* the *book—ugh*!" She slapped the spines in frustration. "How could I have lost it? It was the only thing that mattered."

"It's okay," Jovie said, kneeling and rubbing Ruth's back. She was so frail, her ribs and backbone nearly poking through her pale blue cardigan. Jovie could feel the rattle in her breaths. "Why don't you sit on the couch? I can look for the book. Is there anywhere else you might have put it?"

Ruth took a deep breath and nodded. As Jovie lifted her by her arm, she said, "The other bookshelf, in the den."

Jovie eyed Mason, who took the cue and headed down the hall while she helped Ruth to her usual spot on the couch.

"You want a tonic?" Jovie asked, willing herself to hold back all her questions.

"That would be lovely."

Jovie went to the fridge for a can of tonic water and

plucked a slice of lime from the plastic-wrapped bowl beside the cans. She stuffed the lime into the can as she returned.

"Thank you, dear." Ruth sipped it, and calm spread over her face. "John's favorite drink." It was the same thing she said every time.

Jovie gave her another moment, looking over the bookshelf for any blue spines that mentioned Orders or Arthur or what was the planet? Elysia? That sounded like a name from ancient history. The Greeks, or the Romans, maybe? But she didn't see a match.

"So, you were part of some kind of order?" Jovie asked as she bent to double-check the bottom shelf. "Is that like a club or something?"

Ruth didn't answer. Jovie was just standing back up when she heard the thud of the can hitting the carpet and the hiss of spilling tonic. She turned to see Ruth staring wide-eyed in terror at the hallway, where Mason had just reappeared.

"Harry?" Ruth said in a chilling whisper.

Mason looked worriedly at Jovie. "Ruth . . . ," said Jovie. How could she even see him? "That's, um, my friend Mason. I shouldn't have brought him in, I—"

But then Ruth's face bloomed into a smile. "Little Harry, how you've grown. Is your father here?"

Jovie looked to Mason, who just shrugged. "Who's Harry?" Jovie asked.

"Look, he's right there. Roy's boy. You were always so

good at keeping the baths clean and fetching us towels. I hope you saved those nickels we gave you."

Jovie's thoughts felt jumbled. She pointed at Mason and raised her eyebrows at him as if to say *play along.* "This is Harry? And you know him from the bathhouse." Her thoughts quickly began to organize. "Is Harry short for Harrison?"

Ruth cocked her head. "Why don't you ask him? He's right there."

"Harrison Westervelt," Jovie said. "He would have been a boy back then."

"Harry, I have a picture of your father and my husband," Ruth was saying. "Fetch me that green photo album, dear." She pointed at the bookshelf.

Jovie placed the album in Ruth's lap and sat beside her as she began flipping through the stiff pages of faded old photographs. Jovie caught glimpses of a young Ruth and John at the Eiffel Tower, on some beach shaded by palm trees, at the Golden Gate Bridge.

"Here they are." The page she stopped on held a pair of photos. One seemed to be a postcard, showing an overhead view of a large glass-and-metal structure jutting out from the beach over the water. The other was a photo of young Ruth and John standing by their car in front of an elegant glass entryway. Beside them was a tall, slim man in a tan suit. Over the door was a large script *V.* This must have been the Vanescere Bathhouse.

"Here he is, Harry," Ruth said, pointing to the man

in the suit. "Roy was the one who introduced us to the place, to Arthur. He managed the finances there." Ruth's fingers glided slowly over to John and tapped lightly. Jovie heard a light clicking sound and saw that fresh tears were running down her cheeks. "What a lovely view from those baths," she said quietly. "I remember how much your mother loved it, Harry."

Jovie looked at Mason, who had his arms crossed like he was cold and was looking around awkwardly.

"Harrison's mother," Jovie said, remembering what Sylvan had told her. "She died in the explosion there, didn't she?"

"Oh no," said Ruth, as if this was obvious. "Nobody died."

"I thought . . . ?"

But Ruth shook her head. "That was the story in the papers, but I'm sure, Harry, that your mom and the others ascended just as Arthur had predicted. I know he was a charlatan when it came to the books, but when it came to Elysia . . ." Her voice quieted. "Across the gradient, into the golden light of a better world." Ruth's finger went still. She sat, unmoving.

Jovie waited a moment, but when Ruth didn't say anything more, she asked, "So, you think when the bathhouse exploded, all those people actually crossed the gradient?"

Ruth blinked and looked at her. "Hmmm?"

Come on, Ruth, Jovie thought. She motioned to Mason. "You were talking about how nice it was to see Harry again, from the bathhouse?"

Ruth turned her head slowly in Mason's direction, and seemed to look right through him. Then back to Jovie. "Could you get me a tonic?"

"You were talking about the *Order*," Jovie pressed. "About Harrison Westervelt. Arthur and a blue book."

Ruth stared at her as if she were speaking another language. Then she sighed and looked out the window. "No mail on Sundays," she said. "Always a shame."

"But—"

Mason put a hand gently on Jovie's shoulder and gave her a look. Whatever memories they'd stirred up in Ruth seemed to have slipped away for now.

Ruth got to her feet and crossed the room toward the kitchen. "Thank you for your help, dear," she said mildly. "Bring me my purse so I can pay you."

15

THE JOURNEY

JANUARY 14, 2018
199 HOURS TO BREACH

"That was weird," Mason said as they stepped out of Ruth's house. He shivered, almost like he was cold, and twisted that silver bracelet back and forth on his wrist.

Jovie folded the ten-dollar bill Ruth had given her and slid it into her pocket, eyeing the Barsuda van. It didn't seem like the driver was looking their way, but she lowered her voice anyway:

"How could Ruth see you?"

"Well, she didn't think she was seeing *me*," Mason said. "But I guess she was remembering Harrison and, I don't know, that somehow allowed her to see through the drift. . . . Do I look like him?"

"Not unless you were wearing a tinfoil hat and chewing

blue pills and you were like, seventy. Trust me, it would take a lot for you to look weird." The words had barely left her mouth before her face started to burn. "I mean, you know, to look *that* weird."

Mason glanced at her and smiled. "Thanks."

"But Ruth made it sound like the bathhouse explosion had something to do with the gradient. Do you think one of the storms could have done that?"

"I mean, it's possible. The bathhouse was right on the beach."

"If that's true, then this has been happening in Far Haven for . . . almost sixty years." Jovie glanced at the van. "Except, Barsuda hasn't been here that long, not even close. So what does that mean?"

"I'm not sure," Mason said.

"Let's see what we can find at Micah's house," Jovie said, getting on her bike. "I'm going to act like you're not here until we're past that van."

They coasted down her street. As they rounded the bend, Jovie looked back at the van, but the glare on the windshield hid the driver from view.

They reached the bike path and swerved down the hill toward town at top speed. Mason stood on his pedals, wind whipping his shaggy hair back. He grinned at her, and as they turned onto Main Street, he cut behind her, buzzing her back tire with his front one and causing her bike to shimmy.

"Hey!" she shouted over her shoulder.

"Gotcha."

"Jerk!" She flicked her brakes.

"Whoa!" Mason laughed and veered off the curb into the road. As he hopped his bike back onto the sidewalk, a horn honked.

Jovie stopped to let him catch up. She glanced at the pickup truck that had honked, the driver glaring at them. And then realized: "I think that guy was honking at *you*."

Mason watched the truck go. "Maybe."

"That's twice," said Jovie. "Do you feel different today?"

"Not really. But something does seem different."

"I wonder if it's because we're hanging out. Like, maybe it makes you more connected to the world or something. Sort of the opposite of when I was with you and I could see the drifters better."

"It's possible." Mason looked away from her as he said it, though, twisting that silver bracelet again like a nervous habit.

"Is that bad?"

"No," said Mason. "I just don't want it to mess up my connection to my dad."

"But you do want to be remembered by the world," said Jovie, "don't you? Maybe this is how you fight the drift."

"Yeah, they do—I mean, *I* do, it's just . . ."

Jovie felt a little surge of frustration. "You could ride separately to Micah's, or not come at all, if you think that's better."

"No, sorry, it's just complicated," he said, looking at her meaningfully. "I really do want to go. And I'm glad we're, you know, connecting." He gave her a sheepish smile, which made Jovie's face flush all over again.

"Okay, fine." She rolled her eyes and got back on her bike.

They rode through town and turned into a condominium complex. The units encircled a parking lot, their gray-painted surfaces streaked and faded with age. Jovie locked her bike to the rack and started toward Micah's walk, but paused when she realized Mason wasn't with her.

"I'll catch up in a sec," he said, standing by their bikes. He still looked shaken by being seen, and Jovie decided to give him a minute.

She approached Micah's door and rang the bell. There was no sound inside. When she rang a second time, she heard the slow thudding of feet.

The door opened and Hannah Rogers peered out of the dimly lit front hall. She wore sweats, her hair tangled. "What," she said uncertainly.

"Hi, Mrs. Rogers, it's me, Jovie."

Hannah's lips formed Jovie's name silently. Once, then twice.

"I was friends with Micah."

"Jovie." Her gaze softened, but then she looked past Jovie, out to the street. "Why are you here?"

"I, um, I was wondering if I could visit Micah's room. You know, I've still been putting up flyers, and I was thinking—"

"You remember Micah?" Hannah peered at her.

"Yeah . . ."

Hannah grimaced and put a hand on Jovie's shoulder. Jovie saw that in her other hand, she held a small square scrap of what looked like a blanket, sea blue with drawings of mermaids and frayed edges. "Everyone acts like she never even was. I can't take the looks on their faces." Her eyes fell, and she stepped back and motioned Jovie inside.

"Thanks." As Jovie moved into the dim hall, she held her breath for a moment, nearly overcome by the heavy odor of old pizza and unwashed clothes.

"You used to be here for sleepovers," Hannah said, as if she was reminding herself, "and movie nights."

"I was," said Jovie. "It had been a while, though."

Hannah nodded emphatically, but her eyes also started to tear up. "We hadn't seen any of her friends in so long, a long time even before . . ." She breathed deep. "I always wondered why you two stopped hanging out."

Jovie felt a wave of guilt. "We weren't in touch as much last year."

"She'd been having a tough time, but we never thought,

we never . . ." Her face contorted.

Jovie wanted to ask her why, what had been happening, but Hannah looked so devastated even just by this conversation that all she could bring herself to say was, "I'm sorry."

"I'll take you upstairs." Hannah led her down the hall.

Jovie looked back and saw Mason slipping in.

They passed the kitchen, the counters piled high with dirty dishes and frozen food boxes. Ahead, a TV was on in the living room, showing a football game. There were two recliners aimed at it. Micah's dad, Russ, was sitting in one, his feet up. The folding table between the two chairs was cluttered with beer bottles and stacked bowls. Jovie paused, thinking she should say hello, but Hannah gently gripped her forearm. Her fingers were so cold.

"Don't disturb him," she said, tugging Jovie down the hall. "Seeing you will just remind him. And he gets in a dark place."

Hannah led her up the stairs. Micah's door was closed. It still had that hand-drawn sign on it from way back in sixth grade: *BEWARE OF WITCHES!* She and Jovie had been reading some book series, still such little kids in so many ways.

Hannah stopped a few feet from the door. "Was there something in particular you were looking for?"

"Not really," Jovie said. "I just, um, wanted to be in there for a minute."

Hannah nodded and retreated toward the stairs. "The police said they didn't move anything, so . . . only thing I did was put her journal in there, after it showed up."

"Showed up?" said Jovie.

"Somebody found it and left it in the mailbox. But not till after, when the police had already stopped calling. I looked through it, but there wasn't anything that could tell us where, or why she . . ." Her voice tightened and she sniffled. "You take all the time you need."

Mason had just reached the top of the stairs and pressed himself against the wall as Hannah stepped past him.

"Thanks, Mrs. Rogers," Jovie said.

Hannah stopped. She bit her lip, a shadow crossing her face. "I know you're probably wondering why we stopped updating the web page."

"I know there wasn't any news."

"You don't know what it's like." She blinked back tears. "To want something to be different every single minute and be unable . . . have no power to change it. And to have no one care like you do, everyone just moving on like, 'oh well, that's just how it is, that's reality now,' and even if it is . . ." She shook her head.

"It doesn't feel that way to me," Jovie offered.

Hannah opened her mouth as if she'd say more, but then hurried down the stairs.

Jovie turned to the door. She gripped the handle, her

nerves buzzing. Up until this moment, she'd tried not to consider it, but was there any chance that Micah might just be here, behind this door, invisible to the world?

And yet, though her fingers were wrapped tightly around the spyglass, as Jovie stepped into the room, she didn't remove it from her pocket. One look, and she knew: Micah wasn't here, and hadn't been in a while—the room was too clean, the air too still. There was a faint scent of her: that sandalwood fragrance spray she'd started using, that special clear-skin cream.

But there were no clothes strewn on the floor, no laptop or jewelry or lip balms or purses scattered about. The bed was neatly made, and her desk was completely cleaned off except for her journal, placed perfectly in the center. The chair was pushed in just so. It had never looked like this when Micah had been here.

Otherwise, the room was like Jovie remembered it: filled with light from its south-facing window, though today there was rain pattering against it; the white-painted furniture and pink carpet that Micah had often complained was too childish; the ceiling over her bed still covered with a collage of printed pictures of her favorite singers and movie stars, as well as photos she'd taken. Jovie appeared in many. When they'd had sleepovers, lying on the floor, it was like their past had been a constellation overhead.

But if Hannah hadn't been in here, who had cleaned

up like this? Jovie thought of her own room: just about the only time she really cleaned it was before they went on trips. Had Micah felt the same way? Like she was getting ready to leave?

On the pillow, there was a stuffed alligator Jovie had never seen before. Micah had cleared all the stuffed animals and dolls from her room sometime early in seventh grade.

"Your room is so cute," she'd said of Jovie's room, on that last sleepover.

"Thanks," Jovie had replied, except the comment had put her on edge. She'd known that she was the last kid to still have so many stuffed animals on her shelves, to still have a bin of dolls, to even get them out still, now and then.

"Let's turn it this way," Micah had said as they'd taken a selfie that night, putting those rows of stuffed playthings out of the camera frame.

Jovie remembered the shrinking feeling. She should have been putting her time into fragrance sprays and curling irons and thick-heeled boots. What did it mean that she hadn't been?

They'd rather do something fun, not play with dolls.

One of the texts during their last fight. It had made Jovie feel so small. Like, so much less. . . .

"We should go," she said, turning away from the bed. "There's nothing here."

But Mason was looking at the wall, at a poster of London's Globe Theatre, his head cocked curiously.

"What?"

"Look through the spyglass."

"She's not here."

"I know. There's something else."

Jovie held the device up to her eye, and the room began to ripple in certain spots, like bubbles on the surface of water, only these roiling shapes were geometric, rectangles coming into perfect focus. . . .

The walls were covered with drawings. All of them were done on large, rectangular white paper with a frayed edge, as if torn from a pad. There were drawings taped to the walls, the dresser. Some had been done in vibrant pastels, some in thick black marker, some in smudged pencil, and through the spyglass, their edges glowed with faint rainbow energy. More than ten in all, Jovie thought, which neither Micah's parents nor the police had ever seen.

Jovie stepped to the wall and reached out, her hand a foggy impression. She gripped the corner of one drawing, rubbing her thumb on the coarse paper, and when she lowered the spyglass, she found that she could see the sketch with her naked eye.

This drawing was in pencil. Fluid, curving lines, the shading softened by fingerprints. It was of a beach, with gnarled pine trees at the edges of the paper and waves in the distance. Here and there on the flat sand were large upside-down triangular shapes scribbled dark black.

"That's Satellite Beach," Jovie said, tapping the triangles. "It's not far from where you pulled that woman from the water."

Mason nodded. "That's where the storms happen."

The next drawing she examined was of the beach at sunset, this one done in brilliant pastels, with vibrant reds and oranges and magentas.

"Look." Mason pointed midway up the drawing. There among the colorful clouds were three marble-sized shapes, furiously scribbled in a rainbow of colors.

There were words scrawled across the bottom of the paper, in Micah's handwriting:

ALWAYS AT SUNSET. FOLLOW THEM?

"Are those the lights?" Jovie wondered.

"I think so," said Mason.

She is *a drifter*, Jovie thought, and yet this proof settled like ice inside her.

"They're here, too." Mason was pointing to an ink drawing that depicted a view out a window, with the crisscrossing lines of the windowpanes, and trees outside. Jovie glanced across the room; this was Micah's window. In the center of the drawing were three bursts of wild color, done with watercolors over ink outlines.

"They look like butterflies," Jovie said, tracing her finger over one. The forms had that mirrored symmetry of a butterfly's wings, though they lacked details like antennae or legs.

These same butterfly shapes appeared in nearly all the other drawings, sometimes distant, sometimes close, often in a group of two or three, though in one drawing, there were dozens. This pastel composition seemed to have been drawn from a high spot, maybe the lookout tower on the bluff, and the lights were loosely arranged in a rainbow parade that was streaming out to sea across a sunset sky. Jovie pictured Micah sitting up there, watching this show of lights. Had she thought it was beautiful? Terrifying? Or both?

"They have dates," Mason said. He'd peeled back the corner of one of the drawings. "September fifth."

"Two weeks before she disappeared." Jovie checked the one with the view out the window. A tiny pencil note on the back read *September 14*.

"This one is July fifth." Mason was looking at the drawing with the parade of lights.

"July." That date was before Braiden's party. When had she started seeing them?

Jovie stepped to the desk and ran her fingers over Micah's journal. It was spiral-bound, with the unlined pages she'd preferred. The cover and page corners were wrinkled and stained, as if it had gotten wet, and there were bits of sand here and there. Jovie felt that elevator falling in her belly. Micah always had her journal with her; it wasn't something she would have left behind on purpose.

Jovie flipped it open, turning past dozens of pages of Micah's fluid handwriting and sketches, feeling the urge to read the entries but also feeling guilty for prying. She was nearing the end when a drawing caught her eye.

It showed a street, and Jovie thought it was the view from the tables outside Salt & Sand. The drawing was done in regular pencil except for one figure walking along, who was outlined in overlapping colored pencil lines, like rainbow. At the bottom it read:

LIKE ME?
SEPTEMBER 9

Mason had stepped closer. "That looks like a drifter," he said, echoing her thoughts.

Jovie flipped the page, and her heart caught in her throat. The next drawing was a figure sketched in pencil, looking up at them from the paper. A man in large, bug-eyed goggles. It looked almost exactly like the Barsuda agent who'd been in her yard.

THEY'RE WATCHING ME
SEPTEMBER 12

The next drawing was done in thick black marker lines, and the sight of it made Jovie's eyes prickle with tears.

It showed two people sitting in separate chairs: a man and a woman. The woman seemed to be reading something, the man looking away as if at a television. Jovie felt certain this was the living room downstairs. There was a girl standing in the doorway, arms crossed, a few feet from the adults. She had on a sweatshirt with the hood up. Her face had been left completely blank. This drawing had no title, only a date:

Sept 19

Jovie turned the page and reached the very last sketch in the journal. It was all in pencil and seemed hastily done, and, judging by the blank areas around the borders, maybe unfinished. It depicted the beach again, only this time, the sky and water had been colored in dark with jagged pencil strokes. But then, right in the center of the water, there was a spiral of white, like a galaxy, or a hurricane. Judging by the smudge marks, Micah had first colored the water in dark and then erased to make the spiral. The effect was of a ghostly, luminous swirl of light. Jovie could almost see it spinning.

At the very bottom of this erased disk, there was a small silhouette, as if a person was standing at the foot of that light, or even walking into it. The sketch had no title, and no date.

"Is this the gradient?" Jovie asked.

Mason just looked at it for a moment, his expression fearful. Then he nodded. "I think it is."

Jovie pointed to the little figure at the base of the light. "Is that a drifter?"

"Maybe," Mason said.

"But she didn't follow them," Jovie said, reassuring herself. "She didn't go into that light, because I remember . . . but why would she leave her journal? She never went anywhere without it."

"Once you're in the drift, it's hard to keep track of the things from your life before," said Mason. "Like, you're less aware of them? She might have just misplaced it."

Jovie ran her finger over the page. *I'm sorry.* One of her tears landed on the paper. She wiped it away with her finger, smudging the pencil. She looked around the room: for months, this had been happening to her friend. Micah, the same girl she'd known for years, the outgoing one, the confident one, had been lonely and fading. What had it been like? To be seeing all this? To know you were drifting, and to feel like there was no one who could help?

"If she's been this close already . . . ," Jovie said, tapping the page, "we have to figure out where she is before the next storm." Jovie waved her hand around the room. "Should I show her parents? I could, with the spyglass, I mean . . ."

"I'm not sure it would help," said Mason. "It might just make them feel worse."

Jovie nodded. The only thing that would help was finding Micah and bringing her home.

She tapped the journal drawing. "She was on that

beach," Jovie said. "More than once." She looked around at the drawings on the walls. "I don't see any clues to where she might be now." Jovie closed the journal and slipped it inside her coat. "There might be something in here. I can look later—" Jovie stopped, noticing that Mason was looking out the window, and the color had drained from his face.

"We need to go," he said. "Now."

Jovie followed his gaze and saw that a black van with the *B* logo had pulled up out front. The doors opened and two men got out, along with the woman with the red hair from the hospital. The three strode toward Micah's door, the woman leading the way, the tall man in back pulling large goggles over his head.

INTERLUDE

SECOND TRIAL, JANUARY 1962

PROJECT BARRICADE

REFERENCE CODE: 7

ARTIFACT #02143-2

SOURCE: FBI RECORDS VAULT

CLASSIFIED: TOP SECRET

INTERVIEW WITH ROY WESTERVELT

DATE: JANUARY 24, 1962

LOCATION: PROVIDENCE ST. PETER HOSPITAL TRAUMA WARD, OLYMPIA, WASHINGTON

CONDUCTED BY: SPECIAL AGENTS DARREN LEWIS & TOBIAS WALSH, SEATTLE FIELD OFFICE

TRANSCRIPTION BY: MARGERY CASE

LEWIS: This interview is being recorded at 6:18 p.m., Pacific Standard Time. Present in the room are Special Agents Lewis and Walsh, and Mr. Roy Westervelt, age forty-six, of Far Haven, Washington.

WALSH: Mr. Westervelt, for the purposes of transparency, would you please restate your consent to this interview with a yes or no.

WESTERVELT: Yes.

LEWIS: Now, Roy—can I call you Roy? [inaudible] Swell. You were employed by the Vanescere Bathhouse, which was owned and operated by Mr. Arthur Odegaard. Is that correct?

WESTERVELT: Yes.

WALSH: Why don't you tell us about that, Roy. Start from the beginning.

WESTERVELT: Suppose I could. Don't see what harm it could do now.

LEWIS: On the contrary, Roy. The way I see it, it can only help.

WESTERVELT: [coughing] And how do you see it, agent?

LEWIS: I see a man lying in a trauma ward with third-degree burns over half his body. A man who was the second most senior employee at an establishment that, just two nights ago, exploded in such a fury that it left twenty-six people presumed dead. A man who's facing federal charges for fraud, embezzlement, criminal conspiracy, and possibly murder. You got a young boy. Harrison, that's his name, right?

WESTERVELT: Harry . . . has he been here? Don't want him to see me like this.

WALSH: You don't want him to see you behind bars, either. Little boy's liable to become a ward of the state.

LEWIS: It's not good, Roy, but you know what else I see? I see a man with an opportunity to clear his name, right here and now. Arthur Odegaard, that's the real culprit, isn't it? You were just a simple man who was a whiz at numbers, who fell under the sway of a charismatic cultist. It happens, even to good men.

WESTERVELT: It wasn't a cult. Just a bunch of lonely souls looking for an answer. You ever felt separated from the world, gentlemen? Like you don't belong at your job, in your house, in your family, even in your own skin?

WALSH: Not sure what you're getting at here, Roy.

WESTERVELT: Just that people need to feel like there's a place for them. That's what Arthur offered.

LEWIS: Tell us about it, Roy. Tell us about Arthur.

WESTERVELT: [long pause] I met Arthur Odegaard in '59. My wife read about the spa in one of her magazines. I was working for Boeing at the time, on the accounting team—

LEWIS: That's good work. Steady.

WESTERVELT: Steady, yeah. Stale. And Betty . . . well, we'd lost Harry's younger sister a few years back to a heart defect, and she'd been fading. Felt like living with a ghost more often than not. If a trip to some oddball spa had any chance of brightening her spirits, I had to try. Did you ever go there?

LEWIS: We don't really have time for spa weekends.

WALSH: Busy catching bad guys, Roy.

WESTERVELT: Well, it's quite the place—was. Big atrium, the pools filled with heated ocean water, the glass steaming. With the palm trees Arthur brought in, you could almost imagine you were somewhere exotic.

Anyway, my wife, well, she took a shine to Arthur immediately—what lady wouldn't? He was this strapping, barrel-chested guy. He'd been a surfer with trophies from the North Shore, turned professional diver. Appeared in a movie or two, even met Elvis, had the picture to prove it.

It was enough to make a fella jealous, I'll tell you that. But he said he'd given all that up for something bigger. He invited us to a meeting that night. A real opportunity. And I don't know if it was the heat, or seeing a smile on Betty's face for the first time in who knew how long, but I agreed.

After dinner we found ourselves in this big room that Arthur said was modeled after an Indian roundhouse, but it was decorated in a real eclectic way. There were Hindu statues, and in the center was this bust of some Greek god, a Cynic or something, but carved out of cedar instead of marble. Everything had to do with Arthur's "philosophy," but I didn't really track all the finer points.

WALSH: Just the two of you and Arthur, was it?

WESTERVELT: No, there were three other couples, and it turned out we all had a . . . cloud over us, you might say. The Andersons, they'd lost their boy overseas. The Koswoods, well, the husband had recently been made obsolete when the march of progress reached his factory, and the wife, you could just tell that their marriage fit her all wrong. Another couple, the Murphys, they were just lonely, never seemed to be able to land a friend in their town, always a chill.

So there we all were, and Arthur arrived, dressed real sharp in a jacket and tie, and made his pitch. He said he'd made this profound discovery. That our world was connected to a larger reality, and that from right here in Far Haven, from these very pools, we could access a higher plane of existence. A better place, a paradise. He said it was another planet, a place he called Elysia, and that you could cross something called "the gradient" to get there.

LEWIS: Sounds like standard cult leader stuff. But you bought it.

WESTERVELT: Not at first. But then he took us out to the beach. It was summer, so the sun set late. Arthur had this wild setup in the sand: four of these, well, lenses I guess you'd call them, each a few feet across and held at an angle by a brass tripod. There was one for each couple, aimed out toward the horizon. Behind each one was a blanket. So we sat there, and I think it was Mr. Koswood who was first to complain: "Say, Arthur, the view's all fogged up, can we wipe this mist off?" Arthur told us to be patient. Now, quite a while went by, and even Betty was starting to grouse a bit, when it happened: these lights began to appear. Strange, rainbow shapes buzzing out over the water, that you could only see through those lenses. Sort of looked like butterflies, but much bigger, like the size of giant eagles.

LEWIS: What were they, Roy? Are we talking about some kind of fireworks, or UFOs—

WALSH: Was it the Russians, Roy?

WESTERVELT: Arthur said it was energy. He called them "essences," on their way out of this world, crossing the gradient. He said that if you felt lonely here, left out, if you didn't fit in, it was likely because you were supposed to be somewhere else: Elysia was calling, beckoning you to paradise. He said there was a balance between the different worlds, and that these feelings we had might mean our energy was needed elsewhere. That across the gradient, we would belong.

WALSH: Gotta be frank with you, Roy, this sounds like a tale from a science fiction rag.

WESTERVELT: Be that as it may, you didn't see those lights, didn't feel what they felt like, how they called to you. Made you feel a stirring inside. Like you wanted to follow them.

Then Arthur got real excited and told us to turn our lenses down the beach. And, by god, there, in the surf, we see this fella, or the ghost of a fella. He was shimmering and faint and surrounded by that same rainbow light. As we watched, he looked up, and when another of those essences sailed overhead, he smiled in this real peaceful way and just walked out to sea until the waves swallowed him. "Did you see that look on his face?" Arthur said. "He was ecstatic! He's truly on the path."

Now, not everyone was turned on by this idea—I think the Koswoods got up and checked out right then—but a few were, including Betty, and they wanted to know: How can we get to this paradise? Arthur said they needed to spend time here at the Vanescere, as much as they could manage, preparing to be part of his "Order of the Evanescent," I think he called it. He said a time was coming when the gradient would be fully open, and then, if we were ready, we would ascend.

It's all in his book, if you want to read it. To tell you the truth, I never really got the specifics, because later that very night, he approached me with a different opportunity. He knew I was a numbers man, and he asked me if I might have an interest in running his books. Said he'd pay me double what Boeing could, triple in due time.

WALSH: And that was it? You gave up a life and a steady job at a top company just like that?

WESTERVELT: Nothing is just like that. I liked Boeing, even if the ladder to executive was a mile long, but . . . [pause] You didn't see the look on Betty's face. When you've gone without seeing that kinda light long enough, you'll do anything to keep it shining. And back then, I didn't really believe Arthur's story, even with what he'd shown us. If only I had . . .

So, we moved to Far Haven, took up a little place in town, got Harry set up in school. Betty started spending a lot of time at the spa, but I mostly stayed away. Work got busy as word spread about Arthur's "spiritual guidance." By the fall of '61, there were upwards of fifty people sitting there soaking in Arthur's baths on a given weekend, some of them only visible through this special mask Arthur had. The number changed as people came and went, but it kept growing.

WALSH: What do you mean, "came and went"?

WESTERVELT: Across the gradient.

LEWIS: Now, hold on. We only have records of twenty-six people at the spa the other night.

WESTERVELT: That's just who was there at the end, the people you remember. Probably another few dozen went with the storms earlier that year.

LEWIS: Come on, Roy, if there had been dozens more missing persons in those baths, we would have heard about it.

WESTERVELT: [laughs] No, you really wouldn't. I mean, you've seen the financial records, and you still don't truly understand.

WALSH: We get that you were stealing from the customers. Transferring their life savings into your pockets.

WESTERVELT: It's only stealing if someone's going to miss it. Those people in the baths . . . You can't imagine the stories they told Arthur. Turns out, there are more reasons a person ends up feeling alone and lost from this world than you could ever list. And as they soaked, and faded out of sight and memory—happily, mind you—their money and belongings ceased to matter to them, not to mention that their bankers forgot about their accounts. At that point, we became the caretakers of their finances, effectively. Who could fault us for living well from our efforts? I saw it as a way to honor their journey.

LEWIS: Okay, spare us your noble reasoning. Why don't you jump ahead to the night of the explosion.

WESTERVELT: Well, the storms were getting stronger all through the fall and winter, and more frequent. The night of the twenty-fourth, I came out to see Betty. She hadn't even been home for a couple weeks at that point. Blissfully soaking away, invisible to the eye. . . . Harry had stopped asking about her, too, though I don't think he ever truly forgot her, even if everyone else did.

I was just arriving at the spa when the storm kicked up, and out of nowhere, this huge white light erupts in the ocean like a whirlpool, glowing brighter and brighter and making massive waves. As if on cue, the walls of the bathhouse, which had been designed like giant garage doors, started to lift. Everybody in the baths started to whoop and applaud. Arthur had all those big lenses arranged on the dock, and they were focusing the light even brighter.

And then, out comes Arthur in this crazy suit thing. And he says, "I am the Blue Bathymetrist!" Triumphant, you know.

LEWIS: What kind of suit are we talking about?

WESTERVELT: You know those diving outfits, like you see Cousteau wear? Only this one was made of some shimmery blue material like I'd never seen. He said he'd found it in a shipwreck off the coast, but that the suit came from over there.

WALSH: From across this, um, gradient.

WESTERVELT: Yeah. And then he starts to walk out on the dock, singing this weird song. He went straight out toward that light, and it's swirling brighter and brighter, and the suit starts to light up, too, like it's got circuits in it, but also like it was reacting to the storm. And the wind and the rain are glittering like ice, and lightning starts shooting out of the water.

And then this dark spot appeared, kind of like a pupil at the center of this wild eye, and it's like there's a hole right in the middle of the ocean. And out of it came these two figures wearing suits the same as Arthur's. He strode right toward them, arms out like he wanted to give them a hug. But whoever they were, they must not have been as happy to see him, because next thing you know, they were wrestling.

Meanwhile, the storm was getting worse. I started to feel that light burning my face and arms, and that's when I knew. Whatever this was, it wasn't the story Arthur had told us. Everyone in the baths was still ooh-ing and ahhing, but I started calling to Betty, saying we needed to go. . . .

I'll never forget the look she gave me. It was this polite smile, same as you'd give a stranger on the street, like we didn't even know each other. And then she just turned back to the light. And it was getting brighter and brighter and then it started shooting through those big lenses, like they were focusing it, and the beams started shredding the building. So I ran. And good thing I did, because I was barely out the front doors when there was this shrieking whine. I thought my eardrums had burst. Then a gust of hot wind threw me across the parking lot, clear over the hood of my car, and I rolled onto my back and watched it go.

LEWIS: That's when the bathhouse exploded.

WESTERVELT: When I looked back, all I could see was light and fire. And when it died down, all that was left was the foundation, and glowing puddles of melted glass.

LEWIS: And no sign of Arthur, or your wife, or all those people in the spa.

WESTERVELT: No sign at all.

WALSH: [whistles] Heck of a story, Roy, but come on now. You expect us to believe all this?

WESTERVELT: No, but I can tell you boys that you'd do well to.

LEWIS: Why's that, Roy?

WESTERVELT: Because it's going to happen again. Arthur thought the gradient was a doorway out of this world. And maybe all those people, Betty . . . maybe they really went somewhere better. But I don't know. I think . . .

WALSH: You think what?

WESTERVELT: [long pause] Just that doors open both ways.

LEWIS: What do you mean by that?

WESTERVELT: I'm tired.

WALSH: Come on now, Roy. We're going to need more than this

to keep you from a date at the courthouse.

WESTERVELT: Forgive me, boys, but the courthouse will be fine. The further away from here, from Far Haven, the better.

END TRANSCRIPT

PART II

A LIGHT BENEATH THE WAVES

16

THE INTERVIEW: PART II

JANUARY 18, 2022

"So . . ." Dr. Wells typed for another moment and then looked up. "You and Jovie managed to uncover quite a bit about what's been happening here."

Sylvan shifted in his seat. His leg was falling asleep. "No thanks to you guys."

Dr. Wells smiled at him. "I think you understand why that is. Especially after the 2018 event."

Sylvan remembered the moment, four years ago now, when the house had begun to shake. And the surreal drive around town that next morning.

Dr. Wells consulted her tablet. "Getting back to the prior events: After you recovered from your sickness, you only saw Jovie two more times before she disappeared, is that correct?"

Careful, Jovie said in Sylvan's head. "Yeah," he replied. The real number was actually four. Another good sign that though Dr. Wells knew a lot, she didn't know everything.

"There was January eighteenth," she said, "the night of the next cycle-up storm—I think we both know what happened there—and then the morning of January twenty-second, when she disappeared. And that interaction was as you described: a quick hello, and that was it."

"Uh-huh."

Here—that was what she'd really said—*Take this. Just in case.* And she'd handed him the object he'd kept hidden ever since. He was older now than Jovie had been when she disappeared. She'd seemed so much more mature back then, compared to how he felt now. . . .

"Which means my son has told you everything," Dad said. "Again."

"It does seem that way." Dr. Wells sat back and adjusted her glasses. She brushed a loose curl of hair from her face and gave Sylvan a bemused look. "I bet you wanted to see Jovie more than that, though, didn't you? Help her out with her search."

"I . . . yeah." Sylvan flashed a look at his mom. "But I wasn't allowed to."

"He was only ten," said Mom. "And if I hadn't told him he couldn't, then he might be missing now, too."

"Or maybe *she'd* still be *here*," Sylvan muttered.

"Hey," said Dad, but gently. "Come on."

"I see." Dr. Wells gave Sylvan a sympathetic glance, then looked down at her screen. She typed for a moment, then added, offhandedly, "Must have annoyed you that *he* still got to help her."

Sylvan felt a twinge of nervous energy. "Who?"

Dr. Wells looked up with that grin. "Jovie's other friend. You do remember him, don't you?"

"Who are we talking about?" Mom asked.

Dr. Wells turned her laptop around, and when Sylvan saw the picture there, he understood that he'd never, in fact, been a step ahead of Dr. Wells. "Right there," she said, pointing to the image. "Surely you know who that is."

Sylvan swallowed. "Yeah."

"Can I see that?" Mom asked, leaning forward.

Dr. Wells turned the tablet away and began typing again. "I'm afraid not. But Sylvan can tell you. Go ahead, Sylvan, tell us about your other friend, Mason."

"He wasn't my friend."

Dr. Wells pursed her lips. "No? And why not? He was with you and Jovie at the beach that night. In fact, as I'm sure you've known all along, he was with her when she disappeared."

"Who are you talking about?" Mom said.

"Why weren't you two friends?" Dr. Wells asked. Her eyes were boring into Sylvan now, almost hypnotic.

Don't say anything, he thought, and yet seeing that

picture only rekindled the old, painful suspicion, the one he'd tried not to dwell on for four years:

What if Jovie was wrong?

Mason was the one thing they'd disagreed on. What if that disagreement had been the thing that had gotten her lost?

"I . . . ," he started.

"Yes?"

Sylvan's heart pounded. Sweat broke out all over his body. Would saying anything even help? It hadn't back then. Plus, he would be betraying her. What if, when she came back—*if* she came back—she didn't even *want* to be his friend anymore? And yet . . . what if this was the only way to save her?

"I didn't trust him," Sylvan finally said.

"Oh? Why not?" said Dr. Wells.

Sylvan swallowed hard. "He wasn't who Jovie thought he was."

17

THE ESCAPE

JANUARY 14, 2018
197 HOURS TO BREACH

Jovie stood frozen, staring out the window, as the Barsuda team strode toward Micah's front door.

"Let's go!" Mason tugged her arm, and they darted out of the room to the top of the stairs.

Below, the doorbell rang.

They were just down the steps when Hannah reached the door, and as she opened it, they ducked across the hall into the kitchen. Mason pointed toward the dining room, where sliding glass doors led to the backyard, but Jovie peered back into the hall.

"What do you want?" Hannah was saying.

"Hello, Mrs. Rogers," the red-haired woman said. "Sorry to disturb you. I'm Dr. Wells, from Barsuda Solutions. I'm sure you heard about the recent outbreak of salmonella here in town. We're here to—"

Footsteps shotgunned down the hall, and Micah's father stormed toward the door. "What the hell are you doing here?" he snarled.

"Sir, please relax," said Dr. Wells.

"Is this about our daughter?" said Russ.

"No, sir, we're not here about that—"

"She's not a *that*! She's our little girl, and nobody even bothers to remember her name!"

"I'm very sorry," Dr. Wells said, leveling a steady gaze at the Rogerses. "I can't imagine what you've been through, but today I'm here about one of your daughter's friends, Jovie Williams. She's here, isn't she?"

"What do you want with her?" Hannah said.

"Well, it turns out she's been exposed to the same radiation event that caused last week's problems. She probably seems fine at the moment, but she needs to be quarantined immediately, for her own safety."

Jovie felt a dizzying wave of fear. *Quarantined?* That made no sense. Though Barsuda *had* been checking her well. . . . But her house was nowhere near the school, nowhere near where Mom said all the radiation cleanup had been in the first place. This had to be about the drifters. About Micah.

Mason tugged her sleeve to go. She turned, and when she looked past him, she froze.

The tall man from the team, the one who'd been in her yard, was standing outside the sliding glass doors, with those giant goggles down, looking right at them.

"Back upstairs!" Mason whispered.

Jovie ducked across the hallway, trying to make her footfalls as quiet as possible.

"There," she heard Dr. Wells say.

"Hey!" Hannah shouted.

"Jovie, wait!" Dr. Wells called.

Jovie looked over her shoulder and saw Dr. Wells and the other agent pushing between Micah's parents. At the same time, she heard the squeal of the sliding glass doors opening.

They sprinted to the top of the stairs. "Where now?" Jovie said, breathless.

Mason looked this way and that. Footsteps thumped up the steps. "In here!" He darted into the bathroom, Jovie right behind him. Mason slammed the door and flicked the lock.

Jovie looked around the little space. Her heart was hammering, and she couldn't catch her breath. "Wait, what if I should just talk to them?" Her thoughts were still spinning wildly. "My mom was sick, what if I really am—"

Mason was opening the window. "You know why they're here," he said as he fiddled with the corroded latches on the window screen. "They don't want us figuring out what happened to Micah, or any of the drifters." He turned to her. "And if they catch us, they'll definitely take your spyglass."

The door handle rattled. "Hey, open up!" a man's

voice said from the other side.

Mason was still picking at the latches. He was right, Jovie thought, and she pushed him aside. "Let me try." She gave the screen her best attempt at a kick. It twisted only halfway off—so much for those years of karate back in elementary school—but it was enough that Mason could slam it free.

He slid out onto a narrow, steep overhang above the sliding glass doors. The shingles were slick with rain, and Mason slipped and skidded on his backside, barely grabbing the windowsill before he fell. He slowly lowered himself, let his legs dangle off the edge, and leaped off.

Jovie started out the window. A heavy thud against the bathroom door, and another. The wood splintered.

She edged out onto the overhang and saw Mason standing on the deck below. "Jump down!"

She sat and dangled her feet. With a wicked crack, the bathroom door gave way and the goggle man rushed in. Jovie jumped, but not quite far enough out, and her spine raked against the metal gutter. She landed awkwardly, her ankle twisting, and stumbled back against the sliding glass doors with a thud.

As she pushed to her feet, she looked over her shoulder and saw Dr. Wells and the other Barsuda worker rushing across the kitchen.

"Come on!" said Mason.

Jovie limped across the deck, and they raced across the

small yard. There was a gate in the tall wooden fence, but it was locked with a thick padlock.

Jovie looked behind them. The goggle man was no longer in the bathroom window. Dr. Wells was tugging the sliding glass doors open.

"Gotta go over." Mason grabbed the top of the fence and hauled himself up, then held out his hand.

"Jovie, stop!" Dr. Wells was running across the deck. "We just want to talk!"

Jovie grabbed Mason's hand and pulled herself up, and they jumped over. She scraped her leg on the top of the fence and crashed into Mason as they landed. Her back ached, and for a moment she felt like she couldn't keep moving, but she forced her legs to go, her ankle screaming in protest.

They ran down the alley toward the street. *Almost there—*

The Barsuda van lurched to a stop at the end of the alley. Jovie looked behind them. Dr. Wells appeared at the top of the fence, swinging her leg over. To either side, the alley was bordered by fences and shrubs.

"There!" Mason said, pointing toward a warped chain link fence.

Jovie shifted her weight, and her ankle exploded in pain. "I don't know if I can."

Behind them, the wooden fence shook. Dr. Wells was climbing over.

Mason set his jaw. "Okay. Over here." He darted toward a metal garage door partially hidden by an overgrown patch of bamboo. He flattened himself against the door and pulled Jovie beside him so they were shoulder to shoulder.

"They'll see us!" Jovie hissed.

"Maybe not. Just be as still as you can," he said. "Ready?"

"For what?" She saw Dr. Wells dropping from the fence into the alley. In the other direction, the goggle man was getting out of the van.

When she turned back to Mason, his eyes were closed, his face deep in concentration. His hair was soaked from the rain. He gripped her hand, their clammy fingers intertwining. "Deep breath," he said.

And then Jovie felt a strange sensation, like a wind rushing through her. Her head swam, fingers and toes prickling, and her stomach felt like it had come unmoored from gravity, like the moment when a roller coaster starts downhill. The world blurred around her in a foggy way. The sounds, the feel of the air, all of it grew distant. She wanted to ask *what's happening*, but it felt as if her voice was miles away.

Out of the corner of her eye, she saw Dr. Wells moving slowly down the alley, peering this way and that, squinting in the rain. "Jovie?" she called. "We're not going to hurt you. This is for your own safety."

She was mere feet from them now, and yet Jovie's view of her grew watery. She glanced at Mason; he was still sharply in focus against the blurry world around them. So was Jovie when she looked down at herself, like they were somehow separated from everything else.

I'm drifting, she thought, and the realization made her shake.

"You're in more danger than you realize," Dr. Wells was saying. "But I think we can help each other. Just come out, okay?" She stopped directly in front of them, breathing hard, turned, and looked right at them . . . and then back the other way. "Anything?" she called to the end of the alley.

"No," the goggle man replied.

Dr. Wells cursed to herself and strode purposefully in the goggle man's direction. "Get me a pair of those."

As Dr. Wells passed them and the goggle man turned back to the van, Mason stepped away from the garage door and let go of Jovie's hand. He held a finger to his lips and motioned up the alley in the opposite direction. Jovie nodded and followed. That wind through her was already beginning to calm down, but the world around her remained blurry and distant.

They hugged the fences and overgrown shrubs, then ducked around the corner at the cross street and ran. They kept looking over their shoulders, but no one seemed to be following them. When they looped back around the block to the parking lot in front of Micah's, they halted. The other agent was standing out front right beside their bikes, goggles on.

"We'll have to come back for them," Mason said under his breath. "How far is it back to your place?"

"How long is this going to last?" Jovie asked, ignoring his question.

"Not long—"

"But I don't want to be lost!" Jovie hissed. She hugged herself tightly, shivering.

"You won't be," said Mason. "I just transferred some of my energy to you."

"You can do that? *Make* someone drift?"

"I wasn't certain that I could. But don't worry, it will fade."

"Are you sure?"

Mason's eyes shifted away from her. "Pretty sure."

"What if you're wrong?" Jovie said. "You should have asked me!"

Mason shrugged. "I didn't know what else to do. It was either try this or get caught by them."

"But . . ." Jovie didn't know what else to say. *Quarantine*, Dr. Wells had said. That would have meant taking her somewhere. But where? And for how long?

Her phone buzzed in her pocket. She pulled it out and saw a message from Sylvan.

How's it going at Micah's?

Jovie swiped at her phone to reply, but nothing

happened. She tried again. "Oh my god, not now, stupid battery—"

"It's not the battery," said Mason.

A fresh chill shot through Jovie. "Is it because I'm like this?"

"Something about the drift makes stuff like touch screens not recognize us. I don't know if our fingerprint is less *there*, or if we're just not warm enough."

"Are you serious?"

"Just give it a little time."

"But what if it doesn't wear off?" Jovie said, on the verge of panic. "What if I end up like Micah? Ghost-walking through the world until I'm gone?" Each thought felt like another giant boulder piling on top of her. "What if I start to see those lights and—"

Mason gently put a hand on her arm. "You won't. Just trust me, okay? But while you *are* like this, we need to get out of here."

Jovie bit her lip and nodded, and they crossed to the far side of the street. Keeping behind the trees and parked cars, they skirted the entrance to the alley, where Dr. Wells and the goggle man were still searching.

"Where are we going to go?" said Jovie.

"I'm not sure," said Mason. "I don't want to lead them to the bunkers."

"They might be waiting at my house," Jovie said.

Her phone vibrated with another message from Sylvan. This time, when she touched the screen, it unlocked.

Relief washed through her. "It's working again," she said to Mason. *I'm working*, she thought.

"Told you," he said with a cautious smile, but Jovie thought maybe he looked relieved, too.

She typed:

Hey sorry we ran into Barsuda and they wanted to quarantine me!

Are you ok????

Yeah we got away for now. Trying to figure out what to do next.

Reply dots flashed for a moment.

You should come here! My parents aren't home and they won't be for a couple more hours. And I haven't seen Barsuda around.

"We can go to Sylvan's," Jovie announced.

"Didn't you say he's like, ten?" said Mason.

"So?"

"Just seems dangerous for a kid."

It's dangerous for us, too, Jovie thought. "I think it's our best option." She asked for Sylvan's address, and he sent it, adding:

Come down the alley to the back gate.

Ok be there soon.

They walked in silence for a few blocks. Jovie kept glancing over her shoulder, but she didn't see any signs of the black van. It seemed as if they'd escaped, at least for the moment.

"I don't get it," Jovie said, her thoughts spinning. "Even if Barsuda really is behind the gradient somehow, I've never heard of them quarantining people before, or even showing up at houses like that."

"Maybe they knew what was in Micah's room and didn't want us to see."

This thought made Jovie's heart sink. That would mean Barsuda knew Micah was a drifter, had known this whole time, and yet they'd said nothing, done nothing, allowing her to just be lost, allowing almost everyone in town to forget her and those who remembered her to suffer.

"But why?" Jovie said. "If they know that opening the gradient is making people drift, and making other people in town sick, why are they doing it?"

Mason shrugged. "I don't know."

Jovie considered that maybe Barsuda showing up was a good sign, in a way, like it meant they really were getting closer to finding Micah. Except it also meant Barsuda wanted to keep them from succeeding.

"What would they have done to me?" she wondered.

"Questioned you, maybe even threatened you if you didn't tell them everything."

"Threatened?"

"Not like they'd hurt you, but more like, maybe they have a deal with the police, or the town, you know, to keep what they're doing a secret. It seems like they can do whatever they want."

"But we haven't actually done anything wrong!" Jovie said.

"I know," said Mason, "but it might not matter. They might make something up just to get you out of the way."

Jovie imagined how her mom would react to her being brought home by police, how news of such drama would spread at school. It made her want to give up right now—*No*, she told herself. That was probably exactly how they wanted her to feel. And she reminded herself that this had only happened because they were on the right path.

"Come on," she said with a deep breath and a wary look behind them. The chill of the drift was fading, and she picked up her pace. "Let's get to Sylvan's."

18

THE PATTERN

JANUARY 14, 2018
196 HOURS TO BREACH

Sylvan opened the back gate and greeted them in a whisper: "Follow me, quick."

Jovie was about to introduce Mason, but Sylvan was already crossing the yard in a crouch. "What's going on?" she asked as they hurried along a winding brick path.

"Shh!" said Sylvan, glancing worriedly toward the neighbors' house. "My parents are next door."

"You said they were out!" Jovie hissed.

"It's okay. They're watching the playoff game. They're all glued to the TV."

He led them down a short set of concrete steps and through a narrow door. Sylvan's basement was unfinished, filled with stacks of boxes and bins, but there was one corner that had been enclosed with makeshift cardboard walls that were hung from the ceiling beams with string and affixed to the floor with duct tape. One wall was partially made by the back of a ratty couch, the cardboard taped to it. They entered the space through a narrow gap by the wall. A sign was posted there, with a skull and crossbones and script writing that read:

Beneath that was a set of lines with the heading "club members." Sylvan's name was on the first line. The ones beneath it were empty.

The inside of the space was strung with multicolored lights and a glowing model of the solar system. A little window by the ceiling had been covered with a towel. The walls were plastered with *Minecraft* and Mario posters, various drawings, and, in some places, pages from comic books and graphic novels arranged in sequential tiles. Jovie also noticed a framed photo of a much younger Sylvan with a teenage girl. Jovie guessed this was his sister, Charlotte. She had her arm around him by a Christmas tree, and they were wearing matching sweaters.

In addition to the couch, there were two old folding camp chairs, an overturned box covered with a blanket that acted as a table, and a dresser in the corner with a small fish tank on top. A tetra fish hovered there, eyeing them. The floor was covered in Lego sets and various boxed science kits, their contents spilling out.

"Sorry I didn't clean up," Sylvan said. "This spot actually has the best Wi-Fi in the house. We're right beneath the office, so—"

"Sylvan," Jovie cut him off, "I need to show you something."

"Hold on, me first, I—"

"No, seriously." She handed him the spyglass. "You have to meet Mason."

Sylvan froze and looked around. "He's here?"

"Look," she said, motioning beside her.

"Right there?" Sylvan said, putting the spyglass to his eye.

"Yeah, just—"

He flinched like he'd gotten a shock. "Ohh." He looked for a moment. "I guess it makes sense you'd be Jovie's age."

Mason put out his hand, and they shook as Sylvan lowered the spyglass. "It's good to meet you," Mason said. "Jovie said you've been a big help."

"Yeah, well, I mean, I was the first member of the team, so . . ." Sylvan trailed off. He glanced at Jovie and quickly looked away. "You guys can sit down if you want."

"Thanks," said Jovie. "Can I get the Wi-Fi password?"

"Oh yeah, here." Sylvan stepped past Jovie. As she and

Mason sat on the couch, Jovie heard a tearing sound. Sylvan returned and handed her a sticky note, and Jovie noticed that he had taken down his *Captain Sylver* sign and folded it in half. He slid it beside the dresser before kneeling and opening his laptop on the box table. "So, what happened at Micah's?"

Jovie recounted their visit, though she stopped short of mentioning how Mason had helped her drift in order to escape. She laid Micah's journal on the table and showed Sylvan the drawings. "She was drifting," Jovie said. She turned to the picture of the goggle man. "And Barsuda knew it." Jovie flipped to the last drawing, of the beach and the swirling white light.

"What's that?" said Sylvan, awestruck.

"I think that's the gradient," Mason said.

"We also may have discovered another time the gradient opened." Jovie recounted what had happened at Ruth's house earlier.

"Oh, of course!" Sylvan pretended to smack his forehead. "They never really determined the cause of the Vanescere explosion . . . and the owner, Arthur Odegaard, *did* write a book!"

Sylvan typed quickly and spun his laptop around. It displayed a bookstore page that showed a blue book with what appeared to be a deep-sea diver on the cover, encircled by a rainbow ring around his waist. "It's called *The Blue Bathymetrist's Guide to Planet Elysia*," Sylvan read.

"'A complete guide to preparing your life and body for ascending across the gradient to paradise.'"

Sylvan scrolled down. "Let's see: Published in 1961 by Secret-of-Life Books. . . . I read about this when I was researching the explosion, but it just seemed like some scam or weird cult thing." He turned the laptop back around and typed again. "I can't find a definition for 'bathymetrist,' but bathymetry is the study of depth, like of the topography of the seafloor."

"That book might have some answers," said Jovie. "How much is it? We can use my debit card."

Sylvan clicked a few times. "It's not available from any online sellers right now, new or used."

"Okay, well, we'll keep looking. Maybe I can find Ruth's copy. Do you really think this means the gradient opened way back then?"

"Totally!" Sylvan said, snapping his fingers. "This fits with what I wanted to tell you about! Hold on, let me get to my notes. . . . Okay, here we go: First of all, you were wondering if there were other symptoms in code seven patients, and there are! Besides the cataracts and all the salmonella cases, there have been five cases of really bad migraines and people seeing white flashes in their vision, and four cases of broken bones due to rapid bone-density loss."

"Rapid?" Jovie asked. "Like my mom's cataracts?"

"I don't know, but here's the real thing." Sylvan hopped excitedly on his knees. "We were also wondering if there were code seven cases in 1994, and there were a *bunch*. But it turns out there have only been code seven cases in four years, total. This year, 1994, and . . . want to guess the other two years?"

"Nineteen sixty-two?" said Jovie.

"Correct! And?"

Jovie found Sylvan looking at her expectantly. "Am I supposed to know—"

"Two thousand ten!" Sylvan nearly shouted. When Jovie just kept looking at him, he continued: "What do 1962, 1994, and 2010 all have in common?"

"Tragedies," said Mason.

"Bingo!" said Sylvan. "In 1962, the bathhouse explodes. In 1994, the Ascension Camp incident. In 2010—"

"The Baxter plant accident," Jovie finished.

"I can't believe I didn't see it before!" said Sylvan. "My video series would have been *so* cool!"

"So, wait," said Jovie, "we're saying all these accidents were actually caused by the gradient opening?"

"Yup, and there's even more: Do you remember the date of the Baxter accident?"

"Um, not exactly—"

"It was in January. And so was the bathhouse, and Ascension Camp. And after each tragedy, no more code seven cases show up—like, zero—until the next one of these years."

A ripple of fear spread through Jovie. "Harrison said the storms get stronger until some kind of eye opens, and that's the end, until the next cycle. So maybe it's the last storm in the cycle that does the damage? Except that means something like that is going to happen . . ."

"This month," said Mason. "I just wish we knew when."

"Yeah." Jovie felt some of the wind leaving her sails. Sylvan, though, was still bouncing and looking like he was about to burst. "What?"

"We *do* know!" he shouted, his glasses nearly sliding off his nose. "There's a pattern!" He sighed and looked at the ceiling. "I'm sorry, I couldn't wait to tell you. I mean, it's so obvious once you know what to look for, but of course we didn't know until I found all the cases, but still—"

"Sylvan," said Jovie. "What's the pattern?"

"Okay, so, 1962, 1994, 2010, 2018," he said, counting off on his fingers. "Thirty-two, sixteen, eight!"

"The years in between events?" said Mason. "They're decreasing by half each time?"

Sylvan nodded vigorously. "It's an exponential number pattern! Or at least, it could be. To confirm it, you'd ideally find another event before 1962 that fit the pattern." He was already smiling.

"So, you mean sixty-four years before that?" said Jovie.

"Exactly, which takes us back to 1898. And you *know* what happened that year."

"Unless we don't," said Mason.

"The wreck of the *Endurance*," said Sylvan, "a ship headed to Alaska. It sunk right off the coast! Want to guess what month?"

"January?" said Jovie.

"Yes! It fits the pattern perfectly!" Sylvan looked at them like he was expecting applause.

"Yeah, but does any of that help us with *this* year?" Jovie asked. "With when the next storm will be?"

"Well . . ." Sylvan's face fell. "Not exactly. . . ."

"Actually, it might," said Mason. "The most recent storm was January tenth, and I'm almost positive the one before that was on Christmas Day—"

"Ooh, that's sixteen days between them!" Sylvan interrupted. "When was the one before that?"

"I'm not sure."

Jovie eyed Micah's journal. "Was there one on September twenty-first?"

"That would be . . . ninety-six days back from Christmas. Thirty-two plus sixty-four . . . that fits!" said Sylvan. "Which means there would have been one on November twenty-third, too. You guys, this is totally it!"

"But when is the next storm?" Jovie asked.

"It would be eight days from the last one," said Mason. "So . . . January eighteenth."

Jovie checked her phone's calendar. "That's this Thursday."

"Sounds right," said Sylvan.

"Is that going to be the big storm, when the eye opens or whatever?" Jovie asked.

"I don't know," Mason said.

"Either way, we have to be there," Jovie said, pointing at the gradient drawing, "to make sure Micah doesn't get pulled across."

"Or any other drifters," said Mason.

A silence passed over them.

"Does it seem weird that this is happening on a pattern?" Jovie wondered aloud. "It almost seems like it's programmed."

"Well, a lot of things in nature run on precise clocks," said Sylvan. "Maybe it has something to do with weather patterns, or the rotation of the earth."

Jovie still felt like there was something they were missing. "Was there anyone even living here in 1898?"

"Far Haven was founded in 1873," said Sylvan. "But it was basically just a little trading outpost. Why?"

"It's just, we know Barsuda wasn't here back then." She looked at Mason. "This would mean they're not the ones opening the gradient."

Mason just nodded, his face troubled.

"So, what's the plan?" said Sylvan. "I mean for Thursday?"

"Go to Satellite Beach," said Jovie. She held out the spyglass. "Watch for Micah and the other drifters; make sure they don't cross the gradient."

"And we need to see what Barsuda is doing during the storm," Mason added.

"While trying not to get caught by them in the process," Jovie finished. She looked at Mason. "But Carina said it's dangerous for you guys to get too close to the gradient. Will you be okay?"

"I should be," said Mason. "When we're together, I'm more connected."

"Okay," Sylvan said, scowling, "but we *also* need to figure out how we're going to stop this gradient thing from happening." He tapped his computer screen. "It's made a lot of people sick over the years, not to mention the people who have died in the big storms and however many drifters it's taken. In 2010, the storm was big enough that it caused a nuclear accident."

"Or Baxter is just a cover story," said Jovie, thinking of what her mom had said.

"Either way," said Sylvan. "There are more code sevens this year so far than in any of the other years, which could mean that this final storm will be bigger, too. Not only that, if our pattern is right, this whole thing is just going to happen again, in four years. And then two years after that. Which means more victims and more tragic events."

"We still need some kind of proof to link all this together," said Jovie. "Something we could take to major news stations, so that Barsuda would have to tell everyone what's going on. We could try taking photos or videos of the storm, but people will probably just think we faked them."

"We have the code seven cases," said Mason. "We just need evidence that connects them to the gradient."

"That would be like, the smoking gun," said Sylvan.

"Well, we know more symptoms now," said Jovie. "Maybe they have something in common." She started typing into her phone: *cataracts, salmonella, migraines, white flashes, bone-density loss, memory loss . . .*

She scrolled through the results, and one word combination appeared multiple times. "There is something," she said, nervous energy rippling in her belly, "but it's weird."

"Weirder than what we're already talking about?" said Sylvan.

"Good point," said Jovie, clicking on a link. "All these symptoms have been seen in astronauts who've been exposed to cosmic rays."

"Cosmic rays?" said Sylvan. "Like from space?"

"Yeah." Jovie scrolled down the article. "It says that cosmic rays can create super virulent strains of salmonella, too."

"But that's *in space*," said Sylvan, "right?" He typed for a moment. "Looks like Earth's atmosphere blocks almost all cosmic rays."

Jovie returned to her search results and looked at the next page, then the next. "I don't see any other connections."

"What if that's it?" said Mason. "People think the gradient leads to another world. Maybe it really does go, like, through space, and so it's giving off cosmic rays every time it opens."

"You mean like a wormhole?" said Jovie. "Because that would be completely impossible, right?"

"If it really is cosmic rays, we'd need a way to detect them," said Sylvan, typing. "Some way to get real data we could show someone so they'd believe us." He peered at his screen. "It looks like you either need a satellite or some really expensive equipment—ooh, here's something we could do."

He turned his laptop around. On it was a picture of an old-timey-looking device: a large glass jar with something made of golden metal hanging inside. "It's called a Bennet's electroscope, and it says you can use it to test for cosmic rays. It's not that complicated to build one, and there are instructions online. You just need a big jar, tinfoil, a rubber stopper, and pure gold leaf."

"I don't think I have any pure gold leaf lying around," said Jovie.

"That's no problem," said Sylvan, typing again. "We have a preferred account with Seattle Science Supply." He motioned to the science kits on the floor. "My parents let me order basically whatever I want as long as it's"—he made finger quotes—"'educational.' And keeps me busy. Looks like I can get some gold leaf from there. Then we could build this electroscope and take it with us to the beach on Thursday!"

"We could," Jovie said. She looked at Mason. "What do you think?"

"It's worth a try," he said. "If it works, it might really help us understand how to save the drifters."

Jovie thought of Mason's dad and the drifters in the bunker, of Micah out on the beach. She looked at the drawing in Micah's journal, that swirling light. Could the gradient really be some sort of hole into space? Somehow that possibility made the gradient seem even colder and more frightening than it had already. They still didn't know what was beyond it, or why it might make drifters feel like they wanted to cross it, but Jovie found herself picturing not some welcoming planet, but infinite darkness, frigid cold. . . . "Let's do it," she said. "Thursday."

Sylvan and Mason both nodded solemnly.

A quiet moment passed between them. Jovie looked at the little basement window. Though it was covered, she could tell that the light outside had dimmed. She checked her phone; it was almost four.

"We should probably go," she said, getting up.

"The game is in the fourth quarter, anyway," Sylvan said, looking at his screen.

"Do you think it's safe out there?" she asked Mason.

Mason stood. "We'll have to find out at some point."

Sylvan led them to the door. "I'm going to show the electroscope plans to Ms. Harter and maybe she'll help us. I have science right after recess tomorrow."

Recess. The word triggered a wave of guilt in Jovie. She glanced at the neighbors' house. Beverly would be furious if she knew what they were up to.

"Be safe," Sylvan said as they went up the stairs. "Okay?"

"Okay," said Jovie. "Keep your eyes peeled for black vans."

As she and Mason walked up the street, Jovie peered this way and that in the deepening twilight. The rain had stopped, the cars and streets still with a sheen. It was so quiet—maybe everyone was still watching the playoff game—and yet Jovie felt that tingling sensation again, like she was being observed, and she wondered if it was the town itself, awaiting the return of a force that had tormented it for over a century, and whose destructive final act might be mere days away.

19

THE ENTRY

JANUARY 18, 2018
108 HOURS TO BREACH

April 8

I feel like my life is a little island and I'm stranded, just me, talking to a crab and maybe a pirate's skeleton. Like I don't have any friends, or even parents.

Jovie's SUPPOSED to be my best friend but all she ever wants to talk about is the drama with her parents. I was trying to tell her about last night, about sitting in the freezing rain for over two hours because my dad "lost track of time" like he does.

But all we ended up talking about was how her parents are fighting over her birthday and she thinks that's somehow the most tragic thing in the world, like having two parents who actually want to spend time with her is so terrible. Who cares if they don't like each other! They still care about her.

Ever since camp, it's like I don't know how to talk to her, to anyone. But even when I do, it's like she doesn't listen! I'm invisible with her, just like I am at school, in this house, like I was on that stage, a ghost, haunting the shadows. What do I have to do to be seen? Sometimes it feels like it's not even worth trying. I just wish I had someone to talk to about it.

Jovie lay in bed, reading the page in Micah's journal again, and the pit in her stomach deepened.

The worst friend ever.

She'd had no idea Micah had been feeling this way. But she hadn't said anything! *Or was that because I didn't let her?* Had Jovie really talked that much about her birthday? She remembered how upset she'd been—Mom and

Dad hadn't been able to agree on plans for her birthday night, so she'd ended up having a separate celebration with each of them, both of which felt empty. And somehow, in all of that, they'd never actually asked her if she wanted to do any sort of party with her friends (which only would have been Micah and maybe a kid or two from class, if she'd even gotten the nerve to ask them). Jovie had been so frustrated, of course she'd wanted to talk about it! But that wasn't *all* she'd talked about . . . was it?

Micah had thought so. Except Micah also admitted that she hadn't really said anything to Jovie about her own feelings. And that was new. In the past, if something had bothered Micah, she'd always let you know. When had that changed, and how had Jovie missed it?

The references to *camp* and being *on that stage* must have meant the Shakespeare camp, but Jovie didn't remember Micah talking about that, either. Jovie had assumed camp had gone well—that kind of thing always did for Micah—but maybe something had happened there? Either way, Micah had needed someone, and Jovie hadn't noticed. What kind of friend doesn't realize when their best friend is so hurt?

Jovie slapped the journal closed and got a tissue from her nightstand. *She probably doesn't even want me to find her*, she thought bitterly.

Her phone buzzed with a message from Sylvan:

Firewing to Nightclaw: The fox has the egg. Bring the nest. And the eagle.

This, at least, brought a smile to Jovie's face, even as it triggered a burst of nervous energy. If they were right about the pattern, then the next gradient storm was tonight. Sylvan made it sound like this was an adventure, but Jovie still worried that she was putting him in danger. Was she only thinking about herself again, like Micah had said?

Rain pattered against the window. Jovie peered outside; there was a Barsuda van out front. It had been on her street all week. No goggle-wearing workers in her yard, or at her door, but still, it seemed certain that they were watching her. Maybe she should call this off. . . .

No. Not when they were this close, not when Micah could be lost in this storm. And especially not after reading Micah's journal entry. She replied to Sylvan:

See you there

Jovie got up, shivering in her chilly room, and put on long underwear beneath her jeans and sweater, then carefully loaded Beryl into her backpack. Headlamp: check. Spyglass: check.

She found Mom in the kitchen, back from work and reading on her phone.

"Hey," she said as Jovie entered. "I made oatmeal. Just instant, but I did a bunch of packs at once."

"Oh . . . thanks." They'd barely spoken since Jovie

stormed out of the kitchen on Saturday. Now Mom was smiling and making breakfast?

"I don't have any students this afternoon," she said as Jovie sat down across from her. "I thought we could finally go to Fred Meyer. Didn't you say you needed something there?"

"Oh. Yeah, oil for my bike chain. Um . . ." Jovie shifted in her seat as she decided what lie to go with. "I actually have to work after school. Elena needs me to cover a shift."

"Oh." Mom's eyes fell to her phone. "And I'm working tonight. Well, another time."

Jovie felt a tug of guilt. Why did Mom have to pick today to finally suggest that they do something together? "Maybe this weekend?"

Mom shrugged. "I'm on a double shift Saturday, but maybe."

Jovie's phone buzzed with another message from Sylvan: Don't forget to get the jar!

"I have to go," Jovie said, eating quickly, her hands nearly shaking with nervous energy. "I guess I'll see you tomorrow morning."

"Okay," Mom said, back to scrolling on her phone. "Sounds good." Jovie had bundled up and was opening the door when Mom spoke again: "You know, I'm really proud of how hard you work. You're so motivated. More than I ever was at your age."

Jovie looked back, the guilt tugging harder. "Oh, thanks."

Mom went on, not looking up from her phone: "I know it's been hard with me being sick, and working so much, and everything else." Her voice lowered. "You've had to do a lot on your own."

Jovie felt a lump in her throat. "It's okay," she said. It occurred to her how hard it had been for Mom, too, how hard she was trying all the time, how tough it must have been to spend all her nights working, to provide for Jovie the best she could. A surprising thought leaped into Jovie's mind: *Tell her.* She could just tell her about everything. Stop keeping secrets. Maybe Mom would want to help. She'd definitely be sympathetic to what was happening to the drifters. . . .

But Jovie pushed back the urge. Even if she could make her understand what was really happening, Mom definitely would not let Jovie go through with tonight. She'd say it was too dangerous, or want to call the police, or think the police were in on the conspiracy, and Jovie couldn't risk things going that way.

"Bye," she said simply, and headed out.

She biked into town, to the Red Apple market. In the back corner of the store by the deli was a display marked "Northwest Specialties," which included a pyramid of enormous jars of Geoduck Giant Pickles. They were made of whole cucumbers sliced in half, and the enormous jar was just the right size for the cosmic ray detector.

As Jovie made her way to the display, she looked around with the spyglass. No sign of Micah, of course. If Jovie found her tonight, the first thing she was going to ask was where Micah had spent these last few months.

She picked up one of the giant jars and lugged it back toward the front of the store. She was passing one of the aisles when she halted: at the far end was Mason. He was standing near an old woman with a shopping cart, and was reaching up to the highest shelf for a bag of pretzels.

She'd seen him at the coffee stand twice this week, and they'd planned for him to use his invisibility to be the bringer-of-snacks for tonight's mission. Maybe that was why he was here now. Jovie almost called out to him, but then realized it would seem pretty strange to that old woman if she called to someone who wasn't there.

Except then Mason handed the pretzel bag right to the woman.

"Thank you so much, young man," she said to him. "It was so nice of you to help."

"No problem," Mason said. As the woman pushed her cart away, Mason put a bag of shrimp chips in his back-pack and then walked down the aisle toward the front of the store.

Jovie followed him, but wanted to get past the old woman before she called out to him. By the time she got to the end of the aisle, Mason was striding toward the exit, bypassing the checkout stands. He paused just before he reached the security towers posted on either side of the doorway and fiddled with his sleeve, and then, with a quick glance at the checkout workers, he stepped out. The alarm still went off, but when the clerks looked over, they didn't see him.

"Wanna go reset that?" one said to the other.

Jovie watched him go, then paid for the pickles, but by the time she got out to her bike, Mason had long since left the parking lot.

She biked on to school, but she wondered about what she'd just seen. Mason and his dad had been so lost from the world that they'd drifted from Seattle all the way out on the beach, and yet here he was, being seen once again by a normal person. He was clearly still drifting, though, otherwise those store clerks would have seen him, too. Maybe this also had to do with he and Jovie being friends, like when that driver had seen him the other day. Like the longer they were friends, the more connected to the world he became. If that was the case, could the other drifters find someone to help reconnect them, too?

Although it might not be that easy. There wasn't anyone else around like Jovie, with her spyglass and her connection to Micah, both of which helped her keep the drifters in her memory at all times. This effect she was having on Mason gave her hope, though, that when she did find Micah, she could help her reconnect. And that moment might really be as soon as tonight.

These thoughts made the school day drag by, until Jovie was finally on her way to the elementary school. As she waded through the stream of kids running out, it surprised her how much energy there was in these halls, the walls so bright and cheery with vibrant displays of artwork, the kids and teachers all bouncing around, and it occurred to her: she hadn't seen any children in the drifters' camp. Did only teenagers and adults drift? Kids had parents keeping them attached to the world, organizing their activities, supporting them. Was drifting something that could only happen when you were older, and like, more on your own?

She found Sylvan in the science room, standing over a table with Ms. Harter.

"Jovie, hello!" Ms. Harter smiled brightly, her enthusiasm something that Jovie remembered well, even after a few years. "My goodness, you keep growing. How's middle school?"

"It's all right," Jovie said, unzipping her backpack and removing the jar.

"Well, it's nice to see you two pursuing this unique project," said Ms. Harter. "Though I don't want you to get your hopes up. Even a professional device would have a tough time detecting cosmic rays here at sea level."

"That's okay," Sylvan said, giving Jovie a knowing look, "we just want to give it a shot."

They worked for almost an hour to create the electroscope, first installing a rubber stopper in the mouth of the jar, then sliding a slim metal tube through the stopper and attaching two thin, flat rectangles of shimmering gold leaf to the bottom end of the tube so they were angled like the ends of a wishbone. These lined up with two long tinfoil sticks that stuck straight up from the base of the jar.

"Not bad," Sylvan said, putting the glue gun aside and munching on his third pickle.

"I think you have it," Ms. Harter said, consulting her laptop. "Where are you going to test this?"

"Fort Riley," Jovie said immediately, while at the exact same time, Sylvan said, "Satellite Beach." Jovie frowned at him.

Ms. Harter just nodded. "Well, I can't wait to hear about it."

The two thanked her for her help and headed out. As they crossed the damp parking lot, Jovie asked, "Are you sure you're not going to get in trouble?"

"I'm sure. Technically, I'm at coding class right now," said Sylvan. "It ends at four thirty, and I told Mom I'm going home with Hugo after that; he's in my class. But then I told my coding teacher I couldn't be there today, so he won't call home or anything. The plan is airtight."

Jovie felt a wave of guilt. "That's a lot of lies stacked on top of one another, Sylvan—"

"So what?" he snapped, throwing up his hands. "This is more important. I'm not going to let down the team."

"I just don't want you to get . . ." Jovie searched for a word that wouldn't make it sound like she was being protective of him. "Grounded."

They ducked behind a row of portable classrooms along the edge of the parking lot and reached a chain link fence, the shadowy forest dropping away beyond. The sounds from the rest of the world became distant. Jovie peeled up a loose flap of fencing that accessed a small trail, an escape hatch Micah had shown her back in sixth grade.

"Ready?" she said to Sylvan.

He nodded, but his eyes looked wide with worry as he stepped through the fence. Jovie pushed her bike through, and they started down the trail into the silent forest.

20

SATELLITE BEACH

JANUARY 18, 2018
98 HOURS TO BREACH

They ducked through a tunnel of clutching blackberry vines and emerged on a wide trail. The forest dripped and hissed around them, fragrant with the bittersweet scent of pine. Jovie exhaled a cloud of steam, retied her hair, and put on her knit hat.

"Ready?" she said, straddling her bike. Sylvan moved cautiously onto the seat, getting his feet onto the back fork. "No sudden movements, okay?"

"Okay . . . ," Sylvan said, as if this was a lot to ask.

She pushed off and pedaled standing up. The damp, leafy trail descended through shadowy ferns and pines and moss-covered logs. Jovie swerved now and then to avoid long, slippery slugs that were crossing the trail. The air was completely still, as if time itself could swallow you up here. Jovie wondered if Micah had come this way, her journal under her arm, as she followed those lights.

They passed through a tunnel beneath the road, and Jovie's nerves hummed when she saw a faint line of butterfly shapes painted on the corrugated metal. "Micah drew shapes like that," she said to Sylvan, her voice barely above a whisper.

"Oh," Sylvan croaked in reply.

They reached an intersection where a sign announced that they were entering the state park. Another trail led up the slope toward the bluff. At first, the gloomy spot looked deserted, but as they got closer, Jovie saw Mason standing there waiting as they'd planned. He smiled. Jovie smiled back. "There's Mason," she said, in case Sylvan didn't see him.

"Oh, great," said Sylvan flatly.

Jovie pulled to a stop, her brakes squealing in the still forest. "Hey," she said, pushing a stray lock of hair inside her hat.

"Hey," said Mason. "I brought snacks." He tapped his backpack, then looked around Jovie. "Hey, Sylvan."

"Hello."

"We should get moving," said Jovie. "Sunset is in an hour."

The three walked down the trail, Jovie pushing her bike. The trail dropped into a valley and merged with the overgrown remnants of an old road. The sound of the ocean filtered through the trees, and a cool breeze carried the smell of the sea.

The road crossed a mossy wooden bridge, and they stopped in the shadow of the last gnarled trees at the edge of the wide, flat beach. Distantly, layer upon layer of waves roared and foamed. To their right, the bluff climbed steeply toward Fort Riley. To their left, gentle sand dunes rolled along behind the wide beach, receding into mist. Here and there on the sand were the great waterlogged trunk-and-root bases of trees, inverted like crashed space capsules, that gave the beach its name.

"Look," Sylvan said, pointing, "the bathhouse." Just beyond where the old road ended, or rather was consumed by the sand, lines of waterlogged wooden posts marched into the surf. A chunk of concrete wall stuck out like a jagged tooth.

Jovie got out the spyglass and did a long sweep of the beach, the dunes, and the forest behind them, but no drifters appeared. Though it was early yet. *Sunset*, Micah had written. Jovie felt a shudder of anticipation: this was the exact view in one of Micah's drawings. She'd stood in this very spot, drawn here by those butterfly lights. *I'm here*, Jovie thought.

Just in front of them, a bright orange rope had been strung across the road, with a sign that read:

WARNING

BEACH CLOSED FOR HAZARDOUS CLEANUP

1/17–1/19

Below that was a note to call Barsuda Solutions for more information.

"Looks like we were right about the date," said Jovie. She pushed her bike behind a thick tree and ducked under the rope. She peered up and down the beach. Other than platoons of birds running along the waterline, it appeared to be deserted. "They're not here yet. Where do they usually set up?"

Mason pointed down the beach. "They drive up from the parking lot."

"Okay, let's go." She started out across the sand. The plan was to do a test for cosmic rays as close to the location where Barsuda set up as possible, and then get back to the safety of the trees to watch for Micah and other drifters and observe whatever Barsuda was up to.

The moment they left the shelter of the trees, the wind pelted them with sand and spray. Jovie leaned into the gusts, trudging along, pulling her hat down and her collar up. Sylvan had produced a knit hat and a pair of ski goggles. Mason had his hood up, the drawstring pulled tight.

They made their way to one of the giant overturned trunks and knelt in the hollow behind its gnarled wall of roots, safe from the wind. Jovie unpacked her bag, placing her drone and the giant jar on the sand.

Sylvan pulled a folded-up package from his pack. He passed Jovie a round brass object with a little tab sticking out of the center. "This is a disk sensor that Beryl will carry."

"Why do you call it Beryl?" Mason asked.

"Beryl Markham was a female explorer in the early 1900s," Jovie said.

"Oh, cool. Like Amelia Earhart?"

"Yes, but there was more than one female explorer. And it seemed like better karma to name her after someone who didn't end up lost at sea." Jovie glanced out toward the horizon. Beneath the clouds, an underside of salmon pink had already appeared. Time was getting short. She clipped Beryl's wings into place, turned on the remote, and closed the drone's little claw around the disk sensor. "Okay, she's ready."

Sylvan hauled a fat spool of black electrical wire, nearly a foot in diameter, out of his backpack, and dropped it on the sand with a thud. "That's a thousand feet of two-oh gauge. We couldn't risk going with thinner wire because of the signal degradation over distance." He began uncoiling the wire and handed one end to Jovie. "Attach that end to the sensor, and I'll attach the other end to the top of the jar."

"Nice work, Dr. Tesla," Jovie said.

Sylvan's face broke into a big grin that he tried unsuccessfully to rein in. "Thanks."

Jovie twisted the copper end of the wire around the screw sticking out of the middle of the sensor. Sylvan twisted the other end around the metal rod sticking out of the jar. He handed the spool of wire to Mason. "Here. Don't let it get tangled."

"Yes, sir," Mason said. He winked at Jovie.

"Ready," said Sylvan.

Jovie turned on the propellers and Beryl began to rise. Mason guided the wire through his hands, and Sylvan lay down on his stomach and peered into the jar.

The moment Beryl cleared the stump, the wind shoved it sharply.

"Whoa!" The wire yanked free of Mason's hands, and he scrambled to grab it as it unspooled wildly.

"Sorry!" said Jovie, flicking the controllers and correcting for the wind. She steadied Beryl and sent the drone out over the waves.

"You dropped this," Sylvan said as Mason sat back down. He was holding Mason's silver bracelet—

"Hey." Mason snatched it from Sylvan's fingers. "Don't touch that."

"I was just picking it up for you, jeez," Sylvan muttered.

"Right, thanks," Mason said, sliding it back around his wrist. He pulled his sweatshirt sleeve over it, then found Jovie looking at him. "It was my mom's," he said, and looked away.

Jovie realized Mason hadn't ever talked about his mom. She had the urge to ask him about her, but given his reaction to the bracelet, maybe it would be better to at least wait until they were alone.

"Any readings yet?" she asked Sylvan.

Sylvan pulled a ruler from his pack and lay down on his belly. He held the ruler against the side of the jar, moving close enough that his ski goggles bumped the glass. "Nothing yet."

Beryl's hum grew faint over the wind, the blinking red light now far out over the water.

The wire spun between Mason's fingers. "Not much more," he said.

Jovie paused the drone. "Anything?"

"Nope," said Sylvan, gazing at the jar.

"Well, it's not quite sunset." Jovie held Beryl in a hover and got out the spyglass. She looked up and down the beach. No sign yet of any drifters.

They sat there, wind howling around them, as the light slowly dimmed. Mason opened his backpack and pulled out gummy worms and shrimp puffs, and they munched silently. The sun dropped into a gap between the clouds and the sea, and golden sunbeams sprayed across the sky, lighting the wave caps and the bluff and making the mist sparkle.

"How about now?" Jovie asked.

"Still nada," said Sylvan.

Jovie huddled in her fleece. Even with the windbreak, the cold was starting to seep into her bones. Her butt felt numb, her legs tingling from sitting. "Beryl is down to half battery life," she said, deflated. She ate another handful of shrimp chips.

The sun slipped below the horizon. Color bled from the water and beach, now a world of steely grays and iron blacks. Pink bands cooled to purple overhead. The breeze grew icy teeth.

"We should probably get back to the trees," Mason said. Jovie saw a similar look of disappointment on his face. "We can still do the test from there."

"Wait." Sylvan peered at the jar. "I think it moved—ooh! There!"

The gold leaves twitched and then rose from their resting position until they were pointing straight out, vibrating like hummingbird wings, before falling again.

Sylvan slid his tablet from his bag, aimed it at the jar, and started filming. "It's 5:03 p.m. on January 18, 2018," he narrated, "and we are detecting evidence of cosmic rays on Satellite Beach in Far Haven, Washington, using a Bennet's electroscope that—"

A shrill beeping erupted from Beryl's remote.

"What's that?" Mason asked.

"The proximity sensor," said Jovie. She peered out over the water. Had it been a seagull or something? She saw Beryl's little blinking light, but nothing around it.

"Whoa!" said Sylvan, moving the ruler around. "Nearly a half inch of displacement!"

"Is that a lot?"

"The directions said we'd be lucky if it moved a millimeter!"

Beryl's alert kept beeping.

"I don't see anything out there," said Jovie.

"Try the spyglass," said Mason, holding a hand over his eyes.

Jovie fished it from her pocket and aimed it at Beryl. All was a gray blur—

Suddenly, a brilliant light shot across her vision. "Something's out there!" Jovie checked with the naked eye but saw no source of light. She looked through the spyglass again—

The flash arced through the sky, a buzzing form, pulsing with energy. It sped right past Beryl and continued out to sea.

"Big readings again!" Sylvan said.

"It's the lights," Jovie said quietly. Another one appeared, soaring out over the water. This time, Jovie was able to keep it in her view. It looked just like what Micah had drawn, some sort of flying creature shaped like a butterfly, glowing and vibrating rhythmically in all the colors of the rainbow, almost like it was made of energy.

She passed Mason the spyglass and he tracked them. "Wow," he said, handing it back.

Jovie looked again and could see details within the

buzzing light: lines like wings, like bones, and pulsing moments like lungs or a heart, or maybe circuitry, but also none of those things exactly, either. "They're beautiful," she said. At the same time, she felt a strange chill watching them, and a slight lump in her throat. "Do you know what they are?"

"No one's really sure," Mason said. "Some drifters call them essences."

There was something in his tone, and Jovie felt the same. "They're . . . sad."

He nodded. "Yeah."

"Whoa!" Sylvan shouted.

Another essence arced over the dune and out to sea, right past Beryl, its wings humming. The electroscope's gold leaves danced.

"Can I see?" Sylvan asked. Jovie passed the spyglass to him. "I can't believe this," he said dreamily. "Where are they going?"

"Same place the drifters go," said Mason. "Across the gradient."

The three essences darted in and out of the clouds offshore. Jovie had expected them to fly off toward the horizon, as Micah had drawn, but instead they arced back and began to fly in a slow, bobbing circle together, almost like seagulls over a school of fish.

"I think it's time to go," said Mason.

Jovie tore her gaze away from the essences and saw

that Mason was looking down the beach. A pair of headlights had appeared in the distance. Followed by another. And another.

"They're here." Jovie jumped to her feet, at the same time guiding Beryl back toward shore.

"Wait, hold on!" Sylvan scrambled to disconnect the wire from the top of the jar and pick it up.

They sprinted across the sand, Jovie with an eye on Beryl, Mason wrapping the wire around his arm as he ran, and Sylvan stumbling to keep his balance with the big jar in his arms. Jovie looked back over her shoulder; there were five trucks in a loose line churning up the beach now, their headlights making cones of swirling mist and refracted sand. She could hear their engines growling over the wind.

They reached the old road and ducked into the deep shadows of the trees. Sylvan skidded to his knees, panting. Mason crouched and kept spooling the wire. Jovie guided Beryl closer, glancing at the trucks. Could they see the drone's little red light? A moment later, Beryl crossed low over the sand and landed between them. Meanwhile, the trucks were pulling to a stop not far from where the three had just been.

"Did they see us?" Sylvan asked.

Doors were popping open and people wearing black jumpsuits with the *B* logo were jumping out; Jovie thought it looked like they had pairs of those large goggles on their heads. They busied around the trucks, but none seemed to be coming in this direction.

"I don't think so," said Jovie. She tucked Beryl into her bag and scanned the beach with the spyglass. Still no sign of any drifters. Out over the water, another glowing essence had joined the others in their trancelike circle just beneath the clouds.

The workers hauled equipment from the trucks, silhouetted by the headlights. Some began setting up tall metal towers with lights, arranging them in a U shape facing the water, while others were erecting a small tent with clear plastic walls, and with cots and monitors inside. A third team assembled a large metal platform in the center of the semicircle created by those light towers. There was a shout, and spotlights ignited on the tower tops.

Up on the platform, workers arranged computer equipment, running thick power cables to grumbling generators over by the trucks, while beneath it, others positioned a large device that was covered in a black cloth. It seemed to be shaped like a telescope.

There were more Barsuda workers by the water's edge, spiking posts into the sand.

A deep, heavy thumping sound reached Jovie's ears. A helicopter swooped overhead, a spotlight spearing from its nose, and made a wide circle out over the water. It lowered toward the waves and dropped a blinking buoy, then flew on, dropping others. A bright green laser ignited, connecting these posts and buoys, and drawing a trapezoid over the water.

"Yeah, so . . . ," Jovie said, "pretty sure this is not the kind of setup you use for"—she made air quotes with her fingers—"'cleanup.'"

"Definitely not," said Sylvan.

It was nearly dark, the sky and water melding their colors. A steady drizzle had started to fall. The essences continued to fly in their slow spiral, directly above the center of that laser shape.

Everything seemed to be in place now, and everyone from Barsuda took positions, as if they were waiting for something. Jovie squinted and thought she could make out Dr. Wells standing on the platform, facing the water. Whatever that large device beneath them was, it was still covered in its cloth.

Jovie scanned the beach with the spyglass again. Still no sign of any drifters. But— "We need to get to a better position," she said. "I can't see past Barsuda. If Micah comes from that direction, we won't know until it's too late."

"How about up the bluff?" said Sylvan. "We could get to a high spot with a good view."

"That's even farther away," said Jovie.

"How about that way?" Mason pointed to the dune. A narrow track led up the side, through the grass. "That should give us a closer look."

“Closer?” Sylvan exclaimed.

Jovie bit her lip. “Sylvan, stay here, and keep recording the electroscope.”

“What?” Sylvan’s eyes bugged. “No, Jovie, we should just leave. We have enough data already!”

Jovie looked from his terrified face to the beach. “But we don’t have Micah.”

“You don’t even know if she’s coming!” Sylvan was on the verge of tears.

Jovie put a hand on his shoulder. “I hope she doesn’t. But if she does, I can’t miss her. Stay here, out of sight. We’ll be safe. I promise.”

Sylvan wouldn’t meet her eyes. “You don’t know that, either.”

Jovie led the way up the dune, through the wet sand and blade grass, wind whipping at them. When they’d neared the top of the dune, she looked back. Sylvan was sitting cross-legged in the shadows of the trees, watching the electroscope. She saw him wipe his nose, and that guilty feeling returned. *We shouldn’t have brought him.*

They moved in a crouch, staying on the back side of the dune until they were nearly behind Barsuda’s setup, then they crawled up and peered over the edge.

The whole team still seemed to be waiting around, many of them gazing out at the water, while others were still tweaking equipment.

“What if we see her, but we can’t get to her before

Barsuda does?" Jovie asked, checking with the spyglass again. "You said they just scan the drifters, right?"

"As far as we know," said Mason. "But I don't know for sure if they'll stop her. They may let her go to see what happens. Hopefully we can get to her first."

There was a commotion, and from behind the trucks, a new group of workers emerged, wearing red suits and full helmets like astronauts might wear, with breathing tanks on their backs. They marched in a military line down to the water and spread out at wide intervals along the beach, almost like they were guarding the water's edge.

Dr. Wells surveyed her team, arms crossed.

"What are they waiting for?" Jovie wondered. She checked up and down the beach again with the spyglass.

Just then a glimmer out in the water caught her eye. A white light had appeared beneath the surface, in the center of those laser lines. Through the spyglass, she saw that it was directly beneath the orbiting essences. The light flickered and grew, a golden-white color, swirling like a whirlpool.

Jovie looked around Barsuda's setup. "Did you see them do anything?"

"No," said Mason.

The agents were busy now, aiming equipment at the water. Dr. Wells moved urgently between the workstations on the platform, pointing to screens and giving orders.

The light grew quickly beneath the waves, a spiraling vortex, feathering and writhing on its outer edge, getting brighter and brighter.

"That's it, isn't it?" Jovie said. "The gradient." Mason nodded.

Jovie got out her phone and tried making a video, then taking photos, but as she'd suspected, with the darkness and the mist, things were either too dark or blurry.

She tucked it away and found herself staring into the golden-white light. It was mesmerizing, and Jovie felt a strange dizzying sensation, almost as if it was pulling her. That cold wind rushed through her, and it seemed like if she stood, she might fall right into that light, even though there was an entire beach between her and the water.

Mason put a steadying hand on hers.

"Do you feel that?" she asked him. When he nodded, she asked, "Are you sure it's safe for you here? This close?"

"I'm okay," he said, but Jovie thought his eyes looked fearful as he gazed at the gradient.

Its light grew brighter and overwhelmed the surface of the water, washing out the waves. Jovie looked through the spyglass and saw that the essences were circling closer, dipping and darting as if they were caught in its sway. Now one broke off and dove directly into the center, disappearing in a brilliant flash.

On the platform, Barsuda's workstations beeped urgently, and Dr. Wells and the workers were talking excitedly and pointing at their screens. Jovie wished she could make out their words, but she couldn't over the sound of the wind and the surf and the helicopter.

"I don't think they're the ones doing this," Jovie said. "It looks like . . . they were waiting for it?"

"I think you're right," said Mason.

"But if that's the case, what *is* causing it?"

The swirling gradient light had begun to ripple over the beach and onto the shore, making those red-suited Barsuda workers into little more than shimmering silhouettes. Jovie could no longer look directly at it without squinting so hard that her eyes were almost completely shut.

She checked the beach again with the spyglass; still no sign of any drifters. *Micah*, she thought, *where are you—*

Just then, shouting erupted and radios squawked. Dr. Wells waved her arms and pointed, and she and the rest of the team lowered their goggles over their eyes. The helicopter swung around and aimed its spotlight between the shore and the center of the vortex.

Jovie looked through the spyglass and saw a faint shape wading out into the waves, directly toward the gradient. *Micah!* she thought. How had she gotten past her—but it wasn't Micah. This figure was too tall, their proportions all wrong.

Mason squeezed her hand, and when she lowered the spyglass, she saw that his eyes were wide with fear. "It's my dad."

21

THE TEST

JANUARY 18, 2018
96 HOURS TO BREACH

Jovie watched the faint, flickering form of Mason's father through the spyglass as he pushed out into the waist-deep waves. The nearest two red-suited Barsuda workers had started into the water after him, but Paul didn't seem to notice. His movements had a slow, trancelike quality, and the workers were closing fast; Jovie suspected their helmets functioned the same as the goggles.

"I shouldn't have left him!" Mason said. He started to get to his feet.

"Wait!" Jovie hissed, grabbing his arm. "They'll catch you! They're all wearing those goggles. You won't even get to the water before they see you."

Mason was coiled tight like he might go anyway. "If I

fade far enough, I could make it."

"But then what? If you drift that far, what if you get pulled across?" Jovie's heart hurt for him; she couldn't imagine how it felt to watch someone you love try to leave you like that. *Or maybe I do*, she thought, remembering the afternoon her dad had walked out, but this was far worse. Because Mason's dad was trying to leave forever.

And he's not choosing it, Jovie reminded herself. *He's caught in it.*

Mason pulled against her. "I have to try."

Maybe she should let him go—

But then the red-suited workers had reached Paul. They grabbed him by both arms and started dragging him back toward shore. Jovie could see him struggling to keep going toward the light.

The spotlight swept off Paul and up the beach, and now other agents were hurrying into the surf there, too.

Through the spyglass, Jovie spotted a second shimmering silhouette—but this wasn't Micah, either; it was the woman Carina had pulled from the waves.

"She never remembered her name," Mason said, seeing her, too.

The workers had her in a moment and began pulling her back toward the beach.

"It will be okay, right?" said Jovie, watching them wrestle Paul to shore. "After they scan him, they'll let him go."

Mason nodded. The gradient was reflecting in his eyes. "I think so."

The workers carrying Paul reached the shore and waited for the ones who had the woman. Once they arrived, they stood the two drifters side by side, and one of the red-suited workers aimed a device that looked like a vintage camera at the two. The device had a sleek silver housing and a wide lens, and Jovie saw a light illuminate on the top. The worker moved it slowly up and down in front of the woman, then nodded to the workers holding her; they turned and guided her away up the beach, in the direction of the bluff. The worker then aimed the device at Paul and did the same thing, but this time, the light on top of the device began to flash. The workers all seemed to exchange words, and they guided Paul in the other direction, toward the line of Barsuda trucks. The worker with the device waved, and one of the trucks growled to life.

"What's going on?" said Jovie as the truck spun and backed down to the water's edge. "Are they taking him somewhere?"

Mason's expression had darkened. "I don't know—I haven't seen this before."

"What if they've taken others?" said Jovie, feeling the elevator falling in her belly. "They might have taken Micah, too!"

Mason got to his feet. "We need to hear what they're

saying. Find out where they're taking him."

Jovie saw that most of the workers had raised their goggles and gotten back to their tasks and equipment. She stood and took Mason's hand.

"Ready?" he said.

"Yeah." She looked back down to the trail. Sylvan had moved behind a tree and was watching them. She tried to smile reassuringly and gave him a thumbs-up. He waved his hand as if to say *come back*.

Then Jovie felt that rush of cold, of emptiness, and her heart tripped over itself. It was the same sensation she'd had in the alley behind Micah's house, like the world was distant, but this time she felt something else, too—a tugging sensation in her chest—and her eyes moved toward the swirling gradient. It danced more brightly, seemed more vibrant and alive now that she was like this. It almost felt like it was calling to her, and this awareness filled her with terror.

They climbed down the dune and over the driftwood, then circled around behind the light poles, keeping to the shadows, and neared the truck that had backed down to the water. Two of the red-suited workers were lifting Paul into the back.

The workers had just gotten him in when one of them convulsed and fell face first in the sand. The other waved frantically to his red-suited teammates down the beach, who rushed over. He turned back to the truck, closed the doors, and slapped the side. The truck peeled out in the sand. Jovie and Mason watched helplessly as it roared down the beach in the direction they'd come.

"We'll find out where they're going," Jovie said, squeezing his hand. Mason looked ready to run after the truck anyway, but he nodded, and instead turned toward the red-suited workers who were carrying their injured colleague up to the clear-walled medical tent.

Jovie and Mason crept closer to the tent until they were behind the workers inside. The injured worker lay on an exam table, helmet removed. Her head thrashed back and forth, and she wailed in pain, her arms and legs twitching. One worker seemed to be checking her suit, and now another injected her in the shoulder with a metal syringe. The woman relaxed. The first worker ran a glowing wand-like device over her, while the other traded the syringe for an IV, which he attached to her arm. They were talking busily, but Jovie couldn't hear what they were saying through the plastic wall.

Just then, the woman's eyes blinked open, and Jovie saw that they were clouded over worse than her mom's had been: solid white, like her eyes had been switched with giant pearls. Once the fluid line was connected to her arm, the workers lifted the cot and carried her out toward one of the trucks. Jovie and Mason backed into the shadows, making sure to stay out of their view.

Out in the water, the gradient had only grown, the

waves churning wildly, the light blinding. The wind gusted from one direction, then the next, flinging water and sand, and the clouds directly above the gradient had started to swirl, as if they were caught in its pull as well.

Jovie blinked as a light-headed sensation overcame her. She could see the essences without her spyglass now. There were five of them dancing above the light, brilliant and buzzing and, Jovie thought, singing in high-pitched crystalline voices, though it was something she seemed to feel more than hear. As she watched, one dove into the vortex, and the others glowed brighter, their voices pitching higher—

Mason gripped her hand more tightly, and she realized she had been leaning toward the water. She tore her eyes from the light, and they circled around behind the platform.

The workers beneath it had pulled back the black cloth covering the device. It looked like a large, squat telescope encircled in thick bands of wires. They threw switches, and the device began to blink and emit a deep hum.

Jovie and Mason moved as close as they dared, and strained to hear Dr. Wells and her team.

"Antiproton readings have crested the threshold," one of the agents reported. "We're starting to pick up temporal fluctuations."

"How close are we?" Dr. Wells asked.

An agent peering at a different screen responded, "Approaching seventy-five percent of 2010 levels."

"If the same pattern holds, we're ninety-six hours from full breach," said Dr. Wells. "This will be a good test. Are we ready?"

"Positron field is cycling up, sir."

"Drop the probe," Dr. Wells ordered.

The helicopter fought its way over the center of the gradient and released a blinking object that splashed into the water.

"Readings?" Dr. Wells asked.

"Nothing yet on the video feed, but we are detecting the space-time discrepancy on the other side of the field."

"Same ratio?" Dr. Wells asked.

"Affirmative, sir. One thousand to one."

"I think something's clarifying on the video—" The screen they were watching went dark. "Check that . . . we lost the probe."

Dr. Wells nodded. "Right on schedule. Okay, stand by to initiate on my mark . . . now."

A brilliant beam of golden light burst from the device beneath the platform. The light crackled with sparks and speared directly into the center of the gradient. Jovie felt a hot electric wind. One of the light towers down by the water exploded. There was a *pop-pop* from one of the trucks—its headlights blowing out.

The gradient convulsed, writhing and folding around the beam. The essences scattered, flying off into the clouds.

"What are they doing?" Jovie whispered to Mason.

"I don't know. I haven't seen anything like this during the other storms." He pointed to the device. "Whatever that thing is, it's new."

She couldn't be sure, but it seemed as if the gradient's light had diminished as the beam's light brightened, almost as if the device was drawing energy out of it.

"Status?" Dr. Wells called over the sizzling hum.

"Modeling is true," one of the agents reported. "Almost there—"

Suddenly there was a blinding flash, and a huge concussion knocked everyone backward. Jovie and Mason were hurled to the sand.

For a moment, all sound was extinguished, except for a ringing in Jovie's ears. She saw agents running chaotically but silently. Lights arced overhead, and the helicopter careened past in a spin. It crashed down onto the sand up the beach, its landing skids snapping as it slid to a halt.

Jovie sat up on her elbows, blinking spots from her eyes as sound returned. The telescope device and its golden beam had gone dark, and the gradient was growing with renewed, almost furious energy.

"Reroute power!" Dr. Wells shouted, her team wearing headlamps and trying to restart their workstations.

The generators coughed and groaned, and a moment later, the tower lights flicked back on. The beam burst from the telescope device, even brighter than before, and the gradient seemed to immediately shrink in response.

"It's holding steady now, sir."

But Dr. Wells was shaking her head. "But the damage could be much worse next time. This is going to be useless if we can't solve those power surges."

Jovie found herself staring at the gradient as it shrank and folded in on itself, wilting in the power of that beam, and she felt a wave of sadness, a surprising ache, almost like she wished it would stay. . . .

"Hey." Mason tugged Jovie's arm, and they retreated to the dune. As they slid down the back side, a truck churned through the sand toward the helicopter.

Mason let go of her hand, and she felt her connection to her senses slowly returning. She hugged herself, overcome by a wave of loneliness.

"Don't worry," Mason said, rubbing her arm. "You'll feel better soon."

"I don't like how it feels," Jovie said, shivering. "Is this what it's like for you?"

"Not all the time," said Mason.

Jovie felt a lump in her throat and wiped her eyes. "I'm sorry, I just . . ." She shook her head and took a deep breath. *Have to keep it together!* She looked back out at Barsuda and their device, the brilliant beam and the writhing gradient. "What do you think they're doing?" she wondered. "It almost looks like they're sucking power out of it." Then Jovie remembered her online research.

"Barsuda's other location was called an 'experimental energy site.'"

"Maybe that's their goal," said Mason. "To use it as an energy source."

"So they know all the suffering and loss this thing is causing," said Jovie darkly, "and they're still just interested in using it for power?"

She scanned the beach with the spyglass and saw no sign of Micah or any other drifters. *Because they already have her*, Jovie thought. What else could explain where Micah had been these months?

All at once, the telescope device powered down, and the light beam went dark. The gradient was nearly gone, as if they'd sucked all the energy right out of it. Jovie heard Dr. Wells barking orders, and all around, the Barsuda team began to disassemble their gear.

"We have to find out where they took Paul," said Jovie. At the same time, she checked the woods below—Sylvan wasn't where they'd left him. "Oh no."

Jovie scrambled back down the dune to the trees. Her bike was still there, as was the electroscope, but Sylvan was gone.

"Sylvan?" Jovie called, trying to catch her breath.

"He can't have gotten far," Mason said.

Jovie peered into the pitch-black forest. "Sylvan!"

Engines roared behind them. The trucks were beginning to leave. "Up there," Mason said, pointing at the steep side of the bluff that rose toward the bunkers. "We can use Beryl to see where they're going."

Jovie looked from the trucks to the forest. She'd told Sylvan to stay where he was! But he would be all right for a few more minutes, wherever he was. Jovie nodded to Mason. "Okay, let's go—" Just then, her phone buzzed.

It was a text message from a local number she didn't have saved in her phone, but the second she started reading, she knew who it was from:

> Jovie, is Sylvan with you? He was supposed to go home with a friend but he's not there, and they said they haven't seen Sylvan since school ended. Please let me know ASAP.

Beverly. Oh no. Jovie tried to reply, but discovered that once again, the screen didn't sense her touch. "How long before I can type again?"

"I'm not sure," said Mason. "That was a longer drift than last time."

Jovie felt a squeezing sensation, like everything was too much. She cursed to herself and charged up the side of the bluff, feet slipping in the sand.

They climbed until they reached a high ridge; from there, they could see most of the roads, though downtown was obscured by trees. The drop behind them was nearly a cliff, and the salty breeze lashed them with sheets of rain. The ocean was completely black now, except for the gleam of the lighthouse.

Jovie removed Beryl from her backpack and had her flying in a moment. "There they are," she said as the drone cleared the trees. The convoy was moving toward town, but disappearing behind a hillside. She pushed Beryl higher. "I only have a few more minutes of battery." She rotated the camera, watching for the convoy to reappear.

There was a grinding metallic sound from behind them. Jovie turned to see the helicopter's rotors spinning back to life. The truck backed away from it, and the copter lifted off the sand and limped off to the north, around the bluff, staying low. A moment later, it appeared on Beryl's camera, crossing over town . . . and toward a familiar landmark.

"If you did want to use the energy from a cosmic storm," Jovie said, "what better place to make your base than a power station?" She zoomed in on the Baxter plant. There were lights on around the bases of the cooling towers, and the copter was landing beside them. Now she spotted the line of trucks snaking up the hill in that direction.

"A nice abandoned one that everyone thinks is contaminated," said Mason. "We need to get there."

Jovie shuddered at the thought as she brought Beryl back in. "We can't go now. We need to find Sylvan first, and . . ." She couldn't imagine feeling the cold sensation of the drift again. It had left her so hollow. She suddenly had an intense urge to be safe at home on her couch.

Mason nodded. “It’s okay. I should get back to the bunker soon to check on everyone else. I also need to warn them about the breach. Ninety-six hours, Dr. Wells said.”

“Four days,” said Jovie. “That fits the pattern. Do you think that will be the big storm?”

“With a name like ‘full breach’? I think so.”

Her phone buzzed. Beverly again. Jovie felt a fresh surge of guilt. Sylvan was too young to be out here. She’d known it, and she’d brought him anyway. She finished packing Beryl and hoisted her pack over her shoulder. “Come on.”

They hurried back down the trail. Jovie stuffed the electroscope into her pack and grabbed her bike, and they headed into the woods. Jovie slipped on her headlamp.

“Sylvan!” she called.

The sounds of the beach receded, and soon there was only the dripping of water.

“He could be all the way back to school by now,” said Mason.

“Hopefully,” said Jovie. After another minute of silence and darkness, Jovie paused at a faint sound on the wind; was that crying? “Sylvan!”

She ran ahead, and suddenly, there he was in her headlamp beam, sitting on a log at the intersection where they'd met up with Mason, head down, his arms across his knees.

"Sylvan, hey!" she said, but he didn't react. He just whimpered and sobbed like the loneliest creature.

He doesn't hear me, she thought, *because I'm still drifting.* She ran to him and shook his arm.

"Ah!" He scrambled off the log, then squinted and pushed up his fogged glasses. "Jovie?" he croaked.

"It's me. It's okay."

He looked away and wiped at his eyes. "I was at the beach, and you . . . I couldn't remember why I was there . . . and then there were all those Barsuda people, and that light."

"I'm sorry," said Jovie, rubbing his shoulder. "We were just trying to get a closer look."

Sylvan nodded. "I remember that now." He touched his forehead. "My head hurts, and my knees. Do you think it's from the cosmic rays?"

"Maybe," Jovie said worriedly. "How are your eyes?"

"I think they're fine. I felt so lost," he said quietly, and started to cry again. "I was so scared."

"It's okay. Shhh." She hugged him, her chin resting on his damp hat. "Your mom texted me. She knows you're not at your friend's."

"Oh no."

"Here." Jovie handed Sylvan her phone. He looked at her quizzically. "I can't type yet. You need to tell her that we're okay and we'll meet her at the school, except make it sound like *I'm* the one telling her."

"No! If she knows we're together, she's never going to let me hang out with you again."

Jovie pursed her lips. "She's probably already figured it out."

Sylvan's head fell. "I'll be off the team."

"Start by telling her that I'm really sorry."

Sylvan nodded and Jovie gave him her passcode. He sniffled as he typed. "She's going to kill me." He finished and handed the phone back. It buzzed almost immediately.

I'm on my way.

Sylvan stood and sighed. "Yup, I'm definitely dead."

Jovie turned to Mason. "We should go."

"Me too," said Mason. "When should we meet to go to the plant?"

"How about tomorrow night? My mom usually leaves for work around six," said Jovie. "We could meet up at Salt & Sand, in case they're watching my house."

"Sounds good. Be careful getting home."

"You too."

Mason shoved his hands in his hoodie pocket and started up the trail.

"We'll find your dad," she called after him.

"Yeah." In a moment, he was lost to the dark.

"Let's go." Jovie pushed her bike up the trail, Sylvan

walking beside her. The forest plinked, and a frog gave a lonely croak. Jovie felt like her breaths were getting fuller, the scent of the forest stronger, like she was reconnecting with the world, and the feeling gave her a measure of relief. She tried her phone and found that she could operate it now—except that it immediately proceeded to die from the cold.

"What are you two doing tomorrow night?" Sylvan asked in nearly a whisper as they walked.

"We're going to the Baxter plant. It's Barsuda's base or something. We're pretty sure that's where they took Mason's dad, and where Micah might be, too."

"Is there some way that I can still help?"

"I don't know," Jovie said. "The biggest thing right now is to show your mom you're okay and to not get grounded forever."

Sylvan nodded, but Jovie's words made his shoulders slump farther. "Just be careful, okay? I remember now, watching you and Mason up on the dune, how you faded away, and I felt this big sadness, like I was losing you. . . . I don't want that to happen again."

"It won't," Jovie said, but she felt like her whole body was being squeezed tight as she said it. They'd have to drift to get into Baxter. She'd have to feel that empty chill again. . . .

They continued up the trail in silence. As they neared school, they heard sirens in the distance, seemingly from all directions.

Beverly's car was already sitting there, headlights on and engine running, the only one in the lot. As they walked toward it, the door opened, and Beverly got out and stood with her arms crossed.

Jovie felt like her heart was pressing up into her throat. She stopped ten feet from the car. Sylvan went a little farther before turning to look back at her.

"Sylvan, get in," Beverly said tersely.

"Bye," Sylvan said to Jovie under his breath. He walked to the car with his head down and got into the back seat.

Jovie blinked at tears. "I'm sorry," she said.

The sirens grew louder. Beverly glanced toward the road. "I called Dr. Aaron; they have multiple cases like your mom's coming into the ER."

"There was another storm. They're caused by—"

"I don't want to know, Jovie. Today I was formally reprimanded for looking into the code seven cases. For the searches you guys did without my knowledge. Whatever is happening here is *dangerous*, and you should be staying away from it rather than getting closer."

The tears slipped down Jovie's cheeks, despite how hard she tried to hold them back. "Sylvan has some mild symptoms," she admitted.

"Oh my god." Beverly glanced back at the car.

"His eyes are fine!" Jovie nearly sobbed. "Just headache and achy joints."

"And what about you?"

"I'm okay," Jovie said, but was she? If Beverly knew

what she'd done, fading from the world . . .

"Do you want a ride home?"

"No." Jovie couldn't imagine sitting in their car now. "I'll be fine on my bike."

"I don't like that I have to say this to you," Beverly began, "but please don't contact Sylvan again. At least, not until all this is over. If you want to get a message to him, you can text me."

Jovie nodded. "There's going to be another storm in four nights. It's going to be bad."

"I'm not going to ask how you know that. But if that's the case, stay indoors. Please?"

Beverly slid into the car and drove off. Jovie saw Sylvan looking at her out the window.

She straddled her bike and all at once broke into sobs, feeling even more alone than she had at the very start of her search.

22

THE PHOTOGRAPH

JANUARY 19, 2018
83 HOURS TO BREACH

The sirens died down around midnight. Sometime after that, Jovie finally fell into a troubled sleep, her dreams haunted by swirling light, the painful screams of the Barsuda woman, and the ever-present chill of that wind through her.

The Barsuda van was once again parked on her street the next morning. Once again, when Jovie coasted past on her way to school, the driver didn't even look up, like this was any other day. Yet now Jovie wondered, had that worker been there last night, on the beach, as the gradient swirled?

The school day crawled by, Jovie's thoughts racing. She felt certain now that Barsuda wasn't causing the gradient—and of course, if that were the case, the questions of what the gradient really was and why it appeared in the ocean following such a mathematical pattern remained—but they did seem to be trying to harness its energy with that giant telescope device. The fact that they were secretly using Baxter seemed to support this. And that might explain their secrecy: the search for clean energy was a major focus worldwide—they would want to keep something like this hidden not just from other companies, but maybe even other nations. Jovie had wondered if the town and the police knew what Barsuda was up to; now she wondered if the government did, too. Was this some sort of top secret operation?

Of course, the problem with that was, the gradient's energy wasn't clean. People were suffering because of it. Maybe Barsuda's secrecy was also so they wouldn't get in trouble for the health effects. The code seven illnesses and the drift had been happening since before Barsuda arrived in town, but they could still be blamed for both if people found out, or at least blamed for not doing anything about them. And Jovie thought maybe that was the worst part: Barsuda knew what was happening to people, but all they cared about was their precious energy source, like prospectors hiding a valuable lode of gold. By keeping it a secret, by spinning their lies, they kept people in town from knowing the dangers, kept people like Dr. Aaron and Beverly from knowing how to help people . . . as if Barsuda had decided that the lives lost to the gradient were worth it.

Jovie thought of how sick her mom had been: Barsuda didn't care. All those vomiting kids: still not enough to tell the truth. She thought of Micah, of Mason's dad, of all those drifters in the bunker and however many countless others who had not only been lost over the years but weren't even *remembered* by their friends and loved ones, as if they'd never been . . . none of that mattered to Barsuda, and it made Jovie boil with rage. She wanted them to be stopped, to be arrested, Dr. Wells in handcuffs, her guilty face all over the news.

As Jovie ate lunch on the library couch, she got out Micah's journal and flipped to the last page. Looking at that final drawing was different now. She knew how the gradient could make you feel, the way it made you cold, but also called to you. The way those essences had seemed to sing. . . .

Jovie ran her finger over the drawing, over the little silhouette at the bottom of the page, standing in the white as if it were walking into the gradient. She thought of Paul, wading out into the water, trying to keep going, and a string of sadness tugged inside her—

Except, wait.

She peered more closely at the drawing and noticed now that Micah had actually made little marks on the figure's face: tiny lines like a mouth, a nose, eyebrows . . . as if this person was facing *away* from the gradient, toward Micah.

Barsuda.

Jovie could picture it: Micah sitting on the dune, watching the gradient unfurl beneath the waves, entranced by it, watching the dance of essences overhead. She probably hadn't even noticed Barsuda setting up their gear, lost from the world as she was, until they spotted her. This was the moment. That little figure walking up the beach, getting closer, until they loomed over Micah in their red suit and helmet. . . .

And now they had her, Jovie felt sure of it. It explained why Micah's journal had been left behind, why she hadn't ever made it to the drifter camp, or even to the beach last night . . . and though this made Jovie's blood boil more, she also felt a little surge of hope. Maybe she really was close. Maybe tonight would really be the night she would finally find Micah—

If she wants it to be you *that finds her.*

Jovie's hope cooled. When she and Micah were reunited, she didn't want things to be like they were last spring. She needed to fully understand what had gone wrong in their friendship.

She flipped back through Micah's journal, pushing through the guilt of looking at something private. She arrived at the April entry she'd found the other day and kept going backward. The pages alternated between sketches, sometimes with excerpts of lyrics, and written entries, which might be a few lines or multiple pages.

Jovie had already been over the few months before their fight, but this time she went further back. She'd reached August, the summer before seventh grade, when an entry caught her eye. Micah had written a single sentence in the center of the page, surrounded by a line design that filled every inch:

I AM ROSALIND!

Jovie turned to the next page, and when she read the entry there, she understood:

I'm HERE!

I feel like my whole life has been leading up to this moment, this week. Is that crazy? We had our first meet-up and icebreakers today; everybody has such impressive résumés. One girl did a program in New York. I could tell when I said where I was from that most people had no idea Far Haven even existed. But hey, they will soon, right? Tonight is the big audition for AYLI, and it is my DESTINY to be Rosalind. Wish me luck!

The first night of Shakespeare camp. Jovie did a search and found that "AYLI" stood for *As You Like It*, and that Rosalind was the lead, the smart, witty protagonist who had been played by all sorts of famous people. Of course Micah would get the part.

Jovie could remember Micah's excitement about going to camp, how she'd talked about it the evening they'd had their picnic atop the bunkers. Jovie even remembered feeling a little twinge of jealousy back then: not toward Micah, but toward those other kids at the camp. Micah belonged with them. With the actors, the stars. And for those two weeks, they would get Micah's favorite side of herself, and bond with her about their dreams in a way that Jovie had never quite been able to. Sure, Jovie and Micah had conversations now and then where Micah tried to relate her own stage aspirations to Jovie's interest in music, but Jovie knew it wasn't the same, not even close. Jovie had a little dream about being a musician, but she already felt like it was impossible, given how anxious that one band performance had made her. Besides, she had a fine voice, but not, like, an *amazing* one. Not the equal to Micah's talents.

And so when Micah had talked about the Shakespeare camp, it had made Jovie feel like there was a timer on their friendship, like at some point, Micah's gift would take her away to some exciting future, somewhere Jovie couldn't follow. Had that made Jovie hard to talk to about it? Had she not been supportive enough? Had she been a bad friend when it came to the very thing Micah dreamed of most?

But when Jovie turned to the next page, what she saw totally surprised her.

The entry was a drawing from two days later. Micah had filled the entire page with tiny rain droplets, each one precise and nearly identical. They were falling in tight, perfect lines, except in the very center of the page, where they bounced off a single, soaked word:

CELiA

Jovie searched again and discovered that Celia was Rosalind's cousin, a minor part by comparison.

The next entry wasn't until three days after that, and it was another sketch. It showed the silhouette of a girl's face in the foreground along the edge of the page, shaded like she was standing in a shadow. The girl was watching someone who was out in the spotlight, in the center of the stage, her arms thrown out as if she was in the middle of some great speech. There were faces below in the audience, looking up with adoration. Celia watching Rosalind, Jovie thought. Micah, the star of every show they'd ever done in Far Haven, now in the shadows.

There were no other entries from camp.

Jovie tried to recall when Micah had gotten back. She sort of remembered Micah saying camp had been fine, but nothing more than that. And then nothing really about acting that fall, and she didn't do the big school production the next spring. . . . She must have been way more disappointed than she'd let on. What had that been like for her? To Jovie, being this Celia character sounded easier, but that wasn't how Micah was wired. For her, the big part, center stage, wasn't just what she wanted—it was where she belonged, who she was.

Was that why Micah hadn't talked to Jovie about it? Because Jovie wouldn't have understood? Or had she tried, only Jovie hadn't listened?

Jovie ran her finger down that profile of Micah's face, the girl in the shadows, and she wondered, was that the moment she began to drift? Not to disappear, not yet, but was this the thing that had loosened her grip on the world, made her vulnerable to that pull?

They're already going before they're gone.

I'm sorry, Jovie thought. Those six months she'd wondered about had been nearly a year for Micah, and Jovie had never noticed! Wasn't that what best friends were supposed to do? Except Jovie never would have guessed that *this* was what had happened. It just wasn't one of the possibilities when she thought of Micah. But she still should have noticed that *something* was off. Maybe if she had, Micah would have opened up. And could that have been the difference?

When I find her, Jovie promised herself, *I'll do better.*

When school finally ended that afternoon, Jovie rode down to the music academy. There was only one parent in the waiting area. No one worked the front desk anymore. Jovie entered and slipped past the doors to the practice rooms: Mom was in one, teaching a young girl the flute, and Colin was in the next, teaching guitar. The rest of the rooms, as well as the dance studio, were open and dark. She ducked into the last room and waited.

Just after 4:20, Jovie saw Beverly's car pull up out front. Sylvan got out and came in as she pulled away. He signed himself in on the desk and was just sitting down when Jovie waved and got his attention. He jolted in shock, then looked worriedly out the window before rushing down the hall.

"What are you doing here?" he hissed as Jovie shut the door to the little room.

"I checked my mom's schedule and saw you'd be here," Jovie said. "I wanted to see how you were doing."

Sylvan just looked at her for a moment, like he was in a trance, and then he blinked, and a tear slipped down his cheek. His eyes fell to the floor, his face reddening as he wiped behind his glasses.

"Hey." Jovie put a hand on his shoulder. "What's up?"

"Oh, nothing," he said, his voice dripping with sarcasm. "You know, just got grounded last night and told I can't see you anymore. And then today, Charlotte called to say, actually she can't come up this weekend like she was supposed to because she has some party to go to where she can talk to a talent manager or something. Whatever. Guess your little brother's birthday is no big deal."

"Oh, right," said Jovie, remembering that Sylvan had mentioned his upcoming birthday the other night in the hospital waiting area. "What day is it?"

"Sunday."

"I'm sorry," she said. "That stinks. I'd help you celebrate if we weren't *banned* from seeing each other. What kind of cake would you want?"

"Red velvet's my favorite . . . but Mom says it's too complicated to make." He sat down on the piano bench and opened his backpack. "So, how's the case going? You know, if you can still tell me."

Jovie rolled her eyes. "Of course I can tell you, but nothing's changed since last night."

"Well, *I* made some progress, no thanks to my mom," said Sylvan. "We had library today. Look what I found in the local history section." Sylvan pulled out a beat-up little paperback and handed it to her.

"No way," Jovie said, running her fingers over the laminated cover of *The Blue Bathymetrist's Guide.*

"There's actually not that much in it," said Sylvan. "I've been reading it under my desk all day. It's mostly about preparing to 'ascend,' and there's guides for soaking and meditation, and recipes for weird teas. Also there's a bunch of crazy stuff about what Planet Elysia is like. It says the Elysians give you robes that feel like bubble baths, and their cigarettes are made of a special root that actually makes you healthier and gives you telekinetic powers."

"The aliens smoke?"

"Well, it was written in the sixties. There are coupons in the back, too, like for a third night free at the Vanescere with your receipt for buying the book."

"Does it say anything about what might really be causing the gradient? You know, other than smoking aliens in bubble baths?"

"Not really. There's no mention of cosmic rays, or wormholes, or anything like that."

Jovie flipped through the brittle, yellowed pages. The print was small and dense. She saw that Sylvan had folded down one corner. "What's this one you marked?"

"The book says that's some kind of chant you're supposed to say when the gradient opens. I just thought it was interesting."

Unlike the other pages of dense text, this one simply had a poem:

He came from the depths
And his power was true
With a path to paradise
To free me and you.
Two four three four six one two
The Melody Universal
The Bathymetrist in Blue

Sylvan turned to the piano and started hitting keys, making a sort of jazzy, spooky melody.

"Hey, stop!" Jovie hissed, glancing toward the hall. "Mom or Colin might hear."

"Sorry, I just wanted to see if I got the melody right."

"What melody?"

"*Two four three four six one two,*" Sylvan sang in the same notes he'd just tapped. "Those numbers made me think of the note intervals—we sing them sometimes in lessons to train my ear, you know, like the two of the key, the four of the key . . . Anyway, it seemed kinda jazzy, like something you'd hear back when the book was written, kinda like the theme in a James Bond movie or something. And the next line did say 'melody,' so . . ."

"Ah," said Jovie.

"I know it's stupid," Sylvan said, "but I heard it when I read it, and thought it was cool." His shoulders slumped. "One time Charlotte told me 'music isn't math.' I used to help her figure out her choir pieces, because it's always been easy for me to read music and pick stuff out, even though Charlotte is the one with like, the amazing voice. I think it annoyed her that I was so fast at it."

"But music kind of *is* math, right?" said Jovie, thinking of her own lessons.

"Sorta. But the way I see music . . . it's not like what Charlotte can do."

"Play it for me," Jovie said.

"What?"

"The melody you made for the poem. But *quietly.*"

Sylvan tapped out the series of notes, softly singing the first two lines of the poem along with them. "Like that."

"Well, I think it's cool," said Jovie, "and it *is* very James Bond." She tapped the book cover. "Is there anything else in here?"

"There is one more thing." Sylvan took the book and flipped to the back. "Look at this."

A business card had been taped to the inside of the back cover. It looked new, at least compared to the book, and it read:

THIS GENEROUS DONATION TO YOUR LIBRARY

COURTESY OF:

THE ASCENSION FILES: FREE THE TRUTH!

WANT TO KNOW WHAT REALLY HAPPENED?

WWW.ASCENSION-FILES.NET

"Check out that website," Sylvan said.

"Okay." Jovie typed the address into her phone.

The page that loaded had a retro-looking starry background with a triangular beam of yellow light shooting across it, and the title from the card. Below that was a link in an enormous font that read:

READ THE SCREENPLAY
(AND SUPPORT OUR CAUSE!)

"Is this a link to a movie script?"

"Yeah, but you have to pay to read it," said Sylvan. "Check out the About page, though."

Jovie clicked on it. The page loaded, with the title "About the Authors" and then a photograph of two men. Beneath it, a long paragraph in a tiny font stretched down off the screen, but Jovie's eye fixed on the photo, and her heart began to gallop.

"That's Harrison," said Jovie, tapping the screen. "And . . ." She peered at the photo to be sure what she was seeing.

"Yeah, he looks a lot younger, and a lot less weird," said Sylvan. "I never knew that he had this whole website, never mind that he was a screenwriter. If you read that page, there's a lot about the Ascension Camp parties, and his conspiracy theories about the gradient. Most of it is pretty weird, like there's stuff about Roswell and Elvis and—"

But Jovie was barely listening. The photo did indeed show a much younger Harrison, thinner and with a mop of black hair, but it was the man he was standing next to, who he had his arm around, who had stopped Jovie in her tracks.

"That's Paul," she said, a light-headed sensation washing over her.

"Who?" Sylvan asked.

"Mason's dad."

Jovie saw the tiny caption beneath the photo now, confirming it: *Harrison and Paul, 1994.*

"I thought you said Mason was from Seattle?"

"That's what he said." Jovie's head swam. Harrison and Mason's dad, together . . . the year of the Ascension Camp incident. Mason hadn't said anything about this.

Although, it would have been at least a decade before he was born. "Maybe his dad never told him?" Jovie said. "He could have moved to Seattle sometime after this."

"Still, it's kind of a big coincidence," said Sylvan.

Jovie's mouth was dry. "Yeah. He—" She stopped herself.

"What?"

Jovie had a momentary feeling like she was ratting out Mason, except, no, she wasn't. This was something he easily could have mentioned. "Harrison has come up a couple times and Mason's never said anything about this. Maybe he really doesn't know, but . . ."

"That would be weird, though, wouldn't it?" Sylvan said. "Considering Paul's old friend Harrison is right here in town, and Harrison is so connected to the history of the gradient. And it looks like Paul is, too, if he was writing screenplays about it."

"Yeah . . . but Paul is pretty out of it now. Maybe he didn't think to tell Mason, or maybe he forgot about it."

Sylvan shrugged and stood. "I have to go to my lesson. I can research this some more later. Are you still going to the Baxter plant tonight?"

Jovie glanced at the photo again and bit her lip. "Yeah. We have to." Whatever this meant, it didn't change what they needed to do.

"Okay," Sylvan said with a sigh. "Let me know how it goes, and . . . be careful, okay?"

"I will."

Sylvan went back out front. Jovie waited until her mom had called him into his lesson to slip out.

It was still early to meet up with Mason, so she biked to the little waterfront park by the docks. It had a play structure, a little beach, and a dock of its own. The park was empty on this gloomy afternoon, aside from an adult and a small child throwing rocks into the water and an old man sitting halfway out on the dock with a fishing rod. Jovie walked past him and sat at the very end of the dock, her feet dangling over the oil-sheened, briny-smelling water.

She looked at the website again and started reading the text below that picture:

> Harrison Westervelt and Paul Ellis are the authors of the feature film screenplay STARCROSSERS, as well as the original founders of the Ascension Files: Free the Truth website, dedicated to revealing the truth behind the Ascension Camp incident, for which, notoriously, Harrison Westervelt was WRONGLY ACCUSED and sued. WHAT REALLY HAPPENED? READ THE SCREENPLAY!

The paragraph went on, but Jovie closed her browser and gazed out over the water. None of that was going to help her with tonight's plan. And yet . . . she couldn't help feeling like Mason must have known at least some of this. So why hadn't he told her?

A seal's head slipped out of the water a little ways offshore, then disappeared again. Jovie watched for it to reappear, her thoughts jumbled, and barely registered the sound of footsteps on the dock.

"Hey."

She felt a light touch on her shoulder and turned to find Mason standing there, hands in his hoodie pocket. "Oh, hi," she said, trying to sound casual.

"Saw you sitting here on my way down the trail. I thought we were meeting at Salt and Sand?"

"We were, I just didn't want to go home first. You know, being around my mom and lying about where I'd be tonight." Jovie slid over and Mason sat beside her. "How was everyone at the bunker when you got back last night?"

"Okay," Mason said. "We didn't lose anyone else." He looked out at the water. "I'm worried about Dad," he said. "What they might be doing to him."

"Yeah," said Jovie. She tried to think of something natural to say next, but instead glanced at her phone.

"Is something wrong?" She found Mason studying her.

"Well . . ." Jovie almost just dodged the topic, but decided that would probably just make things worse. She took a deep breath. "Not *wrong*, just . . ." She opened her phone and showed him the photo. "That's your dad, right?"

Mason's face went stony as he looked at it. "Yeah, um, that's him. Where did you find that?"

"It's on Harrison's old website. Did you know he and your dad were friends?"

Mason looked away. "Yeah, I did," he said. "But it was a long time ago."

"I didn't know your dad was from here," Jovie said, and as she did, she realized that these seemed like kind of important details not to mention, especially when they'd been trying to piece together the history of the town. "It says your dad helped Harrison write this screenplay. I think it has something to do with the gradient, and Ascension Camp. Did you know that he knew about all this?"

"Oh man, no," said Mason. He rubbed his hand through his hair, still not quite meeting her eyes. "They were friends so long ago—I think it's been over twenty years—and he really never talks about it. The only thing I ever heard was that Harrison was a real jerk to him. I was thinking of asking him about it the other day, after we figured out that the gradient was happening back then, but he was still so out of it."

"So, you didn't grow up here?"

"No." Mason shook his head. "Dad lived here a long time ago. He moved to Seattle after he and Mom—" Mason suddenly bit his lip and gazed out at the water. His hand moved to the silver bracelet on his wrist and twisted it back and forth.

"Where is your mom?" Jovie asked. "You've never mentioned her."

"She died," Mason said quietly, and a deep shadow passed over his face.

"Oh, Mason, I'm sorry, I didn't know—"

Mason sniffled. "It's okay. I don't really like to talk about it."

He held out his wrist so Jovie could see the bracelet. It was wide and silver, and its surface was smooth except for some engraved markings that looked like script symbols, and that one circular stone, like a dark, polished jewel. "She got this on a trip before I was born," he said, "to East Africa, I think. She wore it all the time, said it was for luck."

"What happened? I mean, if I can ask."

"We got in a car accident," Mason said heavily. He wiped his eyes. "They got me out in time, but not her."

Jovie rubbed his arm. "That's horrible. When was that?"

"Last year," Mason said, and his breath hitched, tears running down his cheeks.

"I'm so sorry."

"Thanks. It's probably what started all this. After she died, we just never really recovered. Paul especially. Sometimes he tells me that he thinks he's going to see her across the gradient. I try to tell him that's not true, but . . . he was probably thinking that last night." Mason breathed deep and straightened his shoulders. "I'm sorry I didn't tell you about Harrison. I just . . . he wasn't nice to my mom, either, and thinking of him reminds me of her. . . . I guess I just wanted to avoid it."

"That's okay," said Jovie. "I had no idea you were going through this."

"I know. I should have said something. If I'd known that Paul knew about the gradient, I would have told you. I'm not sure if he could have helped us, though."

"Well, maybe after we find him tonight." Jovie rubbed his back, and they both gazed out over the steel-colored water. For a moment, Jovie wondered if everything Mason had just told her added up. When had Harrison been a jerk to his mom? Was that also twenty years ago? Did that mean she was from here, too? Also, if Paul had known enough about the gradient to be writing a screenplay about Ascension Camp, wouldn't he have at least somewhat recognized what was happening to them when they'd started to drift?

These thoughts needled her, but another glance at Mason's face, still ashen, the tears only just dried, made Jovie feel like now was not the time to ask any more questions. Besides—she checked her phone and saw that it was almost five thirty—they had a mission to get to.

"So, what's our plan for tonight?" she said.

"We'll have to drift again," said Mason.

"I know," Jovie said, feeling a chill.

"Hopefully they'll be distracted getting ready for the big storm, and we can find Paul and Micah, and then . . . figure out how to get them out." He looked at her and shrugged. "I wish I knew what we were going to find in there. Will they be okay? Are they going to be injured, or . . ."

"Barsuda is probably studying them like lab rats," said Jovie. "You can't exactly have some sort of power supply that also makes people vanish whenever you use it." Jovie imagined Micah in some sort of hospital room, or worse, some kind of cell, being visited now and then to have tests run on her. . . . The thought made her bolt to her feet. "Let's get going. Unless you still want to go to Salt and Sand for some calorie courage."

"I don't think I could eat anything, actually," said Mason. "Too nervous."

"Same," said Jovie.

They left the dock, got their bikes, and met up on the sidewalk. Then they biked out of town and started up the path toward her neighborhood, and the plant beyond that. As they pedaled up the hill, Jovie kept a wary eye on the road, worried that her mom might drive by, but soon they were past her street. A mile later, they turned onto a narrow dirt road that paralleled the barbed-wire-topped chain link fence surrounding Baxter. They bounced up the overgrown, potholed road until the cooling towers loomed overhead. They stashed their bikes in the bushes, and Mason produced a small pair of bolt cutters from his hoodie and set to work cutting through the chain link fence.

Jovie crawled through the narrow gap, and as she stood, Mason came through behind her and grasped her hand. He was already fading, and she felt that hollow wind inside her.

"Ready?" he said.

Jovie could only nod, holding her breath against the chill and telling herself this was it, just a little more, and she would finally find Micah.

23

THE CONTAINMENT ROOM

JANUARY 19, 2018
73 HOURS TO BREACH

The mist had crept in over town with nightfall, obscuring the tops of the great twin cooling towers so much that the red aircraft-warning lights on their rims were only faint smudges. The two towers were connected by a series of low buildings, their paint faded and chipped, windows boarded over with warped plywood, doors barred and covered in warning signs. And yet there was a door near the north tower that was made of spotless polished metal and had a lock pad with a facial scanner blinking beside it.

There was also a Barsuda worker guarding it. He'd been staring diligently at the hillside for hours when he felt an odd chill, a sensation like someone was nearby, but it was fleeting. Probably just fatigue, he thought.

Fifteen minutes later, the metal door opened with a hiss of bolts, and another agent walked out. In the brief moment it took for one guard to relieve the other, Jovie and Mason slipped inside. They pressed against the wall as the guard came in and sauntered down the hall, his boots clacking on the grimy tile floor.

"You doing okay?" Mason whispered.

"Yeah," said Jovie. "Except for, you know, feeling like there's a hole inside me. Is that how it is for you?"

"All the time."

They crept up the hallway, beneath buzzing fluorescent lights, passing doorways into dark offices filled with old, dust-covered furniture, until they reached a pair of elevator doors, next to which a makeshift list had been taped over the original plant directory. All the new locations listed were on floors with a *B* in front of them: basement levels, Jovie guessed.

"Containment," said Mason, tapping the list. "That sounds like where you'd keep someone." He motioned to a stairwell on the other side of the hall.

They descended switchbacking flights of concrete stairs and emerged in a hallway completely covered in plastic sheeting and silent except for the drone of fans. Just then, a burst of metallic grinding drew their attention back to the stairwell. A bright flash of white light came from the lower levels, and Jovie heard sharp clangs and the echo of voices.

"Let's take a look," she said. They descended two more flights, reaching the bottom of the stairwell, only it was no longer the bottom: a large rectangular hole had been freshly cut in the concrete floor, and a narrow metal staircase descended from it, down toward the source of the light and noise. Jovie gripped the metal rails and climbed down, arriving on a grated metal catwalk that hung just beneath the ceiling. Mason joined her and they crouched, gripping the railing.

They were high above a cavern with rough rock walls, its floor dotted with puddles. It was lit by work lights on tall stands. On the far wall was the entrance to a massive tunnel. A narrow set of train tracks led into it, sloping gradually downward into darkness. Workers in hard hats moved between equipment and the rails. Sounds of more workers and machinery echoed from within the tunnel.

"What is this place?" Mason said, then looked up at the ceiling as if thinking something through. "I think the tunnel goes west."

"Toward the water?" Jovie said. "Maybe it's a way to get the gradient's energy up here."

There was a loud clang and the echo of shouting from the tunnel.

"It doesn't seem like it's going to be ready two nights from now," Jovie mused.

"No. Maybe it's for the next cycle."

Jovie shook her head. "Another whole cycle of illnesses

and drifters and they could care less."

Mason tugged her arm, and they climbed back up and returned to the plastic-covered hall.

Light was spilling from a thick glass door just beyond the elevators. They crept over and peered inside. Jovie saw five beds spread out in a line. Each one was enclosed in a plastic tent hanging down from the ceiling, and had a tower of blinking monitors beside it. The beds were empty, except for the last one on the right. Two figures in green scrubs stood there, looking in at the patient and talking quietly, tapping on tablets. They both had those large goggles up on their foreheads. Jovie couldn't quite get a view of the person in the bed.

They waited outside the door, and after a few minutes, the two workers came out. Jovie and Mason slipped in and stepped over to the bed where the workers had been.

Inside was a figure that Jovie guessed was the red-suited woman from the night before, but she couldn't be sure. The woman's eyes and nose were covered in bandages, and what skin was visible on her face was blistered and cracked and bruised a deep purple. Her body had been almost entirely bandaged as well, and there were crimson stains on the bandages at the tips of her fingers. Electrodes ran from her head, arms, legs, and chest to the tower of monitors. There were two IV bags hanging beside her, and a device that seemed to be pumping air to assist her breathing.

"The gradient did this to her?" Jovie said.

Mason nodded. "I think this is what happens if you get too close and you're not a drifter."

"Will she recover?" Jovie wondered aloud, but Mason had already started toward the other side of the room. Jovie tore her eyes away from the injured woman and followed. She peered into the next tent; its bed was empty, yet she noticed that the equipment beside it was flashing and beeping. Suspended over the bed was a strange structure made out of thin metal mesh. It had a curving shape like the outline of a person.

Jovie aimed her spyglass at the bed. It wasn't empty, but occupied by a nearly transparent figure in a hospital gown: an older woman, it seemed, but so dim that Jovie could see the bedding beneath her. At the same time, her body glowed with thousands of luminescent rainbow lines, almost like her skin had become transparent and her blood vessels were illuminated. The glow was brightest behind her eyes, which were open, staring vacantly at the ceiling. There was a swirling center of brilliant light behind them. A patch of light in her chest, too, pulsing like the beating of her heart. The rainbow light raced throughout her arms and legs, while the mesh structure suspended above her surged with the same light in response, as if it was reacting to her.

Jovie thought of those essences on the beach last night, and in Micah's drawings, and a possibility bloomed in her mind: Was that what this woman was going to become? Had the essences once been drifters? Was that how you looked when you actually crossed the gradient?

Jovie's heart beat faster as she watched the rhythmic glow of the mesh cage. She wasn't sure if it was keeping this woman from drifting further, or making her more like . . . this. Or did this have something to do with energy, too? She thought of how those flying essences had given off cosmic rays. Maybe drifters absorbed the energy from the gradient, and that was what made you drift in the first place. Maybe it wasn't about how connected you were to the world, or how lost you were feeling, but just about how susceptible your body happened to be to this strange force. It might be as random as how some people are allergic to something while others aren't. And did Barsuda want to figure out how to stop that reaction, or how to mimic it for their own energy goals?

She eyed the row of beds with fresh fear. Was she about to find Micah in the same condition? And if she did, was there any way back once you were like this?

Jovie moved to the next bed and found another drifter in a similar condition, but it wasn't Micah; it was a young man Jovie didn't recognize. The next bed held a woman Jovie also didn't know. She was slightly more solid, and seemed to be asleep.

Mason stood outside the last tent, his hands against the plastic. Jovie joined him, and through the spyglass, she saw

Paul. She felt a momentary relief that none of these beds held Micah, but if she wasn't here, then where was she?

"It's worse than I thought," Mason said. Paul was slightly less transparent than the others, but he was still dim, the rainbow light pulsing through him with each heartbeat, the mesh overhead glowing in response. He seemed to be asleep.

Mason felt around the plastic and found a seam with snaps that held the tent together. He pulled it slowly apart, and he and Jovie slipped through. "Hey, Dad," Mason said quietly.

Paul's eyes fluttered open, and he peered through the mesh cage suspended above him. His mouth moved like he was trying to say something, but Jovie only heard the faintest of whispers. He winced, and seemed to try harder: "What are you doing here, buddy?"

"We came to find you."

Paul shook his head weakly. "I think . . . I almost drifted. I followed the lights. I was on my way."

"We saw," said Mason. "Hang on, we're going to get you out of here."

"No." Paul reached out, his hand gripping Mason's, luminous lines glowing beneath his skin. "I saw into it," he said, his voice like paper. "There's something on the other side. A place. A shadow on the stars . . ."

"I know," Mason said. "But we need to go right now before they come back—"

"They're trying to keep me tethered here, to this world," Paul said, his transparent eyes flicking to the mesh latticework above him. The light from his mind glowed out through his pupils. "It hurts."

Mason sniffed. "We can figure out a way to bring you back. We just have to—"

"N-No," Paul forced out. "You have to release me. Let me go."

"I can't—"

"There's no bringing me back. This is a one-way trip, and you know it."

"It doesn't have to be," Mason said weakly.

"Please. I'm more there than here now." He smiled, tears rimming his light-filled eyes. "It's okay, buddy. It's what I want. I'll see your mom."

Mason didn't respond for a moment, his eyes welling with tears, too, and it made Jovie ache. She didn't know what to do, how to help . . . Finally, Mason said, "Okay then. Okay."

"Mason . . . ," Jovie said.

He let out a slow, defeated breath. "He's drifted too far." Mason ran his fingers over the mesh cage, the wires rippling with rainbow light.

"But you wanted to save him," Jovie said.

"It wasn't enough," said Mason, his head falling. "I was too late."

"Hey," Paul whispered, gripping Mason's hand. "No. Everything you did . . . this was my fault. I'm so sorry, buddy. About the drugs, about your mom—"

"Don't—" said Mason.

"I made a mess of everything, for so many years . . . but I'm so glad you came back." Paul managed a smile. "Nobody would have remembered me otherwise." He craned his neck and pointed at Mason's chest, at his old Nirvana T-shirt. "So glad we got to see that show together. Those were the times that mattered."

Mason's face crumpled, tears falling down his cheeks. "That was the best."

Paul smiled faintly. "You bet."

Mason sighed. "Okay. It will be okay. I—" His voice hitched and his eyes shut. Jovie put a hand on his back, and he breathed deep.

"Are you sure about this?" Jovie said.

Mason nodded. "Are you ready?"

"I'm ready," said Paul.

Mason squeezed his luminescent hand. "I love you."

"Love you too, buddy. I'll let your mom know you're okay."

Mason nodded, but had to look away, his jaw clenching. He turned to the tower of equipment beside the bed and found the cables that connected the mesh structure. He gathered them, and yanked them all at once. The cage sizzled and went dark, and immediately a bright red light began to flash on the tower, accompanied by a beeping alarm.

Paul let out a long, slow breath. The outline of his

face, of his body, began to fade, while the energy lines grew brighter within him, overwhelming his body. The lines curled together, the light coalescing and beginning to swirl, becoming brighter and brighter, until Paul's body was gone, and there was only this form of pure energy, buzzing and levitating and taking the shape of a butterfly.

Behind them, the door hissed open and Jovie saw the two workers rushing back in. "We've got a situation in the infirmary," one of them said into their watch.

"Come on!" Jovie grabbed Mason's hand, and they retreated through the plastic, flattening themselves against the back wall. Jovie felt the chill as Mason pulled them further into the drift, and the workers rushed past. They tore aside the plastic and lowered their goggles over their eyes as the shimmering essence that had once been Paul rose from the bed, bathing them in light.

"The containment field is disconnected," one of the workers said as she looked over the monitors.

"Plug it back in!" said the other.

"It's too late."

Jovie tugged on Mason's hand and they slid along the wall, making their way toward the exit. But the door hissed as Jovie pushed it open. The workers whipped around, and with their goggles on—

"Hey!" one shouted. "Stop!"

They pushed the plastic aside to come after Jovie and

Mason, but just then, the essence that had been Paul burst out of its tent and buzzed in a frantic circle around the room, cutting off their path to the door.

"Ah!" Its humming wing struck one of the agents and he fell backward, clutching at his chest as if he'd been burned.

Jovie and Mason ducked through the door, and the essence buzzed out behind them and across the hall and into the stairwell, spiraling upward. They ran after it, bounding up to the next floor. Mason was starting up the next flight when Jovie tugged him to a stop.

"Wait!" she shouted, motioning to the hallway.

"We need to get out of here!" Mason said.

"I have to find Micah!"

Footsteps clomped into the stairwell below.

"But she wasn't there—"

"She could be somewhere else!" Jovie hissed. "I can't leave without her." She dropped Mason's hand and darted into the hall, but could hear him rushing after her.

"We might have time to check this floor, but that's going to be it," Mason said from behind her. "If we get caught, all this will be for nothing."

He was right, of course . . . but Jovie imagined Micah becoming one of those essences, her body ceasing to be, her energy leaving the world. . . .

No.

She rounded a corner and ducked into the open

doorway of a dark room. Mason joined her, and they leaned against the wall in the dark and listened, trying to control their breathing. Footsteps clomped by out in the hall. Mason waited another moment, then peered out and motioned for Jovie to follow. They heard rushing footsteps from the direction of the elevators, then the squawk of a radio, and started creeping up the hallway in the other direction.

They passed more dark doorways and locked doors, rounded the next corner, and found an open set of double doors that led into a vast concrete room. The corners were stacked with piles of dusty boxes and rusty equipment, while the center of the room contained two orderly rows of sleek metal tables holding glass cases, all under gleaming lights. Some were filled with water, while others held objects. At the far end of the room, folding chairs were arranged in semicircular rows, facing a series of whiteboards covered in diagrams and numbers.

"We should check another floor," said Jovie, but Mason had turned back toward the entrance to the room, the color drained from his face.

She heard a soft shuffling and turned to see a team of agents, all wearing goggles, some with devices in their gloved hands and others holding white loops that looked like giant zip ties.

"Stay right there," came a voice, and Dr. Wells moved to the front of the group, her goggle eyes boring into them. "We don't want to hurt you, Jovie."

"There's an exit," Mason whispered, glancing behind them.

The team edged closer.

Jovie's heart was beating so fast she felt like it might burst right out of her chest.

"Ready?" said Mason.

Jovie squeezed his hand in reply.

They turned and dashed between the long tables of displays. Boots shotgunned behind them. In the corners of her vision, Jovie saw the blur of agents flanking them on both sides.

Ahead, a green sign glowed over a single door in the far corner of the room. They sprinted past rows of chairs—

"Stop!" A huge heavy body slammed into Jovie. She screamed, and lost hold of Mason's hand, but not before yanking him off-balance.

Jovie and the agent crashed to the concrete floor. Mason careened into the folding chairs, sending them clattering this way and that.

"Run!" Jovie shouted, her body thrumming with pain, her thoughts wild with fear.

Mason scrambled to his feet. Agents were racing at him from both sides. His eyes locked with Jovie's almost apologetically—*why?* Jovie had just a moment to wonder—and then he reached to his wrist, to the bracelet there. His fingers gripped that polished black stone, and he twisted it purposefully. The stone lit up in rainbow colors—

Then Mason vanished completely.

The two agents staggered to a stop in the space where Mason had just been. They turned this way and that, then pulled up their goggles.

Dr. Wells appeared above Jovie, breathless. "You watch that door!" she shouted at one of the agents. "Everyone else double back! Set your scanners to maximum sensitivity. Don't lose him!"

The agent who had tackled Jovie pulled her up by her arm.

"Ow," Jovie grunted, and felt tears brimming in her eyes.

"Easy," Dr. Wells said to the agent. "It's okay, Jovie." She smiled. "It's time we had that talk."

24

THE BARRICADE

JANUARY 19, 2018
72 HOURS TO BREACH

"Here." Dr. Wells returned to the folding chairs, where Jovie was seated, and handed her a steaming mug. "That's highly concentrated truth serum."

Jovie glared at her, and she smiled.

"Kidding, it's chamomile tea. To calm your nerves and warm you up. Didn't have any honey, though. Sorry."

Jovie didn't respond, but she did sip the tea. It helped to warm that hollow chill inside her.

Dr. Wells sat opposite Jovie. She'd pushed her goggles up onto her head and opened a tablet on her knees. "You know, what you and your friend are doing shouldn't be possible. In fact, it flies in the face of everything we've learned about the breach. Where exactly did you meet him?"

Beneath her buzzing fear, Jovie's thoughts were a jumble: Mason fiddling with that stone on his bracelet, the way it had glowed before he disappeared, almost as if it had been some kind of technology. . . . What did it mean? She thought of how that older woman had seen him in the grocery store, but then the cashiers hadn't. How he could push them both into the drift and out again, while Carina and the other drifters seemed unable to control it or to connect with anyone. Suddenly, Jovie wondered if anything about Mason was like the other drifters at all. And if he was different, why? And why hadn't he told her? He'd lied about knowing who Harrison was, he hadn't told her about the bracelet. . . .

"Jovie, the only way we're going to be able to help each other is by actually talking," said Dr. Wells.

"I'm not helping you."

"But I think I can help you." Dr. Wells looked up as an agent arrived beside her. He handed her a rectangular device, shaped kind of like a thermometer, which she aimed at Jovie until it beeped. "Good news, your antiproton fluctuations have officially receded below critical threshold."

"What does that mean?"

"It means your atomic structure is normalizing and you're not going to end up like the transient entities."

"You mean the drifters?"

"Is that what you call them?"

"That's what they call themselves. They're not entities, they're *people*, who—" Jovie caught herself. "Why am I telling you, it's not like you even care. All the drifters, my mom and my friend getting sick, you don't care about any of them as long as you get your precious energy."

Dr. Wells laughed incredulously. "Wait, hold on—what? The drifters and your mother are precisely the reason we're here. We're not the bad guys, Jovie. We're a scientific agency contracted by the United States government to investigate what's happening here and stop it, ideally before anyone else gets hurt."

Jovie tripped over this revelation. "Then why have you been after me? Spying on me? Why are you holding me here?"

"We're operating on top secret clearance, which requires us to be, well, secretive, but I mean, the reason we're holding you here now is simply because you're trespassing." Dr. Wells raised her hands to indicate their surroundings. "This is a private facility. Technically, you've committed a crime by coming in here, though at your age I guess it would only be some sort of juvenile misdemeanor. Regardless, we're having the police come and pick you up, and they'll deliver you to your mother."

Jovie's insides curdled. "My mom?"

"I'm afraid so. We've already contacted her at work. Naturally, we can't allow her on the premises, either, so she'll meet you at home."

Jovie swallowed hard, a metallic taste in her mouth, a queasy feeling sloshing through her. She imagined pulling up to her house in a police car, Mom standing there . . .

"As for why we've been watching you: you've discovered a lot of things that we've been trying very hard to keep secret for public safety," said Dr. Wells. "I have to say, I'm impressed, and since this is the end of the road for you, I thought we could trade notes."

Jovie sipped her tea. She didn't even know what to say.

"You've been looking for your friend," said Dr. Wells, consulting the tablet in her lap. "Micah Rogers. Disappeared September twenty-first."

"More like you took her," Jovie said under her breath.

Dr. Wells shook her head. "We never had Micah here. It wasn't until your principal went to the local police saying one of his students had gone missing, and that he hadn't remembered it happening, that we became aware of her. But I'm afraid Micah's not in Far Haven at all."

Jovie's insides froze. She peered at Dr. Wells. "How do you know that?"

"Here, look." Dr. Wells scooted her chair over and held out her tablet. On it was a map of the area. There were a number of little pulsing dots here and there. "I shouldn't be telling you this, but the monitors we installed on the wells around town aren't for radiation; they're for measuring cosmic rays, which the breach emits. Recently, though, we figured out how to upgrade them to track the drifters. See, here is the group at the bunkers." She pointed to a cluster of glowing dots at the edge of the bluff. "Yes, we know they're there. Seems to be a safe enough location; those bunkers were lined with lead during the Cold War to serve as fallout shelters. And there are a few others, scattered all over town."

Jovie gazed at the dots floating around. "How do you know none of them is Micah?"

"The transients—sorry, drifters—their matter has been altered by the breach. And they, in turn, affect anything they touch or interact with. It leaves behind an energy signature, and each one is unique." She tapped the screen. "I took readings from those drawings in Micah's room and ran them against all the entities in the area. She's not here."

"Then where is she?"

"We have no idea."

"I don't believe you," Jovie said, but even as she uttered the words, she felt the truth settling in her gut.

Micah was across the gradient. Even though Jovie still remembered her, somehow, it had happened. . . . What other explanation could there be? Micah was gone.

It was probably only a matter of time before Jovie would forget her as well.

"I have no reason to lie to you," Dr. Wells continued. "And if we did have Micah here, our goal would be the same as yours. My company was brought in after the 2010 event to try to understand this thing, but just as important, to protect the town and its people. What did you think we were trying to do?"

"Use its energy," Jovie said. "We thought that was why you'd set up here."

"Interesting theory, but no. What we're really trying to do is find a way to close the breach for good, and limit the number of casualties in the process. The drifters you saw down in containment, we want to save them, to reestablish their connection to the world. The technique we've developed hasn't worked yet, but we're making some progress. And until we have something that works, I don't want to go terrifying the general public. The breach doesn't just pose a danger to the drifters; this thing could affect the whole town, if not the entire West Coast, maybe the planet." Dr. Wells leaned forward. "How much do you know about what's happening here?"

"You mean that the gradient has been opening for at least a hundred years, and that it's happening more and more often at an exponential rate?"

Dr. Wells gazed blankly at her for a moment, then nodded approvingly. "Okay then. In that case, come here. I want to show you something." She stood and moved to the nearest of the long metal tables. Jovie reluctantly joined her. On it was a glass case about ten feet long, inside which were pieces of dark, smooth wood encrusted in barnacles. "The cosmic rays produced by the breach—the *gradient*, as you call it—they leave behind radioactive fingerprints. We've been dating the samples we collect. This is a piece of wreckage from 1898."

"The *Endurance*," said Jovie.

"Exactly," said Dr. Wells. "That's the oldest sample we've found, and our analysis indicates that's when this specific phenomenon began, but . . . come look at this." She led Jovie down the aisle, past cases with whale bones, concrete chunks, dried mollusk shells, and starfish skeletons. The next case she stopped at held an ornately carved oar, like you might use in a canoe. Its paint was faded and chipped. "This is from the Coast Salish people, circa 1700. See the carvings?" Dr. Wells pointed to the end of the paddle. Among the carvings of different animals, Jovie saw a line of shapes like butterflies.

"And this, from around the same time." Dr. Wells motioned to the next case, which held a vest made of leather and adorned with intricate multicolored beadwork. Jovie spotted a line of butterfly symbols across the chest. "This is from the Spokane Tribe, hundreds of miles inland from here. Then there's this." Dr. Wells stepped to a case containing an oil painting in an ornate gold frame. It showed a beach and the sea. The sun had just set beyond bands of vermilion clouds, and there in the sky were small versions of the essences. "This was painted in the 1600s, on the northeast coast of Siberia."

Dr. Wells pointed to a word scrawled in the corner of the canvas:

распутывание

"It translates to 'unraveling.' Leave it to the Russians to capture the melancholy in a phenomenon."

Jovie remembered hearing that word before. "What does all this mean?"

"We believe—though we have yet to confirm—that this place, this spot on Earth, or rather, in the fabric of space-time, is a sort of boundary between our universe and others. A region where there is some exchange of energy, as if the borders between universes are semi-permeable, like a membrane. At least, that's what our measurements of the flow of cosmic radiation tell us.

"But you've spent time with the people who are experiencing this firsthand—what do they think it is? I've tried to ask the drifters we've taken in, but they're always too far gone to help us."

Jovie found herself gazing at the painting. She thought of that longing she'd felt on the beach, and the way the essences sang. "Some of them think there's another world over there, a better place, maybe."

"Ah, like that Planet Elysia stuff Arthur Odegaard concocted?"

"Something like that."

"Well, Arthur got that idea from the ancient Greek concept of the Elysian fields, which, get this, were described as being *on the western edge of the earth.* For as long as there have been civilizations, there have been stories about passage out of this world and into another. The Egyptians had Aaru, the place beyond the reeds, and there are countless others. And myths are always at least somewhat rooted in truth."

"Are you saying all these people throughout history knew about the gradient?"

"Perhaps, on some level. There have been humans on this coast for at least twenty thousand years. Word may have traveled, even through the ancient world."

"So have there been drifters all that time, too?"

"I think a certain amount of energy has always departed here. I don't know why a person would be drawn away; I do know that the basic structure of this universe is such that the very forces that made us and everything else are also, on a cosmic scale, pushing us toward isolation and emptiness. Matter follows the flow, out from the big bang itself. In our own existences we are able to fight those forces to a point, to create connection and belonging, but not always."

"Things don't come back around," Jovie said quietly.

"It's not a very comforting thought," said Dr. Wells. "That said, speaking metaphysically, if this gradient is proof of a multiverse, then there could be forces at work that we haven't even imagined yet. Perhaps we do have multiple selves, perhaps those selves are connected on some essential level. It could be that our energy flows between these versions of us; when one withers here, another thrives elsewhere, and draws energy from this world to it—call it a conservation of self. I have absolutely no proof of anything like this, by the way. But that doesn't mean it's not possible. Seeing things like this, drifters and their essences, can make even the strictest scientist wonder." Dr. Wells sighed. "But in the meantime, I have lives to save here, and I'm not even exactly sure what's causing this breach, or when it will happen again."

Jovie found herself on the verge of tears. What they were talking about felt so lonely. . . . *Focus*, she told herself. "We were thinking that maybe the gradient was some kind of cycle," she said, "like with the seasons or the planets or something, because the math is so exact."

Dr. Wells's eyes lit with interest. "Or like something mechanical."

"Is that what you think?"

Dr. Wells tapped her tablet. "I think, whatever the characteristics of this spot, something new began happening here in 1898." She held out a graphic for Jovie to see. It showed a shape like an hourglass on its side, with a brightly glowing bar in the middle. The two wide ends of the hourglass had rounded teardrop sides, and their insides were littered with small dots like stars. "Breach, gradient, whatever we want to call it, the actual data suggests that it's something more akin to a stable anti-matter bridge."

"Is that like a wormhole or something?" said Jovie, thinking of Sylvan's theory.

Dr. Wells pointed to the little glowing cylinder between the teardrops. "That's exactly what it's like, but because of the space-time discrepancy we're reading, we don't think it's coming from another part of our universe, as wormholes are usually theorized to."

"That's what you were talking about with the probe last night?" Jovie asked.

Dr. Wells smiled. "So you *were* there. I thought so."

"I just remember you saying something about time being a thousand to one."

"Yes, as our probes have entered the breach, before they disintegrate, that is, their clocks read a difference in the flow of time."

"So time is faster there?"

"Actually, it's faster here. Time is relative, and just because its rate feels 'normal' to us doesn't mean time would flow at the same speed near a different star or on a different planet . . . or in another universe entirely."

"You think the gradient really leads to another universe?" Jovie asked.

"That's our best guess." Dr. Wells's speech sped up, almost like Sylvan's when he was excited about something. "And the pattern of years between breaches, and of days between storms, is evidence that this bridge between universes is not something naturally occurring. That, in fact, it was made on purpose."

"Made by who?"

"That is the seven-billion-human-lives-at-stake question," said Dr. Wells. "Someone over there chose this spot to try to build their bridge, and their attempts to cross it are becoming stronger and more destructive every time they try."

Dr. Wells moved up the row of cases and stopped beside a tank holding a large fish. Jovie saw that its left eye was actually two eyes overlapping one another, one milky, but both flicking as if working. Half of the fish's lips were missing, revealing its pointy teeth and blackened gums.

"Our analysis of the 2010 event indicates a cosmic ray burst with the equivalent strength of a miniature nuclear blast," said Dr. Wells. "We really have been here cleaning up leftover radiation. And what we are seeing with this current series of storms suggests that the breach in"—she checked her watch—"a shade under three days from now will be even larger, and have the power to potentially sicken or injure the entire town. Further, we have found code seven cases in towns to the north, south, even inland, all at greater distances than in 2010. It could be more than just Far Haven that's in danger. Unless we can stop it."

"Is that what that telescope machine is for?" Jovie asked.

Dr. Wells shook her head. "Next time, just pull up a chair. Yes, that device is nicknamed the barricade. It reverses the flow of energy back through the breach."

"So you're trying to close it," said Jovie. "Like, for good."

"That is the mission, though we have a bit of work left to do in that department."

"And you don't even want to understand what's over there?"

"Of course I do!" Dr. Wells threw up her hands, a note of frustration in her voice. "So much! Every time we send a probe into the breach, I feel like a kid waiting to get out of bed on Christmas morning. I've never wished so hard for something . . . but none of our attempts to gather data have worked. Whatever the cause of this, it remains ever so painfully just beyond our understanding. And I fear it's going to stay that way. Because even if we avoid major damage during this current cycle, all our models indicate that the next breach will be even stronger, and even more dangerous." She put a hand on Jovie's shoulder. "I'm sorry. I know that's not what you want to hear."

Jovie crossed her arms. All of this felt like great weights being lowered slowly onto her shoulders.

An agent walked up to them and waited for Dr. Wells to turn. "Yes?"

"We haven't been able to find the other trespasser," the agent said. "We're getting no readings within the complex."

"All right, keep searching outside." As the agent left, Dr. Wells eyed Jovie. "You may have realized by now that your friend is not like the other drifters."

"I'm starting to," Jovie muttered.

"Did he tell you where he came from?"

"Seattle."

"And he was the one who introduced you to the drifters?"

"Yeah," Jovie said, but at the same time, she tried to hide a realization that hit her like a jolt: *She doesn't know about the spyglass.* "What do you know about him?" Jovie asked.

Dr. Wells blew air out of her cheeks. "Almost nothing. Except that he shows up on our scans now and then, and seems to be able to manipulate his matter phasing, almost as if he can choose to drift or not. No other drifter we've encountered has had even a shred of this kind of control. I would very much like to talk to him about that."

So would I, Jovie thought darkly.

"Sir," another agent called from the doorway. "Local police are here."

"As promised," Dr. Wells said to Jovie. "See? Thanks for chatting with me, Jovie. And I hope you'll take all that I've told you seriously. You've come a long way, but it's time to leave the potentially-world-ending threats to the professionals."

Jovie nodded, but a tear slipped down her cheek.

"I thought our talk would ease your mind."

"You just basically told me that I've lost my friend forever, that my whole search has been pointless."

Dr. Wells patted her shoulder awkwardly, like it wasn't something she was used to doing. "It wasn't pointless. You didn't know, and your memory of her is a testament to how strong a friendship you two had. It's one of a kind, truly."

"What's that supposed to mean?"

"Well, just that, you know, by the time a drifter transitions and leaves this world, they're usually completely forgotten. I mean, as far as we can tell, the forgetting is part of what makes the process even possible. Like the world forgetting them is what frees them. But you hung on to your memory of Micah even after she was gone. Awhile after."

Something about what Dr. Wells was saying tugged at Jovie's mind. "It wasn't just me," she said. "There was a big search for her when she disappeared, like with the state police, and it was all over the news for months."

"Really?" said Dr. Wells. "Actually, that does ring a bell, now that you mention it."

"And other people still remember, if I ask them about her. Like my mom, and the principal."

"That's right." Her brow wrinkled in thought.

"What?" said Jovie.

"It's just odd," said Dr. Wells. "Micah was definitely beginning to drift, those drawings she made prove it, but . . . the forgetting always comes first. And there's never a search for a drifter, because no one remembers that person to even know they're missing in the first place."

Jovie was only half listening. In her mind, all she could see was that very last drawing in Micah's journal. The light in the water . . . and the silhouetted figure who seemed to be emerging from it. If that wasn't actually someone from Barsuda: "What if someone took her?"

"Like a kidnapping?"

"I don't know . . . but I mean, what if they took her across the gradient, *before* she could drift across on her own?"

Dr. Wells cocked her head. "I don't think a drifter could interact with a person like that."

"Then what if it was someone *from* the other side? Like, whoever made the gradient."

Dr. Wells bit her lip. Then, almost to herself, she said, "The Blue Bathymetrist."

"That's from Arthur's book," said Jovie.

"Have you read it?"

"Not really."

"Well, it's bananas," said Dr. Wells, "but Arthur's

whole thing was that when the gradient opened, one of the beings from this Planet Elysia would come through to guide the enlightened to the other side. He called that being the Blue Bathymetrist."

"Okay."

"There's more: In the account from the lone survivor of the *Endurance*, there's mention of a figure in a blue suit coming through the breach. There's also a description of multiple blue-suited figures emerging from it during the 1994 event, although that's not from a very reliable source. . . . Still, all that does point to whoever is on the other side trying to come over here."

Jovie imagined a blue-suited figure grabbing Micah from the beach. "Do you think that could be what happened to her?"

"I'm not sure," said Dr. Wells. "All those accounts I mentioned are from the final breach events, not the earlier storms, and Micah disappeared back in the fall. There's also the minor issue that anyone who gets too close to the gradient, and isn't far enough along in the drift, gets severely injured by the cosmic rays, if not killed."

"But—" A thought had occurred to Jovie, but she stopped herself.

"What?"

"Nothing. Just . . . you're right. There's no real way to know." Jovie tried to sound discouraged, and not to show that her new realization was making her heart pound.

"Doesn't change the fact that she's gone."

Dr. Wells looked at her curiously. "I suppose it doesn't."

"Sir," the agent at the door said. "You want me to bring the police in?"

"No, that's all right." Dr. Wells motioned Jovie toward the doorway. "Time's up, I guess. We have a lot to do and only a few days to do it. Thanks for talking with me, Jovie, and I'm sorry about your friend. Keep safe until after the breach, okay? We're going to be releasing a severe storm advisory for that night. Hopefully it will keep people indoors. I'd strongly recommend you follow it."

"Sure," Jovie muttered. She stood and followed the agent out.

"Jovie." She turned back to Dr. Wells. "You would have been my hero when I was your age. I know what it's like to believe so strongly in something that no one else sees. I also know that in a way, finding out you were actually right only makes it worse. This isn't your fight—but I'm betting a future one will be."

Jovie looked at her for a moment, then continued out. She followed the agent to the elevators, and after a silent ride up, she was escorted outside to where two police officers were standing by a squad car, its lights flashing silently.

"We have your bike in the trunk," one officer said as she opened the back door.

Jovie slumped into the seat and the door thudded shut. She looked at the wire grating that separated her from the front, and Dr. Wells's words—*this is the end of the road for you*—settled more heavily on her shoulders.

But as the car pulled away from the plant and up the dark road, a faint light flickered in the corner of Jovie's eye. She fished the spyglass from her pocket and, after a glance at the officers, aimed it out the window. There, weaving among the trees, was a glowing essence. A name drifted into Jovie's mind: *Paul.* She realized she had already nearly forgotten him. But though his departure had felt powerfully sad back in the containment room, his essence out here, so brilliant and full of light, also filled her with wonder. Was there that much energy in her, in every person? Were they all so luminous?

The police car pulled out onto the main road. The essence arced over the street and darted away into the trees, in the direction of the sea.

Jovie put the spyglass away, and her adrenaline surged with a new certainty: Dr. Wells was wrong. This wasn't the end of the road for her. Because Jovie knew something now, and there was important work to be done.

The realization had come near the end of their conversation, arriving in Jovie's mind like a firework, so bright and urgent that she'd nearly revealed it a moment later.

Dr. Wells had been saying that getting near the gradient could injure or kill you, but if Micah had, in fact, crossed the gradient *before* she was forgotten, and had only been forgotten afterward, that had to mean she survived the crossing in the first place. And while the forgetting suggested that she was drifting now, the fact that Jovie still remembered her had to mean Micah *still* wasn't yet an essence like the one she'd just seen, whose name was already escaping her once more. And *that* meant . . .

The next half hour was dreadful. The flashing of police lights through her neighborhood, being walked to her door by an officer, the sight of her mom in the doorway and the furious look on her face. She grounded Jovie and excoriated her for lying, for causing her to miss work, for endangering their fragile income and making poor choices, while also making sure to heap some of the blame on Dad, too. Jovie was sent to her room like she was a little kid, with no prospect of being out on her own again anytime soon.

And yet through all of it, part of Jovie's mind had been miles away, the gears turning. If she was right, it wasn't too late—Micah could still be saved.

But Jovie had less than three days to figure out how.

INTERLUDE

THIRD TRIAL, JANUARY 1994

PROJECT BARRICADE

REFERENCE CODE: 7

ARTIFACT #98103-5

SOURCE: SCRIPTS FOR SALE

CLASSIFIED: TOP SECRET

STARCROSSERS

A teleplay by

Harrison Westervelt and Paul Ellis

Episode 1: Pilot—Shooting Script p. 87

EXT. DESOLATE BEACH 1994—NIGHT

A wide, empty beach. RVs and trucks encircle a collection of tents, campfires, and chairs. There are dozens of people mid-celebration, with wild kites that resemble butterflies. Many participants have their faces painted blue.

Suddenly, a STRONG WIND, and everyone turns toward the water.

IN THE WATER: a vortex of ghostly light swirls.

IN THE CROWD: Max moves close to Barbara.

MAX

Mom, is this really it?

BARBARA

(*worriedly*)

I think so, honey.

A large wave breaks, and water rushes over everyone's feet, surprising them. The light grows. Nearby, an RV door bursts open and Harrison emerges, dressed in the cosmic blue suit we saw in Act 1.

HARRISON

Everyone! This is it! Proof of what Arthur Odegaard really discovered! We were told a lie about what happened here thirty-two years ago! Some of us lost relatives . . . parents . . . Some of us even watched our loved ones be wrongly accused of misdeeds, but ALL of us lost a chance to truly understand our place in the universe! That there's a place for those of us who yearn! Somewhere we belong!

(*to himself*)

They'll have to listen now.

He turns to Paul, who stands nearby holding a video camera.

HARRISON

Are we rolling?

PAUL

Yessir.

Harrison gazes meaningfully at the growing light.

HARRISON

I'm coming, Mom.

He stabs at the panel of buttons on the suit, but nothing happens.

HARRISON

Come on . . . Arthur, how did you work this thing?

IN THE WATER: the light grows, the surface boiling and the waves increasing.

Harrison gives up on the suit controls and rushes out knee-deep in the waves and holds out his arms.

HARRISON

Our calculations were right! Prepare yourselves—

A wall of water rises out of nowhere and knocks Harrison over. Paul staggers back in the waves. A few of the campers cry out in concern.

Barbara puts her arm around Max and peers at the water. A humming sound is growing—

Suddenly, the white light EXPLODES out into a SPHERE of solid brilliance. A CONCUSSION of energy blasts over the beach. Massive waves begin to crash, rushing up over the fires and slamming into the RVs. The light grows blinding.

A horrific shrieking . . . Paul lowers his camera and sees a woman, one of the other campers, collapsing in the surf with HORRIBLE BURNS.

PAUL

Harrison!

Harrison is getting to his feet in waist-deep water and facing the light. He doesn't seem to hear.

HARRISON

Come on! Show yourselves!

Suddenly, a GUN FIRES.

AGENT TULLY

(*offscreen*)

Everybody off the beach!

Paul spins around to see Agents Tully and Holder charging down the beach.

AGENT HOLDER

FBI! Evacuate the beach
immediately!

HARRISON

No! No one panic! Just—

Agent Holder fires another warning shot.

HOLDER

Now!

BARBARA

Harrison, we need to go!

Harrison looks back at her and Max, incredulous.

HARRISON

Now?? We can't go now! Not when we're
this close!

Barbara grabs Max's arm and drags him toward their RV, but the vehicle is smacked by a wave and TOPPLES OVER with a crash. It is pandemonium now, the crowd running this way and that. Screams echoing. An RV peels out up the beach, while another is overturned and floats in the waves.

Barbara and Max weave their way toward a small hatchback car and jump in.

Agents Tully and Holder wade into the waves toward Harrison.

AGENT TULLY

Harrison! Come to shore! This ends now!

HARRISON

You're ruining everything! You don't understand what's out there!

AGENT HOLDER

This isn't what you think it is!

The sphere of light has grown, its edges enveloping the beach, and now a black center appears, like the pupil of a cosmic eye.

Paul lowers his camera, gazing into it. He sees a field of darkness dotted with faint stars, smeared with green nebula, and yet there is clearly something blocking this impossible sight, some sort of large shadow with a glint of metal.

PAUL

A shadow on the stars . . .

A wave batters him.

In the car, Barbara cranks the ignition, but the car won't start. Water rages around them, up to the doors.

Paul sees this and wades desperately toward the car.

PAUL

Barbara! Max! Get out of there!

MAX

Mom, we need to—

A huge wave crashes and the car is overturned. Suddenly, Barbara and Max are upside-down and water is filling the car from all sides. They struggle with the seat belts, but the frigid water is rushing in.

MAX

Help! Dad!

Harrison turns toward them as if snapping out of a trance.

HARRISON

Max?

He starts toward the car but is TACKLED by Agent Holder.

HARRISON

Let me go! My family!

Paul tries to reach the car, but it is being sucked out into the waves, into the light and closer to that pupil of darkness.

PAUL

Hang on!

In the car, Barbara looks desperately at her son with wide eyes.

BARBARA

Deep breath, Max!

The water fills the car and submerges them both.

Harrison fights, watching the car helplessly, as Agents Tully and Holder drag him toward the shore.

HARRISON

No!

Paul presses out into the waves, he's nearly within reach of the overturned car—

A MASSIVE BURST OF ENERGY lifts him up and throws him back out of the waves. He lands hard on the beach. More blasts erupt, and the agents and Harrison are thrown back, too.

A grinding humming sound like twisting metal assaults their ears. Furious wind—

All at once, sound is extinguished. The waves calm to mere lapping ripples, and an otherworldly silence settles over the scene.

Paul, lying on the sand, manages to rise to his elbows, his arms and face smoking with burns. He spots Harrison and the agents up the beach, unconscious.

Paul turns back to the light. He can only see a faint outline of the car, but what he does see, closer . . .

PAUL

My god.

Out of that pupil of darkness step three figures clad in shimmering blue suits just like Harrison's, but the suits gleam with active circuitry, and the figures wear large helmets. The visors have a reflective surface that hides their faces.

The figures speak in deep voices: an alien language interspersed with birdlike clicks.

Aliens 1 and 2 are holding silver STAFF-LIKE WEAPONS.

Alien 3 steps between them and past the overturned car. It strides to the beach, kneels, and opens a futuristic silver case. From the case, it produces a sleek silver probe, which it sticks into the soil. The device chirps out readings, lights flashing.

Alien 3 nods back to the others, opens a tiny box made of dark metal, and removes a small white sphere like a pearlescent marble. It presses this marble into the sand and then produces a glass dome, like a bell jar, and places it over the spot.

Alien 3 taps invisible settings on the top of the glass

dome, and the interior begins to glow with a warm amber light, and to hum.

PAUL

(*weakly*)

Please, don't hurt us.

Alien 3 cocks its head at Paul, not understanding, then returns to its work. The little device hums at a higher pitch.

Just then, something small shoots out of the sand and unfurls. It is an alien PLANT, with a bluish stem and leaves. It spreads and then blooms, producing a star-shaped, golden FLOWER.

Alien 1 makes a whooshing sound, as if in approval.

Alien 3 removes the glass dome. The flower shudders in the ocean breeze. The tips of its leaves shrivel slightly, but the plant hangs on.

The aliens nod their heads and speak excitedly to one another.

Paul watches, mesmerized. This changes everything.

An alert begins to flash on Alien 2's wrist. Just then, the hole in space behind them WOBBLES precariously, like a bubble about to burst. The aliens call urgently to one another.

Alien 3 quickly inverts the glass dome, scoops up the flower with some sand, and retreats to join the other two. They move into the light—

AGENT HOLDER

Stop! FBI!

Agent Holder has gotten to his feet. He staggers through the waves, his hands up as if in surrender.

The aliens pause, regarding him.

AGENT HOLDER

Tell us why you're here! I want to believe!

The aliens chirp to one another as Holder nears. Then Alien 1 crouches and fires a BURST of LIGHT ENERGY from its staff.

AGENT HOLDER

Ahhhh!

The bolt strikes Holder in the chest and sends him hurtling backward, lightning spiderwebbing all over his body.

AGENT TULLY

Holder!

She stumbles over to her fallen partner, who moans weakly. Blood dribbles out of his mouth. She rises, aims her gun, and FIRES, clipping Alien 3 as they depart. Alien 2 fires at her, narrowly missing.

The aliens retreat into the pupil, and it closes behind them. The gradient shrinks in on itself and vanishes. The ocean is calm again, the sky quiet.

HARRISON

Barbara! Max!

Harrison stumbles out into the surf. Paul looks out at the waves, blinking away the leftover brightness in his eyes, and spots the little car out there, overturned, listing in the waves.

There are the sounds of SHOUTING VOICES from behind. More FBI agents are running up the beach toward them, and the surviving campers are crowding around, soaked and shivering. Many of the RVs are overturned, some with their sides torn open. A HELICOPTER appears overhead.

Out in the water, Harrison reaches the overturned car and peers inside, but it is EMPTY.

HARRISON

Give them back!! It was supposed to be me!

He falls to his knees in the surf, face in his hands.

HARRISON

You were supposed to take me. . . .

Agent Tully walks over to Paul.

AGENT TULLY

What did you see?

PAUL

The truth.

AGENT TULLY

And what truth is that?

PAUL

We've got it all wrong.

They come in peace.

PART III

A SHADOW ON THE STARS

25

THE INTERVIEW: PART III

JANUARY 18, 2022

Dad closed the door and watched out the window. The red glow of the Barsuda van's taillights played across his face. "Are you okay?"

"Yeah," said Sylvan, breathing deep.

"Well, I hope that's the last we see of them," said Mom. "What was all that about that boy? Mason? I don't remember you ever mentioning him."

Sylvan shrugged. "He was Jovie's friend. She trusted him. And he was able to help her. Since I couldn't."

"Hey," said Mom. "What happened back in 2018 was serious. People died. It could have been you."

"But—" Sylvan caught himself.

"What?" Mom asked.

"Nothing."

You're not going to change Mom's mind, he heard Charlotte saying, sometime years ago on one of her rare visits. *She thinks the best way to make something go away is to never talk about it.* But it seemed to Sylvan that the opposite was true. Things that weren't spoken of kept growing, only they did it out of sight, beneath the surface, until soon their roots were everywhere. It was the reason Charlotte never came home anymore. It was the reason Sylvan felt the way he did now, as the people from Barsuda Solutions drove away.

I could have helped.

That thought, which had begun as a little sprout of regret, had, over the years, spread its roots through his mind; even now, it made him ball his fists in a fresh wave of fury.

But he kept it in. He couldn't let his parents know what his plans were, not now, this close to the end.

A silence passed over them. Outside, wind rattled the windowpanes; branches scratched the roof. A storm front would be coming through these next few days, almost like the planet was shuddering at what was about to happen.

It had been a similar night four years ago. Sylvan had been lying on his floor in his room, watching the electroscope. When it registered only a few twitches of radiation, he'd allowed himself to hope: maybe they'd been wrong about the gradient opening. Maybe Jovie would be all right.

But then the house had shaken, and they'd heard a distant rumble and the sounds of breaking glass and car alarms from around the neighborhood. The power had briefly gone out, and not long after, sirens had begun to wail in the distance. Soon, they'd learned from social media that four blocks at the south end of downtown had been damaged in a landslide, part of the bluff at Fort Riley had collapsed into the sea, and three houses had exploded due to a ruptured gas line. There had been twelve confirmed deaths.

For weeks afterward, crews of Barsuda workers had been cleaning up the damage. Satellite Beach had remained closed for months. The lighthouse had been damaged, too, and was still closed to this day, a chain link fence blocking access to the jetty, its little light dark.

It took until spring of that year to dig out those buildings downtown and begin repairs. By then, only a few spots were still taped off by Barsuda crews for cleanup.

Spring had also been the last time an article about a missing girl named Jovie Williams appeared in the *Herald*. That article cited a lack of any new leads, and pointed back to her bike being found in the bunkers as evidence that she'd perished when the bluff partially collapsed. And with that, the world had moved on.

But not Sylvan. He knew Jovie hadn't been in that landslide. Knew she'd left her bike at the bunkers so that she and Mason could go down to the beach on the night the gradient fully opened.

The messages he'd sent her later that night, the next day, the next week, had all gone undelivered. *Because she's over there*, Sylvan told himself. Something had gone wrong that night, and Jovie had ended up on the other side of the gradient. Trapped for these four long years.

Until now. Finally, it was time to get her back.

Forty-seven more hours, Sylvan thought, glancing at his phone. *Two thousand eight hundred and twenty minutes*, his brain added, seemingly always dividing and multiplying the world. These were the final moments of a countdown he'd been keeping for so long.

"I should get back to my charts," said Mom, getting up off the couch. "I'm still behind."

"Any new code seven cases?" Sylvan asked.

Mom shook her head. "Nope. I know that Dr. Wells is concerned that . . . *something* is going to happen, but as far as I can tell, it just doesn't seem that way."

It will, Sylvan thought. . . .

And yet as his parents got up and left the room, Sylvan remained on the couch, feeling a cool surge of adrenaline, and for just a moment, the unspeakable thought returned, the one that caused his heart to fill with doubt. It was silly now, after all these years, all the patient waiting and planning, but maybe exactly because he was so close to the end, the thought had become more urgent:

What if I'm wrong?

After all, when it really came down to it, he had no actual evidence that Jovie was still alive. What if she really did die in that landslide, or got burned by the radiation, or was washed away by the storm? None of those terrible outcomes could be entirely ruled out, could they?

No! Sylvan thrust himself to his feet. None of those things had happened, because Jovie wouldn't have *let* them happen. She was too smart, too determined. He knew she'd survived because she *had* to. He hurried to his room to go over his plan again.

But still, the doubt remained, a tremor inside him. All he could do was try to ignore it, and keep believing for two more days.

26

THE PROFILE PAGE

JANUARY 20, 2018
57 HOURS TO BREACH

The first thing Jovie did when she finally crawled out of bed the Saturday morning after sneaking into the Baxter plant was to peer out her window. There was no Barsuda van. No need to monitor her anymore.

This isn't your fight, Dr. Wells had said.

She also scanned the street with the spyglass, but there was no sign of Mason, either. Jovie couldn't quite tell if the quiver in her belly was disappointment, or relief.

Your friend is not like the other drifters. The more Jovie thought it over, the less she knew what to think.

There was no question how Mom was feeling about the events of the night before. Their only conversations all day were terse reminders that Jovie needed to clean the house and get her homework done, and that she wasn't to go anywhere. And so she'd spent the day staying out of Mom's range, until after dinner, when her taillights had finally disappeared down the road, at which point Jovie and Sylvan immediately got on a video chat.

"Hey!" he said with a big grin.

"Is this a good time?" Jovie asked.

"Yeah, Mom's not home, so we're good." And yet as soon as he said that, Sylvan's face fell and he looked away.

"What's wrong?" Jovie asked.

"Nothing," said Sylvan with a sigh. "Not really."

"Sylvan . . ."

"I was just worried about you last night. Before I got your text this morning, I thought . . . Well, I didn't know what to think."

"I'm sorry. It was stupid to go. Micah wasn't even there."

"No, it wasn't. I know you had to try." Sylvan looked away. Then he shook his head and readjusted his glasses. "What did you find out?"

Even though she was alone in the house, Jovie found herself lowering her voice as she recounted what had happened at the plant, and her conversation with Dr. Wells.

"So," Sylvan said when she was finished, "you think Micah is on the other side of the gradient, but *not* a drifter?"

"Not yet. Or, not completely. Dr. Wells said time

moves differently over there. Like, a thousand days here is only one day there."

"Whoa, that's almost three years per day," said Sylvan. "Well, closer to two point seven five."

"Micah disappeared on September twenty-first. How many days ago was that?"

Sylvan looked at his ceiling, but only for a moment. "One hundred twenty-one."

"So, if time there is—"

"Oh! You want to apply the time variable, right, so that would be one hundred twenty-one times twenty-four . . . divided by a thousand . . . that's two point nine hours."

"So even though Micah's been gone almost four months here, it would only be three hours for her over there. And I think the fact that I can remember her means there's still a chance to save her, but . . ." Jovie trailed off. Thinking of *how* she was going to save Micah reminded Jovie of something else Dr. Wells had said last night.

"What?" said Sylvan.

"It's just that . . . I think Mason might be lying to us." She told him how Mason had used his bracelet, and what Dr. Wells had said about him.

"Yeah." Sylvan made an apologetic face, like this news wasn't a surprise. "So . . . I did some more looking around last night. I'm going to send you a link."

A message arrived. Jovie tapped it, and a social media profile came up. At first, she had no idea what she was looking at, but then a name floated into her mind like a whisper. *Paul.* And then she remembered: Paul Ellis, Mason's dad. She also pictured the night before, the way he'd transformed and floated off.

Paul's profile picture looked like it was from a few years ago, or maybe it was just that his hair was neat and his face clean-shaven; he seemed to be standing with his arm around someone who had been cropped out of the photo.

Then Jovie noticed that his current home was listed as Far Haven . . . not Seattle. Her heart had already started to beat faster as she scrolled down his posts—a Christmas tree, a palm-lined beach, and then she reached a photo where Paul had his arm around a younger man, someone Jovie had never seen before. They were in the stands at a basketball game. There was a name tagged in the post: *Mason Ellis*.

"I don't get it," Jovie said. She clicked on the name and found the profile for a Mason Ellis of Far Haven. But it *wasn't* Mason . . . at least, not the boy she knew. This was an adult. His profile said he lived in Spokane, and he was born in 1991.

"Paul is with someone named Mason here, but he's twenty-seven," Jovie said.

"I know . . . ," Sylvan said again, in that tone like he knew where this was going.

Jovie could see the resemblance to Paul in this young

man's face. She looked at his posts, and the nervous flutter became a steady whir inside her; this Mason had a dog and a boyfriend, and appeared to work with kids, maybe as a teacher . . .

She returned to Paul's page and scrolled back further in time. There were many more photos of Paul and the person who was apparently his son. Skiing, sitting at restaurants. Even further back, and a woman Paul's age began appearing in photos, tagged as Naia Walters. She had her arm around the older Mason, and you could see the family resemblance between them, too.

My mom died, Mason had said.

With shaking fingers, Jovie clicked on Naia's name. Her page had more current posts; she lived in Portland. There were many pictures with that older Mason. Naia and Paul seemed to have separated, maybe a couple of years ago, around the time Paul had stopped posting. . . .

Jovie looked away from her phone, overcome for a moment with a light-headed feeling and a metallic taste in her mouth. "All of it was a lie," she said.

"I think your Mason isn't really *Mason*," said Sylvan. "He's definitely not Paul's son."

"But it doesn't make sense! He called Paul 'Dad,' a bunch of times, right to his face! Except . . ."

"What?"

Jovie tried to picture the times she'd been with Mason and Paul. Had Paul ever actually been fully conscious when Mason called him "Dad"? Jovie didn't think so. But Paul had called Mason "buddy," so they must have known each other well. . . .

"Jovie?" Sylvan asked.

"Sorry," she said quietly. "Maybe he's Paul's nephew or something? They'd been to concerts together and stuff."

"But then, why lie about who he is?"

"I don't know." Jovie remembered that in the bunkers, Mason had referred to Paul as "Dad" around Carina, too. Did that mean he'd also been lying to the drifters?

Jovie continued scrolling down Paul's page.

"I already checked his entire profile history," Sylvan said, "and I didn't see our Mason, or whatever his name is."

She scrolled back to the top and stopped on Paul's most recent post. It was a picture of a sunrise. The text below it read:

> To all those who have extended their love and care before now: Today is a new day. I am facing my demons and beginning the road to recovery. I can't undo the hurt I've caused those around me, and I can't change the history that haunts me, but I can try to change myself. I won't be on here for a while, but know that I am getting better.

That sounded like someone who really was dealing with a drug problem, as Mason had described. And he had been stealing medications and giving them to Paul to treat his withdrawal—Jovie was *certain* that had been real. So were his tears last night, when he'd let Paul go. And yet . . .

Who *was* this boy she'd been hanging out with? And why had he been lying to her?

"Maybe he's, like, in trouble," said Sylvan. "Like, on the run or something."

"What are you talking about?"

"You know, like, shoplifting, or—"

"He's not a criminal, Sylvan!" Jovie said. Of course, she'd seen him steal many things, but all had been to help the drifters. "Maybe he doesn't want to be found. Like, by his real parents, or something. Maybe something bad happened in his past."

"I don't know," said Sylvan, "but . . . I think he's up to something. And I think it has to do with the gradient."

A chill rushed through Jovie, thinking again of the way Mason could control whether he was visible, and extend that power to her, too. . . . That bracelet. Was it from his mom? If not, where had he gotten it?

"I don't trust him, Jovie," said Sylvan.

"Yeah, I know you don't."

"Do you?"

Jovie looked out her window at the dark street. "I don't know. You're probably right . . . but I need him. Micah is across the gradient. And whoever Mason really is, he's also the only person who can really help me find her."

"Thanks," Sylvan muttered.

"Come on, you know what I mean." Jovie rolled her eyes. "He can help me actually get to the breach."

"*To* the breach?" said Sylvan. "Why would you want to do that?"

"So I can get a message to Micah, or at least find out exactly what's over there, or who took her."

"Is that possible?"

"I don't know yet," Jovie said. But she was starting to suspect that maybe Mason might.

"But Barsuda isn't going to let you close enough to—"

"I haven't figured it all out, Sylvan!" Jovie nearly shouted. She lurched up off her bed and paced into the kitchen.

"Okay," he said quietly. "Sorry."

She exhaled heavily. "Look, the gradient is opening in two days. I'm just going to have to find Mason and ask him what the deal is, point-blank."

Sylvan made a face.

"What?"

"It's just that, well, usually when you confront someone about their evil plan, they get angry—"

"He's not some supervillain, Sylvan! We don't even know if he has a *plan*."

"No, but he still could be dangerous. I just think you should be careful. Whatever he's up to, he clearly doesn't want you to know. He already lied to you on the dock, didn't he? Why would he tell you the truth now?"

"Because we're . . ." She was going to say "friends," but were they? If he was keeping so much from her? Jovie dropped down on the couch. "What do I do, then?"

"If it were me," said Sylvan, "and I wasn't grounded, I'd follow him around. See what he's up to."

"You think I should spy on him?"

"He's lying to you already, what's the difference? It's what a good detective would do."

Jovie pursed her lips. She wanted to argue this point, but . . . "You're probably right."

"Or what if—"

"What?"

"Nah, nothing."

"Tell me."

Sylvan's face scrunched. "Just . . . with Barsuda last night, and now all this Mason stuff . . . I know you want to find Micah, but what if you just stayed away instead? The gradient is dangerous. You still have the spyglass, and we still have our cosmic ray data. We could wait until after the breach, and then we can keep researching. We could even get help, like from professional scientists or whatever, like we talked about."

Jovie shook her head. "Sylvan—"

"No, just listen for a second," Sylvan said. "We'd have four years to come up with a good plan. And like you said, for Micah, that would only be . . . one point four six days!"

He looked at her with his wide, young eyes, and Jovie felt a little sting behind her heart.

"It sounds like a good plan," she said finally.

Sylvan's gaze fell. "But . . . you're going to try anyway."

"I don't know if Micah has four years, a day and a half, whatever. So much of the world has forgotten her already."

They were both silent for a moment. Looking at Sylvan, Jovie was reminded of watching Micah's posts from the band trip, and how it had hurt to see Micah going out and doing stuff that she wasn't part of, feeling like Micah shouldn't have needed that, because they had each other. . . . She suspected Sylvan felt that way right now.

"I'm sorry," Jovie said, guilt squeezing her. "You've been a really good friend—I mean, you *are* a good friend, and I probably should be listening to you."

Sylvan nodded, but his face was ashen. "What's your next move?"

"I have to try to find Mason tomorrow. And then I'm not sure."

"Let me know what happens," he said. "And please be careful, okay?"

"I will."

Another silence passed between them.

"I guess I should go," said Sylvan. "I'm meeting up

with some people to play online or something."

"Okay." Jovie felt an anxious storm brewing inside her, a feeling like she was doing something wrong, even though she wasn't. Was she? "Have fun in your game."

Sylvan gave a small nod. "Okay."

He left the call, and Jovie found herself alone in the quiet house. She set about heating up some dinner, and finding something to watch, and ignoring the stillness and silence all around her, as well as her worried thoughts, by reminding herself: *Just two more days*. She was close. She had to be.

27

THE HIDDEN ROOM

JANUARY 21, 2018
36 HOURS TO BREACH

After a restless night, Jovie woke Sunday morning with a grim agenda: as soon as she finished her shift at the coffee stand, she would have to disobey her mom's strict order to come right home, and instead search for the person she'd known as Mason.

But before she could even decide how she was going to find him, he appeared right in front of her.

It had been a slow morning beneath a gloomy bank of fog, with few customers. Elena had been by, seen the lack of action, and promptly announced that she'd be back after running a few errands. Jovie had texted with Sylvan to wish him a happy birthday—his parents were taking him to Olympia for the day to visit the science center and have dinner at his favorite burger place—and she was sitting idly, sipping a mocha, when a voice from the ordering window startled her:

"Hey." As Mason flickered into view, Jovie tried to keep the suspicion off her face. She only had a moment to decide what she was going to do. . . .

"Hey," she replied mildly, putting on an expression of curiosity, and just a little dejection. "You're okay." She crossed her arms. "I didn't know what happened to you the other night."

"I know." Mason held out his hands in a helpless gesture. "I was lucky to get out of there. Hiding in different offices, making my way up to the outside. I saw them put you in the police car . . . but I figured I shouldn't come by your house or anything. In case they were watching."

"Actually, they're gone," Jovie said. "Guess they figured I was no longer a threat now that I'm grounded." Jovie looked at him, waiting. The next thing he said *had* to be about his bracelet, about that look he'd given her, about how he'd just disappeared. . . .

But Mason exhaled. Did he look relieved? "I'm just glad you're okay. I came here three times yesterday looking for you."

Jovie nodded and turned to the espresso machine, fighting the urge to laugh. The feeling tickled her throat, so insistent that she had to forcibly steel her expression.

Every single thing coming out of his mouth sounded *so* false now. How had she ever believed a word he'd said? "Mocha?" she asked, swallowing her urge to confront him.

"Oh yeah, that would be great."

As she started the machine, she added, "I'm sorry about your dad," and glanced at him, watching for any clue.

But the hurt that passed over Mason's face looked real as ever. "I saw him, out in the woods, after. Well, I saw his essence."

"Me too."

"What did Dr. Wells say to you?"

You mean what did she say about YOU? Jovie almost replied. She steamed the milk and put the drink together as she spoke. "I think . . . Barsuda might not be what we thought. Wells said they're trying to close the gradient, not open it. They're not even after its energy. She thinks it's coming from another universe, and that someone or something on the other side is causing it."

"Huh," Mason said, like none of this quite surprised him.

He knows something about this, Jovie thought, *maybe a LOT more than he's saying.* "She thinks the breach could eventually destroy the town, maybe even the whole planet if it's not stopped."

Mason blew air out of his cheeks. "That sounds very

end-of-the-world. Did she know anything about Micah?"

"She said Micah hadn't been there, and she's not in town . . . but I think she's on the other side of the gradient, only she might *not* have drifted there."

Mason's brow wrinkled. "How do you think that could've happened?"

Jovie handed him the mocha. "Maybe whoever is over there, like whoever made the gradient, took her or something. I was thinking: if we could get close enough tomorrow night, we could find out, or even contact her."

Mason sipped the drink. "Legendary," he said, offering her a smile, and she could see that tentative look in his eye, like he was hoping things were okay. She did her best to smile back. "That would be dangerous," he went on. "Barsuda will be looking for us, and you saw what the gradient did to that agent."

"But you could get me close," Jovie said, studying him. "Couldn't you?"

"I think so, but—" Mason looked over his shoulder. A pickup truck was pulling up to the stand.

"One sec," said Jovie.

Mason ducked out of the way, and Jovie served a cup of drip and a muffin to a sleepy-looking older man. The truck had just pulled away when Elena's minivan returned. For the first time Jovie could remember, she was actually back early. But maybe this timing would be perfect. . . .

"That's my boss," Jovie said.

"Can we talk more later?" said Mason. "We could meet on that dock at the park again, or—"

"I'm super grounded," said Jovie. "But what about tomorrow? After school?"

"Sure." Mason looked at his feet. "I guess. That's only a few hours before the breach, though. I have to help the drifters fortify the bunkers, and Carina is worried they won't be enough protection."

The drifters, Jovie thought, *that's what he said. Not "we."* "How about we meet on the trail to the bluff?"

"Okay." Mason nodded to himself like he was doing math in his head.

"What are you up to the rest of the day?" Jovie asked, trying to sound nonchalant.

"Not much. . . . I have a few supplies to get, and then just helping at the bunkers."

Elena pulled around the far side of the stand. Jovie heard her van door open. "You should go before she comes in."

"Right." He breathed deep. "See you tomorrow. I, um . . ." Mason gave her a pained look, like he wanted to say more, but slipped away as the door to the stand opened.

"How's it going?" said Elena brightly.

Jovie steeled herself. She had to act fast. Time to do some lying of her own. She put a hand over her stomach and a queasy look on her face. "Hey," she said weakly.

"Oh, what's wrong?"

"My stomach," Jovie lied. "It's been getting worse all morning. I was fine last night. . . ."

A car was pulling up. Jovie slackened her expression further.

"Here, let me get this one." Elena traded places with her. "Could it be something you ate for dinner?"

"We had leftovers," said Jovie. She leaned against the counter for effect. "I thought maybe the refried beans smelled a little weird, but if you heat them up a bit, it's usually fine."

Elena greeted the customer and started making a latte. "It could also be something infectious," she said, lowering her voice. She glanced worriedly at Jovie's hands. "Whenever one of the twins gets something, they pass it right to the other."

"Yeah. . . ." Jovie tried for her best disappointed tone. "Maybe it's safer if I go?" She touched her belly again. "I mean, I could probably manage—"

"No, you're right," Elena said. "You've covered for me so many times, Jovie. It's no problem."

"Thanks."

Jovie gathered her things, making sure to move slowly, sickly, but once she was outside and on her bike, she pedaled hard.

This trickery would buy her an extra hour. If she sent

her mom a message saying Elena needed her to stay late, that would buy her even more time. After that, she probably had even another half hour of *My phone died* and *We did some extra cleaning.* All of that assumed Elena wouldn't call home to see how Jovie was feeling. Hopefully Jovie could count on her to be as preoccupied as she normally was.

But once she biked away from the stand, Jovie began to doubt her plan: How exactly was she going to spy on someone who she might not even be able to see? And it wasn't like she could sneak into the bunkers without being noticed. What was she really going to learn? *I should've just confronted him*, she thought. Told him all the things she knew he'd lied about, and asked him why. This was probably going to be a waste of time—

And yet, she had just crossed Port Street when she spotted Mason ahead, biking in plain sight toward downtown.

Jovie let him get a little farther ahead, then followed. He wove through downtown, past Salt & Sand, and turned onto one narrow street, then another. When Jovie reached the next corner, she halted sharply. Mason was nowhere in sight, but just ahead, a Barsuda van was parked on the side of the road, and Jovie saw that it was directly across from the Treasure Trove, Harrison's shop. It was a sagging wooden building, like a one-story pioneer house, the rickety sign written in faded script lettering reminiscent of a pirate ride, the small front yard cluttered with junk and half-rusted hulks.

Where had Mason gone? Jovie ducked back into the shadow of the corner building and got out the spyglass. That's when she saw him, leaning his bike against the fence of the yellow Victorian house beside the Trove. He'd made himself fade, and now he ducked between the two buildings.

Why would Mason come here? He'd made it sound like he only vaguely knew who Harrison was, but Paul and Harrison had been friends. Had he come to inform Harrison that Paul had drifted?

Jovie crossed the parking lot behind the corner building and reached the white wooden fence that bordered the Victorian house's backyard. Through the spyglass, she saw the top of Mason's head as he circled around the Treasure Trove. There was a back door as well as a garage, but Jovie saw Mason stop beneath a small window. There was a banging sound, a splintering squeal, and then Mason pushed the window open and hauled himself through.

Jovie stood there for a moment, her mind racing. Why would he be sneaking into the Treasure Trove? She sighed to herself. Too many questions, too many lies. She leaned her bike against the fence and hoisted herself over it, then hurried across the yard of the Victorian house and climbed that fence as well. She landed, out of breath, behind the Treasure Trove, and stood there staring at the little open window. . . .

Five minutes later, Mason slipped back out the window—

To find Jovie waiting, arms crossed.

"Oh hey," he said, his eyes widening. "What are you—"

"No, what are *you* doing here?" Jovie said.

Mason narrowed his eyes at her. "Were you following me?" He glanced up the side of the house like he was thinking of running off.

"I was," said Jovie, trying to keep her voice from shaking, "because you've been lying to me."

"I—"

"Haven't you?"

Mason blurted an incredulous laugh. "What do you think I'm lying about?"

"Your name, for one. You're not Mason," Jovie said, and the shock on his face confirmed it. "You're not Paul's son. I've seen his profile page. His real son is, like, twenty-five."

"Th-That's not right. . . . ," Mason stammered.

"I don't think you're really from Seattle, either."

"I—"

"And you have that bracelet, and the way you control the drift. You're not even a real drifter, are you?"

Mason just looked at her for a moment, gaping. "Why

would I be living in a bunker for months if I wasn't a drifter?"

Jovie glared at him. "Was that story you told me about your mom even true? Or was that another—"

Mason's voice sliced the air like the hiss of a snake. "It was." He narrowed his eyes at her again. "Every word." Jovie saw that his hands had curled into tight fists at his sides, his face growing a searing red.

"Okay. . . ." Jovie felt a flash of nervous energy. She didn't know who this boy really was—which meant she also didn't know if he was dangerous. "Then why did you lie to me about everything else? I thought we were friends."

"We are—" Mason looked at the ground, his expression still furious, but Jovie saw tears rimming his eyes.

She lowered her voice. "We aren't friends if you're lying to me about everything."

"Not *everything*." Mason looked up. The anger had passed, and he just looked so sad. "I loved Paul like a father, but . . ." He looked at the sky and sighed. "You're right. He's not my dad. When I found him, he was so delusional from his addiction that he thought I was his son, his *real* son, even though I'm like, ten years younger. But it would be easy for him to be confused, with our history."

"What history?" said Jovie carefully.

Mason glanced back at the bathroom window. "Could I just show you?"

"Show me *what*?"

"I want to tell you the truth now, but why should you believe me? So, if you come inside, I can show you proof."

"So I just caught you, and now you want me to come into a creepy antiques shop?"

Mason shrugged. "I actually want you to come into the secret basement room of the creepy antiques shop." When Jovie just stared at him, Mason rolled his eyes. "Believe me, I know how that sounds. I'll understand if you don't want to, or if you don't want to see me again, but what I can show you will help with tomorrow night. With finding Micah."

Jovie wanted to shout at him, even to storm off, but more than that . . . "Fine," she said. "Just tell me the truth."

Mason nodded. "Follow me." He climbed back through the window. Once he was through, he turned and offered his hand.

"I got it," said Jovie. She gripped the sill and hauled herself up. It crossed her mind, as she slid through the window, that this was the second time in three days that she was trespassing.

Jovie found herself in a grimy bathroom with stained white porcelain and a chipped tile floor. Mason led the way out into the store, past the tightly spaced shelves stacked deep with junk and coated with dust.

"Harrison isn't here?" Jovie said, whispering anyway.

"He's over at Salt and Sand doing what he does every

Sunday: writing letters to government agencies trying to get information released to the public about Barsuda. He knows they're watching this place. I don't think he's been here in a while."

Mason moved past the counter to a doorway and pushed aside a curtain. On the other side was a room that seemed to be part office, part kitchen, part bedroom. There was a desk piled high with papers—Jovie noticed the words OVERDUE or FINAL NOTICE on many—a little sink and stove covered with dishes and pots and pans, and a cot in the corner with a sleeping bag twisted on top. A mini refrigerator served as a bedside table. The room smelled of unwashed clothes and old food.

There was a map of the coast, like a nautical chart, on one wall. The other three walls were bare.

Mason pulled the cot away from the wall and ducked behind it. He gripped a metal handle that was bolted to the floor and hauled open a trapdoor. It groaned on metal hinges, revealing ladderlike stairs that descended into darkness.

"Down here," said Mason.

Jovie's heart pounded. "How do you know about all this?" she asked.

Mason looked at her with a bitter expression. "I wish I didn't."

Jovie watched him climb down the ladder. Her thoughts were buzzing with a strange mix of confusion and suspicion; they were close to something, some truth, but what? And should she really go any farther? But she dangled her feet over the edge and started down.

She found herself in a low passageway with dirt walls. Long boards had been laid over the hard-packed floor. The air was cool and musty smelling. Mason plugged a string of holiday lights into an electrical outlet that hung from the ceiling and started walking up the passage.

Jovie followed him through the tunnel to a doorway made of concrete blocks that led into an unfinished basement area, empty except for a simple folding table and chair in the center. The walls and floor were concrete; the ceiling was the beams and warped floorboards of the store above. There was another hanging box with a light switch, which turned on a string of naked lightbulbs, casting the space in stark light. The walls were bare except for one corner that had been curtained off with a blue plastic tarp.

Mason stopped at the table. "He's been doing his own research into the storms."

On the table, Jovie saw a map of Far Haven covered in notes and arrows. Most of the marks were on or near Satellite Beach. There was also a small *x* there with an arrow pointing to it, and the word *journal*.

"Harrison must have been the one who found Micah's journal," said Jovie, remembering what Micah's mom had said. "Why would he return it secretly?"

"He's the biggest weirdo in town," said Mason. "He probably figured if he showed up with it, they'd think he had kidnapped her or something."

Beside the map was a plastic instrument with a digital display. It had a symbol at its base that Jovie thought she recognized: *radiation*. Beside it was a handwritten chart with dates and numbers. Jovie saw that the last date was January 22, and it was circled in thick red marker.

Jovie thought of what Harrison had said at the gas station. *Can't screw it up this time.* "It looks like he knows tomorrow night is the breach," Jovie said, pointing to the date. "He might not be as out of it as he seems. Could he be planning something?"

"It's probably for his stupid website," said Mason.

"Is this why you came down here? To see what he knows about the breach?"

"Not really." Mason pushed aside the map, revealing a large black-and-white photo with stained and tattered edges. "This is the Vanescere Bathhouse." The photo showed three long rectangular pools with lap lines, gleaming in sunlight diffused by the steamed-up glass walls. Giant potted palm trees stood in each corner beside sofas covered with pillows. Standing on the balcony in the foreground were two adults and a child, posing for the picture. One adult was in a three-piece suit, while the other was in a heavy bathrobe, his hair slicked back. A tag at the bottom of the frame read: *Arthur, Roy, and Harry, 1961.*

Young Harry, Ruth had said, and peering at the photo now, Jovie thought she could see at least some similarity between him and Mason that would've given Ruth's addled memory that idea.

But Mason was tapping another circle of thick red marker, one that had been drawn over an area of the baths behind the men. There didn't appear to be anything in it.

Jovie was already getting out the spyglass. When she gazed through it, ghostly bathers began to shimmer into view all over the photo: some swimming, some leaning on the walls, one perched on the edge of the pool as if about to jump in. Where she could make out an expression, they seemed to be smiling. There was one woman in that red circle, though she was too distant to see any specific details.

"Is that Harrison's mother?" Jovie guessed. "She died in the explosion. Or drifted, I guess."

"Died," said Mason. "Harrison wanted to believe otherwise, until he saw what exposure to the gradient could do firsthand in 1994. The only way someone could cross the gradient was as an essence, or . . ." Mason stepped away.

Jovie looked up after him. "Or what?"

Mason moved to the corner of the room and pulled aside the blue tarp, revealing a small table. Behind that, hanging from an exposed pipe, was a strange blue suit whose fabric shimmered in an uncanny way. It had a metal ring around the neck; the helmet that likely fit it hung on a hook beside the suit. In the center of the suit's chest, Jovie saw rough stitching made with black thread, as if a hole had been sewn up. Rows of opaque bumps along the arms and legs might have been lights of some kind, and there was a panel on one of the forearms with eight black buttons, smooth and rounded, like oily droplets—or, Jovie realized, polished stones.

"Behold, the Blue Bathymetrist," Mason said.

But even the wonder of this suit—*from another world*, Jovie realized—couldn't keep her attention from the items that were lying on the little table in front of it.

On top was a fresh piece of lined notebook paper with a handwritten note. But it was the item beneath it that caught Jovie's attention: a brittle, yellowed front page of the *Far Haven Herald*. The headline read "'Ascension Camp' Tragedy: Beach Campout Beset by Freak Storm, Over a Dozen Dead/Missing."

Beside the text of the article, there was a photo of three people: two adults and a young teen. The caption read: *Harrison Westervelt, organizer of the event, with his wife, Barbara, and son, Max, both among the missing.*

Jovie ran her finger over the photo. . . .

And then she looked up at the boy standing beside her, his face exactly the same, as if that picture had been taken yesterday.

28

THE CONFESSION

JANUARY 21, 2018
31 HOURS TO BREACH

Jovie just stared at Mason, trying to process it all. The truth was rushing through her, making her head swim.

He looked back at her queasily. "Surprise."

"You . . ." Jovie didn't know where to begin.

"I'm Max Westervelt. Nice to meet you. Um, Mason wants you to know that he's sorry he didn't tell you the truth, and—"

"Stop it!" Jovie snapped. "Don't make it, like, a thing." She looked at the article and the photo again.

The boy she now knew to be Max reached over and plucked the page of notebook paper from the table and folded it.

"What's that?" Jovie asked.

"That's what I broke in here to leave for him. I wrote Harrison a letter."

"Harrison . . . is your father."

Max breathed deep. "Yeah. But now . . . I don't know." He slipped the letter into his pocket. "I think it might just make things worse for him."

"Harrison thinks you're dead," said Jovie. "That you've been dead since 1994. But if you weren't . . . it's been twenty-four years, you—" Her eyes went wide. There was only one explanation, but it still felt outrageous to say it out loud. "You were across the gradient. You had to have been, otherwise there's no way you'd still look the same."

"I'm four and a half months older than I was in that photo," Max said, "but it's been twenty-four years since that night." He looked away. "Two of my grandparents died while I was gone. My favorite record shop, where I used to buy CDs, is gone. . . . I mean, *CDs* are gone." He laughed. "You know Lucia, who owns Salt and Sand? She and I were supposed to go to a Valentine's Day semi-formal dance in February. In *1994.* Now she's almost forty and has two kids my age. I'm not a drifter, but I might as well be."

This felt too big for Jovie to wrap her mind around. The very idea that Max, standing in front of her, was actually from over two decades ago. That such a thing could even be possible. "But you said no one could survive the gradient if they weren't a drifter," said Jovie. "You also said it was a one-way trip."

Max motioned to sit. "Well, you *can* survive . . . if someone takes you across. Someone with the technology to heal your injuries before you die from them."

Jovie eyed the suit. "Someone from the other side."

Max nodded. "They're called Lahmurians."

"Lahmurians," Jovie repeated. "You're talking about—about aliens?"

"I guess, technically," he said. "But they're not like, little green men or anything," Max rushed to add. "They're very intelligent and kind. I was only with them for about eight days—eight days over there, I mean—"

"Time is slower there," Jovie said, and she motioned at Max: "Obviously."

"Yeah, but it was long enough for me to get to know them. They saved my life, and tried to save my mom's, but—" Max cut himself off, and looked away. "It was too late."

Jovie heard the real hurt in Max's voice. "I'm so sorry," she said gently. She pointed to the suit. "What happened to that person?"

"She was the first Lahmurian to try to cross through the portal."

"The portal?"

"Yeah, that's what they call the gradient. Anyway, she was their admiral, back in 1898. She came through and found herself on the *Endurance*. That's where she got shot. Uncle Arthur discovered the suit in the shipwreck, and then he died in it, too, when the bathhouse exploded. My grandfather, Roy, found him in the wreckage before the police arrived, and hid the suit away until Dad got his hands on it."

Jovie looked back at the article. "What happened to you that night? In 1994?"

"We were trying to get off the beach, and our car got stuck in the waves and flipped." Max winced and crossed his arms. "I think, like, if I could have just gotten my seat belt off faster, if I hadn't panicked, I could have gotten us out. I'm a pretty good swimmer, but I had bad burns already, and I just . . ." He shook his head. "Our car was practically in the gradient at that point. The Lahmurians pulled us out and took us across, but it was too late. My mom had already drowned."

Jovie didn't know where to begin. "Who are they? Or, I mean, what do they want? If they're opening the gradient, that means they're causing the drift, and responsible for all the people who have gotten sick or died. . . ."

"They're not trying to hurt anyone," said Max. "That's part of why they sent me back."

"They sent you back?"

"Yeah. So I could gather data to help them figure out what kind of damage they're really causing."

"So," Jovie said, "you're, like, a spy for them?"

"Not a spy. . . . Well, kinda. It was the least I could do."

"But why are they opening the portal?"

"I . . . can't tell you," said Max.

Jovie crossed her arms. "Are you kidding me right now?"

Max ran his hand through his hair. "I want to, I really do. But the Lahmurians don't want me to tell anyone—they're pretty mistrustful of humans. From their point of view, we keep trying to kill them. But that's not why I can't tell you. If you knew, it would put you in danger from Barsuda."

"In case you forgot, I had a nice long talk with Barsuda. I don't think they're actually a danger. Not like that, anyway. And also, if you don't want Barsuda to know, that makes it sound like Barsuda won't like what your alien friends are doing. And since Barsuda is actually trying to protect people here, that makes me think what your friends are doing is bad."

"It's not like that. The Lahmurians are in danger, they . . ." Max paused, collected himself. "I swore I wouldn't tell. And I owe them my life."

Jovie looked from the suit to Max's wrist. "Your bracelet, is it . . . Lahmurian?"

"No," said Max. "It really is my mom's—I mean, it was. It's the only thing I have left of her now. The Lahmurians just added the button to it. It's like a computer chip. It records data, but it also lets me drift. Their tech is . . . just a bit more advanced than ours."

Jovie felt a noisy crowd of thoughts in her head. There was so much more here that she didn't yet understand, but she found that she believed what Max was telling her, what he *would* tell her, anyway.

And yet the same problem still remained: "Do they have Micah?" she asked.

"I think so," said Max. "I mean, I think you're right," he added quickly. "That she's over there."

"Did you see her?"

Max shook his head. "No."

"But why would they have taken her?"

"Maybe she got too close to the gradient and was injured or something."

Jovie thought of Micah's last drawing. "And do you think you could find out tomorrow night?"

Max nodded, but also raised his eyebrows, as if this idea was daunting. "I think I can. Even Barsuda's goggles can't detect me if I put this thing to full strength." He tapped his bracelet.

"Is that how you got back here from . . . over there?"

"Yeah. The bracelet can simulate the way the drift changes a person's matter, and let you cross unharmed—well, aside from some pretty bad nausea."

"Okay." But Jovie also found herself frowning at him. "You *knew* Barsuda weren't the ones opening the gradient the whole time, and you didn't tell me. And what about the drifters? Were you even trying to help them at all?"

"Yes," said Max. "I knew Barsuda wasn't causing the gradient, but I didn't know what they were actually trying to do. And I couldn't tell the drifters the real cause, either, for the same reason I can't tell you. Besides, it wouldn't have changed what's happening to them. What's happening to all of us. . . . But this data can." Max tapped his bracelet. "Once the Lahmurians can analyze the readings I've taken of the gradient from this side, and of the drifters and Barsuda's barricade, they should be able to adjust their portal so it works correctly. And that will stop all this."

"Too late for those who've already gone, though," said Jovie.

"Yeah, but . . ." Max seemed on the verge of telling her more, but instead he paused for a moment before continuing. "The Lahmurians have been trying to open the gradient for a long time. I mean, a long time by *our* time. But every time they try, something goes wrong—you know about all the disasters. I guess at some point, the navy started really investigating what was happening here, and then when the portal—sorry, the gradient—opened in 2010, they launched a small nuclear warhead into it to try to close it. The bomb only made it partially through when it exploded. I guess that was the real story behind the Baxter accident. On the other side, where I was, it severely damaged the Lahmurians' ship. There was a minute there where it seemed like we wouldn't make it. Why are you making that face?"

"I—" Jovie blew air out of her cheeks. "I've lived with the Baxter accident for basically my whole life. Dr. Wells said it was a cover story, but . . . I mean, a *bomb*? The navy could have nuked the whole town."

"Yeah."

"You're sure that's what happened?"

"I was there."

This truth knifed its way into Jovie's thoughts. She thought of how, all throughout her life, her mom had said this was *only Far Haven*, and she realized, too, that Mom had been right to mistrust the Baxter story, that her belief in all that weird conspiracy stuff had been based on a suspicion that had been correct. Everyone in this town had lived their lives and based their attitudes, their fears and dreams, on a story that wasn't true.

People like Dr. Wells said they were hiding the truth to protect people—Max was saying a version of that now—as if that was a kindness, but it still took away people's ability to choose. As a result, everyone in Far Haven had lived in the shadows of those nuclear towers, believing on some level that they weren't quite important enough to be protected, to be valued. It was an attitude that shaped every thought, every moment of people's lives, good or bad. Why try harder, work harder, take a risk, even keep your business open, if this was *only Far Haven*?

It would not have been great news, Jovie thought, to learn that your town might have to be sacrificed in some sort of cosmic conflict that just so happened to be occurring on your shore, but that actually was a very different thing than what they'd been led to believe. If Dr. Wells, or whoever in the town or government, had trusted them with the truth, maybe they would have evacuated by now. Or fought harder to get the gradient properly investigated sooner. But instead that truth hadn't been shared, and so the people in town had made their own: that Far Haven was a place that was lesser, that was lame . . . when really, it was a place that had been deceived. Jovie, her parents, even Micah . . . How had their lives been shaped by this lie? How might things have been different, even in little ways, had they been told the truth?

"Are you okay?" Max asked.

"Not really," said Jovie. She felt a simmering inside, and noticed she was trembling, like she wanted to explode.

"You probably wouldn't believe me, but I was planning on telling Carina about this tonight."

"I wasn't thinking about you," Jovie snapped. "Sorry." She crossed her arms. Her thoughts had left her feeling paralyzed and on the edge of despair. *Come on*, she told herself. She wasn't sure what she could do about the town, about the lies, but she could still try to find Micah, and maybe help the drifters. "You were going to tell Carina *tonight*? That's convenient timing."

Max sighed. "I know it sounds like a lie, but it's true. If the drifters can survive tomorrow night's storm, the cycle ends. It doesn't mean they'll be able to get back to their lives, but it does mean they'll be safer from the gradient, from what happened to Paul."

Max looked away, and Jovie tried to sort through her thoughts for a moment. So much still confused her. "Why did you say he was your dad?"

Max exhaled loudly. He didn't sound annoyed, more just tired, or maybe relieved. "When I went to investigate the drifters, I never thought I'd find Paul with them. But I saw the condition he was in . . . I just couldn't let him go like that." Max's voice quieted. "Paul was a good guy. Always nice to me. He was around our house all the time—I think he even lived with us when I was younger. He would hang out with me, throw Frisbee, talk about school stuff. Dad was always too busy. Paul was nice to my mom, too. They worked on house projects a lot together while Dad was hidden away in his office."

"And he took you to see Nirvana," said Jovie, pointing to his T-shirt.

A smile briefly appeared, and the way it lit up Max's face made Jovie think it was the happiest she'd seen him. "November 1993, Nirvana unplugged with the Melvins opening. That was such an awesome night. Dad would never have done that with me." Max blinked and looked away. "Anyway, there he was in the drifter camp, so much older, and so ill, and . . . I had to do something. I thought if I could help him get better, maybe I could get him out of the drift before the gradient opened again. And as I got to know Carina and the other drifters, I wanted to help them, too. But all of that meant I needed a cover story. So I said I was one of them. Paul had already mistaken me for his son the first time I saw him—he was pretty delirious—so I went with that. Then you showed up that afternoon, and I couldn't blow my cover. Plus, at the time, I didn't think we'd end up being, you know, friends."

"Are we friends?" Jovie asked. "Not sure a mountain of lies is really the best foundation for a friendship."

"I want to be." Max shrugged. "But most of what I want doesn't work out."

Jovie sighed. She felt stormy inside. She wasn't as angry as she had been—she couldn't imagine what Max had been through. Losing his mom, living in an alien world while decades went by here . . .

And yet she didn't want to feel bad for him. She wasn't sure he deserved that just yet, not when he'd been lying to her this whole time about what he knew, while all she'd wanted was to find her friend. "Did you already know all that stuff we were figuring out in Sylvan's basement, about the cycle and the dates?"

"I actually didn't," said Max. "That's the truth. The bracelet is designed to alert me when a storm is going to happen, but only, like, *right* before. I didn't know the math behind it. I didn't know about the health problems like your mom had, or anything about the cosmic rays. I didn't really even know the history of the town. I mean, Dad would talk about that bathhouse stuff sometimes, but I was never really paying attention. He would tell me—when he bothered to talk to me at all—that he was researching a big mystery, that he was going to "uncover the truth," and I saw all the weird stuff on the walls of his office, but I wasn't interested, more just resentful that he chose that over me and Mom."

Jovie found that she believed this, too. "Okay," she said, feeling like her thoughts were full to the point of spilling over. "Back to tomorrow night: you can use your bracelet to check on Micah. If it allows you to cross . . . would it let Micah cross, too? Could you, like, bring her back?"

"Maybe," Max said. "I mean, I probably could."

"Wait." A fresh wave of doubt rushed up inside Jovie. "Is that something you could have done the other night, during the last storm? Could Micah be back here already?"

"Oh, no." Max shook his head emphatically. "Time is only stabilized between the two universes when the portal is fully opened. That *eye* that Harrison was talking about."

"The breach," Jovie whispered.

"Huh?"

"That's what Dr. Wells calls it."

"Oh. Well, during the other storms, there would have been no time for me to cross over and talk to the Lahmurians about getting her back here safely. Those storms are over in like a minute over there, and besides, they're too dangerous for the Lahmurians—" Max glanced at her quickly as he said this, as if he was catching himself.

"What do you mean by that? Too dangerous? I thought the Lahmurians made the portal."

"Oh yeah, but the Lahmurians aren't the same as we are physically. They tried using this technology on themselves," he said, tapping his bracelet, "but it didn't work. They can only come through to this world when the portal is at full power."

"But if . . ." Jovie stopped herself, her thoughts in a knot.

"What?" Max was eyeing her worriedly.

Jovie pictured Micah's drawing, the last one she'd made in her journal before dropping it in the sand. The figure coming out of the water on the night she'd disappeared. "If the Lahmurians can only cross during the full breach, then . . . who took Micah across in September?" Jovie saw a queasy look come over Max. "What . . . ?"

He looked at the floor like he was trying to think of what to say.

"Wait." Jovie felt a fresh wave of nervous energy.

"What are you not telling me now?"

"Well . . ." Max rubbed his hands together. "I told you I got here in October, but . . . there wasn't actually a storm that month. It, um . . ."

"Oh my god." Suddenly, Jovie saw it. Micah's drawing, the silhouette . . . "Was that *you*?"

Max didn't have to answer. Jovie saw it in his face, and his fidgeting hands. "Look," he began, "it was an accident—"

"What did you do to her?" Jovie nearly shrieked, her voice echoing around the concrete walls.

"Nothing!" said Max. "I mean, not really. But I came out of the portal and I was really disoriented and sick, and I fell down in the surf, and . . . next thing I knew, there was this girl kneeling next to me and asking me if I was okay. I could barely hear her, I was so out of it. She tried to help me stand up, and I could see that she was glowing a little, you know, like a drifter, not that I even knew what one was at the time. I tried to tell her to get away, that it was dangerous, but I didn't quite have my balance yet, and she was determined to help me, and then . . ." Max looked at Jovie apologetically. "She got too close. And the radiation . . . So I brought her across. If I didn't, she would have died. It was a snap decision, and I had no idea who she was, I swear. It was just bad timing."

"Bad timing?" Jovie muttered.

She tried to picture it as Micah had seen it: sitting there on the dunes, watching the gradient grow beneath the waves, sketching it . . . and then this silhouette emerging, a boy walking right out of the light, falling to the sand, as Max had just described. Yes, Micah probably would have run to him to see if he was okay, and to get answers about what she was experiencing, and where he was from. But still . . .

"I can't believe you didn't tell me any of this!" Jovie shouted. "We went to the bunker together looking for her. I showed you her picture!"

"I was *going* to," said Max. "But I thought you'd be mad, and—"

Jovie laughed. "Well, there's one thing you were right about."

"But also, I knew that I could figure it out tomorrow night! I was already planning on helping her when I got back."

"Got back? What do you mean? Like, you're going back there and staying there?"

"Well . . . I have to take the data back." He held out the bracelet. "I mean, that's the plan. And we have to analyze it, of course, and see if there's more that we need before next time."

"Next time . . . you mean in four years?"

Max glanced at her, then looked away. "Yeah."

"So wait," said Jovie, "after tomorrow night, you were

going to just be gone?"

Max held out his hands. "I was going to tell you."

"Tell me what? 'Hey, thanks for helping me sneak around and learn some stuff, catch you when you're a senior in high school'?"

"It's not as bad as it sounds."

"Isn't it?"

"I didn't know how to say it, okay? Also, I didn't *want* to tell you. You're, like, the only good thing that's happened to me since my mom, and . . . I didn't want to ruin things until I had to."

Jovie felt her face flush, but then cursed at herself for even feeling that, and kept her scowl. "Until *you* had to. What about me? You're just as bad as everyone else. And what about your dad?"

Max's face darkened. "What about him?"

"He remembers you," Jovie said. She pointed over to the table of charts and maps. "I think he's been looking for you this whole time. For years. He's so sad and broken—"

"You think I care?" Max nearly shouted. "He deserves everything he's been through. The night Mom died, he was more concerned with his stupid discovery and all his followers. I can still picture him, all worried about making this dumb suit work while we were drowning. He never cared about us."

Jovie saw the anger in his eyes, heard the venom in his voice. It seemed so raw, but of course, it was—for Max,

Ascension Camp had happened months ago, not years.

"We shouldn't even have been down there," Max went on. "He knew the gradient could be dangerous. But all that mattered to him was showing off, like he wanted to impress us or something, like that would make it okay that he basically ignored us for years."

"It sounds like he really screwed up," said Jovie. She thought of her conversations with Harrison. "I think he knows it."

Max's gaze fell. "I know he's in a bad way now. But I still can't close my eyes without seeing Mom going underwater, without seeing . . ." He bit his lip. "Did you know there are gravestones for us in the cemetery? They're old enough to have moss. Everyone has forgotten about it, moved on. But not me."

"I'm sorry." Jovie felt herself tearing up. She knew something about what Max was saying. The way people moved on after her parents had separated. Of course, at first, everyone was sympathetic, but then after some amount of time, why *wasn't* she doing better? And this was doubled for Max, who was still so close to what had happened while the world around him was decades beyond it. She couldn't imagine how lonely that must feel. "Is that what your letter to Harrison was about?"

Max rubbed his hoodie pocket, where he'd stuffed the letter. "Mostly. I thought he'd want to know what happened to Mom. But hearing from me would probably just mess him up more." Max pulled the tarp back across the corner. "I do think I can get Micah back tomorrow night."

"Really?"

"She's probably injured from the crossing—it's only been a few hours for her—but yeah. But it's going to be dangerous." Max looked at her, his face serious. "The gradient will be at its strongest."

"And Barsuda will be there."

"I think we can use them to our advantage," said Max.

"What about the barricade?" Jovie asked.

"I might have a plan for that, too. I'll tell you on the way out."

"Okay then." Jovie looked around the room. "While we're here, anything else I need to know?"

Max laughed to himself, eyeing the ceiling, then looked at her. "Just that I'm really sorry."

Jovie finally allowed herself to smile. "I think I believe you."

29

THE VOICE

JANUARY 22, 2018
1 HOUR TO BREACH

Jovie paused in the doorway, looking back over the silent kitchen.

This was it.

Mom had left for work a few minutes before, just after a seemingly normal dinner, during which Jovie felt like she was going to explode the entire time. Trying to talk about her day at school, about normal Monday stuff, while a dangerous date with an otherworldly gateway was mere hours away. Adding to that, the plan that she and Max had come up with involved Mom getting a call from the police yet again. By this time tomorrow, Jovie would likely be discovering a new level of grounding . . . but she would have Micah back. And just in case anything went wrong, the plan had a backup: early this afternoon, she'd secretly met with Sylvan to pass along key information.

Everything was in place. This was going to work. And yet, as Jovie stepped out into the chilly night, the fear rolled through her belly in nauseous swells.

Her neighborhood was still. Barsuda had announced a "strong storm advisory" at the end of the school day, and there had been an alert on her phone. Everyone was being told to stay indoors. But as Jovie pedaled out onto the street, a small movement caught her eye. She saw Ruth in her window, peering out into the night. She raised her hand, like she was waving, and Jovie felt a chill, as if Ruth knew where she was headed, and why.

Town was quiet. A car or two, a nearly empty bus.

"This town and its miserable weather," Mom had muttered to herself as she was leaving, another statement whose downtrodden tone was based in the great lie of Far Haven's past. Jovie had to fight the urge, stronger than before, to tell Mom all she had learned. *Soon*, she thought. *Once I have Micah back.*

As Jovie biked up the winding road to the bunkers, the night couldn't have been calmer: no rain, little wind, just a gentle mist laced with the briny smell of the cove. There was no hint whatsoever of what the universes had in store.

She hid her bike just inside the bunker, then made her way into the dark tunnels, running her fingers along the walls until she found the etched arrows. After her first trip here with Max, she'd drawn a map of the route in her notebook, but she didn't have that with her now. She'd left it behind, hopefully in a safe place. Fortunately, her memory was true, and she soon emerged in the circular room.

Inside was a flurry of activity. Some of the drifters were cooking in the center of the room, but most were working around the perimeter, securing to the wall rusted slabs of metal that looked like pieces of old ships' hulls. The tunnel that led out to the bluff had been blocked off, and a drifter was using a blowtorch to weld one metal piece to another.

Max was with Carina. She was hammering in large metal hooks, while Max organized a series of ropes on the floor.

"Hey," Max said, the only set of eyes not glaring at Jovie as she crossed the room. "How was your day?"

"Oh, just great," Jovie said. "Really got a lot of good learning done at school, you know, not distracted at all. What are you guys doing?"

"Making restraints," said Carina, pausing from her hammering. "So we can lash ourselves down to ride out the storm, just like old sailors. But if Max is right, that will be it." Carina gave him a look as she said it.

"Max," Jovie repeated. "So you did tell her."

Max nodded. "It's been, like, a whole day since I

lied to anyone." He stood and turned to Carina. "We should go."

Carina stood as well. "I guess this is it." She looked around the room. Other drifters had heard her and were eyeing Max with a mixture of sadness and uncertainty. "Thanks for all you've done," Carina said. "Good luck, I guess."

"Thanks." Jovie saw that Max couldn't quite meet her eyes. "Once the gradient is closed," Max offered, "maybe you guys will be able to get farther away from here, and reconnect."

Carina's eyes fell. "One can only hope."

Max looked around the other faces, made a little waving motion, and then turned to Jovie, his face red. "Okay, let's go." He moved to the wall, picked up a long, heavy-duty pair of bolt cutters, and started out.

They headed up the tunnels to the field, then took the path around to the edge of the bluff and started down the narrow, switchbacking trail. The moon flashed from behind high chains of fast-moving clouds. Jovie saw the lights from Barsuda's towers, already glowing through the mist down on Satellite Beach, and she felt a fresh wave of fear.

They reached the beach and trudged through the wet sand, bracing wind in their faces. They passed the bathhouse ruins, then the old road where they had emerged with Sylvan the week before, and Jovie hoped he was staying safe tonight, like he'd promised.

They climbed over the driftwood and up the dune, making their way behind Barsuda's position. They had set up their light towers the same as before the last storm, in a U shape facing the water, with the platform in the center, though this time, the workstations on top were protected by a large plexiglass shield. The barricade device was beneath the platform, aimed at the water. Generators grumbled and vibrated near the trucks.

There was a deep rumble and now two helicopters swooped overhead, then peeled off from one another, hovering to the north and south. A moment later, the lasers lit up from one buoy to the next, making the trapezoidal perimeter atop the water.

Jovie and Max edged their way to a position almost directly behind the platform. Jovie felt Max's hand slip into hers. "We need to be in position before they turn on the barricade." He held up the clippers. "Once it's disabled, I'll head for the water. When the eye opens, I'll go through, tell them what's happening, and send Micah back, all as quickly as I can. She'll be in a suit, so she'll be protected. As soon as you see her—"

"I know: completely give myself away to Barsuda and make sure they understand that she's Micah and not some alien."

"Right. Then Barsuda grabs Micah, and you, and . . ."

"And then you're gone," said Jovie.

"For a little while."

"Four years won't be a *little while*, not here."

"I know. I'm sorry."

"At least I'll know when you're coming back."

"First storm of the next cycle," said Max. "Probably sometime in the late spring? Sylvan can figure it out."

"Right." Jovie couldn't quite meet his eyes. "So, this is probably goodbye."

"I'll miss you."

Jovie just nodded, but when she looked up at him, their eyes locked. Suddenly, she felt an overwhelming flush of heat in her cheeks. Were they—

Max looked away quickly. "We should get to it."

"Right."

He gently twisted the black button on his bracelet. Rainbow light glowed against his fingertip.

He took Jovie's hand, and she felt that cool rush of hollow wind through her, felt her connection to her senses and her skin retreating. All of it made her want to turn and run, but she steeled herself. *One more time, for Micah.*

They crept down the front of the dune, over the logs, and crossed the sand until they were just outside the lights, close enough to hear Dr. Wells up on the platform.

"What's our status?" she asked the two workers sitting at computers in front of her.

"The breach is cycling up to forty-five percent," one of

them replied. "Right on schedule."

Dr. Wells ran her finger over her tablet. "Tell the barricade unit to power up, and move the acquisition team into position."

The workers spoke quietly into headsets. Now the team of agents in their red, astronaut-style suits emerged from behind the trucks and spread out in a line across the water.

"Sixty percent," one of the agents announced. "Rising fast."

Now a glimmer appeared, and the golden-white light began to swirl beneath the waves. The wind increased, blowing sand around them.

"Here we go," said Dr. Wells.

The light grew quickly, becoming blinding, the waves rising and hurling themselves onto the beach with far more force than during the previous storm.

Jovie saw that Max was peering at his bracelet. The button had started to pulse with rainbow light. "Why's that flashing?" she asked.

"The portal is almost open," said Max. He pressed the button for a long moment. "This should let them know I'm coming. Okay, time to do this." Max smiled at her, his features almost completely lost in the gradient light. "I'm sorry I didn't tell you the truth. But I'll get Micah and send her back, I promise. Ready?"

"Yeah," Jovie said.

Max twisted the button on his bracelet again. The world faded further, and that cold wind inside Jovie grew more biting, like there were great mountain passes between her bones, her very cells.

The swirling gradient light began to overwhelm the shoreline, washing away the waves and the beach, ballooning above the water. It was as if, not far past the platform, the world had been erased completely.

Flashing lights caught her eye, and now Jovie could see the essences that were hovering longingly overhead. There were nearly a dozen.

And the chill grew in Jovie, the sense of space, of wind, and an urgent thought spoke inside her. *This is too close . . . too close.*

"Cresting ninety percent," said an agent on the platform. "Radiation levels are approaching redline. It's growing even faster than our model, sir."

Dr. Wells lowered her goggles. "Hold steady."

"Go," Max said.

Jovie nodded and tried to add *I hope I see you again*, but she wasn't sure if the words came out.

She ran across the beach, the world a blurry sketch of light and lines. She moved into the ring of light towers and scanned the sand for the cables that powered the barricade: there they were, thick black lines snaking across the sand. She followed them to the Barsuda trucks, to where they were plugged into a large generator. Its side was tangled with cables hooked into rows of ports. She bent and traced the ones from the barricade, found their connection points, and looked back toward the platform.

Max had positioned himself halfway between the barricade and the generator, the large bolt cutters in his hand. Light was rippling over the beach in furious waves, blurring everything, but Jovie met Max's eye, and he nodded.

Jovie yanked the cables from the generator and threw them aside. Once Max saw that they were safely detached, he clipped them with the cutters. Then he dropped the tool and started toward the water.

Jovie dashed back to the safety of the shadows and circled around behind the platform. She could see Dr. Wells gesticulating, could hear frantic voices, and saw two workers hurrying from the barricade toward the generator, only to stop when they saw where Max had cut the lines.

Jovie spotted Max entering the surf. He was so faint, little more than mist and memory, and he'd passed right between two of the red-suited workers who were lining the water's edge.

Another essence dove into the furious white gradient light. Now another. They wanted to go so badly, Jovie thought, as if they were certain there was something over there, something more.

And the gradient grew faster, and now bolts of lightning shot from its sides. One of the light towers exploded in sparks. The headlights on the trucks burst and, one by one, went dark. Jovie felt a great vibration in her feet. Distantly, she thought she heard a rumbling sound, but when she looked toward the bluff, she could no longer see it. Waves of light were roaring up the beach, over the dune, erasing everything beyond it.

Out in the water, Max seemed to move effortlessly through the waves, which looked less like water now and more like ripples of pure energy.

And beyond him, a new form began to appear, a disk of pure darkness, like a pupil slowly expanding. It was like looking through a hole in the sea, but Jovie saw that it wasn't only darkness in there; there were dots of light, and closer, some kind of structure, a great curving shape, a shadow on the stars.

Max was nearing the pupil, the "portal," he'd called it. On the beach, Jovie saw Barsuda workers frantically unrolling new cable for the barricade, but up on the platform, Dr. Wells stood still, gazing out at the growing portal as if in a trance. Jovie remembered the feeling she'd described the other night, her own longing to know what was over there.

All at once, the pupil stopped growing. Even though they were surrounded by light and energy, the beach seemed to have become almost silent. The portal open, Barsuda waiting . . . two universes connected. Jovie had an urge to get Dr. Wells's attention, to wave her arms and shout and give herself up now. That way she could tell her what Max had said. There didn't have to be a conflict here, did there? If the humans stopped building barricades, stopped firing weapons, maybe they could reach an understanding with these Lahmurians, share technology even, and quickly find a way to stop the drift, the damage, the loss of life.

But Jovie stayed where she was. They were too close to getting Micah now to take that risk.

Out in the water, Max was at the edge of the portal. And beyond him, inside the darkness, Jovie thought she saw silhouettes approaching. The Lahmurians. Max just had to talk to them, and they could get Micah—

"Max!"

The voice jolted her out of her thoughts. It had come from behind her. Jovie spun, squinting through the brilliant white all around her, and saw a large figure half running, half stumbling down the dune and across the beach, a figure who was making no effort to hide himself.

"Max!" Harrison's hat blew off, its tinfoil lining glinting. "Wait!"

He bolted past Jovie. She could see the wild, desperate look in his eyes, and in that moment, she understood what he'd meant at the gas station: *Can't screw it up. . . .*

He'd known Max was here, somehow, and he'd been planning for this moment, to get his son back.

Jovie spun back to the portal, and realized she could

see Max more clearly, as if he'd been pulled closer and made more solid. Like he was *remembered*.

"Max! My boy! I'm sorry!"

With every word, Harrison was reconnecting Max to the world. A look of horror came over Max's face, and Jovie saw him twisting frantically at his bracelet, but it wasn't helping.

"*Stop!*" Jovie tried to shout at Harrison. But her voice was little more than a wind gust.

Harrison only made it a little farther down the beach before a red-suited worker slammed into him, tackling him.

"No!" Harrison shouted.

"Get the boy out of there!" Dr. Wells was pointing emphatically out at the water, and more of the red-suited workers were wading out toward Max, who seemed stuck in place at the edge of the portal, as if he was pulling against an invisible force.

"Max!" Harrison called again, his face coated in sand, struggling against the agent who had him pinned.

"Run, Max!" Jovie tried to call, but it was already too late. Two of the workers had reached Max. They had him by the arms. He was struggling, but it was no use.

And then Jovie found herself running toward the water and out into the foaming waves. "Let him go!" she shouted. "Please!" They had to let him cross!

Jovie heard shouts from behind her—was that Dr.

Wells calling her name?—but she kept running, and now the water began to feel strange, softer, and Jovie felt a burning sensation on her face, but also that pull of the gradient—it was more than just an urge now, it felt like it was drawing her closer to its yawning darkness, the essences singing in the crystal chorus overhead, and all of it made her wild with fear, but she pressed on, racing toward Max.

He saw her now, even as he fought against the workers. "No, Jovie, don't!" he shouted.

Jovie fought on, closer. "Let him—"

A red-suited worker slammed into her from the side, sending her sprawling into the water. The worker's helmet had impacted her head, and for a moment, she lost track of up and down. Then the worker yanked her up to her feet.

"Let go!" Jovie pulled against him uselessly. "You have to let him go!"

"You need to move back!" the worker shouted at her.

And through the blazing white light, Jovie saw spots in her vision, and felt that heat, a burning on her arms and legs, but also in her chest now. *He's right*, she thought. *I'm too close.* Her legs buckled and she fell to her knees. The other workers had Max, and were dragging him away from the portal. It wasn't going to work. *Micah*, Jovie thought. *I'm sorry—*

Just then, a sizzling bolt of pure energy flashed and

slammed into the worker holding Jovie, sending him staggering. Two more flashes—the energy bolts seared through the air and hit the two workers holding Max, blasting them backward as well.

Jovie saw three tall figures in blue suits emerging from the portal holding silver, spear-like weapons, their tips crackling with energy. Lahmurians. One fired again and another Barsuda worker who had been approaching from behind Jovie was sent flying across the water.

Two of the Lahmurians moved to Max. The other stalked toward Jovie, holding the energy spear at the ready.

Jovie saw the two help Max up by the shoulders and guide him toward the portal. She looked at the one looming over her. *Oh no*, she thought—but she couldn't move. Her head fell, and she saw the red splotches on her hands and felt the white-hot burning on her face. The cosmic radiation of another universe scorching her Earth-made cells.

Too close. The pain became its own white light in her mind. She fell onto her side and the waves rushed over her. She couldn't find which way was up or down. Her eyelids began to flutter.

Distantly, she sensed a shadow. The blue-suited figure was bending over her, lifting her up, and turning toward the portal.

No! Jovie thought weakly. *No, please.* But her plea made

no sound, and the figure carried her into the darkness.

Mom . . ., she thought desperately. *Sylvan . . . please remember—*

And then her thoughts were erased by the feeling of her mind and body being stretched beyond their limits, and a great and terrible wind roared between her every molecule, as if she were no longer an object but a direction, a movement, spreading and soaring and picking up speed.

30

THE QUIET COASTLINE

JANUARY 2018–JANUARY 2022

When the gold leaves of the electroscope had fluttered back to stillness on the night of January 22, 2018, and the sirens and car alarms had begun to wail, Sylvan had tried texting Jovie.

> What happened? Did you get Micah? Are you okay?

When she hadn't replied after an hour, he sent another, and then another. He'd told himself that Barsuda must have caught her. He imagined her in some sort of cell, with interrogators visiting her. How long would they hold her? A few hours? Overnight? But then they'd send her home, like last time, right?

When she hadn't texted by the next morning, Sylvan

had told himself that, of course, they'd taken her phone as evidence. She'd have to get a new one, or maybe even wait until she was on a school computer to message him.

When she hadn't texted by the end of the school day, he'd told himself that she likely hadn't come to school, too exhausted, maybe even slightly injured, or maybe so focused on Micah, if she'd found her, or too disappointed, if not, that she just hadn't gotten around to messaging Sylvan yet. Totally understandable.

It had only been in the car that afternoon on the way home from school that Sylvan had finally been forced to accept the nagging, fearful voice inside him, the one he'd been trying desperately to ignore. . . .

"Jovie's missing," Mom had informed him. Her bike had been found in the bunker ruins. Her parents had no idea where she was.

Sylvan had pictured the golden-white light in the water from the night he'd been at the beach, the way it had swirled and beckoned, and thought: *She got pulled across. She and Max got too close.*

As one day had bled into the next that January, and searches for Jovie had come up empty, Sylvan's belief had cemented. Of course, at the same time, so had his fear—*what if she died*—

No. He would not believe that. She *must* have ended up on the other side.

"Is there anything you can tell me that might help?" Dr.

Wells had asked the first time she came to Sylvan's house to interview him, three nights after what she referred to as "the breach." "This is no time for keeping secrets."

"Well . . ." In that moment, Sylvan had made the snap decision to begin the lies. How the last time he'd seen Jovie was Monday morning, on the way to school, and so on.

The truth was, Sylvan hadn't seen Jovie that morning. He *had* seen her, though, at the very end of the day, mere hours before she disappeared.

Eleven-year-old Sylvan had been walking out of his fifth grade class—Mom would be waiting out in the parking lot, as usual—and had just made the turn toward the main doors when he'd heard his name.

"Sylvan!" Jovie was leaning out of the doorway to the girls' bathroom. Sylvan hurried over.

"Hey!" he said. "What are you doing here?"

"Keep your voice down," Jovie said, looking warily around. "We can't trust anyone except each other."

"Oh yeah, right. Okay. So what's—"

"Just listen," she said. "I have something I need you to do. You're the only one I can trust."

Sylvan felt a surge of excitement, but also concern. "Are you and Max still going tonight?" He and Jovie had texted the night before, and Jovie had filled him in on all that she had learned about Mason's real identity and his role in Micah's disappearance, as well as tonight's plan. All of it had blown Sylvan's mind, and made him feel guilty for not putting the pieces together far sooner. He was supposed to be the town history expert!

"Yes, we're still going." Jovie looked up and down the hall again. And then she reached inside her jacket and held something out to Sylvan. "I need you to take this."

It was her investigation notebook. For a moment, Sylvan just eyed it, a lump in his throat. "Why?"

Jovie thrust it to his chest. "In case we get caught. Barsuda will take it if they find it. And if tonight doesn't work, if Max crosses back over and Micah doesn't make it out, well, we're going to need the notes for the next time. Otherwise, we might forget everything we learned."

Four years later, Sylvan could still remember how his heart had been pounding in that moment, and wondered now if that fear had been some kind of premonition. As if by taking the notebook, he had set the terrible sequence of events in motion.

What he said then was, "You should keep it. And if you think you're going to get caught, then maybe . . . don't go." He was unable to meet her eyes. "If it's too dangerous . . . I mean, it is, isn't it?"

Jovie hadn't responded for a moment, biting her lip. "I have to try. Just take it and keep it out of sight, okay? Please?"

No, Sylvan had thought. But he'd slipped it into his backpack anyway.

"Thanks," Jovie said. "Ooh, I have one more thing."

She slung her pack around and removed a small cardboard box and handed it to him. "Go ahead, open it."

Inside was a red velvet cupcake.

Jovie reached out and ruffled his hair. "Happy belated birthday, little brother."

Sylvan closed the lid and threw his arms around her. "Thanks." He wanted to say more, but he didn't know what, and he also didn't want to cry. He *really* didn't want to cry.

Then Jovie said quietly, "Please stay inside tonight, okay? I mean it."

Sylvan leaned into her shoulder. He closed his eyes without realizing it. "Okay," he replied.

"I gotta go." She stood him up. "Don't leave your mom waiting." Then she gave him a gentle push and darted off in the other direction.

And Sylvan had walked out to the car, on the edge of tears, but telling himself it would be all right.

Except then, it wasn't.

In those first few months after Jovie disappeared, Sylvan had been able to make some progress of his own on the case. At first, after Dr. Wells had visited, he'd been too nervous to take out Jovie's notebook, afraid that Barsuda was watching him, that they'd discover it and confiscate it. But a couple of weeks later, he finally dared to retrieve it from where he'd hidden it, deep at the bottom of a bin of Legos in his clubhouse. Among the pages of lists and notes in Jovie's careful, flowing handwriting, Sylvan had discovered two key pieces of information that had given him hope, and would help sustain him through the long years to come.

The first was a hand-drawn map of the Fort Riley bunkers. Jovie had made a dotted line detailing the route from the entrance to the drifters' camp. Beside it, she'd written:

look for the arrows

She'd sketched one below.

In the corner of the map was another curious detail: a jagged line, along with the note:

crack in the northwest corner, where the mask
and the list are

Sylvan had remembered Jovie describing the drifters' mask, the one that worked like her spyglass. He wasn't sure what the list was, but two weeks later, once the road to the state park had reopened, Sylvan had lied to his parents that he was going to the library and biked up there.

The field and parking lot were deserted. Sylvan ducked under the fluttering yellow caution tape, climbed over the chain link fence, and faced the bunkers. He got out Jovie's map and started in.

The musty dark quickly closed in around him, the light disappearing behind him.

Sylvan steeled himself. *Come on*, he thought,

determined to be brave like Jovie. As he inched into the darkness, he sang his Blue Bathymetrist song quietly to himself—"*He came from the depths and his power was true*"—and soon, he found the first of the arrows.

He arrived in what had once been the drifters' camp. What remained could barely be described as a room. One entire side had been ripped away by the landslide. The metal walls had been torn and twisted outward, as if some great creature had taken a bite out of the place, and a chilly, salty wind was funneling in through the hole, peppering his face with sea spray and making the caution tape there flap and buzz.

"Is anyone here?" he called, but there was no reply. What had happened to all the drifters? Jovie had said there were dozens. Sylvan noted the lengths of soaked rope that were still tied to the walls.

By some measure of luck, the landslide's destruction ended just before the crack that Jovie had marked. Sylvan reached into the damp dark and found a plastic bag with the mask and a spiral notebook.

The bag had been punctured, and the notebook was soaked and ruined, but other than being covered in a salty film, the mask was intact. Sylvan tucked it into his jacket, took it home, and hid it in his Legos as well.

The second important item Sylvan had discovered in Jovie's notebook was a small note she'd made to herself in the margin of a page dated January 20. Jovie had made a list after their night inside Baxter. It was a series of questions about how Micah could have crossed the gradient, and how to get her back.

But after a notable space of blank lines, there was one last note, as if Jovie had added it later, that read:

- Are you sure about Mason's abilities?

An arrow curved away from this line, to a tiny note in the margin, which read:

Sylvan is the only one you can ALWAYS count on. Even if he's too young to help.

Sylvan had run his finger over this note, his eyes prickling. *You* can *count on me*, he'd thought, with a certainty that would carry him from one month to the next, and the next, for four more years, until he could be there for her again.

Before that time came, though, Sylvan's life had to be lived.

Sixth grade, seventh, eighth, all of middle school . . . While there wasn't a day that went by when he didn't think about Jovie, Sylvan had to adapt to the reality that, for a while, it was just going to be him.

He spent the first half of sixth grade keeping mostly to himself, doing solo quests in his games. Day after day, through fall and winter, until finally, in the spring, he made some new friends: Lina, Tommy, Jesse, and Arlo. Sylvan met them in band class, and near the end of the year, he had started joining them on their afternoon trips to get bubble tea. The four of them had been friends since kindergarten, and while at first he'd hovered on the edge of their vibrant conversations, almost like he was waiting for something to happen, Sylvan began to push through that wall as spring became summer.

He never felt like he was totally part of their group, but he did feel included. By the middle of seventh grade, almost two years since the breach, Sylvan had grown nearly a foot. He had also gained a shred of coordination and joined the Ultimate Frisbee team. In fact, it turned out that he had a knack for bending throws, for leading runners, for timing. He and Arlo were taking a coding class together and he'd even asked Lina to the winter ball, and somehow found the courage to kiss her during the last song of the dance—though, truthfully, the kiss had landed a little off-center.

All in all, Sylvan had, to his surprise, found himself in the midst of a real life, in the present tense . . . until a couple of months later, in early 2020, when the COVID-19 pandemic had shut the world down. And so began a creeping year at home; his parents always around, everyone in his world on the other side of a screen, there but not. The shared experiences of school, of music, of trips for bubble tea, of days and weeks, of time itself, all lost. So much of the world receded, became foreign. And when Sylvan did go out, the proximity of people made him wary.

Far Haven receded, too. The town had already been a patchwork of boarded-up and vacant storefronts, but many of the businesses that closed because of the virus later announced that they wouldn't reopen. The cove was quiet, the beaches were empty, while the clusters of tents and RVs in their parking lots grew.

When school finally reopened in the spring of 2021, Sylvan found it hard to reconnect. He couldn't quite find that old rhythm with his friends—Jesse and Tommy had been mostly lost to other online friend groups, and Lina had moved away, leaving only Arlo, who he still met up with virtually but whose parents weren't sending him back to in-person school. It was as if that whole life he'd briefly found had been reset. Sylvan couldn't quite feel comfortable in class, in band, in any moment. It was as if he existed separate from it all, drifting along, not really there. It seemed like everyone felt that way to some degree, after being isolated for so long, but for Sylvan, it was more than that.

An invisible countdown had begun in his head, a ticking that had gotten slowly and steadily louder, dominating all his thoughts.

It's coming.

He could feel it on each spring breeze. Despite the reopening of the world, Far Haven still seemed shuttered and quiet, as if the town itself was waiting, day after day, month after month, as clocks, both big and small, cosmic and secret, ticked down.

Finally, one thousand two hundred and seven days after Jovie disappeared, on the night of May 13, 2021, tall, lanky, fourteen-year-old Sylvan snuck down to the basement. His clubhouse was gone, the cardboard walls taken down when they'd had to convert the basement to an office so Dad could work from home. It was okay; Sylvan had preferred being in his own room with a real locking door for a while now.

He made his way over to the closet, which held a few dusty bins filled with his old toys. Mom had been gently inquiring whether he might be ready to donate them, but Sylvan had resisted—not so much because he had any interest in playing with Lego sets or plush Mario characters anymore, but rather because of the items they concealed.

He retrieved Jovie's notebook and the drifters' mask, and then, just after dinner, headed out on his bike, claiming that he was studying at Arlo's, who was allowed to have guests over to his deck. Instead, he rode to Satellite Beach.

On the way, he double-checked the math in his head. Using the date of the 2018 breach, as well as the dates of the Baxter, Ascension Camp, and Vanescere Bathhouse accidents, and researching historical weather data for the years leading up to each event, Sylvan had concluded that each time the gradient opened, the series of storms that led up to it began in May. The first storm of this 2022 cycle should be on this very night.

As he neared Satellite Beach, he felt that old fear rising in him. He pictured the swirling light, Barsuda's helicopter and trucks. It was as if that night had not been years ago, but rather mere weeks. At the same time, he also felt hope. What if tonight was the night that Jovie reappeared? He wasn't sure it would be, or how he could even help if it was, but as she'd said, he was the one she could always count on, so he would be there.

When he arrived at the parking lot, he found no signs for beach closures, and no Barsuda trucks. It occurred to him that he hadn't seen much of them at all these last few years. Of course, Sylvan had largely been stuck at home, and since their well was not one of the ones Barsuda "monitored" for radiation, there wasn't much reason for their paths to cross. But when he *had* been out and about, he couldn't remember seeing a van or a team of workers behind caution tape for quite some time, maybe since the immediate aftermath of 2018.

Well, he told himself, they'd probably been doing the same thing as him: waiting for tonight.

He hid his bike in the dunes and climbed to a secluded vantage point overlooking the sand and surf, where he watched the sun set. He scanned the skies with the drifters' mask until the light faded and the wind grew cold. . . .

But no essences appeared. No Barsuda team.

And no swirl of light in the water.

Sylvan sat on the dark, silent beach until his mom started texting and asking when he was coming home. And as he biked away, he felt a withering chill.

What had he missed?

His math could have been wrong, but that would have been a first. Just in case, though, Sylvan made sure to be right back out on the beach the next night, but there was no storm then, either, no trucks or essences or any sign at all that any such thing would or even could happen.

Sylvan had returned to the beach on the eighteenth of September, to a similar result.

Same for November 21.

"Where are you?" he said to the darkness, his fear now a hurricane inside him.

When there was still nothing in December, the fear became full-blown panic. He had waited four years for this. What had happened? The gradient had been wreaking havoc in Far Haven for over a century, and on an entirely predictable schedule. Had it changed? Had Barsuda altered it somehow with their barricade? Or stopped it completely? What if it was never going to open again? Did that mean Jovie was gone forever?

But I remember her, Sylvan reminded himself. And he'd never needed a Post-it note or a name on his arm to do it. Jovie wasn't forgotten yet. That *had* to mean something.

Maybe, Sylvan thought, the gradient had moved. After all, galaxies were always moving, continents shifted over time. Perhaps its location had changed. And so, on January 8, 2022, Sylvan left for yet another study session at Arlo's, and instead biked up to the bluff, where he sat atop a bunker—it was the same one Jovie and Micah had sat on years ago, though Sylvan didn't know this—affording himself a view of the coastline in each direction.

But the gradient still did not appear.

On January 16, Sylvan set out yet again. This time, however, he didn't head to the beach. *Last chance*, he thought to himself. If the gradient didn't appear tonight, he couldn't see how it was going to magically appear on the night of the breach, which, he calculated, should be in four days. And what would that mean? Would Jovie be gone forever?

"*He came from the depths and his power was true*," Sylvan sang, trying to keep up his failing spirits. "*With a path to paradise to free me and you.*"

He headed up the hill north of town through a light drizzle, and felt a twinge of guilt as he passed the entrance to Meadow Bluff. Jovie's mom had stopped teaching lessons when Jovie disappeared, and Sylvan had heard that she'd lost her casino job not long after that. The music school itself had been lost to the pandemic. Sylvan had thought many times that he should go see her, either to help out around the house, or maybe try to offer her some hope, but he'd found one excuse or another to put it off, before the shutdown let him off the hook. Since then, he'd hoped that he would soon have a reason to visit her with good news.

He turned onto the dirt road that ran beside the old Baxter plant fence and parked at a high point with a good view of the complex, unaware that this, too, was the exact spot Jovie had once been. Maybe, he'd reasoned, Barsuda would be gearing up to go to wherever the gradient location actually was, and he could follow them. This theory of course hinged on Barsuda even still being in town; he'd still seen no evidence of them. And yet, even as he parked his bike, his hopes began hissing out of him like a leaky balloon.

The plant was dark. A section of one of the cooling towers had collapsed over the years. And as the sunset came and went, there was no evidence of a gradient storm, or any activity at all.

Frustration, liquid and hot, rushed through Sylvan. He was soaked, and shivering, and running out of time! *What did I miss?* he thought uselessly. All his waiting and searching, only to end up here, at a dead end.

It was just then, as he was starting to slide off the mask, that he saw it.

The light was faint, flickering. Sylvan nearly missed it; far down by the buildings, a glowing form was floating along. Sylvan peered through the mask. It seemed to be a person, luminous with rainbow light. The figure had arms and legs that were moving in a motion that resembled walking, but it also appeared to be floating across the ground.

The figure slipped into the forest, heading toward the coast. Sylvan jumped on his bike and raced back down the dirt road, pausing every now and then to lower the mask and check the woods. The winter night was so quiet, no birds, just a few frogs, the gentle shush of rain and the dripping sound of water from branches. Sylvan reached the main road, beginning to fear that he'd lost track of the figure— There it was, drifting out of the trees and over the wet pavement. It looked like a young woman.

As she crossed the road, the woman blurred, and it seemed for a moment as if her legs and arms morphed into shimmering, buzzing wings. It was like her human form was a chrysalis she was anxious to burst out of. The wings almost lifted the woman off the ground, only to dissipate, and her arms and legs regained their shape. She reached the woods on the other side and disappeared into the pines.

Sylvan rode back down to Meadow Bluff. There she was again, drifting through the yards, and it was clear that her path was taking her toward the water.

He raced through town and spotted her again near

Potter's Beach, gliding across the meadow through a damp, whipping wind. When she disappeared over the dune, Sylvan coasted down the hill, turning just before the beach lot and heading down to the inner edge of the cove, where the road ended at a small parking lot beside the lighthouse jetty, which had been fenced off since 2018.

Sylvan rolled up to the fence. The ghostly woman was floating out along the jetty toward the dark lighthouse. As she went, her wings grew brighter, her arms and legs less distinct, until she was no longer a human form, just winged, buzzing energy. She reached the lighthouse, circled it twice, and then dove straight toward the ground beside it and vanished.

Sylvan blinked, waiting for the light to return, but it didn't. He removed the mask, gazing at the dark structure. *What would Jovie do?*

Duh, he thought nervously. The answer was obvious.

The fence was topped with loops of barbed wire, which, now that Sylvan thought about it, seemed a bit extreme just to keep the public out. He followed the fence line across the lot to where it dropped down to the narrow cove beach and extended a few feet out in the water. He waded out into the frigid cove nearly up to his waist, holding his phone up in one hand, rounded the end of the fence, and waded back up to the beach on the other side. He looked down at his soaked clothes; it was going to be interesting trying to explain to his mom later.

Sylvan started out onto the jetty, hopping from one giant angled rock to the next. Waves crashed on either side, adding spray to the already-slick rocks; more than once, Sylvan's sneakers slipped and he barely caught his balance.

"*Two four three four six one two*," he sang to himself.

By the time he reached the lighthouse, his teeth were chattering, and he was shivering nonstop.

The entire lighthouse had been shifted on an angle by the 2018 event. The circular path around it was warped and cracked. Sylvan peered through a grimy window and saw that the room inside was coated in dust. He headed around to where it had seemed like the essence had gone—

And nearly fell to his death.

He was teetering on the edge of a hole in the ground, perfectly circular and about five feet in diameter, as if a giant drill had bored straight down through the concrete path and the earth beneath it. The sides were lined with smooth metal, and there was a narrow ladder descending into darkness. Except it wasn't entirely dark down there. Squinting, Sylvan thought he could make out a faint light. And there was a distant sound: the humming of fans, or machines. On closer inspection, Sylvan saw that there was a half-moon of thick metal on one side, set into grooves. It looked like a cover that could slide closed.

Was this built for the essences? he wondered. He couldn't be sure, but *who* built it seemed obvious.

Barsuda.

And if the essences were heading this way, that meant the gradient was down there, somewhere.

It's been here all along, he thought, *just underground.* Somehow, Barsuda had altered its location. Sylvan wondered how they'd managed such a thing, though *why* they'd done it seemed obvious: this was clearly protecting the people of town—there had been no code seven cases, after all—but it was going to make getting to Jovie much more difficult.

He was so fixated by this strange structure that he barely noticed the flicker of light from the windows of the lighthouse behind him. Like a flashlight beam, angled upward, as if someone was coming up from below.

Sylvan ran back down the jetty as fast as his shivering legs and slippery-soled shoes would carry him. He misjudged a jump and scraped his knee and tweaked an ankle before he finally reached the fence and waded once again into the icy water. He didn't look back until he was on the other side.

Two beams of light were sweeping around the base of the lighthouse.

Sylvan had just begun to catch his breath when a car door clunked shut behind him. He whirled and saw that a Jeep had arrived in the lot while he'd been gone, and now a figure was approaching him.

"It's okay," a man's voice said, "I'm not with them."

Sylvan turned on his phone flashlight and illuminated a hulking man in a long duster coat, high rubber boots, and a plaid hat with earflaps. Harrison Westervelt, now with a scraggly salt-and-pepper beard, was carrying what looked like a large shard of glass, its edges thickly wrapped in duct tape. It gleamed with an oily rainbow sheen.

He motioned toward the lighthouse with the shard. "Uh-huh. That's where they go now. Down down down." As he spoke, Sylvan saw that his teeth were stained bright blue.

"Have—have you seen them here before?" Sylvan stammered, trying to swallow his nervousness.

Harrison nodded and his eyes glistened. "My fault."

Sylvan checked over his shoulder. The two lights were still near the lighthouse and didn't seem to be getting any closer. "What's your fault?"

"Everything," he said. "Can't ever get the timing right."

"Timing?" said Sylvan.

Harrison gazed out at the water for a moment. Sylan almost prompted him again, when he finally said: "It's my fault about your friend, too. I told her to stay away, but I should have known better. Shouldn't have waited so long. I was sure it was him, even after all this time. . . . But I got distracted by the eye . . . hesitated, then it was too late."

"Do you mean . . . Max?" Sylvan asked.

Harrison nodded. "I tried to reach him, but it only made things worse, and then they took them."

Sylvan, his heart already pounding, thought he understood. "You were there when Jovie and Max crossed the gradient."

Harrison nodded. "Lost him again."

"Do you know what they're doing down there?" Sylvan asked, pointing to the lighthouse.

But Harrison was turning back toward his car. He motioned for Sylvan to follow. "I have something for you."

Harrison opened the back of the Jeep. Inside was a bright red vintage suitcase. He flicked the latches and opened it.

"It never worked for me, but maybe it will for you."

Inside the suitcase was a blue suit with a helmet that Sylvan recognized quite well. "Is that *the* suit?" he asked.

Harrison held it up by its shoulders. "Uh-huh."

"What am I supposed to do with it?"

Harrison nodded with his chin toward the lighthouse. "Use it to save them."

"Okay, but you just said it doesn't work."

"Arthur could make it work. He could make it *sing*." Harrison closed the suitcase and handed it to Sylvan. "Maybe you'll have better luck."

"Um, thanks," said Sylvan.

Harrison shut the back of the Jeep and moved around to the driver's side door. "If you find your friend, tell her I'm sorry."

"What about Max?" Sylvan asked. "Do you want me to say anything to him?"

Harrison paused. His lips parted like he was about to reply, but then his gaze fell and he was silent for a moment. "It won't do any good," he finally said. "I know what he's going to do. And I don't blame him." And he slid into the Jeep and drove off.

Sylvan watched him go for a moment, considered the suitcase in his hand, then got on his bike. The lights were gone from the lighthouse, but he kept checking over his shoulder anyway as he biked home, holding the handlebars with one hand, the suitcase swinging awkwardly beside him.

Two nights later, January 18, Dr. Wells arrived at Sylvan's house for her interview, and Sylvan answered her questions, and kept his secrets, all the while counting down the hours in his head until he could finally try to save his friend.

31

THE STARLESS NIGHT

JANUARY 2018–JANUARY 2022

"Jovie?"

Her eyes fluttered open. Even that small movement caused a throbbing ache through her skull. Her vision was blurry; Jovie's whole body felt that way, as if she'd been hastily reassembled after breaking into a million pieces.

"Hey, Jovie."

She was on a warm, soft surface—a bed. She rolled over onto her side and focused on the person beside her.

"M-Micah?"

It was her. The face, the voice she knew from so many afternoons and classes and sleepover whispers. Her hair was loosely tied back, and she had dark circles under her eyes, and there was dried sand stuck to her sweatshirt, a few grains still on her cheeks and in her hair.

"Hi." Micah broke into a grin and threw her arms around Jovie as she sat up. Her hair still smelled like the coconut shampoo she used, and Jovie felt the months they'd been apart like it had been years, and yet also no time at all. The two feelings spiraled together in a rush as Jovie hugged her back.

Micah pulled away and blew a loose strand of hair out of her eyes. "I can't believe you're here." She spoke quietly even though the room they were in seemed to be empty, and Jovie tried to push aside a tremor of fear about where she was, and what had happened to her. "How did you find me?" Micah asked.

"It's a long story." Jovie grimaced as another wave of pain washed over her. She pushed up her sweatshirt sleeve and saw faint pink streaks up her arms. She felt another tender area on her neck. Jovie ran her fingers gently over the streaks. They tingled, like the echo of a much worse pain, and she remembered how red they'd looked back on the beach, how brightly they'd burned.

"I had those, too," Micah said. "They've been in a couple times to treat you."

They. Jovie remembered the figures in the blue suits. She looked around the small room they were in. Its floor and walls were made of dark metal. There were two of these beds, a small table, and a large, round window. "Where are we?"

Micah blew air out of her cheeks and responded in a cowgirl accent. "It ain't Far Haven, that's fer sure." She helped Jovie to her feet and guided her to the window.

When Jovie saw the view, she felt woozy again. Outside was a vast field of darkness, with only a few faint stars here and there. She thought of those photos from telescopes that showed their own universe littered with uncountable stars and galaxies, and she had an immediate feeling of emptiness here, like there should have been more stars, more *something.* The darkness was faintly lit by long brushes of green nebula in the distance, but otherwise, there was only a heavy sense of nothingness.

Micah must have noticed her expression. "I felt the same way the first time I saw it. Doesn't look like any view of the night sky I've ever seen."

"It's another universe," Jovie said quietly.

Micah blinked. "Okay . . . I just figured we were somewhere *else* in the universe, which seemed bad enough. Are you serious?"

Jovie nodded. "But it's so empty." She placed her head against the window's smooth surface. The side of the ship—for that's what this was, she realized, a spaceship—seemed to be curving away from her in all directions, and she remembered that glimpse she'd had of a shadowy shape through the portal. It had appeared circular; maybe this ship was shaped like a sphere. There were also enormous curving arms coming off it and arcing around, almost like a sea creature. The ship was bigger than any structure she'd ever seen, and its hull was pure black.

A shadow on the stars.

Jovie wavered on her feet, sensing the endlessness all around her, beneath her, a void she could fall through forever.

Keep it together, she thought, gritting her teeth. She removed the spyglass from her pocket, put it to her eye, and found that here, her entire field of view was in crystal clear focus.

"What's that?" Micah asked.

"It's how I could see the drifters," she said.

"Drifters?"

"The people who became invisible, like you," Jovie said. "There were more of them . . . camped out in the bunkers."

Micah nodded. "Did you find them with that?"

"Yeah, basically." Jovie looked at the device in her hand. What did it mean that everything was in focus here? She noticed now that the metal that made up the walls of this room appeared to be the same color as that of the spyglass. She held it closer to the wall—well, not exactly the same, but sort of—and as she did, little lights appeared in the wall by the spyglass. They looked like droplets of neon, and seemed to be shooting along in small tubes, only lighting up when they came close to the spyglass. Jovie moved it an inch away, and the strange circuitry dimmed. Moved it closer, and it grew brighter.

But it wasn't just the wall. The spyglass was glowing, too. Jovie rotated it and saw that there was a line of glowing green light on the little cylinder itself, just beneath that etched inscription. It was a series of symbols, none that Jovie had ever seen. Why were they appearing now? Was this alien language? Was the spyglass *from* here?

Jovie moved it away from the wall and the symbols faded. She eyed the door across the room. It didn't seem to have a handle. "Are we locked in here?"

"Yeah," said Micah. "The creatures—I mean, people? They look humanlike . . . humanoid? Is that the word?"

"They're called Lahmurians," said Jovie.

"Would have been nice if they'd told me that," said Micah. "I don't think we're their prisoners, exactly. It seemed more like they didn't know what to do with me. I was really starting to lose my mind before they brought you in. Longest hours of my life."

Hours. Jovie felt a fresh chill. "How long have I been here?"

"Let's see." Micah pulled her phone from her pocket. "About eight hours. You didn't happen to bring a phone charger, did you?"

"No. . . . What does your phone say the time and date is?" Jovie asked cautiously.

"Um, six thirty a.m., September twenty-second." Micah shrugged. "Not sure if my parents even noticed that I wasn't in my room last night, but when I don't show up for breakfast, they are going to freak—wait, why are you looking at me like that?"

Jovie tried to compose herself. "It's just . . . time works differently here than back home. You, um, you've actually been gone longer than you think."

"Okay . . ." Micah's brow scrunched. "How bad is what you're about to tell me?"

Jovie took a deep breath. "You've been missing for four months."

Micah froze for a moment. Then she laughed in disbelief. "What? I was sitting on the beach, like, just last night, and—"

Jovie held out her phone, displaying the January date. Micah stared at it. "There was a search for you, for weeks," Jovie said, deciding to skip the part where Micah had been forgotten, at least for now. "I put up flyers, your parents set up a website . . ."

Micah crossed her arms. "This can't be happening." Her eyes glistened with tears. "You're joking, right?"

"I'm sorry." Jovie rubbed her shoulder. "But I'm here now, and we can get back, except . . ." She trailed off as a chill of understanding flooded through her. If she'd been asleep for eight hours . . . "It's already been almost a year."

She felt a surge of terror and guilt. Her mom, her dad. They would be so worried—*would've been worried, months ago.* How were they now? Resigned? Devastated? They'd already lived a year thinking their daughter was missing, with no idea what had really happened to her, day after day, with more days passing almost by the minute. Jovie slumped back onto her bed.

Sylvan was right, she thought. *This was too dangerous*. Did he even still remember her? Did her parents?

"I never thought . . . ," Micah said quietly. "I didn't really know what was happening to me, and I was seeing these lights that felt . . . I didn't know it would lead to this."

"You couldn't have known," said Jovie. "That's part of the drift. You don't really realize it's happening."

"The drift," Micah repeated. "I felt like my life had become this dream."

Jovie looked around and saw her backpack lying by the bed. She opened it and got out Micah's journal. "Here."

"No way." Micah took it eagerly and ran her fingers over the cover.

"I, um . . . I looked through it. But only because I was trying to figure out what had happened to you."

Micah leafed through the pages. "That's okay."

"I also, well . . ." Jovie forced herself to continue. "I wanted to say that I'm really sorry, about last year. That I wasn't there for you." She motioned to the journal. "I know you were having a tough time."

"Oh." Micah shook her head, but didn't look up. "I guess that was a long time ago now."

Jovie tried to remind herself that Micah hadn't spent four months here thinking about this; for her, she'd only left Far Haven and her life less than a day ago. "Corey told me about that night when your dad left you at practice."

Micah rolled her eyes. "Yeah, when you're already in a bad way, it doesn't help to have a dad going through an idiot phase."

"She told me about Braiden's party, too, and I read about the Shakespeare camp. I should've realized something was wrong after you got back," Jovie said. "But you probably felt like you couldn't talk to me about it, because of how I was being about my parents."

"You had a good reason to be upset." Micah stood and stepped to the window. "I didn't feel like I could talk to *anyone* about it. Everybody would just have told me that it was okay, you know? That just being at that camp was good enough. Plus, it was only my first time there, so really I was dumb to ever expect that I could just walk into the best camp in the state and get the starring role."

Jovie nodded. "That probably is what I would have said. You're *so* good at acting—sorry, I guess that's exactly what you're talking about."

"None of that would have changed how much I wanted it," said Micah. "I thought I was good enough—I mean, I know I'm good—but then, to meet all those other actors, and see how talented they were . . . I felt like

I was shrinking, like the world was growing giant around me, but not in the good way, like you always hear about, like how there's all this opportunity and you can chase after your dreams, or whatever." Micah hugged herself, that faint green nebula light on her face. "This was like, the world was *too* big, and I was small, too small to ever be seen. Like, *really* seen. And it was so scary, like: What if I did the best I could do, and there were still more talented people? People who were better than me, no matter how hard I tried? What if my dreams were really *their* dreams, and I wasn't ever destined for that? It was so defeating, but then also lonely, because everybody in Far Haven thinks I'm this big star . . . so either they're wrong and I'm a fraud, or I'm wrong and not strong enough to deal . . . I just didn't want anyone to know."

"I know about some of that," Jovie said. "The shrinking part. I mean, I feel that, but for me it's just in regular old life stuff, not like, big-time acting stuff."

"That doesn't make it any less important."

"I wish I'd asked you about it."

Micah glanced at her. "I don't know if I could have explained it. Not back then, anyway. And then the feeling got worse, all last year. . . . I know I was a jerk after the band trip, but I just felt like, last spring, everything from my clothes to my room to my family . . . school, our dumb town, it was all just *irritating*. Like I was allergic to my whole life, and I had this constant feeling like I was on the edge, like something had to change, anything. I guess the camp really started it. But then . . . being with Isla and Corey, being one of *those* kids, that didn't fit me right, either, and then I started to feel like nothing did, and like there was nothing I could do about it. And maybe it would just keep getting worse and worse. . . ." She motioned to the ship. "And then it did."

"I should've noticed," said Jovie. "I think I just figured you were okay, like you're always okay."

"I know that's what people thought, but I never actually felt that way. And it gets lonely, feeling like everybody thinks you have it all figured out, that you're going to *do big things*; you don't want to let them down. But also, being anything less than that seemed like it was *not* an option." She sighed and sat back down across from Jovie. "I guess if I had really tried to tell you that, you would have gotten it."

"Maybe."

"But instead, I went and sulked inside my own head so bad that I got myself lost in another universe."

"No," said Jovie, motioning to their surroundings. "This wasn't your fault. Just because you were having a hard time doesn't mean you deserve to have this happen. It's *this* thing's fault you ended up here." She added under her breath, "And Max's."

"Who?"

"The guy you tried to save in the water during the light storm."

"Wait, you *know* him?"

"I thought I did? I think I do, now. He helped me find you."

Micah flipped to the last page of her journal, the drawing of the white light with the little figure. "I have always been a sucker for a cute boy in peril."

"*Kinda* cute," Jovie said under her breath.

Micah's face suddenly lit up in that familiar old way. "Wait, are you two—"

"No!" Jovie's cheeks turned bright red. "He was a total jerk. But he's helping these people here, and he was lost like you." *And me*, Jovie thought with a fresh chill. How much more time had passed at home just while they'd been talking? "He actually ended up here back in 1994."

Micah flashed a sly grin. "So you have a crush on a thirty-seven-year-old—"

"He's not thirty-seven!" Jovie said, smiling in spite of their predicament. "And it's not a crush."

There was a sound like a low-pitched chime, and the door slid open. Max was there, hands in his pockets, a sheepish look on his face like he was stopping by their lockers at school.

"Hey," he said.

"Hey," Jovie said, but her attention was fully on the tall, blue-suited figure standing beside Max.

"This is Iris," said Max. "She's the leader of the Lahmurians on this ship."

Iris's suit was covered with glowing lines of light. She wasn't wearing a helmet. Her face was humanlike and yet not; her skin had a sort of geometric pattern to it, almost like scales, but smooth and soft-looking. She had two eyes, though she didn't have defined irises and pupils the way humans did. Instead, there was the white of the eye and then a metallic silver disk in the center. Her mouth and ears looked human enough, as well as her nose—except there seemed to be a second smaller nose above the first, just below her forehead.

Iris began to speak, and at first Jovie heard the sounds of her alien speech, but then a moment later, a voice spoke from her suit, which must have had some sort of translating system.

"Please know that Iris is not my exact name," she said, "but a close approximation based on your limited language." She looked Jovie up and down. "You look as if you are recovering. How do you feel?"

"Fine," said Jovie. "I think."

This seemed to satisfy Iris. "We will be back for you when the next trial is ready."

She turned abruptly and left.

Max watched her for a moment. "She really is more friendly than she seems." He stepped into the room. "How are you doing?" he asked Jovie. "I saw that you woke up."

"Saw?" said Jovie.

Max looked away. "The rooms have monitors. I mean I wasn't, like, *watching*."

Jovie glanced at Micah, who had that grin again. *Stop!* Jovie tried to say with her eyes, overcome by an irrational urge to smile even though this was no time for that. "We were just talking about you," Jovie said to Max, trying to keep it serious.

"Great," he said flatly. "I'm glad you're okay."

"*Mostly* okay, except for the part where I'm in another universe."

"It was the only way to save you. Leave it to my dad to screw things up, again."

Jovie pictured Harrison running desperately across the sand. "I think he was just trying to get you back."

Max shook his head, like that idea was baffling to him. "I'm sorry for you, too," he said to Micah. "I didn't mean for you to end up here."

"It's okay." Micah shrugged. "It's not like you asked me to come closer to that giant swirly thing in the water."

"Where are we?" Jovie asked. "Exactly?"

"This is one of the Lahmurians' generational ships. They've been on it for centuries, looking for a new home for their people. It's pretty amazing, actually. Gardens, parks, different sections are like different neighborhoods. They have this big biorecycling system, sort of like a forest. . . ." Max's eyes fell. "That's where I buried my mom."

"Your mom died here?" Micah asked.

"She died in the water, near the gradient," said Max. "I'd only been here for, like, a day when Iris took me down to the recycler and we covered my mom's body with this cloth full of seeds." He fell silent for a moment, looking at his feet, then shook his head. "It was a lot. And my dad's fault, no matter how sorry he might be."

Jovie thought of what she'd just been saying to Micah, and that no matter what mistakes Harrison had made—a lot, it sounded like—no one could've really expected *this* to happen. So much of it was out of their control: each of them like a tiny stick caught in the flow, sucking them toward the waterfall. . . . *Except for me*, Jovie thought, thinking of how she'd run directly at a portal. *I'm the only one dumb enough to end up here on purpose.*

"So, what's the plan for getting back?" Jovie said to Max.

"The power systems are rebooting now," he said. "The next cycle to open the portal starts in twenty-three hours, and Iris has agreed to send you both back then."

"So, we just have to wait around for a day while three more years go by back home?" said Jovie.

Max shrugged. "There's no other option. I gave them all the data I recorded about Barsuda's barricade system, and they're figuring out how to override it. Oh," Max said, as if remembering something. He reached into his hoodie pocket and removed a parcel wrapped in something that looked like foil but unfolded silently, revealing three green rectangles. "I brought a snack for you guys. It's like an energy bar." As he passed them out, he added, "I'm also supposed to tell you that there's a bathroom, the next door down. The door to this room won't be locked anymore now that you've been deemed a non-threat."

"So they think," Jovie said, and they all shared a smile. Jovie bit into the bar. It tasted sweet but also a little bitter, sort of like dark chocolate with a hint of seaweed. "How exactly does an alien bathroom work?"

"It makes sense, mostly," said Micah. "Turns out, we have similar plumbing."

The three of them broke into a laugh.

"Do you have a room like this?" Jovie asked Max.

"Yeah, it's down the hall. And I got permission to take you on a tour of the ship, if you want."

"Maybe later." The food was helping, but Jovie felt a fresh wave of exhaustion and despair washing over her. It was really hitting her now. *Four years.* She could almost feel them passing like a wind through her. All the kids she'd gone to middle school with would be out of high school. And her parents; she remembered being at the hospital when Mom had been sick, thinking of Mom on a spaceship, about to leave her. But she'd had it backward; *she'd* been the one who was going to leave, and now her parents had no idea where she was. She lay back on her bed. "I think I need to rest."

"Okay. I'll come back when it's time to head up to the bridge," Max said.

When he was gone, Micah shut the door and lay sideways on her bed, looking at Jovie. "You just passed up a private tour of a spaceship with a time-traveling boy."

"I'm just not really feeling in a touristy mood." She thought of her room, her bed, her kitchen with its broken stove, and was surprised how powerfully she wished she were back there.

"Well," said Micah, taking on a British accent, "even though I saw him first, I must report that he only has eyes for you, my dear."

"Stop."

"What, why wouldn't he? You figured this all out. I never could have done what you did."

"I just wanted to find you," said Jovie, and yet she thought for a moment that it was also something more than that. Like, the idea that the world could just lose Micah, could move on without her—something about that had been unacceptable.

They lay there for what felt like forever. Jovie slept now and then, and in between she and Micah talked, Jovie catching her up on the details from school that she'd missed, the shows she'd been watching, and there were moments where it felt like they were back on Micah's bedroom floor, late at night, talking quietly so as not to wake her parents.

But there were awkward moments, too, when they touched on the months when they hadn't been speaking before the drift. It still hurt, and yet it also felt so long ago now, sitting here beside her best friend and talking just like they used to, that Jovie found herself wondering how they had ever let that happen.

And when the conversation ebbed, Jovie would hear the hum of the ship through the floors, and see that starless sky out the window, and feel a deep tremor of fear. These weren't just normal conversations they were having in their bedrooms, or at the tables outside Salt & Sand. They were still a long way from home.

Finally, many dark hours later, Max and Iris returned.

"Time to go," Max said. He was carrying two blue suits, and handed one to each of them.

Jovie and Micah slipped them on and then met him outside, and they walked up the hall in nervous silence.

32

THE CAVERN

JANUARY 20, 2022

The night of the breach, Sylvan arrived home from school, rushed to the bathroom, and promptly threw up. He cleaned himself off, then leaned against the counter and stared into the mirror. His eyes had deep purple rings around them, his skin slack and pale, his hair a mess. He'd barely slept, barely been able to eat, and forget paying any kind of attention in class.

How did Jovie do it? he wondered.

He opened the medicine cabinet and shook out two pink tablets of stomach medicine. At least it tasted kind of minty. "She's counting on you," he reminded himself in the mirror. "You can do this."

But do what, exactly? That was still a mystery. One he had mere hours left to figure out.

The house was quiet. Mom was at the clinic, and Dad was in his basement office, still in meetings. He might not have heard Sylvan come home, and even if he did, it probably hadn't registered that Sylvan wasn't at jazz band practice, like he should have been. As long as he got back out of the house fast, he should be in the clear.

Had his parents even realized what night this was? The meeting two nights earlier with Dr. Wells had no doubt raised their suspicions, but with the lack of storms and code seven cases, and with their lack of knowledge about the larger pattern over the years, they'd have no way to know that the breach was tonight. And they knew nothing of Sylvan's trips out for the previous storms. They might just be waiting for some sort of warning from Barsuda, like in 2018, but there hadn't been one yet.

Whatever they're doing beneath the lighthouse, Sylvan thought, *maybe it's working.*

But what did that mean for finding Jovie?

Sylvan slipped up to his room and put on his long underwear beneath his clothes. He grabbed his back-pack, then retrieved a large black duffel bag from the back of his closet. It was one that his dad used to use for work trips. Inside were the drifters' mask and the Blue Bathymetrist's suit.

Not that he knew what use the suit was going to be. In the brief time he'd had to study it, he hadn't yet found a way to activate it; he'd been spending most of his time the last couple days making sure to get all his homework and chores done, so that he would appear normal and fine and utterly unlikely to be sneaking out tonight. He had actually put it on once, only to find that while the suit basically fit—the arms and legs were a little long, and the fingers were *very* long—the helmet wouldn't seal into place unless he could get the automated clamps working.

He had fiddled with the pad of buttons on the arm a bit, and almost immediately discovered something rather astounding. The eight buttons each made a faint tone, one note in a major scale. And while that had rather fascinating implications for the connections between humans and the beings who'd made this suit, no single button seemed to actually do anything. Sylvan had tried a few different combinations, but those hadn't worked, either.

Maybe it would automatically turn on when it got near the gradient or something. *If I can even* get *near the gradient.*

Back in the kitchen, Sylvan penned a note saying that he would be at Arlo's to study again, and that they were getting pizza. He looked at what he'd just written and froze for a moment. *What if I don't come back, like Jovie?* But he couldn't say anything *now*, or it would blow his cover. He could maybe send them a text, but would there be cell service in what he could only imagine was a secret underground facility? Or in a wormhole?

I'll be back, he said to himself. *With Jovie.*

Sylvan set out into the night. For the first few minutes of his bike ride, he felt like he might just have to pull over and vomit again, but by the time he reached downtown, he was starting to feel better. "*He came from the depths and his power was true*," he sang to himself, and even smiled a little bit. Finally, after all this time, that feeling of excitement had returned! Venturing into the unknown, just like those weeks with Jovie four years ago. He'd missed it more than he'd realized.

It was a chilly, misty afternoon. Sunset was still an hour away, so Sylvan's plan was to get some food at Salt & Sand. It seemed like a move Jovie would have made.

"What can I get you?" the barista asked when Sylvan reached the counter. She had a distracting array of facial jewelry, and seemed cool in that particular way that always made Sylvan feel like he was not. But hey, did *she* have a transuniversal space suit in *her* bag? Was *she* about to infiltrate a secret government lab?

Sylvan pushed his hair out of his eyes and tried to seem relaxed, confident. "What would you recommend for someone who needs to be sharp? But, like, without dairy."

The barista eyed him. "For you, my dude, I'm thinking a doppio."

Sylvan nodded. "Nice." And as the barista moved to the espresso machine, he added, "Make it a double."

The barista smirked. "You got it, boss."

A few minutes later, Sylvan was sitting at a window table with the coffee and one of the café's giant blueberry muffins. He sipped the small cup of jet-black liquid and did his best not to spit it right back out. It was the strongest thing he'd ever tasted. Was this pure espresso? He did a search for "doppio," and only then did he learn that the word already meant "double," which meant he had ordered four shots of espresso, or approximately two hundred and fifty milligrams of caffeine. He was going to be sharp, all right. He might even be able to open the gradient with his mind. Also it tasted kinda terrible. But then he noticed the barista eyeing him, so he continued drinking it like it was exactly what he'd meant to order.

He checked the weather reports, but the forecast for tonight was still calm. He looked around online for any storm warnings, but found none. That worry crept back into his thoughts: *Is tonight really the night?* Yes, it had to be. But some sort of sign would've been nice.

He'd just finished his muffin, and maybe managed to achieve a feeling of calm despite the caffeine coursing through his system, when Mom called him.

Sylvan considered not picking up, but that would only make him seem guilty.

"Sylvan, where are you?" She sounded frantic.

"I'm just, um, at Arlo's," he stammered. "I left a note, and—"

"I've been stopped on the highway," Mom said over

him. "There are state police here saying the road is closed due to a tsunami evacuation. Where are you right now?"

"Tsunami?" Sylvan repeated. "Was there an earthquake somewhere?"

"I don't know. But they're telling us we have to turn around."

Suddenly Sylvan's phone buzzed, and his screen was covered over with an alert.

TSUNAMI WARNING IN EFFECT. FOLLOW EVACUATION ROUTES IMMEDIATELY. THIS IS NOT A TEST. REPEAT . . .

He looked up and heard every other phone in the café buzzing with an alert tone, too.

"Um, looks like we're closing, everybody!" the barista said, putting down her phone and quickly untying her apron. Everyone began hurrying to gather their things and make for the door. Cups clattered; a glass shattered.

"Are Arlo's parents home?" Mom asked. "Can you leave with them?"

"Oh, um . . ."

"Hey! Double doppio!" the barista shouted. "Get moving!"

Sylvan covered his phone as she spoke. "Sorry, Mom, yeah, they're here."

"Okay, I'll call Dad. You go with them and update us."

"Okay." Sylvan slugged down his espresso, nearly gagged, then picked up his bags and rushed outside.

All around, people were hurrying up the sidewalks, doors were slamming, and cars were tearing up the streets.

Sylvan's phone buzzed with a text from Dad.

Are you seeing the alert? Mom says you're going with Arlo's parents?

Sylvan just stared at the phone, his brain spinning like a stuck hard drive. He went back to his browser and did a search. Then social media. Still no earthquake or tsunami reports there.

Meanwhile, a police car appeared at the end of the street, rolling slowly, its lights flashing, and its loudspeaker blaring: "*Please evacuate the area. This is a tsunami warning. All buildings must be cleared immediately.*"

Another message buzzed, this time from his mom.

SYLVAN WHERE ARE YOU? I messaged Kayla and I know you're not at Arlo's!

Oh no. Sylvan glanced at his bike. Back to his phone . . . He heard a thumping sound now. A helicopter, somewhere overhead.

This wasn't a tsunami. *They're clearing town for the breach.* Vanescere, Ascension Camp, Baxter, 2018 landslide . . . It was always the breach. This time, too. He was sure of it.

And so, as the police car rolled closer, Sylvan crouched behind the café chairs. His phone buzzed again, this time a message from his dad:

Sylvan please answer!

If I don't go now, Sylvan thought, *I'll never get out there*.

He swallowed a swell of nausea, and typed a message to both his parents.

Guys, I'm ok, and I'm sorry, but

But what? he thought. There was only one thing he could say. The truth.

I have to go help Jovie. I'll be careful!

Holding his breath, he pressed send, then switched his phone to Do Not Disturb. When the police car had passed, he darted out from behind the tables and toward the cove. He left his bike; cars were still pulling out everywhere, people rushing to pile things into trunks, and on foot he could stay low, weaving between the frantic adults, scared children, barking dogs.

When he reached the cove, he saw that the docks and the park had been completely blocked off with police cars and a fire engine. There was also a police boat out on the water, its lights flashing. Sylvan sprinted across the street and climbed down the rock wall to the narrow beach. The sunlight was quickly dimming to dusk, and the lighthouse was close to a mile away. He ran along the sand in a low crouch, stumbling now and then on barnacle-crusted rocks, his bags thudding against his back.

Soon, the sounds of car horns, sirens, and announcements faded behind him, and there was only the lapping of the water, the motor of the police boat, and now and then the whupping of the helicopter as it made one of its sweeps overhead.

After fifteen minutes, he reached the jetty park. There was a police car in the lot. Sylvan crept to the fence, only to see that the tide was higher than it had been last week. How exactly was he going to sneak out to that tunnel and climb down that ladder if his entire body was soaked and freezing?

He slung the duffel off his shoulder and pulled out the blue suit. He put his arm into the sleeve and reached into the water. His hand remained dry.

"Okay then," Sylvan said to himself, already shivering. "*The Bathymetrist in Blue*," he sang to himself.

He took off his sweatshirt and slid into the suit. It fastened together with two magnetized strips up the side and along one arm. Once the suit was on, he stuffed the helmet and the drifters' mask into his backpack, stashed the duffel in the rocks, and started into the water. The suit gave his movements a little more drag, but it kept him dry as he waded out chest-deep, rounded the fence, and climbed up the other side.

He made his way carefully out along the jetty in the deepening twilight. Ahead, the lighthouse was quiet and dark. There was a light moving on the water beyond it. Another patrol boat, Sylvan guessed. Now and then, the helicopter swooped by, just beneath the clouds.

"*He came from the depths and his power was true*," he sang to himself as he bounded from rock to rock, his voice quavering with nerves. "*With a path to paradise, to free me and you.*"

As he neared the lighthouse, he almost laughed: this was by far the craziest thing he'd ever done. But whether it was that, or the truly eyeball-shaking amount of caffeine that was now fully hitting his system, Sylvan felt a rush of confidence. He was going to make it to the gradient, and he was going to find Jovie, and nothing was going to stop him—

But that feeling crashed to a halt a moment later, when he arrived out on the little island where the lighthouse stood, and found the entrance to the tunnel shut tight.

Sylvan stared at the disk of smooth metal for a moment. Then he crouched and ran his fingers around the edge. The disk was beneath the rim of the tunnel, so there was no way to get his fingers around the edge, and there were no visible controls for opening it.

He retreated to a cleft in the nearby rocks where he was mostly hidden from the lights of the boats and the helicopter, put on the drifters' mask, and waited, thinking, any minute now, an essence would come, and that lid would have to open. But a minute quickly became ten, and meanwhile, twilight had drained to night. What if, Sylvan thought, after all this, he was simply stuck sitting out here as the gradient came and went?

Finally, almost a half hour later, an essence appeared. It floated over town like an ember, and as it got closer, Sylvan saw that this one had no vestiges of its human form. But he still wondered: Who had this person been, and what had happened to make their grip on the world slip free?

A humming vibrated the rocks, and the smooth metal lid slid open. The essence spiraled around the lighthouse, then dove straight into the metal mouth, its light dancing on the sleek surfaces.

A moment later, another came, this one from over the high point of the bluff . . . then another. These two arrived at the same time, and for a moment, spiraled together, like two hummingbirds eyeing the same flower, before they darted down the shaft, one after the other.

Sylvan moved to the edge and peered down the shaft. His heart crept up into his throat, and a dizzy feeling flowed through him. *This is it.*

Just then, he felt a hot stinging wind on his face. He staggered away and lowered the mask in time to see another essence buzz down the tunnel. He touched his face and felt a raw spot on his cheek. He remembered Jovie's description of the Barsuda agent and her terrible burns. He was never going to be able to get down there without risking those things frying him.

But wait: Sylvan realized the essence had brushed his shoulder and arm as well, but had left no mark there.

The suit had protected him.

If he could wear the helmet, he could get down—but that meant he had to figure out how to get this thing working. Sylvan stabbed at the panel of black buttons on the forearm again. They made their faint whistling tones. He tried each one, tried two simultaneously, then three. There had to be a sequence, but nothing he'd tried yet had worked, and with eight buttons, there were over forty thousand possible combinations.

"Come on," he said to it. There was some pattern, he knew it, and this was supposed to be what he was good at! He tried every other button, knowing that wouldn't be it: the first one, then the third. The second, then the fourth . . .

Wait.

He tapped the second and fourth buttons of the top row. Then the third. Those notes, and the intervals between them . . .

"*Two four three four six one two.*" The words from the poem in *The Blue Bathymetrist's Guide* floated across his lips. Could it possibly be?

Music isn't math, Charlotte had said.

But both were language.

The Melody Universal, Arthur had written.

Sylvan spoke to himself as he tapped the buttons in the order of those note intervals: "Two four three four six one two."

Lines of light burst up the arm of the suit, streaming out from the panel through all the seams, and the suit began to hum.

"Yes!" Sylvan shouted.

He ran back over to his backpack, traded the mask for the helmet, and pulled it on. It hissed and locked into place. "YES!" he shouted again, then winced, as his voice was very loud in here.

Red symbols were flashing across the inside of the helmet's visor, and at the same time, Sylvan noticed that his chest was feeling tight, like he couldn't get enough air. But then the suit hummed loudly, followed by a whoosh, and the symbols began to change from red to green. Sylvan's breaths felt fuller, his head clearer. *It's adjusting its systems to me*, he thought. Very. Cool.

Light caught his eye, and he turned and watched the next essence zip into the tunnel. This helmet worked just like the mask. He stuffed his backpack beneath the rocks, then stepped to the rim of the tunnel.

"*The Melody Universal*," he sang to himself, nearly laughing, "*The Bathymetrist in Blue!*"

He started down the ladder, and had just dropped below the lip of the tunnel when the next essence streamed by. While he was protected now from any burns, the waves of its energy still shoved Sylvan sideways. His foot slipped, a hand came free, and for a moment he swung, dangling, before grabbing on again.

After that, he moved slowly, pausing to hold on tight to the ladder whenever an essence passed.

The suit's lights illuminated the dark. Sylvan's breathing was loud in his ears. After a few minutes of climbing, the tunnel began to curve. Soon, it was horizontal, and Sylvan could walk in a crouch. Ahead, he could see the exit: a circle of white light.

He reached the end of the pipe, and what he saw made his breath catch in his throat and his heart race. He was gazing out over a massive, spherical cavern. The back half of the cavern, where he was located, had roughly carved rock walls, while the front half was lined with smooth hexagonal tiles of polished, shimmering metal. In front of these tiles was the gradient, seemingly floating in the air, spinning vertically, its light feathering. It looked like a miniature galaxy suspended there, blinding, dazzling, but also writhing, like a caged creature. With each spin it surged and grew, but at the same time, the wall tiles behind it surged with light of their own, as if matching its energy. *Containing it*, Sylvan thought. *Holding it here.*

In front of the gradient, and aimed directly at it, was a massive machine like a three-headed telescope. It hummed and buzzed, the coils and panels of circuitry on its side blinking and glowing. *The barricade*, Sylvan thought. He'd read a description of it in Jovie's notebook. Only this version looked way more advanced and powerful than the one Jovie had seen four years ago.

A catwalk led back from the new barricade to curving rows of workstations protected by walls of thick, clear material. Dozens of workers moved urgently between consoles and screens, every one of them dressed in a red suit with an astronaut-style helmet. In the center was a raised platform that looked like the command station.

A large digital clock on the wall was counting down. It had just dropped under five minutes.

An essence darted past Sylvan, out across the cavern and directly into the swirling white vortex.

This facility was clearly containing the gradient; that explained the lack of illnesses and storms this cycle. But that worried Sylvan: Would Jovie even be able to get back through? Or, if the gradient had opened down here on the prior dates, had Jovie already returned? Were they holding her somewhere? The only way to find out was to get closer.

He spotted a set of metal stairs that descended the back wall. If he took those and then hugged the wall, staying behind the banks of equipment, he could get himself close to that giant barricade machine. He slowly edged out of the tunnel and descended the ladder. He reached the catwalk and turned toward the stairs—

A light speared onto him. Sylvan found a drone hovering in space directly across from him. "Don't move, kid," said Dr. Wells's voice from the drone's speaker.

Oh no! Footsteps approached, and Sylvan saw two

red-suited Barsuda workers coming toward him, each holding some sort of wand that Sylvan could only assume was designed to subdue him if he tried to run. All he could do was stand there, legs quaking.

The workers took him by the arms and led him down the stairs, between the rows of workstations, and then up onto the platform where Dr. Wells stood.

"Sylvan," said Dr. Wells, speaking through her helmet's intercom, over the humming and wind around them. "I came to your house, now you've come to mine. Nice suit." She reached out and tapped the stitched-up hole on the chest. "*He came from the depths and his power was true* . . . and all that. What on earth are you doing here?"

Sylvan felt his fear abate just a bit. "I have to help Jovie," he said, speaking loudly through the helmet of his own. He glanced through the thick shield of clear material that was protecting them, at the spiraling light storm. "Did she come back yet?"

Dr. Wells pursed her lips and looked at him thoughtfully. "No. But if that was her plan, we haven't exactly given her the option."

"You have to let it open!" Sylvan said. "At least long enough for me to get her back!"

"We're approaching forty percent," one of the workers sitting in front of her said.

Another streak of light caught Sylvan's eye. He turned

and saw a pair of essences arcing across the cavern. They dove into the gradient vortex with a flash of light, causing sensors to flash on the monitors.

"That right there is exactly why we can't," said Dr. Wells. "Every one of those is a person we are losing from this world. And we have about thirty drifters in containment who we're trying to keep from the same fate. We estimate that over two hundred souls were lost to the drift in 2018. This time, we've increased the power and effectiveness of the barricade eightfold, and we've still lost close to a hundred. We don't know who they are, or where they came from. And we don't remember them afterward. But each crossing is recorded in the data, and the data doesn't lie."

"So why not try to talk to them?" said Sylvan. "To whoever's over there?"

A humming vibration shook the room, causing the platform to wobble. A curl of energy licked away from the gradient and strafed the ceiling. Dr. Wells leaned over the controls for a second, speaking in the ear of one of the workers sitting there and pointing at a screen.

Then she stood and sighed. "I would love to do that, believe me I would. I want to see the inside of that ship over there and communicate with those beings more than you could know. The glimpse I had of it when the breach opened four years ago . . . I see it every night in my dreams. I want so badly to trade suits with you and see another universe, to know all the truths that would be revealed. When I imagine it, it's as hopeful as I've ever felt."

"Fifty-two percent," one of the workers called.

"But I'm not going to do that," Dr. Wells said heavily, and Sylvan thought he saw sadness in her eyes. "Because that ship has latched onto us like a tick, and it is sucking the very lifeblood of our world. I don't know if that is their intention—I suspect it's not—or if they even understand the effect they're having on us, but our modeling shows that if we were to let them fully open the breach, it would mean the deaths of thousands, at a minimum, maybe even the destruction of our planet, our solar system. So we're going to do the only thing we can: we're going to blast it off our hide once and for all."

"You tried that before and it didn't work so well," said Sylvan, remembering what he'd read about the nuclear warhead in Jovie's notebook.

Dr. Wells cocked her head. "You mean the navy? Believe me, I would have advised against that." She motioned to the barricade. "Our methods are much more advanced."

A bright flash made them wince; one of the hexagonal panels on the wall had burst into flame.

"Will the barricade destroy their ship?" Sylvan asked.

"I have no idea, but what happens to their ship is beyond my mission."

"But Jovie's over there—"

"That may be true," said Dr. Wells, "but she is *one soul*, Sylvan. Our job is to save hundreds of drifters, the people of Far Haven, the entire planet. It's not kind, I know. It's simply the math."

"Your math," Sylvan muttered, "not mine."

"Seventy-five percent," said the worker. "Here it comes."

The vortex writhed and seethed, light spiraling around it like solar flares, and at its center, a black disk began to grow. *The eye*, Sylvan thought, and the sight of it filled him with fear.

Dr. Wells clapped him on the shoulder. "I'm sorry, I really am." She turned to the agents. "Prepare to fire."

The giant barricade device glowed more brightly, and a deep humming shook the walls of the cave.

No! Sylvan thought desperately, gazing into the pupil. He glimpsed faint details on the other side, dots like stars, green streaks like nebula . . . This couldn't be happening! After all this time, and all his waiting and searching, here he was, about to lose someone again, and unable to do a thing about it. Charlotte, Jovie, and now Jovie all over again—

"Sir," one of the workers said, "the antiproton levels are starting to drop."

Suddenly, the gradient's light dimmed sharply. A great, teeth-grating whine washed over the room, and the vortex seemed to slow to a stop, only to begin spinning in the opposite direction. Wind gusted around them, as if it was being sucked into the gradient. The panels behind it began to pop and spark.

"What's happening?" Dr. Wells called.

"We're getting strong antimatter readings," one of the workers said. He tapped rapidly at his controls and then turned to Dr. Wells. "Whatever's on the other side . . . I think it's leaving, sir."

The light spun faster, its edges curling inward, the pupil shrinking.

Dr. Wells looked almost longingly at the vortex. "They finally got the message."

Leaving?! Sylvan gaped at the light sucking in on itself. *No!* He looked around; Dr. Wells and her workers were all transfixed either by the vortex, or their screens. . . .

Sylvan grabbed the railing of the platform and vaulted over the side. The drop was farther than he'd anticipated, and he landed in a heap, his ankle screaming, but shoved himself to his feet and sprinted between the rows of workstations, toward the barricade and the gradient.

"Sylvan!" Dr. Wells shouted after him.

He glanced over his shoulder but didn't see any workers in pursuit. Some around him were looking up as he raced past, a boy in a strange, oversized alien suit. He vaulted the little set of stairs that led to the catwalk, then crossed it to the platform that held the giant three-headed device. He circled around it to the far side and leaned against the railing. From here, he could reach out and nearly touch the blinding, spinning light.

Sylvan could feel the heat even through his suit. At the same time, his visor was dimming, adjusting automatically, and he was able to see through the light into the shrinking pupil. Was that the ship on the other side? Were those people standing there? But the view was fading. . . .

"Jovie!" he called. "Wait!"

He leaned farther out, reaching. Though the gradient was shrinking, its light was whipping all around him in violent waves of energy, and though the suit protected him physically, he began to feel a strange sensation, almost like a humming, in his arms and legs, even in his bones, as if the gradient was pulling him, or inviting him, and he thought he'd never been more scared, but he swallowed and stood his ground.

There were definitely figures over there, and he thought he even heard the faintest echoes of voices, but everything was light and wind now, whipping and flashing. He leaned even farther, pushing his gloved fingers into the wild light.

"Jovie!" he called as loud as he could into the storm. *Please*, he thought, reaching . . .

33

THE CONDUIT

JANUARY 2018–JANUARY 2022

Max led Jovie and Micah through curving corridors. The walls were made of smoky black metal crisscrossed by networks of thin tubes through which pulses of neon light zipped back and forth, like little messages. The tubes reminded Jovie of blood vessels, as if this ship were somehow alive.

They passed through a large cylindrical space ringed with walkways. Jovie looked down and saw dozens of levels below them. There were figures moving here and there, but fewer than she would have imagined for such an enormous ship. At one point, through a wall of floor-to-ceiling windows, she glimpsed a fabulously tall greenhouse with spirals of plants with blurry leaves ascending staircases of clear cascading water. At another point, she could see down into a great hangar full of what must have been spacecraft of all sizes.

They also passed a vast, silent room with fields of what looked something like mushrooms growing in dim light. Pathways curved through the fields, and in one spot, a group of Lahmurians were gathered around what appeared to be a body wrapped in a shroud. Jovie saw that Max was eyeing this space sadly.

"Is that where your mom is?" she asked.

Max just nodded and looked away.

Soon they arrived in a great circular room. It had a clear-domed ceiling that afforded a panoramic view of the nearly empty universe. Jovie's chest tightened at the sight of all that empty space; the loneliness seemed overwhelming.

On either side of them were curving workstations occupied by Lahmurians in their blue suits. At the far end of the domed room was an enormous trapezoidal structure that looked like some kind of doorway. Its sides were made of sleek metal and threaded with circuitry that glowed a liquid silver color. A thick, inky blackness swirled inside it.

Max led them to Iris, who stood at a central workstation facing this doorway. She began to speak, and a moment later, the voice came from her translator. "Our systems are almost charged up and ready to begin the next trial."

Jovie looked over the shoulders of the beings sitting

in front of Iris. They were moving their fingers within holographic displays filled with charts and meters. One of the floating displays showed an hourglass shape that reminded her of what Dr. Wells had shown her inside Baxter: two universes, connected. Jovie looked around the domed room, at all the Lahmurians working quietly and intensely, and sensed a heavy mood among them.

"Is that what makes the gradient?" Jovie asked of the doorway with its liquid darkness.

"That's it," said Max.

"More accurately, it is our portal through this convergence zone, where the borders of many universes meet," Iris said.

"Ooh, like the Four Corners," Micah piped up. When everyone looked at her, she added, "It's in the Southwest. You can touch four states at once. Sorry, I don't know why I brought that up now; it's the terror talking."

"Why are you trying to get into our world?" Jovie asked.

Iris made a thoughtful face, as if she was weighing whether to offer an explanation. "You are aboard the generational vessel *Deliverance*," she said. "Of the many universes that converge here, preliminary tests revealed that only yours has a basic chemistry and physics similar to our own, and your planet in particular contains the conditions most favorable for us to establish a settlement."

"You want to live on Earth?" Jovie asked.

"Yes. At least until we've repaired and refueled our ship, at which point we could seek out a less inhabited option."

"Why can't you stay here?"

Iris motioned toward the dome overhead. "Your universe is thirteen or so billion of your Earth years old; this one is over twenty trillion. And it is dying. It has been eons since the expansion of space moved all other galaxies beyond where they can even be seen, never mind reached, while in the meantime, billions of stars in our own galaxy have died and none have formed. This is one of the only quadrants left with any visible stars, and they are merely leftover neutron stars. None of them have habitable systems. We were forced to leave our own planet over five billion years ago, and that planet itself was the fourth we had colonized since leaving our original home world."

"You've been on this ship for over five billion years?" said Jovie.

"Our ancestors were stored as digital codes of our essential proteins; you call it our DNA. *Deliverance* is one of many ships that left our world, all heading in different directions in search of a new home. The ship printed our great-grandparents upon finally reaching what its models indicated was our best chance at a new planet, but we were unable to colonize it successfully. Ever since, we have been searching for something, anything, before our fuel stores run out . . . and at last we detected this convergence point."

Jovie crossed her arms, looking out at the mostly empty space with fresh dread. "So, what happens if you can't get into our universe?"

"We will likely die out. Not only have our fuel stores run low, but on the fourth trial of the portal to your world, our ship's drive system was severely damaged." Iris sighed. "We were able to repair everything except for the attenuating conduit, a precision instrument that is utterly irreplaceable out here. We can't leave this spot now, even if we wanted to. Which is why, with each trial, we have been rerouting more of our fuel stores and processor banks to the portal, in order to shorten the recharge time and make it more powerful."

"We noticed the pattern," Jovie said. "But each time your portal gets stronger, it's also hurting more of our people."

"Yes, so I have heard." Iris seemed to purse her lips. "I am sorry to hear about your mother and the other sick people, but we have almost one hundred million Lahmurians on this ship. And given that we have not heard from any of our sister vessels, we must assume that we are the last of our kind."

"But there's the drifters, too," Jovie said. Iris just looked at her. "There have been hundreds of them, maybe more."

"Yes, the creatures made of light," said Iris. "Max told

us. But the number is still statistically insignificant."

"But . . ." Jovie thought of what Dr. Wells had said. "If you open your portal at full power, it could be many more—it might even destroy the whole planet."

"Is seven billion '*statistically significant*'?" Micah added.

Iris looked at them for a moment. "We have tried to make contact with your people on more than one occasion during our trials. In doing so, we have been attacked multiple times. An atomic weapon, the most recent attempt to destroy us, was what damaged our drive. We would have been happy to coordinate our crossing in the safest possible manner, but we are being treated as a threat."

"Because you are," said Jovie. "I mean, that's how it seems from our side."

"I understand that your people fear us passing into your world, but I'm afraid we must insist. We would make every attempt to coexist peacefully with humanity, and to find a home of our own, as I said, but I cannot let my civilization die out." Iris turned to the workers in front of her. "Are we ready?"

"Yes, sir."

Great green flashes sparked out in space, and Jovie saw three of the enormous curving arms of the ship moving like tentacles toward one another, their tips firing green energy bolts. The bolts grew blinding, meeting at a central point where a pure white glow like a miniature star began to bloom. Here inside the dome, the inky darkness within the trapezoidal doorway began to brighten and swirl, taking on an appearance more like dark clouds. The air hummed and crackled with energy.

Just then, there was a flash of color out in space where that miniature star was glowing: a rainbow streak of light burst out of it that for a split second held the shape of a butterfly, but then it quickly dissipated into a thin stream of sparks. Another appeared and disintegrated in the same way, making a tendril of energy that shimmered like stardust as it flowed across the vast darkness.

Jovie watched the stream of embers drift past the dome, and felt a lump in her throat. "That's what happens to the essences?"

"Yeah," said Max quietly.

"Those are people?" Micah asked.

"They were," said Jovie, and her sadness grew.

"What's happening to them?"

Jovie thought of the drifters in the bunker. She thought of Paul, becoming light, telling Max he'd see his mother. Of that woman trying to walk into the sea. Arthur, Harrison, all those smiling faces in the baths, even the urge Jovie had felt herself when she'd been near the gradient. They'd all been wrong. There was no Planet Elysia out here. There were no planets at all, no stars, no warmth, no future. That sense that there was something better here was a lie. The gradient was the end, the essences nothing more than seeds on the wind, with no soil to be found—at least, not here.

"Unraveling," Jovie said quietly.

"If they remain here, yes," said Iris. "There is no belonging left in this place. But it is possible that their energy will travel through this convergence zone to yet another universe. It does seem to have direction as it emerges. Perhaps that means it has a destination."

"When one withers here, another thrives elsewhere," Jovie said, remembering what Dr. Wells had said. Yet the lump remained in her throat. "But the person they were on Earth, the life they had, that can't be saved."

"I'm afraid not," said Iris. Lights began to flash urgently on the holographic displays. Iris spoke with her team, then turned back to the humans. "Please move yourselves into position."

Max touched Jovie's arm. "Ready?"

Jovie thought he looked kind of sick, but she nodded and turned to Micah. "You?"

"Um, yes, please," said Micah. "Is it really going to be 2022?"

"First, it will be May 2021," said Max. "As the portal cycles up, it tests the connection briefly. That's what causes the cycle-up storms."

"Can you send us back through one of those?" Jovie asked.

"That's the plan," said Max. "But the time fields won't

be stabilized yet, so there's like two seconds when you can go through. So we need to be in position. Come on."

"What about Barsuda and the barricade?" Jovie asked.

"We've analyzed Max's data," said Iris. "If they follow their pattern from the last cycle, they will wait until the portal crosses the seventy-five percent threshold to fire their barricade."

"And the portal doesn't get that strong until the January storms," said Max.

"Though I'm sure they will be there on the beach to greet you when you return," Iris added.

"But what about when it does open that far?" Jovie asked.

"We have altered the portal's parameters, and we believe we can override it."

Max led them around the workstations and across the room until they were standing in front of the towering trapezoidal portal doorway. From this close, its roiling clouds looked more like mist, yet also like fabric.

"Okay, helmets on," said Max.

Jovie slid hers on, and Max tapped out a pattern on the wrist panel. "Huh," Jovie said as the suit hummed to life and the helmet clicked into place, hearing the same melody Sylvan had played for the Blue Bathymetrist poem.

"What about you?" she asked Max once he'd activated Micah's suit. "They have the data now, right? You can come back with us?"

Max's mouth scrunched. "This trial might work. But if it doesn't, we'll need to figure out a new strategy, so—"

"But what about your dad?" Jovie said.

"I . . . ," Max began, but he couldn't finish.

Jovie frowned at him. "So, it's 'See you in a couple years,' then," she said. "That's what you're really saying?"

"I'm sorry," Max said. "I'm just not ready yet."

She looked away. "Fine."

"Jovie—" He was cut off by a great gust of wind from the portal that made them stagger.

Jovie's breaths echoed inside the helmet, but she could still feel the cold from the portal through her suit. "It's going to get chilly," she said to Micah as the wind began to rush through her.

Micah bit her lip. "I remember."

The portal swirled before them, growing brighter. Distantly, the light outside the ship grew. Another essence burst through the light, streaking overhead. Jovie watched its embers separating, dimming . . . *Home*, she thought, and she suddenly wanted little more than to be back in her tiny, rainy town.

"Here it comes," said Max.

The view through the portal began to sharpen, and now Jovie could make out shapes on the other side. Except . . . it didn't look like the ocean, but rather, she saw what looked like rock walls, like a cave. "It looks different," she said to Max. "Doesn't it?"

Max peered into the swirling clouds. "Maybe Barsuda built something more elaborate?" He shrugged. "You're going to find out in a second."

"Is it safe?" Micah asked.

"I think so," said Jovie, still unsure of what they were seeing over there, but Dr. Wells and her team would be there, and while they didn't want the Lahmurians crossing, they'd certainly welcome Jovie and Micah back . . . wouldn't they? She looked down at her suit. *Will they even know it's us?*

"Okay." Max gave her a gentle push on the back. "This is it. Deep breath."

Jovie felt the wind rising, swirling, and that sense of a rush inside her, of being in a flow, and fear gripped her. *Not unraveling*, she told herself. *Returning.*

"Counting down . . . ," Max said, watching pulses of light pick up speed on his bracelet.

She was another step closer when, out of the corner of her eye, Jovie noticed Max turning toward Iris with a concerned look on his face.

"What's—"

Max was cut off by a deafening shriek, and Jovie felt a burning sensation like the air all around them had ignited. A burst of wind and energy shoved them backward. Jovie lost hold of Micah's hand, and the three of them sprawled to the ground. Jovie pushed up to her elbows, her head pounding, and heard the Lahmurians frantically calling to one another, and alarms resonating throughout the domed room.

Iris appeared beside them, hauling Max to his feet. "You have to move back!" She and Max helped Jovie and Micah up, and they rushed back to the workstations.

The portal was seething with sparking energy. Out in space, the white disk of light was folding in on itself, as if a giant hand was balling it up like paper. Iris barked commands, and the system cycled down to dark. Alarms continued to sound, and the Lahmurians moved urgently about. Jovie saw more than one of the workstations smoking, and a team was running toward the dome, where a crack had appeared.

"What happened?" Max asked.

"Was that Barsuda?" Jovie asked. "I thought you said they wouldn't fire the barricade yet?"

Iris finished a tense back-and-forth with one of her team and then turned to them. "This is something different from what you observed during the last cycle. Something stronger, and . . ." She trailed off, glancing at the holographs on the workstation. "We will find out more in a moment. Cycling up . . ." Iris pointed at the holographs in front of her team and barked additional commands.

"Is that a good idea?" Jovie looked back at the portal, thinking of what she'd glimpsed in the clouds. Those walls that looked like a cave . . . "Remember that tunnel we saw, beneath Baxter?" she said to Max. "What if they were building something new down there to stop the gradient?"

But the system was already beginning again, the arms in space firing their green beams, the white disk of light appearing, and the portal here inside the ship beginning to glow and swirl with clouds. The floor hummed with energy now, this cycle stronger than the last. A circuit on the wall shattered and showered sparks.

"Should we get in position?" Max said to Iris.

"Stay back this time," said Iris, "until we know what's happening."

The light of the portal grew, and Jovie just had that sense of being able to see those outlines on the other side again, the form of a cave, and maybe even machinery there, when the technicians in front of Iris began to shout frantically.

A sizzling sound buzzed their ears, and once again, there was a deafening shriek. This time, lightning bolts shot out of the portal, raking the walls and workstations.

"Get down!" said Iris.

The system went dark again. Smoke filled the room, and Jovie heard moans and cries of pain.

Iris got to her feet, barking commands. One of her workers projected a giant holographic image up into the air in front of them. It depicted a massive mechanical structure with a central core that was glowing red-hot.

Jovie guessed that it was their engine.

"They're reversing the flow of our energy in a new way. It's pushing our antimatter engine toward critical overload," said Iris. "They're not just trying to block us this time. They're trying to destroy us." She shouted frantic orders at her team. The system began to cycle up yet again.

"You can't keep doing this!" Jovie said, even though the words filled her with fear. "You have to stop, don't you? Try again later?" *Two more years*, she thought with a chill that nearly made her stagger.

"We'll have barely any fuel left after this cycle," said Iris. "This is it. If we fail now, we're as good as dead."

"But if you keep trying, you might be destroyed," said Max.

One of Iris's workers pointed to the large glowing holograph, talking rapidly. Iris peered at it, and after a thoughtful moment, she nodded grimly. "There is another option. We can counteract their attack by ejecting our engine's antimatter core into the breach."

"What will that do?" Jovie asked.

"The resulting explosion should open the portal and stabilize the time field long enough for our ship to fly through."

"If you do that, what's going to happen to our town? To our planet?" Jovie tried to imagine a ship this size bursting through the gradient—how could that even work?

"There will be collateral damage," said Iris.

"Don't," said Jovie. "Please."

"It cannot be avoided now."

The next cycle ramped up, only for them to be blasted back by whatever Barsuda was doing on the other side. Jovie, Micah, and Max ducked as more lightning savaged the room, carving black gouges into the walls. Circuits popped and smoked; an entire bank of consoles burst into flames. An enormous crack zigzagged across the top of the dome, and Jovie heard a sound like escaping air.

Iris shouted to her workers and pointed at the giant schematic of the engine.

Micah gripped Jovie's hand. "We're not going home, are we?"

"Please turn it off," Jovie said to Iris.

Iris ignored her and kept giving commands.

Jovie turned to Max. "You have to make them stop!"

"What do you think *I* can do?" said Max. He motioned to indicate the Lahmurians all around them, the cracked dome overhead. "Even if they did listen to me, they're fighting to survive here."

The workers busied themselves at their stations, and a section of the giant holograph zoomed in and showed what must have been the internal workings of the engine, parts here and there flashing red, indicating damage. Iris pointed at the image and spoke urgently to her team.

Outside, the portal system was starting to cycle up

again, but now there was a grinding beneath their feet, jagged and jarring. The entire floor began to shake violently. More alarms sounded on all sides.

Jovie's eyes darted wildly around the room, from the fires to the portal, up to the cracked dome, and to her friends— But just then, out of the corner of her eye, something caught her attention, something she only barely noticed in the chaos, but that made her turn and peer at that floating holograph of an alien engine. . . .

"Wait!" Jovie shouted, and tugged on Iris's arm. "What's that?"

Iris turned to her. "What?"

"There!" Jovie pointed to the center of the holograph, to a curved rectangular panel surrounded by circuitry that was glowing red. Etched into the center of the panel was a small series of symbols. No, not symbols—they were human letters, in English, and Jovie had seen them before:

PROPERTY OF F.D.L.

She fumbled in her pocket and pulled out the spyglass. "That's the same inscription that's on this!"

Iris looked from Jovie's hand to the holograph. "You can read those symbols?"

"It's our language," said Jovie. She pointed to the words on the spyglass. "See?"

"That's impossible. It—" Iris spun and snapped a command at a technician in front of her.

The schematic zoomed in again, this time through that rectangular panel. Here, amid a complex array of what looked like lenses and prisms, there was a single item glowing bright red: a cylinder.

"May I have that?" Iris asked. Jovie handed the spyglass to her. She turned it over in her fingers and held it up to the schematic. "This is an attenuating conduit. Who gave you this?"

"I don't know," said Jovie. "Someone who knows how your engine works?"

"Our antimatter drive was created a hundred generations ago," Iris said. "There is no one on this ship who knows much more than its basic function."

"Could that thing fix it?" Max asked.

Iris gazed at the spyglass. "It is possible."

Jovie looked back at the holograph and her head swam, a fuzzy feeling like there was a larger *something* she couldn't quite see. All this time, she'd had a piece of an alien spaceship in her possession. But not just any piece. *The* piece that this ship, the one that was causing the gradient, that had caused Micah's disappearance, desperately needed. How could that be? Had whoever had given it to her known she would end up here?

One of Iris's team shouted, then lunged at them. Iris, Jovie, Micah, and Max fell back just as a huge bolt of energy sliced the workstation in half.

Jovie pushed up onto her elbows to find the holograph

gone, the workstation in flames, the room choked with smoke. Whatever the case with the spyglass, however *any* of that was possible, there was only one thing that mattered right now. "You can have it," Jovie said to Iris. "If you promise to use it to try and find another universe. Or, at least, another way into ours. Somewhere safe, away from Earth. . . . Please."

"I could just take it," said Iris, getting to her feet, the spyglass clutched in her gloved hand.

Jovie stood up and faced her. "We may be statistically insignificant," she said, "but if one little human like me can fix your ship, just imagine what each of the other lives you save could do."

Iris gazed at her thoughtfully, then around her damaged ship. She closed her fist around the spyglass. "*If* this works . . . we will try another way."

"Thanks." Jovie smiled, and yet Micah squeezed her hand. "What about us?" Jovie asked Iris. "How will we get back?"

Iris pursed her lips in thought. "If we let the portal cycle up again, but cut the power just before they have been firing on us, it may confuse them for just long enough that you can get back. It will be a matter of seconds, again."

"That doesn't sound great," said Micah.

Outside, the arms of the ship began to fire their green energy once more.

"I would suggest you hurry," said Iris. "Farewell." She turned and strode toward the corridor, the spyglass in her hand, calling to other workers to join her.

"Come on," said Max. Jovie held Micah's hand, and they ran in a crouch through the wreckage to the portal. Its metal sides were cockeyed and sparking. The clouds in the center were boiling with light and dark flashes of lightning.

"This doesn't look great!" Micah shouted over the yawning of wind, the crackle of fires, and the hum of energy.

Jovie peered into the clouds and saw brightening on the other side, those outlines of walls, of machinery. "I can see through!" Jovie said. She turned to Max. "Ready?"

But he'd stopped a few feet from her. And then she saw the look on his face.

"What are you doing?" Jovie shouted. "You can't *still* stay with them! There won't be another chance to come back!"

Max looked away for a moment, and when he met her eyes, she suddenly knew what he was about to say. "I know."

There was a zap and a bright flash, making everyone shield their eyes. The floor shook.

"I'm going with them," said Max. "I'm dead over there. Mom's gone, Paul too. And my dad, he . . . he's so broken."

"But he wants you back!" Jovie shouted over the wind.

Max shook his head. "He thinks he does, but it will just be the same as it was."

"You don't know that."

Max's eyes trembled. "Look, when I was back, it just . . . it all fit me wrong."

"Not all of it," said Jovie. "You helped the drifters. And it might not ever be great with your dad, but it could get better. And if it doesn't, you have me."

"I don't know." Max turned toward where Iris had departed—

"Max." Jovie lunged and grabbed his hand. "Just because you ended up here doesn't mean it's where you're meant to be. You can make a different choice. Come with us. Come back. I know you can make it work. I'll help. Plus, free mochas."

"I'll help too," said Micah over Jovie's shoulder. "Honestly, whatever you need, because I think this thing is closing, and I'd really like to not be stuck here forever."

The air just above them lit with heat and fire, and they were all sent staggering. The view through the portal had clarified—Jovie thought she could even see the outlines of people—but just then, outside, the ship's arms stopped firing . . . and that view of the cave back home immediately started to fog over. *It will be a matter of seconds. . . .*

She looked back at Max, still holding his hand, wishing there was something she could say.

Then the slightest grin appeared on Max's face. "Will they still be *legendary* mochas?"

She rolled her eyes and yanked him toward the portal. "Come on already!"

Max twisted the stone on his bracelet. Jovie squeezed her friends' hands tighter than ever and lunged into the dying portal.

Light flooded her vision, and there was that sense again of being within a breeze, separated into molecules, all moving at incredible speed—

But suddenly, a wind roared. Jovie felt like they were fighting a great current that was pushing them backward no matter how hard they struggled.

"It's not working!" Micah called.

Jovie pressed forward with all her might. *No!* They were slipping backward, the portal closing, and she couldn't stop it. She pushed desperately toward those distant outlines through the fog, but they were fading, their world . . .

Please—

"*Jovie!*" a distant voice called.

And then, a blue-gloved hand burst through the clouds, grabbed her suit collar, and pulled them all through.

34

THE REUNION

JANUARY 20, 2022

The first thing Jovie saw was Sylvan, his wide eyes behind a big helmet. Jovie, Micah, and Max toppled over him, and they all landed in a heap on a metal platform.

Jovie staggered to her feet, feeling like she was made of rubber, to find herself standing in a cavern beside what appeared to be a supersized version of the barricade.

And then Sylvan was throwing his arms around her. "Jovie!"

Their helmets knocked together, and he nearly made her fall over again and—*whoa*, he was taller than her now.

"Sorry," he said.

Jovie turned to see Micah and Max getting up. "You guys all right?"

"Are we?" Micah said woozily.

"Come on, let's get back," Sylvan said, tugging Jovie's arm.

They followed him around the barricade and across the catwalk. When they reached the main floor of the cavern, they turned back to the gradient. It was curling in on itself like a whirlpool siphoning away. Wind sucked toward it, pulling Jovie off-balance, but its power lessened by the second, from a gale, dying to a breeze. In a moment, it had shrunk to the size of a basketball, its wind quieting to a whisper. The sight caused a surprising lump in Jovie's throat.

"Bye," she said to herself.

The gradient winked out completely.

The cavern became very quiet.

"Is that it?" Sylvan said.

"I think so," said Jovie.

"Finally." Sylvan removed his helmet. Jovie took off her helmet, too, and looked at him. He was the same Sylvan—with his glasses and overwhelmed expression—but also, this older boy now.

"Who's this?" said Micah. She'd removed her helmet and was retying her hair. "Another boyfriend?"

"Another?" Sylvan glanced around Jovie at Max. "Oh, hey," he said coolly. "You made it, too."

Jovie rolled her eyes. "Micah, this is Sylvan." Jovie looked over his blue suit, identical to theirs. "What are you doing here?"

"I have so much to tell you," Sylvan said.

"Me too. But . . ." She hugged him. "Thanks, little brother. Or big brother now, I guess."

"No problem," Sylvan said in nearly a whisper.

"Guys," said Micah. "Where are we?"

Jovie looked around the massive cave, then at the multiple figures in red space suits standing there staring at them. "This is not the beach," she said.

"Are we, like, in trouble?" said Micah, eyeing all those Barsuda workers.

"Less than you were a minute ago." Dr. Wells pushed between the agents, wearing a helmeted suit of her own.

"Who are these guys?" Micah asked.

"Remember Barsuda Solutions?" said Jovie. She motioned to the cavern. "Actually not just a clean-up company."

"I'm Dr. Wells, and you must be the famous Micah Rogers."

Micah looked uncertainly at Jovie.

"They're on our side," said Jovie. "Sort of."

"Ah." Micah nodded, then narrowed her eyes at Dr. Wells. "How famous?"

Jovie gave her a look and elbowed her.

Dr. Wells peered past them, to where the gradient had been. "Are they gone?"

Jovie glanced back at the empty spot, feeling another tug of loss.

"They're gone," Max said.

"For good this time," Jovie added. "She promised."

"'She'?" said Dr. Wells.

"The leader of the Lahmurians."

Dr. Wells considered this. "And you believe them?"

Jovie nodded. "I helped fix their ship."

Dr. Wells just gazed at her for a moment. "Well, it appears I was wrong—this was your fight after all. And yours." She nodded to Sylvan. "And then there's you," she said to Max.

"Leave him alone," Jovie said, seeing the uncertainty in Max's eyes. "He's been through more than you can imagine."

"Understood." Dr. Wells looked over their shoulders once more, and an odd expression crossed her face. Jovie wondered if it was longing. "I hope you'll tell me all about it," she said softly. "Do you think you can do that?"

"Can we see our parents first?"

Dr. Wells nodded, then shook her head, as if coming out of a trance. "We'll call them right away. In the meantime, we have a lot of data to crunch here, so I'll give you guys some time to rest up before we officially debrief."

"So . . . we can go?" said Sylvan.

Dr. Wells laughed. "No, of course not! We have to put you in quarantine, in case you brought back any trans-universal microbes or pathogens or anything else."

"But I didn't even go over there," said Sylvan.

"No, but you did just remove your helmet and started hugging potentially infectious subjects."

"Oh yeah."

"You'll be together, though," said Dr. Wells, "and there's Wi-Fi."

Dr. Wells led them out of the cavern to where a small electric transport car on rails awaited. They rode through a tunnel at a steady incline, reaching the spot beneath Baxter that Jovie and Max had seen years before. They took an elevator up, and soon found themselves in a room with a bunch of single beds and a bathroom. On one wall, a window looked into an area with chairs, where, as Dr. Wells explained, their parents could see them. There was an intercom system on the wall. Jovie felt that elevator falling in her belly at the thought of seeing her parents, who had lost her for four years. She couldn't wait to see them, and yet she felt so bad for what she'd put them through. . . .

"Hey, check it out, snacks." Sylvan was perusing the items on a table along the wall. There was a small refrigerator there, too. "And sodas." He cracked one open, took a big sip, then looked around. "This is extremely weird."

"We were just in a room like this," Jovie said, "in another universe."

"But with a better view," Micah added.

"Were you guys really on a spaceship?" Sylvan asked.

"A generational ship," said Max. "The Lahmurians

used it to transport their civilization around their universe for over five billion years."

Sylvan's eyes lit up. "How did it work? Did they have stasis pods? Hypersleep?"

"Frozen DNA," said Max, "thawed out and grown by robots."

"Whoa," said Sylvan. "Nice."

"They let you keep the bracelet," Jovie said. And the way Max looked at her . . . She added, "Is there another secret mission we should know about?"

"No," said Max. "Seriously, I think Iris forgot about it with everything happening." He ran his finger over it. "Or maybe she let me have it because it was Mom's."

Jovie wondered if Iris would be that forgetful, or sentimental. "So, no plans to jump universes if things don't go well?"

"No plans." Max smiled at her. "Yet."

They opened sodas and bags of chips and traded stories. When it was Sylvan's turn, his tales about the four years Jovie had missed left her feeling hollow and wistful, even the part about the long, strange time when a disease had made it so no one could leave their houses, and apparently, things still weren't quite back to normal. Jovie had to remind herself that she hadn't missed those years of her own life, but what would it be like to go forward without those experiences that everyone else had shared? The world was going to be very different out there. It was all going to be so much.

Then she thought of what Max had said: *When I was back, it all fit me wrong.* Micah had said a similar thing. What if they couldn't make it work, what if they never did feel like they belonged again, now that they were here? Once you left the world, could you ever really come home to it? Or were you always destined to feel adrift?

Jovie looked around this strange room-out-of-time, at the friend she'd lost for months, at the other who'd lost her for years, and at the one she'd just found. They fit each other, at least. Maybe not perfectly, and maybe not forever. But if they could each be one person for the other, and if they could each hear what the other was trying to say, and listen carefully for what they couldn't say, then they could make their own gravity, their own little cosmic spiral, each with a place in its orbit.

And who knew? Maybe it would be even better than it had been. Jovie knew she could've been a better friend, but she also knew she could cross universes, if needed, to make things right. Of course there would be forces that would try to pull them apart. Probably not something as fantastic as a portal between worlds, but what about high school, or college? Would they eventually end up on opposite sides of their own little universe?

As scary as that might be, Jovie realized she'd been wrong: things *do* come back around, only they come back changed. But that was the point of the journey. And the power of being there for one another, as best you could.

"Jovie said you're like, an amazing actor," Sylvan was saying to Micah.

"I'm all right," Micah said, flashing Jovie a look, and Jovie felt a burst of worry—this was exactly what Micah had been talking about—and yet Micah's gaze had that old flair, that brash confidence that was so *her*, like she could handle anything. Jovie was so glad to see it again that it made her feel like she had it, too.

"Because I was wondering if you would ever be interested in doing voice-over work," Sylvan went on.

"I thought you were all into video games," Max said.

"Actually, lately I've been running a YouTube channel, where I have like, five thousand subs, and I play the new Zelda game and do running commentary on the history of the character and all the Easter eggs from previous games. So having a guest voice actor could be cool—"

"Hey!" Max snapped his fingers. "I know what that is. I used to play Zelda."

Sylvan's eyes lit up. "Which game?"

"The new one," said Max, "*Link's Awakening*."

"Dude," Sylvan said as he seemed to put things together. "You probably mean the old version on Game Boy."

Max's face fell. "Oh yeah, I guess."

"No," said Sylvan, "that's cool! Those old games are super hard and convoluted. I bet you know all the old-school secrets. This could be a very interesting video series."

"Interesting to who?" said Max.

"Oh, I know tons of people. . . ."

As Sylvan continued, Micah got up and sat beside Jovie. She dug into her pocket and held out her earbuds, still flecked with sand. "Want to get caught up on all the music we missed?"

Jovie got out her phone and saw that it was at 10 percent. "We can probably get a couple in before it dies."

"How about this: we just do the first minute of each song," said Micah, "and we'll rate them yeah or nah. You can always tell by the end of the first minute."

Jovie smiled, a warmth blooming inside her. "Okay." They each slipped in an earbud and she pressed play, and they sat there, smiling, music in one ear, Sylvan and Max's increasingly incomprehensible conversation in the other.

Jovie suddenly had a strange feeling like she was viewing her life from above, in it and apart from it at the same time. Despite all they had just seen and done, in this universe and beyond, she might just remember this moment the most. This room. These people. It didn't matter what was happening anywhere else, or what had happened before, or even what would come next.

Just this, she thought, looking at her three friends. *Just hold on to this.*

EPILOGUE

JANUARY 2024

The girl had been lost for some time.

She knew that no one meant for it to happen. That it was no one's fault but her own. After all, the world was a crowded place, and all the messages were clear: you had to do your best, get to the top, don't fall behind, let your voice be heard, show 'em what you got, and on and on, the expectations piling up. . . .

And it had terrified her all her life, a fear like a shadow, always right behind her, because the girl had known earlier than anyone else that she couldn't keep up, would *never* quite be able to. Like whatever it was you had to have to be able to do that, to belong, she didn't have it. Which made her wonder: Where could someone like her fit in?

But then she heard of a place.

The butterflies told her. They'd been appearing

outside her window for some time.

Follow us, they would say, *we know the way.*

And so, eventually, she did.

From her house, down her street, out of her town, through a moonlit dark that stretched into three sunrises and sunsets, until at last she reached a vast, desolate shore.

It was twilight, and the rumpled clouds were striped with oranges and reds. The waves roared, and a relentless wind stung her eyes. The girl stopped when her sneakers hit the foaming surf; she barely noticed the water, as she was already feeling a different chill, like a wind through her.

The butterfly she'd been following proceeded out to sea undaunted, and was soon lost in the gleam of the setting sun.

This way, it called back to her. And the girl took a step—

But she hesitated, feeling something both sad and elated at once, like a deep breath that was also a gasp of fear. She looked back over her shoulder. . . .

It's okay, she thought to herself. Whatever was out there would be better. It had to be.

The clouds began to lose their fire. The waves cooled to purple, to silver, to a bottomless black. The wind sharpened like a blade, and the mist gathered deeper shadows.

This way.

The girl stepped farther into the waves. The water rushed over her ankles. *Goodbye,* she thought, but the word was carried off by the wind.

She'd gone two steps farther out when a new light appeared, only this one was flying toward her, not away. And it wasn't flashing with rainbow color; it was buzzing. The light stopped in front of her and hovered. The girl held up her hand, and the light spoke.

"Hey. Are you okay?"

Actually, the voice was coming from behind her.

A hand fell on her shoulder.

The girl whirled to find a boy about her age standing in the surf. He had a shaggy mop of dark hair and wore a long brown coat, like something a cowboy might wear. It was a bit too large on him.

And he could *see* her.

"It's okay," he said. "You don't have to go out there."

The girl tried to speak, but her voice came out a croak. When had she last talked to anyone?

Now a girl appeared beside the boy. She was taller, and wearing the oddest thing, like a magnifying glass that covered her whole face. She was smiling—the mask made her smile appear comically large—and she held out a blanket. "I know what you're feeling," she said. "I felt it, too. But there's nothing for you out there. I know it seems like there is, but trust me: what you're looking for is here."

The girl took the blanket, and the boy guided her out of the surf. Suddenly, she could feel the chill in her feet, the grit of the sand, the tug of her wet jeans, and she wondered: What had she been thinking? She turned back toward the water and saw the light that had flown toward her, and could tell, quite obviously now, that it was a drone, its little propellers buzzing.

The two teenagers led the girl up the beach to a fort built from bleached driftwood logs that looked like dinosaur bones. A warm orange light glowed inside. Just beside the short doorway, another girl stood, piloting the drone with a remote control. She had her hair back in a ponytail, and wore a ratty puffer jacket. "Hi," she said with a gentle smile. "I'm Jovie. We have some hot chocolate inside." She peered into the fort. "Sylvan, anyone else?"

The girl ducked through the doorway and found a portable space heater giving off just enough warmth. A tall, lanky boy sat cross-legged on the sand, studying a tablet.

"No more readings," the boy—Sylvan—said. He motioned for the girl to sit.

"How about light storms?" said the other boy, ducking inside. "Wormholes? Anything? I'm Max, by the way," he said to the girl.

"Negative," said Sylvan, and let out a relieved sigh. "Antiproton readings are back below detectable levels. Ladies and gentlemen, I think that's it for this evening's activities." Sylvan picked up a pen and wrote in a little beat-up notebook.

"What's the count?" Max asked.

"Four found," said Sylvan, glancing at the girl. "Eighteen essences observed. That's approximately . . . an eighty-five percent drop from what Dr. Wells told me in 2022. I'd say that's ample evidence that our trans-universal convergence zone is no longer being actively engaged by an alien ship. Well, that and the lack of scary light storms in the water."

"I told you she'd keep her word," said Max.

Sylvan craned his neck to look out at Jovie. "Does this mean Dr. Wells is going to want her stuff back?"

Jovie came in, holding her drone, and removing something that looked like an oversized camera lens from its claw. She sat beside Sylvan and handed him the device, which he promptly slipped into a black velvet case. Then she started folding the drone's wings. "She said to keep it as long as we thought we needed it." Jovie eyed the girl. "I don't think we're quite done needing it. Or maybe I just like being here with you dorks." She smiled at the others as she put the drone into her backpack. Sylvan handed her the notebook, which she stowed as well.

"Any word on what good ol' Barsuda Solutions is up to these days?" Sylvan asked.

"The last time I heard from Dr. Wells, she said she was back in Juliette, at their site there. She said she'd had a big breakthrough that she wished she could tell me about, but it was"—Jovie made air quotes—"'classified.'"

"'Breakthrough' like they're trying to break through universes again?" said Sylvan.

"Technically they were always trying to close it," said Jovie, "but yeah, I wouldn't put it past them."

The tall girl entered and sat with them. She picked up a thermos. "I'm Micah," she said, passing the girl the top. "Here." She poured hot chocolate into it. "This is the secret elixir of recovery."

"Micah . . . ," said Jovie, rolling her eyes.

Micah made a thoughtful face. "Oh, right. Yes, just hot chocolate, my apologies." She winked at the girl.

They were quite crowded in there, but it was warm, and the girl didn't feel threatened. In fact, she had started to feel a hungry growl in her belly. When had she last eaten?

"How are you feeling?" Max asked.

"I'm okay, I think." A question occurred to her now, one she somehow hadn't thought of until this moment. "Where am I?"

"As far from interesting as one can get," Micah said.

"This is Far Haven, Washington," said Jovie. "West of everything. Do you remember coming here?"

"Sort of," said the girl, "but I'm . . . I'm not sure from where."

"That's okay. Do you know your name?"

The girl thought for a moment. And another. She could nearly picture the word, but it kept slipping from her grasp, and now a panicked feeling began to rise inside her. "No . . ."

"That's okay, too," Jovie said. "It will come to you. It just takes a little time."

"This is going to sound weird," said Max, "but could I hold your hand?" He held his own out and showed her a strange bracelet on his wrist, like something the girl's mother would wear, except this bracelet had an oily black stone on it. He twisted the stone, and it began to pulse with rainbow energy. "I can help you remember."

"Okay." The girl took his hand and noticed that hers felt warm in his.

"Try to picture your room," said Max. "Or maybe your favorite spot in your hometown. Or a person who you can remember yourself with. And then just try to be there."

"I don't understand," the girl said, that panicked feeling whirring faster. "What happened to me?"

"You got caught in a current," Jovie said. "It's not your fault. And we know how to help. All of us have been in it, too, to some degree."

"Who are you?"

Sylvan, who was still fixated on his tablet, pointed back behind his head. The girl saw a sign hanging on the wall, a slab of driftwood with words painted on it.

"'League of Transient Detectives, Limited,'" the girl read. She saw that below it, their four names had been written on lines, like they were all members.

"That is definitely not our actual name," Max said.

"Sure it is," said Sylvan, typing away.

"Our name can't be 'LTD, Ltd.,'" said Max. "It's redundant."

"Or slyly poking fun at organizational structures as a concept, while also being memorable," said Sylvan.

"Or maybe just confusing," said Jovie.

"I liked 'Castaway Club,'" Micah said.

"That sounds like a restaurant," said Sylvan.

"'Memory Guild' was clearly the best," said Max.

"I love that band," Micah said, and elbowed him playfully.

"Hey," said Sylvan, "if any of *you* want to make a sign, feel free."

"Anyway," Jovie said pointedly, "Max can help you reconnect, and then we can help get you home."

The girl nodded, but at the same time, she looked over her shoulder with the strangest thought: she'd hoped to catch a glimpse of those glowing creatures one more time. They had seemed so lovely. . . .

"I know it's hard," Jovie said gently. "You've probably spent a long time feeling like you don't belong, like you weren't a part of the world around you. But that's the drift talking." She motioned to her friends, to the crowded fort with its warm light. "And this is how we fight it."

The girl nodded. A sadness welled up inside her, and before she knew it, tears were slipping from her cheeks.

"It took all of us a while," Micah added. "Everyone feels it from time to time, but that's natural. And when it happens, our job is to remind ourselves that we have each other, that we're still together, even when we're drifting."

"We're like the Great Pacific Garbage Patch of friend groups," said Sylvan.

"I get why you like that analogy," said Jovie, "but there's got to be one that doesn't include garbage."

"Fine, I'll work on it. In the meantime, we're a regular old bunch of totally normal high school kids who spend their nights out on the beach searching for the unseen. As you do."

"As you do," said Micah, toasting with her hot chocolate cup. "Speaking of normal life, I have to get to rehearsal by seven, which doesn't seem possible without noodles. Anyone else? Max?"

Max checked his phone. "I think there is noodle time before Dad needs the Jeep back."

"How goes clearing out the shop?" Jovie asked.

Max shrugged. "It is a never-ending process, now that he's got the new job. Each of those shelves is packed so deep, it's taking forever. Plus, there's Mom's memorial anniversary this weekend."

"We'll be there," Jovie said.

"Thanks. So will the real Mason, by the way."

"Ooh," said Micah. "Are you ready?"

"Yeah," Max said. "I think I know what to say. And I have the concert shirt and a bunch of Paul's things from Dad's. It might jog his memory."

"Good luck," said Jovie.

"What time is your band practice, Joves?" Micah asked.

"Eight. Sylvan, do we need to get the PA?"

"That's a negative; it's already at the practice space."

"You guys ready for the gig?" said Micah.

"I think so," said Jovie.

"Remember, half of stage presence is remembering that the crowd actually wants you to succeed."

"I know," said Jovie, a nervous look passing across her face. "It's only my mom's café. It will probably just be the baristas."

"No way," said Sylvan. "I have like, twenty subs who say they're definitely going to make it."

"Oh, because your subscribers are *so* reliable," said Jovie.

"Well, I'll be there." Micah turned to the girl. "How about it: Do you like noodles? This town has historically specialized in fast food only, but since we closed the breach—"

Sylvan interrupted, coughing into his hand, "Saved multiple universes."

"Right, since then, there's been a little more life here, including a decent noodle bar. You game?"

But the girl hadn't totally been listening. That warmth from Max's hand had spread, and she'd found a place in her mind, a room that she knew, where she belonged—it was actually a few places blended together—and it filled her with such relief that she wondered how she'd lost it to begin with.

She held her breath for a moment. Searching, so close . . .

And then, she knew.

"Rosa," she said. "My name is Rosa."

AUTHOR'S NOTE

If you wish to learn more about the mystery of F.D.L., please refer to the Chronicle of the Dark Star, a trilogy that begins with *Last Day on Mars*, as well as the standalone novel *The Fellowship for Alien Detection*.

For more information on Barsuda Solutions . . . please stay tuned.

ACKNOWLEDGMENTS

Any time a writer can actually finish a novel, it probably means that story was the right one for them to be working on at the time. I have never felt that more than with this book. Writing a story about the search for belonging and about nurturing relationships felt particularly meaningful during these last difficult years.

At many points, it seemed unlikely that I would be able to find the bandwidth to get this thing done, but here it is. I am so grateful for the support, love, and patience of my family and friends, and to the readers who have reached out, often just when I needed to hear it, asking me when the next book would be done already. Thank you to my incredible editor, Jordan Brown, for his excellent counsel and tireless belief in this story; to my amazing agent, Robert Guinsler, for keeping my head on straight; and to the teams at HarperCollins and Sterling Lord Literistic for helping to make this book a reality. And thank you to the librarians, booksellers, and teachers who have helped so many of my books find their readers over the years.